D0734886

THE
UNWANTED

THE
UNWANTED

a novel

Christiaan Barnard
& Siegfried Stander

David McKay Company, Inc.

NEW YORK

Dedicated to my children and,
in gratitude, to the handful of colleagues
who helped with information
to make the writing of this book possible
—Christiaan Barnard

Authors' Note

Hospitals in South Africa pattern themselves on the British model. For reasons of verisimilitude, this book retains terms of South African usage. For readers who are unfamiliar with these terms, here is a short glossary:

SISTER: A graduate nurse, usually the senior member of the nursing team

HOUSEMAN: An intern

REGISTRAR: A medical resident

CASUALTY: Emergency Ward

MEDICAL FIRM: Medical team

QUALIFICATION: Graduation from a university

Inevitably, certain of the incidents described in this novel are founded on the factual experiences of the authors. The characters in the work and the situations in which such incidents occur, however, are entirely imaginary and are not intended to refer to any living person or actual happening.

PROLOGUE

NOW

That familiar smell, a mixture of antiseptics, polish, disease, and fear, was in his nostrils as he turned the corner. A nurse, hurrying the opposite way, recognized him and flattened herself against the wall. He gave her an absent-minded smile and turned left without having to think where he was going.

At the end of the corridor he came to a maroon door, made of wood and sliding on metal rollers. He pushed at its weight and it rumbled aside.

Another smell. Sickly sweet. No amount of antiseptics could ever obliterate the unmistakable stench of death.

And yet the room to which that stench clung was white-tiled, brightly lit and cheerful. An African with sloping wrestler's shoulders was working alone at a marble-topped table among an array of human organs. He looked up at the intruder and lowered his sword-bladed knife.

The white man pulled back a jacket cuff irritably to look at his watch.

"Morning. Isn't Doctor Innes here yet?"

The African's broad face remained expressionless, but there was a faint air of rebuke in his voice.

"Good morning, Professor van der Riet."

"Good morning, William," the white man said hurriedly.

"Doctor Innes phoned, Professor. He said he's held up at a meeting and he won't be here till half-past."

Deon van der Riet checked his watch again. Twenty minutes to wait. To waste, in fact, for it was too late to go back to the theater and there was nothing of particular importance to do in the meantime.

"He has to do a post-mortem on a child by the name of Daley for me. Pamela Daley. Have you opened the body?"

"No, Professor."

The African nodded toward a bundle on a second table. The white shroud had been partially unwound, and when Deon approached the table he saw the bleached face of a child below stringy hair.

The dressings on the front of the chest had been removed in preparation for the autopsy. He glanced down at the closed incision and the neat pattern of sutures showing black against the skin.

Why had she died so suddenly? She had been doing well during the first twenty-four hours after the operation. Then . . . gone. He was more and more convinced that the cardiologist had been wrong; that he had misinterpreted the high pressure in the pulmonary artery.

He looked at the face again. There was nothing of life in that stillness.

He had been told a story once of a famous sculptor commissioned to do a bust of the Pope. The work extended over many sittings, and the artist grew to know each plane and hollow of his eminent model's features. When it was done the likeness was precise. But then the Pope died and the sculptor was recalled to prepare a death mask. He was dismayed to see how little the marble face he had created resembled the mask modeled from the flesh. Finally he realized the truth: there had been no failure of skill on his part; the first time he had captured the breath of life; the second time it had been absent.

Perhaps, Deon mused, it is just as well that this change takes place. It gives to the dead the faces of strangers.

He checked his wristwatch once more and turned away, pursing his lips in annoyance. He should have stayed in the operating room. Now he could no longer quite account for the urge that had made him want to attend the post-mortem in person. He had been angry at losing a patient and had needed the satisfaction of being present when the autopsy knife would disclose that the mistake had not been of his making.

Pamela Daley had died. And everything with which she had laughed, wept, run, and cried out in joy would be removed for use in a demonstration to the medical students clustered around the top table, or watching on closed-circuit television. Her organs would become exhibits to illustrate interesting aspects of an interesting disease. They would not seem to have anything to do with life, the life which had once been that of a child.

He had to go.

He would phone Innes later to find out what the autopsy had shown.

The outer door grated harshly on its rollers and he looked over his shoulder, expecting to see Innes. But instead it was Professor Martyn, the head of pathology himself, who came into the mortuary. He was speaking

4

very seriously, with small, contained gestures of the hands, to a long-limbed man in a dark suit who walked beside him and inclined his head attentively.

Deon's sense of shock, almost of dread, was visceral.

My God, he thought. Philip.

He felt a moment's absurd longing that his presence should somehow remain undetected. That Martyn and the stranger should be so engrossed in their conversation that he could slip away without anyone noticing. That they would pass by as if he had become invisible.

The two turned inquiringly toward him. Martyn looked jittery. The other man's face was grave and composed. He had long features; almost an Arab look, with that dark skin and black hair.

But he's gone gray at the sides, Deon thought with a touch of alarm. Gray, and he's my age. Well (self-reassuringly), not quite my age. Two years older.

"Deon," said Martyn, "I didn't expect you here."

"No. I was waiting for someone."

"I see. I wonder, have you met Professor Davids?"

Martyn turned back to the dark-skinned man and now their eyes were compelled to meet, directly and frankly.

"Professor Davids, Professor van der Riet," Martyn said.

"Philip," Deon van der Riet said tentatively.

They were both smiling now, an identical, questioning smile.

"Deon," the other man said.

Both laughed lightly, as if at a well-remembered joke. They shook hands.

"It's been a long time," Deon said.

"A long time," Philip said.

"Twenty years?"

"That's right. I left at the end of 'fifty-four."

"Yes." Deon spoke with a tone of wonder. "Lot of water under the bridge since then."

Philip appeared to ponder over the phrase as a serious and profound statement. He nodded.

"A long time," he said.

Professor Martyn had been looking anxiously from one to the other as they spoke, seeming to fear something potentially dangerous, a spark which could cause an explosion. Now he broke in, obviously relieved, as if he had by his own valiant efforts succeeded in averting disaster.

"I hadn't realized you chaps already knew one another," he observed brightly.

"We qualified together," Deon told him. "And we were housemen together here as well."

Martyn looked properly astonished and impressed. "Good heavens, eh!" He looked around at the room. "So you probably had lectures right in here."

"It's been modernized a great deal," Philip said. He pointed at the amphitheater that surrounded three sides of the table upon which the African had arranged a systematic display of heart, lungs, kidneys, and liver. "All that is new since my time."

"Oh, of course," Martyn said hastily. "It was all put in after I took over the department." He moved toward the television control unit, beaming. He relished any opportunity to show off his equipment. "It saves a lot of time, you know. William here removes the organs before the class starts and puts them out. It means the lecturer can spend all his time teaching. And naturally all the students have an equally good view."

With an awkward sense of guilt Deon remembered the day (twenty years ago? More—twenty-three or twenty-four) when Philip and other members of the class who were not white had been turned away from that maroon outside door because a white body had been lying on the table inside. Was the new arrangement, with television and all the rest of it, a neatly contrived way of avoiding this? For, once the organs were out on the slab, who could tell whether the body that had contained them had been white, yellow, or black? Only William.

The flood of memory, once it had found a breach in the dam, would not be stanched:

Philip in class in his thin, worn jacket and trousers, asking the questions no one else had thought to ask.

Philip intent over a microscope; brown hands making delicate adjustments.

Philip on the day they graduated, his back stiff as he kneeled to be capped.

Philip . . .

Deon spoke to Martyn, almost harshly in his need to escape the torrent.

"I'm waiting for Doctor Innes. He was supposed to do this PM for me. It's a child we operated on yesterday for a VSD, ASD, and high pulmonary pressure. The cardiologist said it was due to flow. She was doing well, but she went into ventricular fibrillation last night and we couldn't restart the heart. Now Innes hasn't turned up. Think you could just open the chest and look at the heart and lungs for me?"

Martyn glanced at Philip. "I think we have time, don't you, Professor?" He called the African. "William, get me an apron and gloves, will you?" Then he turned back to Deon and said chattily: "I was really only looking after Professor Davids while Hugo Gleave is getting things organized for the lecture. You've heard he's lecturing today?"

"Professor Gleave sent us an invitation."

"Are you coming to it?"

Deon hesitated. "I doubt it. I don't think I'll be able to make it. I did a mitral annuloplasty at the children's hospital this morning and I left there before the kid was out of theater. But Doctor Robertson will be there from our department." He asked Philip: "Remember Robby Robertson?"

"Robby? Yes indeed."

"He's my deputy on the cardiac team now."

"Really? I didn't know that."

"Yes. Hasn't changed. Still the same old Robby."

"He was always a great joker."

"Still is."

Martyn had tied on his apron and was wriggling his fingers to improve the fit of the latex gloves. They watched as William moved the body into a position on the white marble slab where Martyn could reach it.

"Okay. Switch on the tape recorder," the pathologist told the African, and Deon and Philip withdrew out of range of the microphone.

They could hear Martyn's droning voice: ". . . body of a well-nourished female with certain skeletal abnormalities . . ." as they stood awkwardly together.

Or perhaps, Deon thought, glancing sideways at the hard face and calm eyes of the other man, I am the only awkward one here. Can it be that I am the only one who remembers? Now the moment had come and he did not know how to deal with it. His throat was dry. He coughed.

"You did pathology yourself, didn't you?" he asked in a low voice. Anything to make the past go away; to stop that flood. "Before you went into genetics, I mean."

Philip faced him at once, smiling.

"That's right. I went to Edinburgh from here, if you remember? Then I spent a year in France and finally Canada, of course."

"I see."

Martyn had cut the costal cartridges on each side and was removing the breast bone.

". . . evidence of the recent operation with a fibrinous pericardial exudate present," he confided to the microphone.

7

"But I assume your lecture today will be on genetics," Deon said, acutely conscious of the artificiality and emptiness of the words.

"Yes." Philip did not seem to notice his embarrassment. "It's a pity you won't be there. I'll be dealing with new theories on the origin of congenital abnormalities. You should find it quite interesting, I imagine."

"I'm sure. Only problem is that I'm a bit worried about this kid we operated on this morning." Deon ended with a shrug and a vague gesture of regret.

This meeting was a mistake. He had planned to avoid the lecture and had thought that by sending Robby as a substitute he would not be missed. But now he was face to face with Philip it was difficult to maintain the pretense. Especially when Philip was clearly pleased to see him.

Deon was saved by Martyn, who beckoned and said portentously: "Here we are. The heart and lungs."

Deon moved up beside the pathologist and looked into the gaping empty chest. The heart lay on a wooden table which straddled the corpse's legs. When last he had seen it it had been beating regularly, giving life to the body that contained it. Now it was motionless and all his labor, designed to save it, had been in vain.

Martyn had cut the heart away from the lungs and dissected the pericardial sac. He opened the right atrium, washing away blue blood clots with water from a thin rubber hose. He dictated as he examined the interatrial septum where Deon had closed an aperture.

"The suture line in the foramen ovale appears intact."

Using scissors, he cut across the tricuspid valve into the right ventricle, then alongside the septum down to the apex of the heart, opening up the right ventricular cavity.

"There is a plastic patch over a ventricular septal defect in the outflow tract of the right ventricle. This is intact."

Again he rinsed with the slow stream of water, hunting in between the heart's muscle bands and the septum. Then a curious expression, both elated and apologetic, appeared on his face. He looked round at Deon.

"There's another big defect down here."

Deon stared incredulously. It was impossible.

"There is a second ventricular septal defect lower down in the muscular septum," Martyn said into the microphone, his eyes still on Deon. "It has not been closed. It measures approximately . . ."

"My Christ, I missed it!" Deon said roughly. "How the hell did I miss that?"

Martyn withdrew his gloved hands and asked: "Does that explain it?"

8

Deon nodded morosely. "Ja. That was why the pulmonary artery pressure stayed so high after the operation. And that must have caused the ventricular fibrillation. I don't know how I could have . . ." He shook his head, unable to complete his sentence.

"Do you mind if I leave the rest of the PM for Innes to finish?" Martyn nodded briskly at the African. "Right, William. Please explain to Doctor Innes when he comes." He walked across to the washbasin, peeling off his gloves, leaving Deon and Philip together beside the child's body.

Deon shook his head again. "Missed it!"

"One of the chiefs at McGill always tells his students: 'If you want to play with the big boys you must expect to get hurt,'" Philip said after a while. His voice was gentle and Deon gave him a stricken look.

"I wondered why the blood coming through the left ventricular vent was blue. But I didn't do anything about it. It was venous blood all the time, being sucked through the defect. And for God's sake I should know by this time to look for an explanation for anything unusual. I should have known there was another defect."

"It was those muscle bands that hid it."

"All the same I should have known and looked. I shouldn't have missed it."

Philip pondered, then said judicially: "No. Probably not."

The scrupulously honest reply was so unexpected and at the same time so reminiscent of that Philip of twenty years ago that Deon could not keep from smiling. On sudden impulse he said: "This lecture of yours. What time does it start?"

Philip examined the wall clock.

"In fifteen minutes."

"I'd like to attend. But I'll have to make a phone call first." Deon looked at the clock too.

"I'd like you to come," Philip told him.

A welcoming committee had formed in the foyer in front of the elevators. Deon saw the waiting group as he came down the corridor ahead of Philip and Martyn. There was a strange air of animosity and tension about them; a stiffness in the way the men held their bodies. Deon's quick eyes searched curiously among them.

Old Snyman, grizzled and neat as a squirrel, was feigning indifference. Dr. Malcolm, the hospital superintendent, appeared flustered and cross. The Dean, Professor Levin, and Professor Gleave, chief of the Department

9

of Genetics, were speaking to Malcolm very seriously. Robby Robertson, red hair thinning at the temples, grinned impudently at the superintendent's evident discomfort.

As Deon approached, the Dean's normally placid voice rose sharply.

"Look here, Mac, this man is a graduate of this very university. If there's any fuss about him lecturing here, I promise you you'll have my resignation by this evening. Damn it, man, this is the university hospital, not your damned Whites-only opera house! Clear it with your director yourself, if you want to. But I positively . . ."

He broke off at a frozen-faced signal from Gleave and looked over his shoulder in confusion.

Gleave left the group hurriedly to come forward, hand outstretched, hastily arranging a smile of welcome.

"Hello, Professor Davids," he said, his voice warm. "Nice to see you here. It was kind of you to spare us the time. Sorry I couldn't take you around, but there were some things I . . . ah . . . had to arrange. Thanks for looking after him, Jim."

"Pleasure," Martyn said.

"And Deon," Gleave went on. "Nice of you to come. You've met, have you?"

"Yes," Deon said.

"Let me introduce you to the other people here, Professor Davids."

Gleave moved off fussily and Philip walked beside him tall and at ease, a faintly quizzical smile on his face as he exchanged greetings. Deon wondered if he too had overheard the Dean.

Professor Snyman nodded brusquely as he shook hands.

"Davids. I remember you. Mid-fifties, eh?"

"I qualified in 'fifty-three."

The old man nodded again. "Yes. Remember you well. You were one of our top boys."

Philip Davids looked at him good-humoredly and then around at the wide foyer.

"I didn't expect ever to come back here," he said.

None of the white men said anything in reply.

Elevator lights flashed and a bell clanged. The steel doors opened with a bang. Professor Gleave dashed forward to hold them open with a foot.

"Gentlemen," he said pleadingly. "If you please, gentlemen . . ."

The whole group began to move toward the door, jostling politely, one standing back for another until Deon put an arm firmly behind Philip's back and forced him into the lead. Gleave beamed gratitude and good cheer all around. He was last into the elevator, pinned in a corner, far from the buttons.

"E floor!" Robby called out cheerfully from the front, thumping the buttons with one fist. "Leeches and waterworks!"

There was a hesitant laugh. The hematology and urology departments were housed on the fourth floor. Robby had a license to clown, even when his jokes were hackneyed.

The doors banged again and they rode upward in the constrained silence of comparative strangers who find themselves suddenly too close together. Territory, Deon thought. Traveling jam-packed like this is an infringement of territory. Worth a study.

"I'm afraid I have one little hardship for you, Professor Davids," Gleave was saying, his voice hushed and self-conscious, as if he was overaware that everyone else was listening. "The press, I'm afraid. They got to hear about your lecture, so we had to arrange a bit of a press conference, if you don't mind."

A stricken look at once appeared on Dr. Malcolm's face. The superintendent had a profound distrust and fear of reporters and photographers.

Gleave spotted the look and said acidly: "You people were told about it, Mac."

"I know," Dr. Malcolm mumbled, not in the least placated.

"After all," Gleave continued, maliciously pleased to have found a way of needling the superintendent, "this is the kind of news these chaps like, isn't it?" He said, as if quoting from imaginary headlines: "Coloured doctor, now world-famous geneticist, returns to lecture at his own alma mater."

Deon found himself wincing. Gleave was fiercely protective of his friends and causes, but he wasn't renowned for his tact. Malcolm's face had turned a dull red. Deon glanced at Philip, standing crushed up against him. The high-boned face was impassive.

He's grown thin too, Deon thought. Gone gray and grown thin. You think of yourself as still being young and suddenly a voice from the past declares: You are old.

Old Philip. It's been a long time. He felt a sudden rush of affection and warmth and slapped the man beside him lightly on the back.

"Nice to have you back," he said.

Philip turned to look at him and the skin around his eyes crinkled in an understanding smile.

"Nice to be back," he said.

The elevator stopped with a jar and a shudder and the doors flowed open. They stepped out in strict order of protocol, the guest once again in the lead; Professor Gleave, as host, at the rear.

Philip stopped and glanced around with a half smile.

"Hasn't changed." He examined the cream-colored walls. "Even the paint's the same."

Dr. Malcolm, misunderstanding and scenting further disparagement, said huffily: "We repaint constantly." He adopted his guided-tour voice. "And in fact a great number of things have changed, Professor Davids. The hospital has almost doubled its size since you left. For example, we have a completely new outpatient department where we handle close to fifty thousand patients each month. We have a new obstetrics block as well, and Professor van der Riet's new cardiac block will be completed in eighteen months."

The patronizing tone annoyed Deon. "They told us that eighteen months ago," he said.

Malcolm glared at him.

"That's very interesting," Philip said. "Obviously you're doing marvels here."

"We plan for the future," the superintendent told him loftily.

"I can see that," Philip said with great sincerity. He turned to smile again at Deon, mending whatever breach might have occurred. "You certainly deserve a new cardiac unit."

Deon nodded absently. Something was bothering him.

"Come on, Professor," Gleave said jovially. "Let's go and face the music. I've got them in the small lecture room. Remember it?"

He led the Coloured man away down the passage and Philip allowed himself to be led docilely. His rangy body moved easily under the fashionably cut suit.

That's it, Deon thought. Ease. He's at ease with himself. In complete control. He was always stiff and angular, self-conscious. He has become self-assured over the years. That's it, but that's not all of it.

The missing fragment worried him like a toothache. It was so close, so close. Yet he couldn't quite put a finger on it.

He remembered he had a call to make. There was a telephone at the entrance to the main lecture theater. He murmured a vague, all-inclusive "Excuse me," and walked quickly away.

The final-year students who were to attend Philip's lecture were all inside by now. A lazy hum of voices came from behind the closed door. They had been herded neatly out of the way. Special occasion. You didn't want odd bods cluttering up the place when the top brass arrived. He smiled ironically at the thought that he, too, was presumably counted as one of the top brass. He wondered what these kids really thought of them all. The boys with their untidy tangles of hair and the girls with their cool eyes. Probably, he told himself, it hasn't changed all that much. There's probably quite the same mixture of irreverence and respect. He picked up the receiver, still listening to the voices behind the door.

They seem a lot more confident than we did, he thought. More aware. But are they really? Isn't that confidence a screen each generation puts on to hide itself from the critical gaze of the preceding one?

He put the thought aside as he dialed the number of the children's hospital. Would it have been better to replace the mitral valve? He had deliberately preserved it because the child was from the country, where it would have been difficult to insure that anticoagulant therapy was properly regulated. But perhaps he should have replaced it anyway. The leaflets had been badly scarred by rheumatic fever.

He was put through and spoke briefly and urgently. "Peter? That mitral valve. How are things?"

The very precise voice at the other end said: "He's awake, Deon. Everything seems okay. The venous pressure is ten and the left atrial down to fifteen."

"What was it?"

"Twenty-five. The mean arterial is seventy-five."

"Peripheral circulation all right?"

"It's fine. And I've just seen a chest X-ray. The heart shadow is a lot smaller."

"Sounds all right. I'll be at a lecture over here at the hospital if you need me."

But when he put down the receiver he was still uneasy. The discovery that he had missed the ventricular septal defect had unnerved him. He was always doubtful and unsure after losing a patient and especially so when death could have been prevented.

Could it ever really be prevented? He had often seen how thin a line separated them: failure and success; death and life.

Nevertheless he should have paid more attention to that blue blood. Somehow his mind had refused to accept its importance. And so the child had died.

Very deliberately he turned his mind away from this thought to another cause of concern. Peter Moorhead was on duty. What was wrong with Peter these days? He'd have to pull himself together. He had always been

13

one of the best surgeons on the team. But he was slipping. That bitch of a wife, probably.

Deon considered for a moment telephoning his own wife. Then he looked at his watch and decided that she would probably be out. Bridge afternoon. Or garden club afternoon. Or book club, or something.

His eyes were drawn to the bronze bust that had guarded the entrance to the lecture room for God-knew-how-many years now. He wondered how many students, or lecturers for that matter, knew whom it represented. He had looked once, long ago, but for years he had passed by without sparing it as much as a glance. He looked attentively now at the empty eyes and the forward-thrust jaw. A plaque on the gray granite base informed the curious that this was James Redwood Collier, C.B.E., D.S.O., Ll.B., M.D., F.R.C.P., Hon. F.R.S.M., first Professor of Medicine at the university, 1920–1937.

He had been top brass too, in his day. He had walked these corridors, demanding respect and filled with his own importance. And now all that was reduced to bronze. A bronze bust passed daily without a glance.

Well, Deon thought, that's how it is.

Another memory from long ago came back unbidden. Robby—the same red-haired, bespectacled Robby, but in an earlier edition: second-year anatomy class—holding up a skull and, predictably, declaiming Hamlet's graveyard speech. They had all laughed, for he could be funny even doing the predictable. Suddenly he had become serious and had put down the skull and had said quietly, almost as if speaking to it alone: "'As I am, so was he. As he is, so shall I be.'"

"Where's that from, Rob?" someone had called out. But Robby had shaken his head and continued with his work, which had been the dissection of the layers of the extensor muscles of the forearm.

Deon saluted the frozen image of Professor James Redwood Collier solemnly and went back down the corridor. The press conference was still in progress. He stopped at the door of the small lecture room.

Philip's audience consisted of three young men, who managed to look both bored and alert at the same time, and two women, a blonde and a tall, plump woman with hair pulled severely to the back of her head. One of the men had a big press camera slung on a strap over his shoulder.

"For the last few years I have concentrated mainly on experimental genetics," Philip was telling them. "At present we're concentrating on getting information about the transmission of genetic information and about ways in which this mechanism can go wrong."

The blonde, who wore an abundance of eye make-up, sighed theatrically.

"Professor Davids, could you explain that in simpler terms? We're not all doctors."

"But I take it you are science reporters?"

"I usually do fashion stories for the women's page," she told him earnestly. "There wasn't anyone else free to cover this story."

The other reporters laughed in an embarrassed way and Philip smiled too and told her, tolerantly: "Then perhaps you'd better stick to describing the clothes I'm wearing."

The plump woman had spotted Deon at the door. She nudged the photographer.

"Professor van der Riet," she hissed.

The journalists looked at him calculatingly, and Deon pretended not to notice. But the woman reporter strode up to him. "Excuse me, Professor," she said. "Would you mind . . . if you would . . . we'd like a picture of you and Professor Davids together. If you don't mind."

Philip had joined them, and she smiled uncertainly, now including him in her request.

"Why?" Deon asked.

"Well, I mean, it's . . ." She was flustered. "Well, I believe you were at school . . . I mean at university together."

Deon caught Professor Snyman's sharply supercilious look.

He shrugged. "All right." And at once, deferentially toward Philip: "If Professor Davids has no objection."

Philip smiled and shook his head.

The woman was fussing around, lining them up. The photographer crouched and aimed. The flashgun flicked once, twice. They blinked in its glare.

"All right?" Deon asked in tones of dismissal.

But the reporter was persistent. She had her notebook out and was fumbling with a ballpoint pen.

"Just one or two questions please. If you don't mind."

Deon lifted his eyebrows questioningly at Philip and the other man nodded.

"Just one or two," Deon said.

"Professor Gleave tells me you have known one another for a long time."

She watched them expectantly.

"Yes," Deon said.

"You graduated here together?"

Philip glanced at Deon.

"It goes much deeper than that," he said. "We've known one another for a very long time indeed."

The woman looked mystified.

"As students, you mean?"

"We grew up together," Deon told her tersely.

"Grew up . . . ? How . . . ?"

"We were born on the same farm," Philip said.

She seemed to think she was being teased, and flushed. "I don't quite . . ."

Philip relented. "On Professor van der Riet's farm," he told her. "His family farm, rather. In the Beaufort West district. My . . . my parents . . . were Coloured people who worked for Professor van der Riet's father. We were both born there." He smiled at Deon. "But I am a bit older than he is."

"But that's fantastic! It really is!" She was bubbling with enthusiasm and scribbling rapid notes. "I had no idea. And you both decided to become doctors?"

"Yes," Deon said.

"You decided together? I mean, when you were both still children on the farm. Doing operations on the farm animals and so forth. Dreaming about becoming famous doctors one day."

"It didn't happen quite that way," Philip said gently. "We did play together, certainly. But I can't remember that we ever talked about becoming doctors."

"I wanted to be an engine driver," Deon said.

The woman looked resentful again, as if she disliked her concept of events being disturbed. She had large brown eyes in a rather bovine face.

"In fact, it was quite a surprise to meet up again as students," Philip told her. "I had left the farm when I was twelve, you see. My father died and my mother came to Cape Town to work."

"What kind of work did she do?"

"She was a housemaid on the farm. But here she worked in a factory."

"That's fantastic!" The woman was filled with fresh enthusiasm. "A domestic servant. And her son becomes a famous professor."

"You could," Philip said courteously, "put it that way. And now you will have to excuse us."

He took Deon's arm behind the elbow and they walked away from the reporter, heads slightly bowed, walking slowly and with dignity, talking in low tones, as befitted men of their standing.

"Nosy bitch," Philip said.

Deon laughed sourly.

"You can tell them a mile off. Always hunting for an angle. The hell with the truth."

"I guess you're accustomed to this sort of thing?"

"You seem to have to face quite a bit of it too."

Philip made a gesture of dismissal.

"Geneticists are dull beasts, you know. Even when you manage to drag them out of their labs they're tongue-tied and boring."

Deon chuckled, but he was thinking of something else. That's it, he thought. That's the difference I was looking for. Tongue-tied. It wasn't that he was ever inarticulate, but he used to guard his tongue. There was always a reserve. That's gone. He doesn't mind what he says and to whom he says it. He has put the past firmly behind him. He is his own man. "I heard that your mother was ill," he said.

"That's why I came back to South Africa," Philip said with a certain dry emphasis in his voice.

"How is she?" Deon asked quickly.

"Not too well, I'm afraid. There's no doubt about the diagnosis. It's cancer all right. And she's not very strong. She's had a hard life, you know."

It was hard to tell whether his expression was accusing or defensive.

"I know," Deon said. There was a brief silence between them.

"But she's cheerful," Philip said. "She gets around. She sees people." He added confidingly: "I wanted her to come to Canada. Years ago. Everything was ready for her there, but she wouldn't come. This was her home. This was what she knew. So she wouldn't come."

"Old people get that way."

"Yes. I guess they do."

Deon confided in his turn. "My own mother is here too, now."

Philip's eyes flickered slightly, but he hid his surprise.

"Really? Here in Cape Town?"

"Yes. I fetched her from her brother. He was getting too old to look after her properly. She had a stroke, you know. Anyway, I've got her in a good place now. In a home. They've got good nurses there and they're kind to her."

"That's something," Philip said slowly. "Growing old is tough."

"Being born is tough," Deon said.

They both laughed and the awkward moment was past. Professor Gleave came bustling up importantly. "We're ready to start, Professor Davids. Will you excuse us, Deon?"

"Right."

17

Deon started to walk away. Then he turned back toward Philip. "I'd like to see you again. After the lecture."

Philip was being ushered rapidly toward the side door.

"Fine," he called back.

"Dinner. Dinner at my house tonight. Can you manage it?"

Philip hesitated. Briefly he resisted Gleave's urging. "I'd like to," he said. "Thank you."

"Excellent. I'll pick you up afterwards."

"Thank you very much."

Professor Gleave was an intense but nervous speaker, with a habit of leaning over the lectern as if it were another cause he was about to embrace.

"It is my great pleasure to introduce Professor Philip Davids, our guest speaker . . ."

Deon listened absently to the predictable phrases of ringing praise. Gleave was a short, broad man with the eyes of a visionary. Genetics was his passion, and his devotion to it was made all the more profound by the fact that some adherents of other medical disciplines tended to regard it with a degree of disdain; as an amusing toy with which to tinker when you were not involved with the stern realities of diagnosing and curing real disease.

Bringing Philip, with his Nobel Prize nomination, here today, had been a triumph. Gleave's bearing, as he ended his introduction, made this clear.

There was a rustle of anticipation and some sporadic handclapping. Philip waited, head down, for the applause to die before he looked up and slowly, with an air of utter confidence, scanned the rows of white faces (and the few darker ones; a handful of them in a row beside the aisle) above him. His voice, as he began, was low pitched, so that the audience had to be silent and to strain a little in order to hear him.

Deon recognized the professional speaker's trick with a small smile and settled back to listen.

"At the risk of being obvious," Philip was saying, "I want to remind you that the work of most doctors consists of applying recognized treatment to bring about the cure of recognized diseases." A slight, effective pause. "However, it is when such treatment does not exist that we find ourselves asking the questions: why did this patient get this particular disease and why did he get it at this particular time? At this stage we enter the field of medical genetics."

A beam of sunlight, golden and heavy with dust motes, lay at an angle across the room, from one of the high windows down to the wooden lecture stand in front of Philip. He shifted his notes out of the bright patch of light.

Outside lay the sticky heat of a Cape summer afternoon. It was warm in here too, and Deon, who had spent the morning in an air-conditioned operating room, began to feel drowsy. His mind wandered.

He thought again of the telephone call he had received this morning, just as he was about to start scrubbing.

His secretary had spoken to him first, sounding guilty and very apologetic.

"They're waiting in the operating room, Jenny," he had said brusquely. "Can't it wait?"

"I'm awfully sorry, Prof. But I've got a Mrs. Sedara on the line. She says she's an old friend of yours. She's from overseas and she has to speak to you urgently."

"Sedara?"

"Yes, Prof."

He looked down at the shiny surface of the telephone stand, seeing his face reflected in it at an odd angle. He frowned and repeated the name to himself. It wasn't familiar. He could not remember a patient of that name, and the "old friend" was certainly exaggerated. Possibly a chance acquaintance from some trip or other. Some people were odd about claiming intimacy based on nothing more than a casual meeting. But Jenny was usually astute about weeding out those.

"All right. Put her through."

The woman's voice was remarkably deep and she spoke slowly, rounding out each syllable.

"Professor van der Riet?"

"Speaking."

"Hello, Deon."

Slightly off-balance, he said: "Uh . . . hello."

"You don't remember me, do you?"

"I'm afraid not."

"Patricia. You knew me as Patricia Coulter."

Dubiously: "Patricia."

Then it registered and his heart seemed to make a convulsive leap.

"Trish! My God! I . . ."

"Trish. That's right."

Philip made some observation which caused an amused hum among his audience and diverted the course of Deon's thoughts. He listened distractedly.

"They ran into this Cambridge pub," Philip was saying. "And Crick shouted: 'We've found the secret of life.' Of course no one took the slightest notice, because English pubs are accustomed to cranks making profound statements."

Philip smiled easily at the renewed laughter.

"But in fact Crick was not far wrong, for what he and Watson had done was to delineate the molecular structure of deoxyribonucleic acid. And this substance, DNA, is indeed the key or, better said, the code, to all life."

A pause, to let the thought penetrate.

"Well, bacteria have it, viruses have it and every other living thing has it. The basic mating event is the coupling of two molecules of DNA, which then split and recombine with each other. And that, essentially, is all there is to sex."

Trish, Deon thought.

I had almost forgotten her.

He had remembered the voice perfectly then, of course. A voice from the past. From twenty-one years ago, to be precise.

"Well I'll be damned," he had said. And, lamely: "Where on earth did you spring from?"

"I've only just arrived in the Cape," she told him. "And I must see you. Please."

"Why, of course, Trish."

"I need your help. May I see you?"

"Sure," he said, with undue emphasis. "Sure. Of course."

"Where would be best? And when?"

"My office, I think. It's in the medical school."

"Thank you. It's very kind . . ."

"Not at all," he interrupted. He wished to end this conversation now, as quickly as courtesy allowed. "I'm operating tomorrow morning. How about the afternoon?"

"Yes."

"Tomorrow afternoon at three o'clock."

"Thank you."

"That's fine, then," he had said heartily.

"Thank you, Deon," she had said. "Good-bye."

"Good-bye, Trish."

Another muted, anticipatory laugh from the crowded banks of seats behind caused Deon to sit up sharply. Philip's face was bland, but his eyes were lively. What had he said to cause amusement? Something about Tristan de Cunha and a naval base. But Deon hadn't quite caught it and already Philip had moved on to something else.

"Let us sum up our knowledge of the nature of genetic disease. On the simplest level we may find a discreet change in only a single gene, resulting nevertheless in the transmission of incorrect information, with widespread consequences. One example of this form of disease is hemophilia, which is transmitted by females to males. The most famous carrier of hemophilia was Queen Victoria who, through her offspring, was said to have waged biological warfare on the royal families of Europe."

More laughter from the back benches and a number of stiff smiles at the front.

"On the other end of the spectrum are genetic diseases gross enough to be detected by microscopic examination. One finds, for example, surplus genetic material leading to profound consequences such as mongolism. Recently it has been discovered that twenty-five per cent of spontaneous abortions are associated with various abnormalities in the chromosome."

Deon's attention began to drift. He had not intended to come to this lecture.

He reflected briefly on what Philip had said: on the odd fact that shifts in the genetic pattern, so minute that they could at best be detected only by the lens of a microscope, should nevertheless have vast and imponderable consequences on human fate.

Things merely happen, he thought. Formless things come to shape the pattern of our lives.

BOOK

I

THEN

SPRING

One

He ran all the way up the stairs without touching the bannister, swinging to the outside round each turn so that his shoulders bumped against the wall. On the third-floor landing he almost collided with an elderly, dumpy sister. She threw up her hands and hissed in dismay. He side-stepped her, mumbling an apology. She turned to glare but already he was gone, racing up the remaining flight.

When he reached the fourth floor he was slightly out of breath and yet triumphant, as if he had proved something, even if only to himself. A handful of other students stood at the entrance to the lecture room corridor and some turned to stare at him in a puzzled way. It was only five to twelve. There was no reason to hurry. He composed himself and pulled back a jacket sleeve to examine his watch, as if he might have mistaken the time and this was the explanation for his undignified haste. He nodded to one or two of the students and received forgiving nods in return.

He had no desire for conversation, however, so he went by them and walked up the passage past the hematology laboratory. One of the lab technicians was very pretty. By force of habit he glanced in through the door, but the girl was not in sight today. He noted his own sense of disappointment and at once the thought returned, like a monotonous bell sounding in dense mist.

Five days.

Hell, that's nothing, he tried to tell himself, but the inexorable bell clanged again. Five days.

To avoid thinking about it he went up to the notice board beside the lecture room door and pretended intense interest in its announcements.

He stood there quite still, staring at the notices without seeing them, a tall, sandy-haired young man with a spare face and somber eyes that could become fierce as fire. His hands were in the pockets of his white coat and he fingered his stethoscope absently. The green trim of the coat marked him as a student and the plastic badge on his lapel announced him to be G. P. van der Riet. The initials stood for Gideon Paulus. In his first year he had for a time been half-heartedly nicknamed "Jeep," but the students had soon enough reverted to calling him Deon, the name by which he had been known all his life.

The notice board was plastered with the customary appeals for blood donors and earnest exhortations from the Christian Students Association. He continued to stand there in front of them while his classmates filed past in chattering groups or in preoccupied solitude like his own.

With a start he realized that he was alone in the corridor. Momentarily worried that he would really be late, he hurried into the lecture room behind the others. A tight knot of half a dozen men up at the back, at the top of the banked rows of seats, broke apart and all of them laughed loudly. It must have been a good story. Robby was the joker. The freckled, pinched face was impassive as always after Robby had said something amusing, but his eyes gleamed behind his spectacles.

One of the six at the back spotted Deon and raised a beckoning hand. He pretended not to notice, however, and crossed the floor to the left. Here there were fewer students: the solitary ones, the serious ones. Their notebooks were already open before them, their pens poised, their expressions intent.

He slipped into an aisle seat near the front and glanced along the row. Another small and tight group had gathered here. But its members were silent, as always. Two Indians: the man with a closely trimmed moustache and shy eyes; the girl attractive, but with a face that she always kept meticulously blank. The remaining five were all Coloured, all men. The one nearest to Deon turned to him as he took his seat. His pale green eyes gave a look of startling intensity to his dark face.

Deon smiled briefly at him.

"Philip," he said, drawling the name slightly so as to stress each of the two syllables.

Pale eyes examined him. Then Philip Davids smiled in return.

"Hello, Deon," he said in his light, dry voice.

Their eyes met, but then the smiles became strained; no more than a contortion of lips and face muscles. They glanced away simultaneously. Deon made a show of opening his briefcase and setting out papers and pen.

He felt obliged to try to break the barrier between them. But, he thought crossly, it shouldn't all have to come from one side. After all these years, the man should know I'm not trying to patronize him.

It had been easy back on the farm. Philip had been "Flip" then. The difference between them was clear—one was the son of the master and the other the son of the master's servant—but it had not seemed very important. They had been friends. When there was trouble they were in it together, and they were often beaten together too, for Deon's father believed in swift retribution. *Kweperlat,* Deon thought, and the word brought a wry smile to his lips. He associated it with homely and familiar things. But certainly the association was not entirely happy. They had to cut and bring the supple switches from the quince trees beside the water furrow themselves. A couple of well-aimed lashes could make your tail sting for ten minutes. He could remember standing with Flip behind the dam wall that was their customary refuge, both rubbing their behinds and trying not to betray themselves with the unmanliness of tears.

Then they had been friends, although they were not equal. Now they were equal but no longer friends. They shared a bench in a lecture room and the fear of the examinations ahead. They shared present duties and burdens and the dim but enchanting visions of the future. But they were not friends. Not beyond the surface.

The hum of conversation dropped to respectful silence. Deon saw that the side door had opened and that the short, dapper professor of surgery was already in the room. His private secretary was still with him, like a cumbersome barge in tow behind a fussy tugboat. The old girl always seemed reluctant to surrender her professor for even this one hour a day. The class watched with expectant amusement as the two went through their routine, waiting for the moment when Professor Snyman would make an irritable gesture of dismissal with one small, well-groomed hand and old Mother Arensen would clump out disconsolately on her flat, sensible shoes. The professor pointed at the door with his wad of papers and a student in a nearby row jumped up quickly to close it on the sight of the secretary's retreating back and her brown tweed skirt.

The lecture room was small and sparsely furnished. Professor Snyman walked up to the table in the center of the floor with an air of immense concentration, strutting like a game cock. His great crest of iron-gray hair completed the barnyard image of ruthlessness and aggression. The pun of his name in Afrikaans—the coincidence of a surgeon being called a cutting man—always pleased new students. The joke wore thin once they met up with the old man and realized that his tongue could cut as effectively as his knife.

27

Funny how we always speak about him as "the old man," Deon thought. He can't be all that old really. Probably only in his mid-forties. It could be because of the prematurely gray hair, but it has something to do with his bearing too, and his show of utter confidence.

Professor Snyman put down his papers as if making a revelation, then pushed his spectacles firmly back on to the bridge of his nose and looked up at the rows of faces behind the tiered benches.

"You will be glad to know," he said in his high, forceful voice, "that we are nearing the end of our surgery course." He paused and scanned the faces slowly. "Of course," he added in a slightly lower, almost conversational tone, "there are some of you who will be returning to me for another six months next year."

There was a low laugh, not free from apprehension. The reexamination for those who failed was taken in mid-year. And even the best could fail; even the brilliant ones could fall victim to the paralysis of exam fever.

Professor Snyman had taken a full measure of enjoyment from his ominous little joke. Now his voice became brisk.

"We are concluding the course with five lectures on pediatric surgery." Another pause, brief this time. His head was cocked as if he were listening to a silent roll of drums. "No one these days will dispute the need for suitably trained pediatricians to care for the sick child. Yet in the field of pediatric surgery we are, to coin a phrase, still in our infancy."

The slim Indian girl on Deon's left leaned forward over her notebook to scribble something, and he was momentarily irritated. What is she taking a note of this time? Surely to heaven not the old man's weary pun? She was one of those who wrote down everything, as if by the act of writing they could imprint knowledge on fickle memory. But he had to admit, grudgingly, that it worked for her. She was well up at the top of the class, not far below Philip.

Now he had better concentrate on what old Snyman was saying. Tracheo esophageal fistula. What the hell was that? He looked down at the desk, which was scarred with names and initials and dates as generations of students had practiced their surgical skill with scalpels and pens. Among the names some anonymous wit had painstakingly scratched out the sentence: "Prof. Morris is mad about sex." The professor of psychiatry was a stern, doctrinaire Freudian. Deon grinned.

Five days, memory reminded him. The grin changed to a grimace. There was nothing funny about sex. Not today. And it certainly hadn't been funny last night.

He had spent a busy evening helping in Casualty. There had been a drunken gang fight down near the railway line and several heads needed stitching. A drizzle in the late afternoon had made the roads slippery, causing a couple of rush-hour traffic accidents. No one had been seriously injured, but the half-dozen victims sat silently on the hard benches of the waiting room, watching with that curiously glazed, detached look of all survivors as the business of patching and mending went on cheerfully all around them.

In among the drunks and the cuts and the bruises, Deon had worked hard at charming a nurse who had started night duty in Casualty that week. She had plump little buttocks and velvet-smooth hair. She was amused but seemingly immune. Next year it would be different. He'd be a full-fledged doctor then. Now he was just another medical student and ranked only fractionally above the hospital porters in her eyes.

In fact, apart from being allowed to stitch up one scalp wound, the work he did was humiliatingly little more than that of a porter, and by ten o'clock he was tired of pushing trolleys and drip stands. He was doing revision on cardiology and should still be able to put in a couple of hours of serious studying tonight. He walked cheerfully past the now-darkened medical school and down side streets toward the beckoning lights of the main road. Through the door of a Greek restaurant came the smell of hot oil and fishcakes. He found himself hungry suddenly and was tempted to go in and order a toasted cheese sandwich and coffee. But he had only a couple of quid left of this term's allowance and he was saving it for something special. When would the Casualty nurse have a night off? She might be more responsive with a meal and a few glasses of wine inside her.

He turned through the garden gate and went around the house toward the miniature plot in the backyard. It was really a dressed-up servant's room, which he had inherited from a man who had qualified.

Next year, when he himself had qualified, he would have the car his father had promised him as a graduation present and he'd be more mobile. Pity he would have to move to the housemen's residence. What was the use of being a doctor if you had to live in a monastery like a first-year student?

He unlocked the door and felt for the light switch. At once, even before the light went on, he had a primitive sense of apprehension, a feeling that he was not alone.

He tensed instinctively, back to the door, hands half raised. He was relieved to see that it was only Trish. She was lying on the narrow single bed, looking up at him, eyes screwed up against the sudden glare. Her long dark-red hair was spread over the pillow in an attitude of abandon, but her body was stiff and she had all her clothes on. She had not even bothered to take off the gray-green raincoat.

"Well!" he said. He managed a weak smile. "Hello."

He took off his own coat and hung it tidily on the hook behind the door. The sense that something was wrong had not yet left him entirely. He needed time to recover.

"This is a surprise," he said with forced geniality.

The girl watched him from the bed without speaking.

"How did you get in?" he asked.

"Mrs. Mac gave me the spare key."

"Oh, my God!" He was thoroughly dismayed. "You shouldn't have asked her." His landlady was inquisitive enough about the nocturnal activities of her student tenants. This would give her absolute confirmation of her suspicions.

"I wasn't going to wait in the rain," Trish said calmly. "I told her that."

Undoubtedly she had. And she was probably the only person arrogant enough to persuade the old woman to give up that key. Strange girl, with that mass of auburn hair and eyes that could be as aloof and cold as a cat's and yet on other memorable occasions had grown huge and gentle. She made love when she wanted to with a ferocious need but Deon at times had the uneasy feeling that he was an intruder.

"Well, welcome anyway," he said awkwardly. He went to the bed and leaned over to kiss her. Her lips were unyielding under his. So it was going to be one of those nights. Hands off.

Then why had she bothered to come? Annoyed, he tried to force her lips apart but she clamped her mouth tight and turned her head away.

"What's wrong with you?" he asked. Moving to his desk, he lifted the weighty textbook of medicine off his chair and pushed his lecture notes to one side. He had to work tonight. He couldn't waste time talking art and life with frigid women.

She was only Patricia Coulter, nobody very special. Her old man had a chemist shop. A year ago when he had met her, over a couple of beers at the Pig and Whistle, she had been "Pat," exactly like any other Patricia. She was in her second year at the art school and had been to France and Spain for a year before coming to university. He had liked her. There was that hair, a narrow face that was intriguing rather than pretty, and a small-boned, restless body. Her forthright political views both horrified and fascinated him, for his own were in a state of flux. He had cultivated the air of being a busy medical student, above trivialities like student politics. She had forced him into a reluctant defense of the Nationalists whom his father had worked to bring into office four years before. Finally he had started to ask himself questions, and she had been good at providing answers or at holding up his own overfacile answers to scornful scrutiny.

She was equally merciless with herself. At her age, twenty-two, he would have expected her to be ready to discard some of her independence of spirit for the stability of home and family. But she did not compromise. If anything, she was becoming even more contemptuous of permanence and security.

A symptom of her need to change was the new nickname, on which she insisted. He had found it rather touching at first. She was growing away from her origins and so was he. It amused him to humor her and call her Trish.

But now he was not in the least amused.

"What's wrong with you?" he asked again.

She swung her slender legs down off the bed, saw that he was looking at them, and tugged with pointed modesty at the skirt of the raincoat. The suggestion that he was somehow being ungallant annoyed him even more. He considered telling her bluntly to leave; that he had work to do.

Then she said in a flat voice, without preliminaries or subterfuge: "I'm pregnant."

He felt as if he had walked into a room he knew well in the dark and, confident of knowing the position of each familiar object, had immediately bumped into a wall that had never been there before.

"You're what?"

"Pregnant," she said with the same unnatural calm. "I can't be absolutely positive, but I strongly suspect it."

"But how the hell . . . ?"

His lips twisted in a humorless smile.

"You should know."

He fumbled behind him for the chair. In doing so he bumped clumsily against the desk and a row of propped-up textbooks tumbled with a crash. Flustered, he bent down to retrieve them and saw with a sense of foreboding that on top of the pile, open at the title page, was a book on gynecology and obstetrics.

His mind was starting to function again.

"How can you be sure? How long have you . . . I mean . . . when were you . . . ?"

She saw his embarrassment but did nothing to help. He had not observed before that she had the capacity to be cruel.

For some reason it occurred to him that he had never seen any of her creative work. Was she a good artist? He had no idea. He had never asked her to show him any of her work and she had never volunteered. In fact he really knew very little of what went on inside her beyond what she chose to show.

He had his own observations and reflections on the strangeness of human nature. With shame and a sense of shock at discovering cowardice in himself he remembered the impulse that had come to him as she made her bald announcement. Deny it, a betraying instinct had tempted him. Put up a bold front and say it has nothing to do with you.

Of course he would not consider doing it; would never think seriously of deserting her. Yet the hint of treachery had been there and he could not deny it.

He forced himself to be cool and professional.

"How long is your period overdue?"

"Five days."

He almost laughed aloud in his relief.

"Five days! But, my dear girl, that's nothing. Hell, you gave me a fright. Five days is nothing at all."

An assessing, slightly derisive look.

"It is for me. I'm never a day over."

"Take my word for it. Five days is absolutely within normal limits. Absolutely."

"It's never happened before."

"That's no reason why it shouldn't happen now. You can't make absolute statements about the human body. It's queer and unpredictable. But anyway you don't have to worry. Not yet."

"Not yet." She echoed him obediently enough, but her tone hinted that she thought herself more knowledgeable and wiser than he, for all his professional expertise.

Ignoring her, he pursued the diagnostic trail.

"In fact, worry may be the clue. You've been worrying about it and that quite often has the result of delaying things. You could even skip a period entirely because of worry."

"I wasn't worried five days ago."

"Perhaps you were, without realizing it," he said, trying to be rational, reasonable, and reassuring all at the same time. "It could be due to a deepseated neurosis of which your conscious mind is not even aware."

"I don't need any of your glib amateur psychoanalysis now, thank you very much," she said angrily, showing emotion for the first time.

His anger rose in reponse to hers. "Look, this isn't exactly an occasion for getting off little snide remarks. If you're pregnant, all right, we'll do something about it. But in my opinion, even if it is only an amateur one as you point out, there's no reason for concern at present."

She bit her lip and turned her head away.

"I'm sorry."

He shrugged.

"I mean it," she said, and still would not look at him. "I'm sorry I said that. I didn't intend to say it."

He saw why her face was averted. She was crying.

"Pat!" he said in remorse, and it seemed as if the old name was the key-word, the open sesame to the dark cave of loneliness, for she flung herself across the bed and wept in earnest.

He stood beside her, irresolute, and after a while touched her shaking shoulders tentatively.

"Trish," he said.

She shook her head, trying to choke back her weeping.

"Darling Trish. Don't cry. You don't have to worry. I'll think of something."

She raised her head to look at him then. Her hair had come adrift and hung limply and straggly in her face. She did not attempt to push it back but stared at him through the hanging strands as if through a curtain that divided them.

"Help me," she said. But she said it more as a question than an appeal. "Help me, Deon."

"Of course," he said quickly. Too quickly. "Of course I'll help you."

She looked at him for a moment longer and the question was still on her face. Then her expression became remote once more. She looked away.

He stroked her shoulder and some of her fear communicated itself to him; as if fear were a skin that could be rubbed off. He could feel the tide of panic and then of naked, stomach-gripping fear rising within him.

"Don't worry," he said, and even to himself his voice sounded thin and taut, unconvincing.

"We cannot afford to say: 'Don't worry,'" Professor Snyman was saying. "The problem will not solve itself."

The unexpected echo snatched at Deon's thoughts. He looked at the little man down below, startled.

"Surgery on children, especially on neonates, has to be recognized as a different field from surgery on adults," the professor said. "We will need a

33

new breed of surgeon, working together in a new kind of team, in order to achieve this."

Obviously the old man has been going on about his hobbyhorse, Deon thought. That was fine; there probably hadn't been much more than generalities.

But now he had to concentrate.

Professor Snyman surveyed his class once more, heavy eyebrows swiveling like questing antennae. He turned away and began to fuss with the slide projector.

"I'm going to show you some of the things with which we shall have to contend," he said over his shoulder. He picked up a slide, peered at it and slid it into its slot.

"Lights!" he called out. "Lights!"

The wintry sunshine through the high windows was still too strong for his liking, even with the room lights off. He fretted, making shooing gestures with his quick hands, while the shutters were closed. Finally, satisfied with the half dark, he switched on the projector. He had put the slide in upside down and there was a snicker from the top rows which faded at once when he turned, scowling. He corrected the error, his back stiff and indignant.

A comparative table, now right side up, showed on the screen.

"Here we see something of the incidence of congenital abnormalities," Professor Snyman said. "You will note that approximately four percent of infants are born with extensive deformities. Very few of these cannot be saved by surgery. On the other hand most of these anomalies are invariably fatal if not corrected. This is particularly true of five groups."

He walked up to the screen, and the graph was obliterated by his shadow, made huge by the angle of the light beam from the projector. He stood in the light for a moment, his back to the class, as if enjoying the spectacle of being twice life-size. Then he stood aside and tapped at the reappearing graph.

"Intestinal atresia," he said. "Until a year ago the mortality rate here in Cape Town was one hundred percent." He paused, nodding his head for emphasis. "One hundred percent," he said in tones of awed discovery.

The lecture room door opened and the resultant shaft of light dimmed the image on the screen. Professor Snyman swung on his heel to stare at the intruders. A nurse had come in, leading a small girl by the hand. The child wore a bright scarlet dressing gown. She stared around her, lips parted, then looked up at the nurse for reassurance.

"I'm not quite ready to demonstrate this case," the old man said crossly. "But wait here anyway, nurse. And please try to keep the child quiet."

Philip's voice said softly in Deon's ear: "Excuse me."

Deon looked at him, momentarily startled. The Indian man and girl and the other Coloured men were on their feet too, standing behind Philip, waiting to pass. Then Deon understood. The patient was white. He swung his legs into the aisle, out of the way, and sat waiting in embarrassment as each of the seven students filed quietly past and went up the steps and out through a door at the back. Then he stared with a measure of resentment at the nurse and the solemn-eyed white child.

The nurse was hardly worth staring at. Short and plump, with her uniform exactly at regulation length, four inches below the knee. What was the beauty Robby had spotted on the nurses' noticeboard the other day? An admonition to nurses about evading the dress rules. How had it read? "Nurses must wear uniforms four inches below the patella." But in place of patella, the kneecap, some ignorant secretary had typed "pasella," which was the Zulu word for a gift. Deon smiled inwardly. Funny how it was always the pretty ones who tried to make themselves prettier, with a hemline sneaked a little higher or a cap offset just that small amount to avoid the stereotype. The plain ones stayed plain, as if they didn't really care. Probably they made better nurses. And yet he'd noticed that wards where pretty nurses worked were invariably more cheerful than the others. The patients might die, but at least they died happy.

The fat nurse, self-conscious under the critical stares of dozens of pairs of eyes, looked down at the ground. She had black, thick brows, now drawn together in a mutinous frown.

For some reason Deon felt joy rise inside himself like a bubble. It was going to be all right. He would telephone Trish immediately after the lecture and she would give him the good news. There would be no need for anything drastic after all.

He glanced down at his watch. Ten minutes to go before Snyman finished. By now Trish would be home for lunch.

"In the remaining few lectures," Professor Snyman was saying, "we will discuss some of the malformations in detail and discover how the surgeon may step in to correct the mistakes of nature."

I haven't taken in a single thing he's said, Deon thought. But the sense of joy persisted. What the hell; he'd compare notes with one of the other students afterward.

"Before we end, however, I want to show you an interesting case which came up the other day," the professor said. He motioned the nurse and the

35

child toward him. "When we consider the complexity of the creative process, it is a miracle that the results are so often perfect. Sometimes, however—and we have evidence of it in the body of this child—the lines get crossed."

The child and the nurse both watched him darkly. He reached out to hold the child's hand.

"Terry is six years old. Recently her mother noticed a lump on the right side of her lower abdomen. The doctor, on examination, found this to be cystic in feel. It was about as large as a medium-sized orange, moved around freely, and could be pushed down into the pelvis. I'm sure you will all agree that these are the characteristics of an ovarian cyst. The nature of the growth, however, is clearly revealed by this X-ray."

He touched a switch and the X-ray screen flickered, then glowed whitely. Professor Snyman took a plate from its envelope and flicked it professionally under the clips.

Deon could see the shadowy outline of the child's pelvic bones.

"Mr. . . . ah . . . van der Riet," Professor Snyman called out.

Deon snapped into awareness. Had the old devil noticed that his attention had been wandering? He stood up slowly.

The professor beckoned peremptorily. "Come out, man. Come out. No one's going to eat you. Come down here and have a look and tell the class what you see."

Deon, now almost as self-conscious as the nurse had been earlier, climbed warily down the steps. He bent down next to the X-ray viewer, noting the small cradle of the pelvis and the shadow of the spine. There was something. He peered closer, taking his lower lip between his teeth and gnawing at it. There. Down on the right-hand side, low down in the pelvis. He stared at it in growing horror.

The professor was growing impatient.

"Come on! Tell the class what you see."

Deon pointed at the shadow.

"Here," he said. "In the pelvis. Teeth! I see teeth!"

TWO

The telephone rang, on and on.

Was there no one to answer it? He imagined the bell ringing in an empty house.

But was the repetitive buzz the actual sound of the bell at the other end of the line? He had read somewhere that a ringing tone was no more than confirmation of an electrical connection and that it really came from the telephone exchange. Like the nerve connections to the brain, he thought at once, and could almost see the appropriate diagrams in Gray's *Anatomy*. Page a thousand and something in the neurology section. Two diagrams on opposing pages showing the motor and sensory tracts; thin colored lines weaving delicate patterns like the branches of stylized trees. He would be in trouble if there was a question about the nervous system in the Medicine paper. Bernstein's lectures had bored him and he had stopped attending. Now he would have to leave it to chance and hope there would not be a question on it.

Damn this phone. Would no one ever answer?

There was a click and then her voice, raised in question.

"Hello?"

He had the coin poised, but fumbled with it momentarily.

Again, "Hello?"

He dropped the coin into the slot.

"Hello, Trish," he said eagerly.

"Oh. It's you." Her voice was dull.

He knew.

He felt a rush of nausea, light-headedness, and fought to keep himself under control, to betray nothing.

37

"How are you?" Calculatedly brisk and cheerful.

"Fine," she said listlessly.

He was immediately angry. Why couldn't she try, at least?

But she had said "fine." Perhaps he had misinterpreted the way she had said it. Perhaps she had meant exactly that: fine. Everything's fine. There's nothing to worry about. Perhaps she was forced to be guarded in what she said.

"Listen. Is there someone with you?"

"With me?" She sounded surprised. "No." And after a moment's pause. "My mother has gone out. I'm alone."

"Oh."

He knew, but he was compelled to go on with it; to continue to the last, the ultimate point of pain and absurdity.

"And . . ." He did not know how to phrase it. "Have you any news?"

"News?"

Was she stupid? Or being deliberately obtuse?

"You know. Has anything happened?"

"Oh."

Again she paused. He could feel his pulse fluttering in his throat.

"No," she said.

"I see."

For a little while neither of them spoke. He held the receiver slightly away from his head. It was damp against his skin. He had been sweating in the stifling confines of the call-box. The cupped receiver made a hissing sea-sound. Like the sound of distant surf you heard when you held a sea shell over your ear. He remembered that his father had a collection of the big convoluted shells they called "perdekuile." He and his brother had helped collect them from the rock pools at low tide, one summer holiday at the beach. His father put them in a row on a shelf in the porch room he used as the farm office. When Deon longed to be at the sea again he would take down one of the shells and hold it to his ear and hear the slow sound of waves.

"Hello?" Trish said, again on that note of worried interrogation.

"It'll be all right," he said into the receiver, almost roughly, as if by being emphatic he could force something to happen.

"If you say so." She was trying to be cool, but he could hear from her voice that she had been crying again. Oh, Christ.

"It'll be all right. You'll see."

"Yes. Maybe."

Now he was in a hurry; anxious to be rid of her.

"Listen. I have to go."

"Tonight?"

"No. I can't . . . I . . ." He sought quickly for an excuse. "Look, I'm going to be pretty late tonight. I have to do some work with Robby."

"All right."

"Tomorrow maybe," he suggested, with a sudden resurgence of pity and affection and even (he had in all honesty to admit) a degree of desire. "Perhaps we can fix something for tomorrow evening. I'll ring you."

"You'll know where to find me." She gave a small laugh, intended to be brave, but he understood the implicit reproach.

He said: "Fine," and was aware and ashamed of his own deceit, but did not care at this moment. He needed to end the conversation immediately. "See you. 'Bye, now."

" 'Bye."

The click of the receiver was like the sound of a key in a lock. Briefly he felt free and unencumbered. But at once the leaden weight of guilt and responsibility returned.

He let the spring door of the phone booth bang behind him and walked slowly out into the sun. Something reminded him of his father, something briefly glimpsed, like the quick flash of sunlight on the windscreen of one of the cars moving on the city streets far away across a barrier of buildings.

The shells. Something to do with the shells.

It had been on a morning during the long summer vacation of his second year. A Saturday morning, he remembered now, as it all came back with a rush. Late in the morning, for he had showered and changed into tennis clothes. He was planning to make a lunch of bread and sliced cold mutton and then he was going off to spend the afternoon at the Verster farm. The Versters had a tennis court and pretty twin daughters.

But his father came from outside on to the wide, cool porch and looked at the white shirt with its little design of laurel leaves and the neatly pressed shorts and socks and newly cleaned tennis shoes, and his lips moved very slightly at the corners.

"You're very smart," he said. He used the English word "smart" to underline the irony.

Deon flushed. There had been something in the air since the beginning of the holidays: something between him and his father; a dry, static-charged feeling which needed only one abrasive touch to produce a spark.

"I'm going to tennis," he said.

"So I see," his father said.

39

One of the Coloured laborers came around the corner of the house. He carried his stained, torn hat respectfully in both hands. He stopped at the steps, looking up at the white men.

"Jantjie says the pump down behind Long Hill is broken," van der Riet said.

The Coloured man grinned at Deon, showing uneven yellow teeth.

"I'm going down now to see to it," van der Riet said. He looked at the tennis clothes again. "Are you coming to help me?"

"I was going to play tennis," Deon said sulkily.

His father turned half away. "If your brother wasn't at that ram sale I wouldn't have to ask you."

"Boet is the farmer. Not me."

"Where do you think the money comes from to keep you at the university? It's about time you see where it comes from." His father shrugged. "But if you'd rather play tennis . . ."

Deon worked his shoulders angrily.

"You don't leave me much choice, do you?"

His father looked at him from under his brows. "Do not," he said levelly, "speak to your father in that tone of voice."

Deon changed back into khakis with bad grace. His father was waiting for him at the gate. He was driving the old Chevy pick-up that they used around the farm. Deon climbed into the cab beside his father without saying anything. Jantjie sat at the back among the toolboxes and spanners and monkey wrenches. He leaned against the cab and his hat was pulled down over his eyes. His face had a dreamy, contented look. He was going to ride out to the pump and back; not have to walk as usual. His bare toes were dusty and horny like the wrinkled heads of the tortoises one found in the veld.

The road was badly corrugated and the Chevy bounced on its worn springs. The tools banged and clattered in their steel boxes at the back, so that conversation was difficult. Deon was grateful for this.

They went down past Long Hill, which was not really any longer or more remarkable than any of the other stony ridges that here and there broke the monotony of the wide, flat land. His father stopped once, at a spot where the jackal-proof fence had become slack, so that Jantjie could refasten a dropper pole.

They found that a bearing had gone and that the pump's main gear was partially stripped. His father whistled cheerfully between a gap in his teeth as he and Jantjie struggled to remove the damaged gear, levering it a fraction of an inch at a time. His father was at his best when dealing with large and difficult mechanical problems. He had a folding stool with a leather-thong seat which he carried everywhere he worked on the farm and he sat on this now, leaning forward between the pump and the diesel engine that drove it, working at the gear with the big screwdriver and a tire jack.

"It's coming," he said, and to Jantjie, who was using too much force at his end, "Careful, baboon." Warning and abuse were both good-natured. Jantjie grinned and spat in the dust.

There was no room for Deon to do much of anything except to watch them and hand on tools as they were required. He stood looking over his father's shoulder. The elder van der Riet had taken off his hat, and the band of skin around his forehead showed up startlingly pale by contrast with his deeply tanned and weathered face. Deon noticed, with a slight sense of shock, that the dark hair was thinning on top.

His father changed sides to reach the lower end of the gear. He looked up. There was a smear of grease across his jaw, where he had absent-mindedly wiped away sweat.

"So," he said. "And what else did they teach you this year except how to cut up dead bodies?"

The tension had gone. They were father and son, and friends as well.

"Oh, histology, biochemistry, and so on. The subjects are anatomy and physiology, of course. But they include all kinds of other things. Anthropology and evolution, for instance."

"Evolution." His father said it as if it were a comic word. "Don't tell me they teach you that nonsense too."

Deon attempted a light, disbelieving laugh. "Well, naturally. It's part of science, isn't it?"

"A story about men coming down from the monkeys? Science? It's a funny kind of science."

"It's not quite as simple as that. That's part of it, but it's a lot more complicated."

"I'm sure they make it sound very complicated," his father said drily. "All those clever professors. If they make it complicated, it sounds more scientific, not so?"

"Perhaps. But the point is that it's been proved scientifically. It's all true."

"True? It's true, is it?" He spoke to Jantjie. "Tap it on your side with the cold chisel and the little hammer. Not too hard."

"Of course it is," Deon said.

His father gave him a quick, quizzical look. "Is it true because the professors tell you so?"

41

"You don't understand. All the evidence is there, all interlocked. It's all logical. It's like a chain which you can follow from beginning to end by looking at each of the links."

"All right, give me a hand here," his father said. The three of them eased the heavy, oil-black gear out of the pump block.

"Then you'd better explain it to me," his father said. "But remember that I'm only a simple farmer, so you'd better not make it too complicated."

Deon groped through half-remembered lectures for an example. "The shells," he said with sudden inspiration.

His father looked at him blankly.

"Shells?"

"Yes. Like the shells you've got in the office. The perdekuil shells we brought from the bay, remember? Well, that type of marine shell has remained basically unchanged ever since Cambrian times. And that's almost six hundred million years ago." He looked triumphantly at his father.

"The professors must be very clever to know what happened such a long time ago."

Deon's body stiffened. He did not like being laughed at.

"You won't understand if you don't want to," he said sharply. Then he added quickly, noting the small warning frown which had appeared between his father's eyebrows: "These shells didn't evolve because they didn't have to. Their life didn't change so they didn't change. But other forms of life had to adapt because perhaps their circumstances changed. They had to adapt to survive. That's called the process of natural selection."

He went on explaining with enthusiasm while his father listened with grave good humor, meanwhile examining the rest of the pump for further damage.

"You see," Deon said at last, "it's the only possible explanation for everything."

His father glanced at him. It had become very hot in the cramped corrugated iron pump room and all three of them were sweating now. Jantjie gave off a smell of woodsmoke and old clothes.

"It's very interesting about your shells and your what's-it-mates."

"Primates. Apes."

"Whatever it is. But don't fool yourself into thinking that shells and apes explain everything, my boy. Just remember one thing. And that is: In the beginning God created the heavens and the earth."

Deon made a flapping, dismissive gesture. "That."

"That," his father said, and this time his voice was a little tighter. "That

42

was what you were taught to live by and what I have lived by and my father before me and his father before that. And don't forget it."

Deon shrugged. Perhaps he had been more disrepectful than he had intended, but now he could not back down.

"It's not my fault I was taught to believe in fables."

"Do you speak of the Word of God as a fable?" Now the voice was hard and ringing, like the sound of the cold chisel when it had struck metal.

"Look, Father, everyone knows that the Bible isn't literally true. It's a collection of all the old stories . . ."

"Have you become a communist at that English university? You are mocking the Word."

They faced one another across the grimy, rust-streaked pump case, angry as strange dogs with a fence between them. Jantjie looked from one to the other as they spoke. His face showed fright.

"You have been mocking what I believe," Deon retorted bitterly.

His father appeared to reflect.

"That is true," he said then, very slowly, as if it was painful to form and pronounce each word. "I am sorry for it."

Deon was briefly nonplussed. But he was still very angry. "That doesn't change anything. The point still is that the Jewish priests collected legends from all over, from other tribes and countries, and they put them all together, and so the Bible is nothing more than . . ."

"I will not have blasphemy on my farm," his father said. His face was white and strained.

"Is it blasphemy to speak the truth?"

"And Pilate said to Him: 'What is truth?' "

"Quoting texts doesn't prove anything."

"Better to speak of holy texts than of shells and monkeys."

"You don't understand," Deon said wearily.

"Perhaps I don't understand you. But I do understand this. We need the Word. We are straying children of the world and our little minds rebel against the purpose of God, or we betray him through our deeds. Only the Word can help us stay on His path. You will become a scientist, not a farmer. Boet will inherit the farm because he is the eldest. But in the eyes of God there is no difference between you, provided you carry out His will."

Further argument would serve no purpose. Scientifically, what his father was saying amounted to nothing. It was a lot of meaningless cant which anyone trained in logic could have torn to shreds in a matter of minutes.

But his father would never be convinced. Once his mind was made up about something he couldn't be budged, not even by a team of oxen. This stubbornness was a family trait, a characteristic failing of which all of them were perversely proud. There was even a story about this very borehole. It had been put down by his grandfather forty-one years before. The water diviner had come and gone and had proclaimed that there was no water. His grandfather was sure the water was there. "Drill the hole," he said. The drill had gone down to eighty feet, which was as deep as any borehole in the district, and they hadn't found anything. The drilling foreman wanted to stop then, but his grandfather van der Riet had said, "Go deeper." They went down another forty feet and still there was no water, only layers of granite and gravel. By now the foreman was rebellious, but his grandfather had stood by the machine with his arms folded and said, "I'm paying for it. Go deeper."

At a hundred and fifty-five feet they found water so strong that the test pump couldn't drain it in a week.

Someone nudged Deon from the back. He turned, startled. It was Robby, clever, serious Robby, who hid himself behind a screen of jokes and wisecracks. He grinned at Deon.

"Relax, old son. It might never happen."

"It's happened," Deon said, and laughed to complete the joke.

Robby laughed too. "I'm going down to the cafeteria. Coming?"

"Ja. Okay."

They walked together down the steep steps. Robby talked idly about girls and drinking. Deon's replies were vague. He was still thinking about his father.

That was his father. People called them the "Hard-headed van der Riets" and his father was proud of it. A thing was right or it was wrong. And he knew which at once. After that, nothing could move him.

Would he condone the fact that a son of his, a van der Riet of Wamagerskraal, had slept with a girl and made her pregnant and that he had not the least intention of marrying her? Would he even understand that such a thing could happen?

Never, Deon thought. Never in a million years. Never even (with some pride that he could make a joke at a time like this) in six hundred million years.

They stopped just inside the cafeteria doorway, swiftly surveying the rows of formica-topped tables. The Coloured students had taken over their usual place beside the door. Two of them sat hunched over a chessboard

44

and the others watched the game in silence. In a far corner Philip Davids sat alone at a table. A textbook was propped in front of him and he was reading as he ate. He did not look up as they passed on their way to the serving counter.

They returned, carrying their plates (curry-and-rice day today; the Malay chef was good with curry and rice) and Robby made to pass Philip again, heading for a table against the wall. Deon forestalled him.

"Here," he said, and pulled out a chair at Philip's table.

Both Philip and Robby looked at him, faintly surprised. The races were equal here, true, but there was seldom any easy mingling. Six years ago, when he first came here, Deon had been irritated to see people with dark skins sharing with whites. It had chafed especially to see Coloured men and white girls together. Some of the girls made a point of being elaborately friendly toward the Coloureds. He had been prepared for it in theory, of course, for he had chosen to attend the university here. But still, theory and fact did not quite balance. A sense of tension and resentment remained, even today, and even if he was the only one aware of it.

Now he was uncertain why he had chosen to sit at Philip's table. Perhaps it was because of what had happened in class earlier. And perhaps not. However, he sat down determinedly, and after a fractional hesitation Robby followed his example.

Philip was eating sandwiches from a brown paper bag. He flicked a hand at crumbs on the table, then, still looking at Deon, pushed his textbook out of the way to make room for their plates. Deon glanced at the cover.

"How's it going?" he asked, with a nod toward the book.

"All right," Philip said. He sipped slowly and deliberately from a teacup made of thick china with the university crest on the outside. Finally he asked: "You?"

"Oh, okay. I'm working in cardiology."

"Uh-huh."

The noncommittal air annoyed Deon and he could not quite keep the sarcasm out of his voice.

"Of course, you don't have to worry, do you?"

Philip said nothing. He toyed with the sandwiches. They were made of thick slices of coarse, home-baked bread. Deon could not make out what was in the filling, but it smelled like fish. Snoek-fish perhaps. The Coloureds liked snoek.

Robby looked at them both with interest, as if he had sensed something he did not understand. Then he began to eat rapidly.

To make amends for discourtesy, and also because the sandwiches had reminded him, Deon asked: "How's your mother?"

"Fine, fine," Philip said. "She is fine."

There was constraint in his voice, so Deon was forced to go further. "Where do you live now?"

"Same place. Same house. Still in District Six."

"Is she in the same job? At that fish canning place?"

Philip nodded. He sipped more tea, and the cup masked his face.

"She really has been pretty marvelous. The way she's seen you through university, I mean." Deon was aware that his enthusiasm might ring false, but nevertheless he was sincere. "She can't earn much at that factory. It couldn't have been easy."

Philip was silent. He looked down at his sandwiches. He had not taken a bite at them since the other two had joined him. His hands rested lightly on the table beside the paper bag.

"I know you've won scholarships and all that," Deon said lamely, hoping he had not blundered. "But it still must have meant a lot of sacrifice."

Again Philip did not speak, for so long that Deon was convinced he had misunderstood; that he saw insults where none had been.

But at last Philip said, in quiet agreement: "It wasn't easy."

"That's it," Deon said, relieved and emphatic. "That's what I mean."

Philip glanced at him, then over his shoulder at the chess players. "Your father helped a lot too," he said casually.

Deon blinked in astonishment and half rose from his chair. "What?"

Again that calm scrutiny.

"Didn't you know that?"

"My father? Are you sure?"

Philip nodded abruptly.

"He helped us. I wouldn't have made it through the first two years if he hadn't."

"Well, I'll be damned."

"Didn't you know about it?"

"Not a word. Not till this minute."

Deon chewed a mouthful of the yellow-brown meat and rice mixture, grateful that his eating could serve as a pretext for silence. His father had done that and never mentioned it. Not that he would have mentioned it, for he was not like some people who found it difficult not to praise their own philanthropy. Still, it was amazing to think that he could have decided to give money toward the education of a young Coloured man then, six years ago, in 1948, when racial feelings were being whipped up; when he

46

himself was doing his fair share of the whipping. (They had wanted him to stand as a candidate in the election that year but he preferred to remain where he was: chairman of the local branch of the Party; the man in the seat of power; the man who made other men candidates.) It showed a degree of detachment that was unexpected. No. When you came to think about it, it was the opposite of detachment. His father believed that charity began at home, and Flip was a boy from Wamagerskraal, even if he was only a Coloured. The obligation was feudal.

Nevertheless it was surprising and a pleasing thing to know.

"I'll be damned," he said again.

Perhaps Philip noticed a touch of self-congratulation in his voice, for he said, as quietly as always, but with a certain dry emphasis: "We were very grateful for the help."

"Well, perhaps he thought he owed . . ." Deon said confusedly. Philip's ironic inflection made him resentful. You may be so smart, but don't forget it was van der Riet money that brought you here, my friend, he thought. And then was immediately ashamed of the thought.

"You must take me to visit your mother someday," he said with attempted warmth.

Philip smiled. "Yes. Someday."

Robby intervened, with well-judged diplomacy.

"Has one of you guys got spare notes on diseases of the blood?" he asked. "I lent mine to Dave Fowler and the bugger has gone and lost them."

"You can have mine," Philip said.

"Or mine," Deon added quickly. "I've finished with them."

For a moment it seemed as if the need to be generous might give fresh reason for disagreement, but Robby resolved the issue by nodding his acceptance and thanks to Philip.

"That reminds me," Deon said. "What was old Snyman's lecture about?"

Both looked at him strangely.

"I wasn't really listening," he explained. "I was thinking about something else."

"You're bluidy confident at this stage of the game, m'lad," Robby grumbled in a fair imitation of the pessimistic Scots burr of the assistant professor of medicine. He grinned. "Och, it was no' much. Lot of bull about pediatric surgery." His voice grew sharper, more enthusiastic. "But hell, wasn't that quite an X-ray, huh? That kid's."

"What was wrong with the child?" Philip asked.

Deon and Robby looked away awkwardly.

47

"It's bloody idiotic," Deon blurted out finally. "I don't know why you guys don't ignore the whole business. What difference would it have made to that kid if you hadn't left the lecture room?"

Philip examined his angry face very calmly. "Those are the unwritten rules. And I don't think any of us seeks martyrdom through breaking them."

"You're simply bowing to apartheid, that's all."

"Well, there is little we can do about it. It is the only condition on which we are accepted here. We may not examine white patients."

There was a long, strained silence. Then Philip shrugged. "What's this X-ray you're talking about?"

Robby was clearly happy to change the subject.

"You tell him," he said, nudging Deon with a bony elbow. "You spotted it." He grinned. "I'll never forget old Deon's face when he saw that X-ray." He put on a leering vampire face, then twisted his features to show the supposed reaction, a look of abject terror. He laughed out loud, so that the woman at the cash register turned to frown at them. "Go on. You tell him."

"It must have been an ovarian cyst with teeth inside it," Deon said shortly.

"Teeth!" Robby mimicked Deon's horror-stricken voice. "I saw teeth!" He chuckled.

"Some brilliant G.P. insisted she'd swallowed the teeth and that they had perforated the bowel. Fortunately they brought her here and the gynecologists made the right diagnosis," Deon told Philip.

Philip nodded. "Cystic teratoma of the ovary. Portions of an underdeveloped twin."

"You can't tell this bloke anything." Robby shook his head admiringly. "Go on, Professor. Tell us what you are spotting for the surgery exam."

Philip smiled and as always when his rare smile showed he suddenly seemed far younger, more like the farm urchin Deon remembered.

"I wish I knew." He finished the tea and pushed the cup away. The sandwiches were still uneaten. He began to crumble one of them thoughtfully. "You know, I wonder if that really is the answer."

"What do you mean?" Deon asked.

"The theory that the tumor is a mixed-up growth from a cell which should have developed into the twin of the child."

"That's what the books say," Robby interrupted him.

"And what if the books are wrong?"

Robby cocked an eyebrow at him. "You ask questions like that, and you with your examinations hardly three months away?" He drew his chair

48

firmly and briskly closer to the table. "Till after November you give the answers the books give."

Philip's mouth turned down obstinately, but he did not say anything further.

Deon and Robby ate in silence for a time. Deon found the food tasteless, a soggy mass in his mouth. He splashed ketchup from the bottle, pushed it around his plate, tested a mouthful or two. It was still bloody awful.

"If you really think about it, it is like performing an abortion, isn't it?" he said.

The other two stared at him blankly.

"Well, what I mean is if that tumor is the twin, then cutting it out is the same as doing an abortion."

"Hell, isn't that a bit far-fetched, Deon?" Robby said and carried on eating.

Philip, however, looked interested.

"It's a point. But I don't think it's valid. The cyst isn't a fetus. It has no chance of being born and it couldn't achieve separate existence."

"I guess that's right," Deon said.

He pushed his plate away. He couldn't stomach any more of this stuff today. He looked across at Philip, at his alert face, in which only a slight bluntness betrayed his mixed blood.

He's a Coloured, Deon thought. That's why I sat down at this table. Coloured people know about this kind of thing. It happens to them often enough, God knows. Perhaps he knows someone I could go to, someone who can fix things.

"Speaking of abortions." He made his voice studiedly casual. "I wonder how I would react if an unmarried girl approached me to help her."

"If her life or health is in danger, yes," Philip said promptly "In any other circumstance, no."

"I know. That's what the book says. But you've been asking if the book is right. Can't you envisage any other situations where an abortion might be advisable?"

"Such as?"

"Social situations, for one. A woman's health isn't the only thing at stake, you know. Her place in society might be jeopardized too."

"Then she should practice birth control."

"And isn't abortion just another means of birth control?"

"I've given you that answer already. A fetus can exist independently, so it has a right to be born."

"That's a very legalistic argument. But what of that unborn child's right

49

to a decent existence? Even if you can't guarantee him love; if all you can promise is a miserable existence; must you still guarantee him life?"

"It's not our business to judge. Our business is to preserve life."

"Oh, you're so pure and so righteous," Deon said sneeringly.

Robby sat up with a jerk and uttered a protesting half laugh. "Hey! Steady on," he cautioned. He looked a little anxiously across at the group of Coloured students around the chess players.

Deon controlled himself with an effort. "Sorry. But that kind of attitude gets me. It's the way my father thinks. This is God's will and so, by God, you'd better like it."

"Religion doesn't come into it, Deon," Philip said. The fingers with which he was folding the sandwiches back into their bag had started to tremble slightly. "It's simply what I believe. We haven't trained to become doctors in order to become executioners too."

"You're twisting my words. All I'm saying is that society has a right to decide. Even an individual has the right to decide whether or not it should be burdened with yet another life."

"I'm not twisting your words at all. What you're suggesting is that a woman has the right to barter that life for social esteem. Or even for a holiday overseas. Or a new car."

Deon looked away. It's all very well for you, he thought. He knew that his face was red with anger and shame. "It's easy enough to talk when you're not faced with it. But that woman may be your patient. Don't you owe her a duty?"

"I suggest you blokes drop the subject now," Robby said. His eyes were serious behind his glasses.

"Truly, Robby, I believe this," Philip told him earnestly. "Our sense of values has become distorted. We treasure things above our fellow humans. Abortion is just a symptom of this. What do you think would happen if someone had to start slashing at the Mona Lisa with a knife? They'd kill him. But they would stand by with equanimity while an abortionist destroys another perfect creation."

"Just a minute," Deon said heatedly. "There's only one Mona Lisa, and let's face it there are enough bloody human beings on this earth."

Philip smiled slightly, as if he had set a trap and the victim had walked into it. "That one fetus you're destroying is unique too. And perhaps it could have been a greater genius than da Vinci."

The smile was what made Deon say bitterly: "Or else it might have been a Coloured slum child who ends up a drunkard and in jail."

The words were hardly said when he wished them unsaid. He was still angry and a pulse was hammering away at the side of his neck. But he had not intended to wound. Robby was frowning distantly at one of the caricatures of long-ago members of the medical faculty which decorated the cafeteria walls. He seemed to be pretending he hadn't heard or noticed anything, or that it was no concern of his anyway.

Apologize, Deon told himself. Tell him you didn't mean that. But he was unable to get the words out.

The apology was forming on his tongue when Philip stood up, not overquickly but with firm emphasis in every movement. The chair legs made a scraping sound across the floor.

"Please excuse me," he said very coldly and formally.

He picked up his book and his bag of sandwiches, made a small bow in Robby's direction and turned away without looking at Deon again.

Deon's regret was instantly replaced by anger. Damn you too, he thought. Bloody jumped-up Coloured. If it wasn't for the van der Riets you wouldn't be here anyway.

"You were a bit rough on the poor bloke," Robby said.

"What do you mean?"

Robby saw Deon's face and looked away. "Well, it's none of my business," he said awkwardly.

"Look, I'm not getting at him because he's a Coloured or anything like that," Deon said tersely. "But I can't stand people who get all noble and righteous."

"All right, all right." Robby examined Deon's face again and his eyes were shrewd. "Bit edgy today, aren't we? Had bad news?"

"No, it's just that I . . . oh, I guess cramming's getting on my nerves."

"Uh huh. You wouldn't be needing a reliable telephone number, would you?"

"What do you mean?"

Robby laughed.

"Oh, come now. Who do you think you were fooling with all that chat about distressed mothers-to-be?" He leaned forward with an air of mock mystery. "I've got a friend with a friend. Do you want his number?"

"I don't know," Deon said. He was torn between the desire to confide and his pride in his own self-reliance. "I'll let you know."

Three

A quiet street, with trees and neatly clipped hedges and tidy gardens behind the hedges. It was dark now and only a few scattered lights shone on the trees and the hedges, but Deon could imagine it as it would appear by daylight. There would not be many children, or even the sound of their voices, for this was not one of the young, open suburbs. This was a locality where people settled after going on pension; where they retired for a middle-class old age after a middle-class life—the bank accountants who somehow never became managers, the senior clerks, the businessmen who had never built up giant companies.

It was far too nice here, Deon thought. One imagined old ladies come to tea with delicate cream scones and dignified old men going off to play bowls and fat Coloured servants coming in twice a week to char. You thought of people doing nice things: growing prize roses or knitting woolen toys for charity or collecting stamps of the British colonies and dependencies.

The whole atmosphere was wrong. It should have been a slum street, with snotty-nosed children screaming and obscenities scrawled on gray walls. People should have been watching suspiciously from down the road, fingering the knives in their trouser pockets. It should have been a place of dark doorways and boarded-up windows and smells and furtive noises.

However, this was it: Gardenia Road (all the streets in the suburb had flower names), and he had checked and double-checked the name board at its entrance.

He came out from under the shadow of the fine old oak where he had been standing, watching, for the past ten minutes (feeling the same surges of panicky indecision as on that first day he had waited outside the chemist shop, hoping the man assistant would come to the counter so that he could go up and ask for a package of condoms in a hoarse whisper) and crossed the road purposefully. Number 15 had a clipped hedge like the others, and the house was partly hidden by rows of shrubs among which a crazy-paving path wound in tight curves. Deon hesitated with one hand on the white-painted gate, checked the number (tidy brass numerals on the white wood-work) once more and looked toward the house. Light shone in one window, visible through the shrubbery.

The gate opened without squeaking and he went up the path, hearing his own footsteps almost as if they were coming from ahead of him, as if someone was preceding him.

A wide, old-fashioned porch with squat pillars. He climbed the highly polished steps carefully and crossed slippery tiles to the front door. The doorknocker was in the shape of a brass dolphin. He pushed the doorbell button beside it and heard a bell jangling, far away inside the hoase. The narrow panels on each side of the door, inset with odd-shaped panes of col-ored glass, reflected the dim glow of the streetlight and he could not make out the pattern.

He rang the bell again, and, finally, heard shuffling sounds behind the door. A light was switched on and he could see now that the colored-glass panels were in the shape of two ships, clipper ships, with spread yellow sails against an azure sea.

"Who is that?"

A woman's voice. An old woman's voice; suspicious, blurred, as if she had forgotten to put in her false teeth.

He had memorized the farcical exchange of passwords.

"I'm a friend of Peter's," he said. His throat was dry, so that his voice cracked on the last words and the name came out like a cough. He cleared his throat hastily. "Of Peter's," he repeated, in case she had not heard.

A waiting silence.

"I don't know anyone by that name," the voice said finally. It sounded firmer now. Perhaps she had put in her teeth.

"Peter sent me," Deon persisted. "I'm supposed to ask for Joan."

Again a pause.

"I don't know any Peter. And no Joan. You'd better go away."

Very firmly and emphatically. But the voice contained some other qual-ity. Fear. Merely the fear of an old woman confronting a possible intruder? Or was it something else?

"Honestly, I won't harm you," Deon told her. "I telephoned a number and the man there gave me this address and the message. That I was a friend of Peter and that I had to ask for Joan."

"Telephones. Peter. Joan," the voice said crossly. "I don't know what you're talking about."

But she sounded less sure of herself and Deon was confident enough to continue.

"I'm really not going to do anything. I'm not from the police, or anything like that."

Sharply: "What've the police got to do with it?"

"I'm sorry," he said humbly. "I didn't mean to put it that way." He paused, searching his mind for some means of reassurance. "Look, won't you just open the door please? Just give me a chance to explain."

"No."

He was helpless, trapped.

"Well, hell, what else am I supposed to do? I gave the message, didn't I? I'm a friend of Peter and I'm looking for Joan."

"I don't want any men here," the woman said in tones of extreme loathing. "I don't want men here at all, do you hear me? Go away."

"Look, I've only come to ask about . . . about a certain thing. A friend of mine wants something, so I've come to ask about it."

"I don't want any men here," the woman said furiously.

"Honestly, I'm not trying to interfere." Frankness was the best policy, he decided. "Look, I'm a medical student, so I know about these things. I simply want to make sure everything is all right."

"I don't know what you're talking about," the woman said quickly from behind her door with the brass dolphin for a knocker.

"I wanted to check that, you know, it's all sterile and so on." He added lamely: "That everything will be all right."

"I don't know what you're talking about and you'd better go right now. Or else," as if on inspiration, "I'll call the police."

His eyes opened wide in sudden alarm. What if this was the wrong house? Could he have misunderstood the directions? Possibly he had made a mistake: there were two Gardenia Roads; the other one was the right one, the slum street with the dark hovels and the lurking evil which he had expected, not this tidy, cloistered home for the aged.

He had better get the hell out of here, before the old bitch really called the police.

"I'm sorry," he called. "I'm going now. I'm sorry I bothered you."

"Go away," the woman said from behind the door.

* * *

The voice on the telephone was the same one as yesterday. Foreign-sounding, but not an accent Deon recognized. German or French he would have spotted at once, but this had a Latin quality. Not Italian. Something else.

"Yes," the man on the phone said.

"Look, I phoned you yesterday," Deon said urgently. "About a certain matter."

A long pause, so that he eventually said: "Hello? Hello?"

"I am here," the voice said evenly. "Who is that speaking?"

"My name is Deon. I spoke to you yesterday."

"Yes. I now remember you."

"Well, something went wrong. I went to the address you gave me and I said what you told me to say, but they wouldn't let me in."

The man on the telephone laughed sharply. "You were foolish, my friend."

"What do you mean?"

"I told you to send the girl there. Not for you to go."

"But I simply wanted to . . ."

"What you want is no matter," the man broke in harshly. "I said for the girl to go. We do not like men meddling, do you understand?"

"The woman at that place wouldn't even open the door."

"That's right," the alien voice said. "She is now very angry and suspicious. You were foolish to go."

"I'm sorry. All I wanted to do was to make sure everything would be properly done. That conditions would be sterile."

The voice became hostile.

"What would you know about that?"

"Well . . . I . . . I'm a medical student, actually."

"I see." In long-drawn syllables, as if for reflection. "A medical student. Why don't you do it yourself?"

"I . . . I can't do it."

The other man chuckled. "Scared, huh?" He was contemptuous but indifferent.

"It's not exactly that," Deon said, trying to express it precisely. "It's just that I don't believe I should."

"Sure," the man said. Not even indifference. There was a quality of total disdain, of not caring in the least which way the world went, even were he to go with it. Deon hoped he would never have to come face to face with this man.

"Look," he said. "You've got to do it for us."

"Sure. But you shouldn't have interfered. Now it will cost more money."

"That's all right." Perhaps he had made the concession too readily, but he was beyond caring.

"Good." The voice had become very crisp now; explicit, so that the accent was almost lost. "What you have to do is to speak to your friend again."

"My friend?"

"Your friend." A trace of hostility, of newly wakened suspicion. "The one who referred you to us."

"Referred" was an unusual word for a stranger to use. Was this man a doctor? Well, there was no purpose in speculating.

"Of course," Deon said. "I'll do that."

"Good. I will also phone to make sure it is all right. Then you phone me again, maybe in a month."

"A month?" Deon could not keep the panic out of his voice. "But, look. It's already . . . it's more than two months now."

"You shouldn't have interfered," the foreign voice said, relentless as a beating drum. "I told you to send the girl."

"All right. I'll do as you say. But can't you hurry it up a bit?"

"Do as I say and then we see. Phone on Thursday. Same time."

Deon was conscious that he had lost whatever bargaining position he had ever possessed. He did not care.

"All right," he promised devoutly.

There was a sharp sound in his ear as the line was cut without farewells. The summary dismissal seemed to him to define his position exactly. His job was to pay the piper and let others call the tune.

It hurt his pride to realize this, but wasn't it really exactly what he sought? To have the decisions made for him.

He walked out past the porter and was given a brief, disinterested glance. Another student like so many others. For once he was glad to be an unknown, one of the herd.

He passed the big gleaming cars of the consultants parked in their reserved bays. Here was a circle of lawn, surrounded by low walls, where gardeners worked assiduously and where no one else ever came. On the lawn were benches where no one ever sat. He chose one of these now with as much deliberation as if life itself might depend on the choice.

"Why don't you do it yourself?" the foreign-sounding voice had asked with contempt.

Deon rose to his feet at once. He could not sit still.

"Why can't you do it, Deon?" Trish had asked him.

He crossed the hospital drive without looking, so that an incoming ambulance had to swerve to avoid him. He jumped for the pavement as the ambulance driver honked and cursed.

"Why can't you do it, Deon?" Trish had asked trustingly. He was capable, skilled, a doctor in all but name.

He had talked vaguely and nervously about not really having enough experience. He knew what to do in theory, he explained, but in practice, it would be a different matter altogether. He would find someone safe; he would make very sure of that. She needn't be worried. It was better to leave something like this in the hands of, well, not exactly experts, but at least they would be experienced hands. They did this sort of thing all the time. There was nothing much to it really. Naturally, one wouldn't go to a nasty-looking customer. But quite a lot of these people were doctors even. Or nurses and so on. They knew all about asepsis and what to do afterward and all the rest of it. He would arrange all that, the hospital and so on, and she'd be back on her feet in a day or two. No trouble, no trouble at all. Truly, Trish.

He was uncomfortably convinced that his despairing ramblings did not delude her in the least; that she saw through the layers of lies and deception to the small mean core of truth—that he was afraid.

"Scared, huh?" the man on the telephone had said in emotionless comment.

Are you afraid? Trish had asked with her eyes.

Afraid to risk performing an abortion? Or afraid to say: "Let's get married and to hell with it"? Another question, however: would she want to marry him? This new Trish whose eyes had seen and fathomed and understood, with neither resentment nor pity.

Would it work? She could be moody too. Even plain bloody at times. She was an artist, with an artist's peculiar vision. Would she make a doctor's wife? He tried to picture her as part of the small-town practice that was his ambition. Would she take kindly to calls in the middle of the night, interrupted meals, evenings when he was too tired to do anything but sleep? He doubted it. She had always lived in cities. How would she adapt to the smaller, tighter-bound circle of small-town life? She would be critical of morals and conventions and politics. Nor would she hesitate to say what she thought. She would make enemies and the practice would suffer.

No (with a measure of relief), it could never work.

Be honest, he told himself. You're finding excuses.

What if I am? They're valid. They're reasons, not excuses.

Well, then, do the damn thing yourself.

I can't. What if something went wrong?

Ah! Now we get to the crux.

He remembered that he had been watching operations in the gyne theater that afternoon. He was pleased and excited, for the surgeon had allowed him to scrub in and hold a retractor during a hysterectomy. The surgeons had gone off home and he and a houseman named Malan were waiting in the doctors' dressing room. It was still early in the year, February or March, and Malan was proud of having qualified and a little pompous about making sure everyone called him "Doctor," but he was a nice enough guy once you got to know him. He was putting Deon through a sham but extremely strict oral test and Deon had managed to plod through the whole procedure for retained placenta when the telephone shrilled. Malan had sighed and reached for the receiver and said "B-ll" in a bored voice. Deon, watching him from the side, had seen his neck muscles stiffen and had seen him slowly straighten up in his chair, until he was sitting perfectly erect.

"Yes," he said, his voice husky. "Yes, Doctor. Right away, sir."

He held the receiver suspended in the air for a moment longer, then put it down with an odd air of menace. And at that moment they both heard the wolf howl of an ambulance siren, far away at first, then, abruptly, much closer.

"What's up?" Deon asked innocently.

Malan had looked at him as at a stranger, as if he found difficulty in remembering who Deon was or what he was doing here.

Then he snarled: "Get off your arse, boy. We've got to go to Casualty. Incomplete abortion. Bled pulseless."

"Sure," Deon said, still not particularly concerned. He got up from the table on which he had been half leaning, half sitting. "But what's it all about?"

Malan had snatched up a white coat and pulled it on hurriedly over his surgical gown. He was already halfway out through the door.

"Piet Dannhauser's daughter," he said over his shoulder. "Incomplete abortion."

Deon caught the fever of the houseman's concern and trotted to catch up with him as he hurried down the corridor.

"Not really Dannhauser's daughter."

"Ja. That's what Rosenthal said."

"Was it Rosenthal who spoke to you?"

"Ja." He shook his head in weary acceptance of folly. "Can you imagine it? The bloody father owns half of Cape Town. But when the silly little bitch gets up the pole she's too scared to tell daddy, so she goes to some cheap knitting-needle merchant." He headed down the stairs at a fast clip. His heels beat a rapid and precise tattoo on the tiles, as if in counterpoint to his frustrated anger. "People like that should be hanged," he said. "Bloody murderers."

They came into the Casualty department as the ambulance bringing the Dannhauser girl drew up at the entrance. Malan beckoned unnecessarily to the porters with the trolley, and Deon saw that the Casualty sister, with unerring instinct, was already on her way to the door. Nurses too. A staff nurse, two trainees. A Casualty officer came out of his office at a half run.

Deon was shoved unceremoniously out of the way. Students had no place in a crisis. Humbly he took his place among the other onlookers, the waiting patients.

The trolley came back, being wheeled fast. He caught sight of a girl's face. White. White as a sheet of blotting paper. Dark hair, fashionably short-trimmed. There was a blood-stained blanket over her body. The sister, angrily, as if somehow offended by the sight, spread another blanket to hide the blood.

The porters and the trolley with its motionless burden and the accompanying nurses and Malan went hurriedly up the corridor. One of the nurses ran to hold open the swinging door at the farther end and then they were gone from sight.

Deon walked slowly back up to the gynecology floor. Hemorrhage, he thought, the most common complication resulting from a bungled abortion. If the patient doesn't bleed to death, she very often ends up with a renal shutdown. Other possible complications? Infection, leading to a septic abortion that may result in pyemia or septicemia. Which, again, could end fatally, or else result in sterility.

What was the girl's name. Nadine, Nerina . . . something like that. Nineteen or so. He'd seen her picture on the social pages of the newspapers. Spectacularly beautiful, with dark eyes and dark hair. Only child, if he remembered rightly. The man who married her would get all that and if not exactly half of Cape Town then certainly more than a fair share of it. There was going to be hell to pay over this.

Now under the shade of the trees, as he stood looking up at the massive façade of the hospital and at the entrance where the ambulance had stopped that night early in the year, he remembered with cold clarity that Narina Margaret Dannhauser, aged eighteen, had died from renal shutdown exactly four days later. And if Patricia Coulter, pharmacist's daughter, aged twenty-two, died as well, would there also be hell to pay?

One thing was certain: he, Deon van der Riet, would stand a grave risk of never being permitted to practice medicine.

And that was it.

God help me, he thought. And at once: are you actually praying? You, who have rejected the God of your father. Still, God, whatever or whoever you are, if you are, help me.

Shall I tell her: have it. It's your child; our child if you like. Have it and love it and cherish it, although I won't be there to share it with you.

He smashed a fist into an open palm in a fury of indecision. An African gardener, digging with a spade among the flower beds, watched him with frank curiosity and he walked on, away from the trees, pretending not to notice the black man's stare.

Why had he waited so long? He'd been a damn fool about that too. At an earlier stage it would have all been a lot less complicated. But he had waited all the same, with a vague hope that it might all prove to be a mistake, that everything would be solved of its own accord.

Trish had lashed out at him one evening for this very reason. They had been sitting at their usual corner table in the coffee shop near the flat, empty cups in front of them, both enveloped in moody silence. They seldom went anywhere these days: an occasional cheap meal in a restaurant; the odd meeting for coffee, or a drink when he was affluent. He had to spend most of his time studying, he explained, and this was true enough. She accepted the explanation readily and with apparent indifference. One afternoon she had taken him to a student art show and he had wandered around bemusedly, looking at the weird swirls and splashes. He had liked a few realistic paintings, some nudes and landscapes, but he was totally baffled by the others and told her so. She shrugged and did not try to explain them. He had forgotten to ask if any of her own work was on display, and afterward was afraid to ask.

Trish had swirled the dregs of her coffee cup and had asked shortly: "What are we waiting for?"

He had tried to fence.

"What do you mean?"

She put down her cup irritably. "You know."

"Well, are we absolutely sure it's necessary?"

"After six weeks? And swollen breasts, morning sickness? What more do you want?"

"Well, I'm getting it fixed. You don't have to worry."

"You've been saying that for a month. Do you think if you ignore it for long enough it will simply go away?"

60

"It's not like that at all. You know it. I'm just as worried as you are."

She had laughed harshly and said, with conscious crudity: "Not for the same reason, chum. You haven't got a little bastard growing in your belly."

He had looked round furtively in case someone at a neighboring table might have overheard, and she had intercepted the look and again given that hard, dry laugh, then pushed back her chair.

"Let's go," she said. "I'm tired."

I'm tired too, Deon thought. God knows, I'm tired of it all. There's only one way out. Let's get it over and done with.

He sat in the little Fiat, borrowed from Robby, fifty yards from the entrance to Gardenia Road. At first he had stopped right on the corner, under a lamppost, but after a time the brightly shining light had taken on a positively accusing glare, as if he were the victim in the spotlight at a police grilling in one of those second-rate American crime films Trish and he sometimes went to see. So, circumspectly, he had backed the two-seater into the shadow, but close enough to enable him to keep a watch on the corner.

He hoped it was going to be all right this time. The bastards were keeping him on a string. As if they enjoyed the spectacle of him hopping around like a laboratory rat being given tiny electric shocks to condition it for some experiment.

First he had been obliged to go back to the general practitioner whose name Robby had given him. The doctor thought the little problem could be sorted out. It would, however, be best to wait a few days, old boy. He would first have to sort of pour oil on troubled waters, ha! ha! So it would be best to wait a few days before proceeding.

Although circumstances had altered somewhat, their earlier arrangement about the hospital, etcetera, could be regarded as still in force, provided there wasn't any more silliness or anything like that. His eyes had flickered toward his receptionist, coming into his consulting room with a file, and he had smiled thinly and said how nice it had been to see Deon again and be sure to ring him when required, ha! ha! and cheerio, old boy, and the best of luck.

However, the man on the telephone had made Deon wait a whole week and no amount of pleading would shift him. Then the price was up by another five pounds. He hadn't argued about it, so suddenly it would cost an additional five pounds. Finally he had been given, grudgingly, a date and told to send the girl ("and the girl alone, all right?") and the money to

61

Gardenia Road. That date had been for Tuesday, three days ago, and he had sat waiting here in an agony of suspense, but glad to have got to this stage, glad to have it almost done.

After only five minutes Trish had come round the corner.

The light from the streetlamp had been momentarily bright on her dark hair as she stopped to look for him. Lord, he thought, that was quick. Obviously that old crow works like greased lightning. Trish had seen the Fiat and had come toward it, walking fast. She was wearing a wide green skirt and a matching jersey top; it was her one concession to vanity, for she knew how well the color set off that marvelous hair. He had leaned over to open the passenger's door and she had got in beside him without saying anything.

"Okay?" he had asked anxiously.

She had shaken her head, still not speaking.

"Oh, hell. What's wrong now?"

"I must come back on Friday."

"But why?"

"That's what she said. She wants to be sure. So it's Friday at the same time."

"Haven't they done enough checking?"

"Nothing before Friday."

An alarming thought had occurred to him.

"And the money?"

"She kept it."

"And what if she disappears with it?"

She had turned to him with a look of faint amusement.

"Then you'll have to tell your father the exam fees have been raised again, won't you?"

He had no particular wish to take the subject any further. He would have to fake some kind of receipt to cover the story he had told his father; the reason he needed thirty pounds so urgently.

"What's she like?" he asked with real interest. The voice behind the door that night had left him with an impression of a bedraggled crone, slavering over toothless gums and with shrunken, clawing hands.

"Oh, quite nice," Trish said unconcernedly.

"I mean, what does she look like?"

"Look like?" A slight frown of concentration. "Well, she's . . . she's oldish, I'd say."

"Very old?"

"No." An emphatic shake of the head. "Oldish. Middle-aged. About . . .

62

oh . . . fifty, I guess. She dyes her hair blue," she added quickly. "Otherwise she's quite nice."

"At least she looks efficient?"

"It's hard to tell, isn't it?" Trish had said in a small, still voice.

He hoped to heaven the woman was efficient, blue-rinsed hair or not. He glanced at his watch again, as he had done a dozen times in the last five minutes. Trish had been gone for more than ten minutes, almost fifteen. Something must be happening this time. Surely it couldn't be another false alarm.

Footsteps approaching from behind. He looked in the rearview mirror. A uniform, passing a brightly lit shop window and the light reflecting on polished brass, on leather belt and holster. Policeman! Christ!

He sat, in frozen fear, clutching the steering wheel, as the constable came closer with leisurely strides. Don't be a blasted fool, he told himself. It's just a cop on his beat and he's looking for thieves and robbers and murderers. It has nothing to do with you.

Yet he could not control his terror. He sat staring rigidly ahead while the policeman came up beside the car. He did not dare to turn his head to look in case his face should betray him. The footsteps appeared to slow down, to hesitate (if he talks to me, if he says anything, I won't be able to reply, my tongue simply will refuse to function), and then went by, regularly, unhurriedly.

Deon watched as the policeman walked away and disappeared down the street.

More footsteps, quick and light. Trish. He had not even seen her turn the corner. He tried to look at her face, but she was already past the lamppost and it was too dark to tell anything from her expression.

He got out to open the door for her, but she was too quick and was already opening it herself by the time he reached her. He held the door open.

"Okay?"

She nodded without looking at him.

"Are you sure?"

She climbed into the car, lifting her skirt (green again, but a different one, with a small white flower pattern) carefully clear of the door.

"Sure," she said then, her voice strange.

He closed the door and walked around the back of the Fiat. His mind was a jumble of elation and shame. He got in behind the wheel. There was a strong smell of disinfectant. He started the engine and switched on the headlights and drove off.

They traveled in silence for a while.

"Where are you taking me?" she asked, still with that stranger's voice.

"To the flat," he said. "That's the plan, isn't it? You'll stay there till . . . well . . . till it happens."

"All right," she said.

Apathetic, he thought. That's the word. She's become passive, as if she's prepared to be carried wherever chance takes her. She's never been like this before.

"Do you want to tell me about it?" he asked.

She shook her head. He turned a corner and steered into the busier traffic on the main route to the city, glad to have to concentrate on driving.

Then, surprisingly, she said: "It wasn't so bad."

It had been said casually, almost reassuringly. She's trying to encourage me, he realized, and was touched.

He tried to match her light, untroubled air and laughed a little, fondly. "Not as bad as you expected?"

"No."

After a little she went on, as if under compulsion. "I had to take off my panties, you see, and then she let me lie down on the floor, and . . ."

"On the floor?" he said anxiously.

"Oh, she put down a lot of towels first." She made a gesture of nonchalance, a quick flicking movement of her wrist. "Sterile towels, I suppose they were. It was all very clean. She wore gloves too. Rubber gloves."

"That's a consolation."

"Yes. Well then I had to lie down on these towels and sort of . . . you know . . . lift myself and open . . . my legs."

"Yes, of course," he said hurriedly.

"Then," she said, as if he had not spoken, "she smeared on some cream, disinfectant cream of some kind, I suppose, and then she took this thing, this instrument . . ."

"Syringe," he told her, driven by furies of his own.

"This thing, whatever it was, and she pushed it in. She was quite good about it, she didn't hurt me. But I didn't want to look. I didn't look."

She paused, as if to recall something. When she went on, her voice changed, as if deep and chill waters from the floor of the ocean were welling up to the surface.

"It didn't hurt. It was only sort of . . . uncomfortable when she squirted in the stuff . . . I think it was oil of some kind, that's what it felt like."

Deon listened helplessly to the irreversible, irrevocable flood of words coming from the girl with her placid face.

64

"Then I had to lie like that for quite a bit, it must have been about five minutes I guess, kind of arching my back so that the stuff wouldn't run out. Not that it hurt or anything," she said in growing horror and torment and self-doubt. "It was simply a bit uncomfortable, like it would be if one had to have an enema, I suppose."

Please, Deon wanted to say to her. Please stop it. You don't know what you're doing to yourself. But he was stricken and silent.

"After five minutes she did it again," Trish said, as if she could not quite believe what she was saying. "She used the same thing and the same stuff, but I wouldn't look. Not that it hurt or anything, but I didn't want to look."

The girl was silent, as if thinking back about what she had said, wondering if there was a significant detail she had left out.

"That was all," she said, in the same disbelieving voice.

Please don't let her get hysterical now, Deon prayed. Don't let her start screaming here in the street.

She turned to look at him for the first time since she had got into the car. He did not dare to return her glance. Please don't let her get hysterical.

But her voice had returned to normal and matter-of-fact tones when she said quite slowly, "It was horrible." She nodded reflectively. "Horrible."

He was dreaming about Trish, that she was about to leave on an aircraft and that he was trying to reach her, to tell her something vitally important. But people kept getting in the way, kept blundering into him, and he grew more and more angry and anxious, for she was gradually moving farther away. Suddenly all the people were gone and he was left standing alone, watching the aircraft carrying her fly away until it was only a speck in the distance. He was crushed by the weight of intolerable sadness. Then someone screamed and he looked, startled, to see whether the plane had crashed. Someone screamed again and he woke, sitting up at once in the makeshift bed on the floor.

His own bed, where Trish had been sleeping, was empty. The sheets had been flung back, as if she had been in a hurry.

Then she screamed a third time, from the bathroom.

She had started to bleed before reaching the door; he could see stipples and small pools of blood in a trail leading toward the bathroom. She had closed the door, however, and now no sound came from behind it.

He jumped up from the floor and ran, wrenching open the door, prepared to find disaster.

65

She was standing in the tiny room (it had been designed as a servant's toilet and contained only the bare essentials: a cold water shower and a toilet; his landlady's only extravagance had been to have the place painted a peculiar shade of violet) with her back to the door. Trish had taken off her pyjama trousers and they lay, a blood-stained bundle, in a corner. Blood was flowing slowly down the inside of her bare legs too, but she paid no attention to it. She was staring at the toilet, not moving.

He looked over her shoulder and saw why she had screamed.

Somehow (perhaps she had tried to rise, to call him; perhaps there had been pain at the moment of parturition and she had made a movement of rejection and revulsion) the fetus had landed on the edge of the toilet seat.

The thing, smaller than his thumb, lay curled up in the classic position, legs and arms drawn together. The placenta had fallen inside the bowl, so that the baby seemed isolated and whole, perfect except for its size.

He must have made some sound then, perhaps of pity or grief, for Trish turned and looked at him. "It's dead," she said, as casually as she might have remarked about the state of the weather, or exchanged a greeting with a chance acquaintance.

He took her roughly by the shoulder, turned her round, forced her out through the door, back into the bedroom. He had put out pads and towels in readiness; now he made her lie on the bed and packed pillows and towels under her. He was busy and professional and did not have to think.

"Your tights," he said. "Those ballet things. Where did you put them?"

She nodded toward her suitcase. She lay back on the bed, her eyes wide, her hair lifeless, a sheen of sweat on her forehead. She watched him moving about and appeared content to let him take control.

"All right," he said. "I'm going off to phone now. As soon as I've raised the doctor I'll take you to the hospital. There's absolutely nothing to worry about now. It's finished and done. Do you understand?"

She nodded like an obedient child.

"All right. The worst of the bleeding will stop in a moment. Then I want you to put pads all around you and put on the tights. Don't get up, I'll get them for you. Pull them up snugly round you. Okay?"

She nodded again.

"Fine. Then I'm off to phone. I won't be a minute."

There was a telephone booth three blocks away. He drove the little Fiat with the gas pedal way down, its engine roaring in the empty street.

He was brisk and professional again on the telephone and the doctor responded with equal imperturbability. He would be leaving for the nurs-

66

ing home within fifteen minutes. There would be no problems. The staff there were geared to cope with the occasional unfortunate miscarriage. See you in a little while, old boy.

Trish was lying in exactly the same position as when he had left. She turned her head when he came in but did not move otherwise.

"Okay?"

She nodded.

"That's fine," he said cheerfully. "The doc is on his way and I'm taking you in in a minute. Put on those tights now."

He smiled at her and went to the bathroom door, which had been left standing silently ajar.

"Good. You get yourself ready."

He smiled again and went into the bathroom, closing the door behind him. There was quite a bit of blood on the floor, but that he could mop up later. First things first.

He unrolled a length of toilet paper and folded it into a wad. He looked at the thing on the edge of the toilet seat. It was pink and smooth with that huge head and the small limbs, exactly like the pickled specimens in the pathology museum. Trish had obviously got her dates wrong after all. This must be at the beginning of its twelfth week.

He looked at it and saw that it was a boy.

He used the wad of paper to push his son into the toilet and then threw the paper in as well and flushed away the contents of the pan without looking again.

SUMMER

Four

Deon noticed, with surprise and a trace of concern, that his father was breathing hard by the time they reached the beginning of the final flight of steps. His nostrils flared with each forced breath, and Deon was reminded of a patient with pneumonia. Johan van der Riet was sweating too; a fine beading sweat showed on his forehead below the brim of the black hat. And yet it was not a particularly hot day.

Well, he's getting on I suppose, Deon told himself consolingly. He's sixty now. No. Sixty-one. Not all that old, but it's not young either. Strange that he seldom thought of his father as aging or changing in any way. Yet he *had* changed, Deon observed now, almost as if seeing with a stranger's insight. The eyes, now deep-sunken, were still sharp. But the nose stood out like the beak of a bird of prey. And the face, always hard and resolute, had become leaner, the craggy bones more pronounced.

The old man stumbled slightly as they climbed toward the classical pillars at the head of the steps. Deon put out a hand but his father shook it off, frowning quickly and crossly. Boet, on his father's other side, saw the gesture and grinned at Deon.

They climbed up to the entrance of the great hall in silence.

People were starting to move in through the doors, but most of them still stood in groups on the steps or beside the pillars: self-conscious graduates in their gowns; relatives proud; the university staff indifferent, wishing the whole business were over.

"Do you want to go in now?" Deon asked. He looked at his watch. "It won't start for another twenty minutes."

"We'll wait here for a bit," his father said. He put a finger in under his collar, then took off his hat and wiped his face carefully with a

68

handkerchief. He saw Deon watching him and added, "It's hot in this Cape of yours. Even hotter than the Karoo."

"It's very humid today," Deon agreed.

Boet had been watching the girls in their sleek-fitting dresses. Now he gave a sudden snort of laughter. "Look who's coming. Flip and old Aia Mieta."

Philip Davids was coming slowly up the steps. The elderly Coloured woman on his arm looked flustered and nervous, as if, despite all assurances, she remained uncertain whether she was really entitled to be here.

"Look at the way she's dressed," Boet said derisively. "A Hottentot stays a Hottentot."

Certainly Philip's mother appeared to have mistaken the occasion. Her long, wide-swinging skirt would have been fashionable in a ball-room five or six years before. Her garden-party hat dated from an even earlier period. Among the small, close-fitting hats the other women wore it was comically ostentatious.

More people were staring. Deon saw smiles that masked condescension behind a guise of pity.

He was bitterly angry. He looked down at Philip coming slowly up the steps with the frightened, quaintly dressed old woman at his side. You obstinate bastard, he thought. Why couldn't you have told her? Why couldn't you have seen that she was properly dressed, guarded her against making a fool of herself?

"She has every right to be here," he snarled at his brother. Boet turned, incredulous, his face starting to go red. His mouth opened as if he wanted to retaliate, but he did not utter a sound.

Philip and his mother were halfway up the last flight now and suddenly the woman faltered, almost at exactly the same spot where Johan van der Riet had stumbled a short time before. Philip held her arm and stopped and looked up for the first time, as if to judge how far they still had to climb.

His expression was strange. Ashamed and awkward and yet stubbornly defiant. As if he were saying to the disdainful assembled whites: Go to hell. Each and every one of you go to hell.

That dress and that hat were castoffs. A frilly and flouncy ball gown, worn once years ago, now discarded as hopelessly unfashionable by some indifferent giver; a hat taking up useless space in a wardrobe. One might as well give it to the Coloureds, they do so like bows and satin roses and things, don't they? They were castoffs but they were the best she had, and Philip was too proud and too stiff to pretend differently.

Deon began to move almost before he had made any conscious decision.

He was aware of his father's frown and his brother's stare, but he was already moving away from them, going steadily down the steps toward where Philip stood with his mother. Philip watched his approach gravely.

They had not spoken since the day in the cafeteria, had avoided one another even in the enforced companionship of classes. Their eyes had met by accident at times, and always one of them had looked away.

Now they faced one another. Philip's brows were slightly arched; his eyes still held the question. Deon was calm and assured. He held out his hand.

"Good morning, Philip," he said. And to the bewildered woman: "Good morning, Mrs. Davids."

She mumbled shyly in reply, not looking at him. He stepped down beside her and turned to put a reassuring hand on her elbow. Her arm was thin and bony under his fingers. He could feel that she was trembling.

"Let me help you," he said, and he and Philip went up the steps together, the frail old woman between them. Deon looked up at the people above. There were no more smiles on those smug faces.

Boet was staring at him, still slack-jawed with astonishment. His father was looking away into the distance, at the faraway mountains, as if he had observed nothing.

Deon stopped in front of his father, forcing Philip and the woman to halt as well. "Father," he said. "You remember Mrs. Davids? And Philip?"

His father's eyes did not shift from their remote contemplation of the steel blue mountains.

"Master," the Coloured woman said softly, almost entreatingly.

Van der Riet did not speak, nor did he look at her. But he nodded stiffly, and then she and Philip had passed by and still his deep eyes were on the mountains.

"What the hell did you do that for?" Boet whispered furiously.

"I told you," Deon said. "She's got more right here than you. It's her son who's a doctor."

"That doesn't mean you have to . . . What kind of man are you?"

"I'm a doctor and he's a doctor."

"And are you a bloody kaffir-lover too?"

"That's enough," their father said sharply. His dark gaze went from one to the other, neither approving nor disapproving. "Remember, you are brothers," he said. He turned toward the door through which Philip and his mother had already disappeared. People were starting to gather round it. "I think it is time to go inside."

* * *

70

In the rows of soberly gowned, solemn-faced young people it was difficult to recognize the flamboyant medical students of a few weeks ago. Almost, Deon thought, as if the examinations had in fact been the purgatory most of them had anticipated, had been the flame that melted away the dross and left behind only pure metal.

Boy! he thought. Are you dramatizing! Don't be silly and sentimental about it. Everyone is a bit overawed, naturally. You can't quite believe it's happened and you get a bit keyed up. Which is probably the reason I did what I did.

But he was not yet ready to start thinking about this, so he gazed up at the great arched slabs around the semicircular windows and then at the people.

Across the aisle sat the engineering class; diagonally across and to the front were the arts graduates. Only a few girls wore their hair long and he thought he could pick out Trish's dark head among them, although he could not be sure.

He did not particularly want to see her or to be seen by her, however, so he turned in his seat to look back toward the door.

He saw Philip's mother, sitting by herself at the end of a row far to the back. Scattered through the hall were other isolated pockets of Coloured people and Indian women in saris with brilliant trimmings. Soon the pressure of space compelled some white person to take an adjoining seat, but an invisible barrier remained.

He scanned the rows of business suits and delicately shaded pastel dresses, searching for his father's hawk face. Couldn't find him. Had he gone up to the balcony by mistake? Then he saw the long body. His father was at the entrance to one of the raised side bays, which were reserved for V.I.P.s. He was arguing with a gowned usher who had turned his back. The usher kept pointing at the admission ticket, which was the wrong color, and van der Riet waved the ticket at the quietly insistent young man as if it were something of no consequence and beneath his dignity even to consider. Eventually he gave up, however, and stamped off into the body of the hall, turning to give the usher one final glare. Boet walked sheepishly behind him.

They found two vacant seats in the midst of a group of middle-aged, obviously wealthy couples. Deon could imagine the fashionable "grad" talk which would be in progress, of parties and dances and of university celebrities referred to by their first names and the hyperbole of adjectives, everything "smashing" and "fantastic" and "fabulous." He wondered what his father would make of it.

71

Four worried-looking lecturers were counting the seated graduates row by row and laboriously adding up the total. Deon could imagine his father's contempt. He wouldn't even hire these people as sheepherders. If they couldn't count straight when people sat lined up in tidy rows, how would they ever be able to tally a milling mob of sheep?

He grinned, and Robby, farther down in the same row, caught the grin and returned it.

We're doctors, Deon thought in sudden exultation. The hell with everything else; we're doctors. Or about to be.

He imagined the light touch of the academic hat on his bowed head.

"I dub thee knight." It should be a sword, something really dramatic. "Arise, Sir Deon."

He grinned again at the absurdity of his imagination, but the elation remained. He could feel the startling sting of tears behind his eyes. My God, if they don't start now I'm going to start bawling like a baby.

Abrupt peals from an invisible organ amplified by the broadcast system saved him from this indignity. The audience rose as the academic procession began to wind its way up the aisle to the roaring strains of "Gaudeamus Igitur." The venerable Dean of the Faculty of Engineering, blind as a bat but vain about wearing spectacles on public occasions, took a wrong turn and had to be helped back. The procession filed on to the stage and the organ changed to the opening chords of the national anthem. Halfway through the first verse Deon thought he could hear his father's voice ringing up above all the others. Puzzled, he stopped singing to listen.

Of course. The English people around his father would hardly be singing or perhaps only moving their lips in token. His father's blood would boil at the imagined insult and he would bellow out "Die Stem" as loudly as he could in retaliation.

Deon smiled to himself in wry appreciation. Let's face it, he thought, it takes an awful lot to subdue that old boy.

People sat down, and the wooden folding chairs made a long rattling sound like that of a stick drawn swiftly along a paling fence.

The slow dignity of the ceremony unfolded, ritual by ritual. Finally the guest speaker was introduced. He was a visiting academic from some British red-brick university and he possessed a long sandy-colored lock of hair that he kept flicking nervously out of his eyes. He had a tendency to swallow his vowels, so that the speech was hard to follow. It seemed to consist of an earnest exhortation to various races in southern Africa to mend their respective ways. Deon hoped his father would be unable to make head or tail out of it all. If he was made angry enough he might quite easily demand the right to reply to the speaker.

For a while he listened with attempted concentration to the mumbled pleas for sanity and perspective and watched the visiting professor flicking back his sandy forelock. If it bothered him so, why didn't he have it cut off?

He could see the back of Philip's head, five, six rows to the front; the dead straight black hair, the rigid head. He appeared to be listening with his full attention.

At least I think I've patched up things between us, Deon thought, remembering Philip's half smile of acknowledgment. Something good has come out of what I did. Probably we won't ever see one another again, after leaving here today, but at least we won't be parting as enemies.

Philip had been secretive about his plans, but apparently an all-black hospital in the Transvaal had accepted him as a houseman. There had been talk, too, about a study grant from either France or Germany. If it was true, he deserved it. He had the brains and he worked like a slave. Good luck to him, wherever he goes.

Again the thought intruded: why did I do what I did?

I wasn't out to ingratiate myself or to make a stand, a declaration of attitude. Nor was I merely trying to restore a broken friendship. It wasn't a calculated answer to Boet's jeers or a gesture of spite toward my father. Not even pity or anger at those mean, detestable smiles. It was something about the look on his face as he turned toward us; that look that admitted shame but at the same time expressed fierce and indomitable pride.

He doesn't give up, old Philip. He never admits defeat.

Deon remembered the day of the jackal hunt. How old had they been then? It was before he went to school so he was probably about seven and Philip (who had been Flip then) about nine. Quite right. He had gone to school the following January and in the first term at school his mother had gone away. He remembered boasting about the jackal to bigger boys at the farm school and one of them who was fat, although everyone thought he was very strong, had called him a liar. Boet, who was in Standard Four, fought with the fat boy, who was in Standard Six, and beat him, so that he went crying to the teacher and the teacher beat them both for fighting. Boet was greatly admired for beating a boy two years older, and the jackal story was lost somewhere in the general adulation. Deon considered this very unfair, but he gained by it too, for people had a healthy respect for both of them for a long time afterward. It didn't pay to mess around with the van der Riet boys, not even the little one. Then his mother went away and people felt sorry for him and he had a very easy time at that school.

The jackal hunt, however, happened before he went to school. He and Flip had made new bows and arrows that week, bigger and more powerful than any they had ever made before, using strong, whippy boughs from a pepper tree and stringing them with strips of sinew which Flip's father, who did all the butchering on the farm, had cut specially for them. They made arrows out of dry reeds and gave them metal heads: steel fencing wire hammered flat and shaped into barbs. The feather flights for the arrows came from Deon's mother's chicken run.

Flip knew the secret of making the right poison. He mixed the white milky sap of a succulent plant which grew at certain places in the veld with other things, but Flip would never tell him all the ingredients, for this was a secret of the Coloured people and if they told strangers about it the poison would lose its strength. At the age of seven Deon believed him implicitly, for Flip was nine and he knew.

They had gone out into the veld that morning after Deon's mother had made him a jam sandwich for his lunch. They walked to the stone koppie which was named Long Hill. A dry riverbed lined with stunted thorn trees wound past the base of the hill. They sat in the shade of the trees waiting for the doves that always came here after they had been to water at the pump. Flip killed two doves with his catapult and Deon broke the wing of a third, so that it went fluttering off on the ground under the trees. Flip was on it in a flash and wrung its neck with a twist of his wrists. Deon made a fire while Flip plucked the three doves. They roasted them there in the shade and ate them contentedly and afterward shared the jam sandwich and a bottle of cold tea Flip had brought.

Then they walked for a time along the pebbly bed of the river with their bows strung and arrows ready. Flip carried the poison in a tobacco tin, for it had to be wet when you shot off the arrow. If you painted it on too early the poison would dry on the arrowhead and then it was no good.

They pretended to be hunting springbok, but even Deon realized this was only make-believe, for the springbok were far too fast and alert to give them even a remote chance of getting close enough for a shot.

They walked in the hot sun down the riverbed between the two lines of trees and looked for springbok tracks on the sandy patches between the pebbles. After a while Deon began to lose interest. He wanted to go back home and do something else, play some other game. His father had made him a fine wagon with real spokes on the wheels and a wagon tree with yokes for the oxen. Under the yokes he and Flip used dolosse, which were the knuckle bones of sheep and which made splendid oxen. Behind the dam wall, where the soil was moist and cool, they had laid out a maze of roads and hills on which the wagon could journey. It was very hot here and he thought longingly of going home and playing behind the dam.

Then Flip stopped and stood in a slightly stooped position, looking down at his feet.

"What is it?" Deon asked.

Flip pointed wordlessly at the neat, splayed track in the sand.

"Jackal?"

Flip nodded.

"It went past here this morning."

"How do you know?"

Flip nodded again, mysteriously.

"I know."

"We'll have to go and tell my father." Jackals were ruinous among the sheep. Traps were set regularly when they were known to be about, and Johan van der Riet paid a bounty of a shilling for every jackal tail brought to him.

"I think he's gone up on the hill," Flip said. "He went past here early this morning, and he was running that way. I think he's lying in a hole and tonight he'll come out and hunt the sheep."

"Well, we must tell my father about it."

"Let's go and hunt him ourselves."

Deon looked at him doubtfully. "How? We haven't got a gun."

Flip held up his bow, with the arrow notched.

"With this."

"You think you can kill a jackal with that thing?"

For an answer, Flip pulled back the bowstring and aimed at a tree twenty paces off. The arrow sped straight and true and hit the tree with a dull *thwock* sound, four feet from the ground. They walked up to it. The head had gone in to an inch behind the barb.

Flip cut the arrow out of the thorn tree with his pocket knife and said with conviction, "You've only got to get through his hair and skin. Then the poison will kill him."

"You'll need dogs and so on to get him out of his hole."

"We'll wait at the hole till he comes out."

Deon looked at the Coloured child in astonishment. "But that'll be tonight. Jackals don't walk in the daytime. He'll stay in his hole till tonight."

Philip's face was set and determined.

"That's all right. We'll wait till he comes out. There's a moon tonight and we'll be able to see to shoot him."

"I still think we should go home and tell my father," Deon muttered.

Flip looked at him with disdain.

"You go home if you want to. I'm going to hunt that old jackal."

After that, of course, there was no alternative.

They tracked the jackal as it had crossed the riverbed and gone under the trees where the undergrowth was thickest. Here it had obviously waited for a while, perhaps alarmed by something. Then, as Flip had predicted, it had climbed the slopes of Long Hill.

Tracking was difficult as the jackal had not run straight but in loops and curves. The veld was stony and it was difficult to search far ahead because of the Karoo bush which hid the spoor. They toiled up the hill in the heat, sweating now, dark stains on their backs and the armpits of their khaki shirts (Boet's and Deon's old clothing was given to the Coloured children) finding a track here and there among the bushes.

Once Deon stopped, disheartened, and wiped his face on his sleeve. "No, man. We'll never get this jackal this way."

Flip's expression did not change. "Go home if you want to."

At last the spoor took direction. Flip looked up at the crest of the hill. It was table-shaped, like most other koppies in this part of the Karoo, but there was a low cliff immediately below the summit and this was broken and fractured by long clefts in the rock face.

"He's gone into one of those," Flip said with satisfaction. "Now we must go very slowly and softly till we find the right hole. These jackals hear very well. If he hears us, he'll stay in his hole."

The tracks led to a narrow split near the center of the cliff. They searched for signs indicating that the jackal might have emerged from his hide, but there was nothing to be found.

No sound came from the dark hole.

Flip jerked his head in summons. They moved off to a safe distance.

"All right," Flip whispered in Deon's ear. "He's there all right. Do you see those rocks there, on the left?"

Deon looked and nodded.

"We're going to sit in behind those rocks. When he comes out we'll see him in the moonlight. I'm going up and then you come after me. Don't make a noise. And don't talk once we're behind the rocks."

Deon nodded and Flip gave him a final approving glance and was gone from his side, moving fast but soundlessly up the steep slope. After a brief wait Deon followed, trying to move quietly too, alarmed once when pebbles slipped under his feet and went bounding downhill. Fortunately they caused less commotion than he had feared.

Then they were safely hidden in the shelter of the rocks, breathing a little harder with excitement and the exertion of the climb.

Flip squatted behind a boulder, resting his back against the rough stone, in a position where he could see the jackal's hide, although it was at an acute angle. Deon joined him there, also leaning against the rock.

For a time they watched the crack in the cliff face expectantly, but Deon grew tired of this and instead sat looking out over the veld. It was bluish-brown and hazy in the distance and the horizon was crinkled with heat. From this height one could see faraway hills and the red snake of the road curving between them. The lines of the camp fences marched regularly over the brown veld. Many farmers did not bother to fence their camps, or did not have the money to do it, and as a result they lost hundreds of sheep to the jackals. But his father believed in doing things well and properly so he had fenced his land, even if it meant going without a new automobile or spending money when it was hard to come by during the bitter years of the depression. When the depression was at its worst, during the time of the great drought, his father had gone to work on the roads with a pick and shovel for half a crown a day. But he had never given up, had never abandoned his land and gone to the city like so many others.

Deon sat looking out over the veld with the fences drawn across it as if marked with rulers.

Then Flip's head moved quickly and Deon sat up too, suddenly alert.

But it was only a rock rabbit which had come out onto a ledge to sun itself, had spotted them, and gone scampering back to the protection of its burrow. Normally they would have tried to shoot it but with bigger game in prospect they were not going to waste arrows on a mere dassie.

It grew very hot as they waited through the long afternoon. Deon's legs became cramped from crouching and finally he stretched them out, although this meant he could no longer see the entrance to the jackal's hole. The heat made him sleepy and he found his eyes closing every now and then. Suddenly he sat up with a jerk and realized he had been asleep. He must have slept for a long time, for the sun was low over the flat horizon and they were in deep shade, here under the side of the cliff.

Then he became a little frightened, for he realized that his mother would have started to worry about him and his father would be home by now, wanting his supper and becoming anxious too, and angry.

He glanced sideways at Flip. Flip had never moved. He sat in the same crouching position, head watchfully cocked, bow and arrow resting in readiness on his knee, the open tobacco tin with the secret Coloured poison at his side.

They waited while the sun lingered and then went quickly down behind the flat edge of the earth, like a candle being slowly snuffed out, leaving a last narrowing band of red and orange all around the sky. That faded too and it was dark and they could see the stars.

The moon rose, a little past its full. A flight of birds went by, wings rustling in the night silence.

Deon shivered. He pretended it was only the cold. He was hungry and very thirsty, for they had not had anything to drink since sharing the bottle of cold tea after eating the doves. That had been before midday. The plan had been to drink water at the pump, but because of the jackal they had not gone near the pump today.

The moon climbed steadily through the milky sky. There were fleecy, scattered clouds very high up. Perhaps there would be thunderheads tomorrow, and rain. He hoped it would rain. There was a special, enormous joy in watching the dark clouds with their high-piled crowns moving in slow progression over the plains. When the slanting rain began to fall you ran for cover on the stoop before it caught you, and you watched as a sudden gust of wind set the quince avenue dancing and swirled dry leaves across the farmyard. There was that smell of water on hot dust. Then the storm would start in earnest and the rain would roar on the corrugated iron roof.

Flip nudged him, very gently, and he almost jumped. Flip put a finger on his lips and pointed toward the jackal's hide.

At first Deon could see nothing except darkness, for there was an overhang which partly shielded the cliffside from the moon. He was about to shake his head, and then he was not sure. Had there been something? No. Yes. Yes. A movement. Something had moved in the shadows.

Flip's hand had already reached out, dipping his arrowhead into the tin with the poison, then dipping it again to make sure. He nocked the arrow and braced himself against the rock to steady his aim. Hastily Deon followed his example. His hands were trembling and he rapped his arrow against the side of the tin, so that it made a faint metallic click. He looked apologetically toward Flip, but Flip had hardly noticed. All his attention was on the entrance to the cleft in the rock.

They waited.

Movement again, unmistakable this time. Slow, cautious movement down in the shadow cast by the overhang.

Almost before they had expected it, before they were ready, the black-backed jackal moved full into the moonlight and stood on the flat rock in front of its hide, standing sideways before them, its head slightly raised and ears pricked.

Deon heard the twang of Flip's bowstring and shot off his own arrow an instant later. At once there was a faint yelp, like a dog kicked unexpectedly, and a snarl. And then the jackal vanished; was gone like a gray ghost, as if it had never been.

Deon was on his feet, running.

"I got him!" he shouted exultantly. "I got him!"

He began to search in the shadows, expecting to find the body of the slain jackal already there.

Flip followed more slowly.

"I got him!" Deon said, doing a little war dance of triumph and excitement.

"Yes," Flip said slowly. Then, even more slowly: "I think I got him too."

"I'm sure I got him," Deon said aggressively. "I heard him make like this when my arrow hit him." He imitated the jackal's yelp. "How far will he run?"

Flip shrugged. "A long way. That poison doesn't work quickly. But he'll be dead by morning."

"Only by morning?" It had gone flat.

"Yes. Now we'd better look for the arrows."

They found one arrow almost at once. The head was still on it so this meant the barb had not struck home and it had missed.

"I'm sure I hit it," Deon said stubbornly.

They used identical arrows and exchanged them freely. There was no telling who had used which.

They searched again and found the remaining arrow; only the reed shaft this time. The head was gone.

"He got it all right," Flip said with immense satisfaction. "That old jackal's dead now."

"I'm sure that was my arrow," Deon said.

Flip looked at the moon. It was high in the pale sky. "We'd better go home now," he said.

Deon's father met them halfway with the car. The headlights and spotlights were all on and there were men carrying storm lanterns and other men on horses and both of them were thrashed right there in the veld, thrashed thoroughly and seriously with a broad leather belt before they even had time to start explaining about the jackal. Deon had to go to bed without supper, but later in the night, much later, after he had cried himself to sleep, his mother came to his room, the outside room off the back stoop which he shared with his brother when Boet was not at school. She brought him a piece of biltong and a handful of the little sweet cakes she baked, and while he ate he told her about the jackal. He told her the whole story from beginning to end and she said, "Yes," every now and then; "Yes," but she was not really listening. She sat there at the end of his bed, a pale, thin, listless woman, not really listening to his tale: not even looking at him, really, but gazing with empty eyes beyond him into a place of silence and solitude.

He told his father the story too, the next day, when his father's anger had diminished. At first his father was short with him and then he was inclined to joke about it. But when he saw that Deon was absolutely serious he sent one of the farm workers up to Long Hill to follow the jackal's spoor. The man came back with the dead jackal in the early evening. He had tracked it all day and found where it had gone to earth in an antbear hole. He had to dig it out of the hole and when he got it out at last, dead of the poison, the arrowhead was still imbedded in the tough skin, behind the shoulder.

Van der Riet had made a few joking remarks about Nimrod and about the Great Jackal Hunter, but Deon could see that he was proud. That Sunday he overheard him telling a group of other farmers the story, outside church.

His father paid him the shilling bounty money with great solemnity and Deon gave Flip half of it. He felt a little guilty about taking all the credit for the hunt. He knew that if it had not been for Flip he would never have stayed up on Long Hill in the night. Also, although he had been adamant that it had been his arrow which had hit and killed the jackal, he could never be completely sure. Flip was the better shot and had shot first, when the jackal was standing quite still. But one couldn't tell, for the arrows were indistinguishable, and there were times when he was utterly convinced that he had seen his arrow strike at the moment the jackal had yelped.

The following January he went to school, and during the first term his mother had an attack of nerves and left the farm suddenly for a holiday with her brother and his wife in the Transvaal. Two months later she wrote the letter to the dominee; the long and rambling letter which announced her intention never to return to her husband and made the frightening and incomprehensible accusations against him which convinced the dominee and everyone else in the neighborhood that the woman had become a little mad. There was much head shaking about it among his father's fellow-elders in the church, and the dominee came to read him the mad letter and to ask whether there was anything he could do, whether his intervention could be of use in persuading the wife to return. But his father had said in a black voice: "She has made her choice. She will never set foot on this farm again."

There was general sympathy for his father after this, for people liked a man who had iron in him, who could voice a curse and never relent. The dominee had pleaded for mercy and compassion, of course, for that was his calling. But even he had been secretly impressed and had gone around saying there was one thing about Johan van der Riet, he was a man of his word.

Everyone knew his father was a stern man, even a hard man at times. But he could be kind; he helped his neighbors when they were in trouble without expecting anything in return. In any case, the wife had known all this; she had lived with him for twenty years and had learned that his strength came from that fierce will to survive and accomplish and dominate. Without it he would have gone under in the bad years, like so many others. She had known that for twenty years, and suddenly she had left him, even abandoning the two boys, the youngest hardly at school yet. You could forgive everything else; could blame her desertion on her nerves and her madness. But you could not condone leaving a man with two small children to bring up all on his own. She destroyed any sympathy there might have been for her by leaving the children.

Why? Deon wondered. Why did she do it?

He turned in his seat to glance back toward his father, sitting in his dark suit among the lighter hues of the fashionable university crowd all around him, like a disdainful eagle in a cage of chattering parakeets.

He looked at his father's severe and secret face. There was no answer on it; or at any rate none that he could read.

Why did she leave?

How had he felt then, at the age of seven? He could not remember. There had been a vague sense of loss, of incompleteness, but he was involved in the new world of school and after a while the sadness had been forgotten too.

Perhaps Boet knew more about it. He had been thirteen then and must have picked up small bits of information and been able to interpret them as a child of seven could not do. But Boet had been away at school too.

They had never really discussed it, perhaps out of some vague feeling of respect for their father's personal life. It's funny, Deon thought; Boet's my brother and yet I don't know him at all. Philip was my playmate and I know him far better. Boet and I are two people apart. I see him on the farm during the holidays, and I drive around with him to look at the sheep or the fences or the grazing, and we go out hunting together. Occasionally we've been to a dance together at Beaufort West with Liselle. She'll make him a good wife, although she is a teacher and has a few little affected graces that get on my nerves so that I cannot really talk to her for very long. No more than I can talk to him for very long. Let's be very honest, he thought. I cannot talk to him at all. We have nothing to say to one another.

He shrugged away the thought and gave his attention to the earnest English academic who had by now moved on to the special problems of African culture and who was still going flick, flick, flick with his forelock.

Deon glanced at his watch again. Five more minutes, by most graduation day standards.

We're doctors! Can you beat it! Bloody doctors.

He shook his head in disbelief. Six years of it and now, it was done. Although there had been times in the last few weeks when he had doubted seriously whether it would ever be over.

He had done well with his major cases. Or perhaps he had simply been lucky, for all of them had been pretty straightforward. In surgery he'd picked up a classic hyperthyroidism. He'd read the literature only a night or two before, so he had all the answers down pat. He could see the glint of approval in old Snyman's eyes when he was dismissed, and he'd gone off feeling well pleased with himself. However, he'd had hell scared out of him by the gynecology professor. The old man had the unpleasant habit of driving around and hunting for any final-year student he could find, then loading the poor devil into his car and taking him off to the nearest hospital for the ordeal. It didn't matter how earnestly you explained that it wasn't time for you to do gyne-obstetrics and that in fact you weren't even in his group and Dr. So-and-So was supposed to be your examiner. The old man simply refused to listen, so the students had learned to keep a sharp lookout for his car.

But that day Deon was coming down the hospital stairs when the old boy pushed through the usual cluster of patients at the admission desk and there was no time to evade him.

"Ah, van der Riet," the professor said with grim pleasure, "I've got just enough time to give you a run-through. Come up to the ward with me."

Deon had to think fast.

"Sir, I must tell you I've just been up to see Doctor Robinson."

"Well, what of it, fellow? What of it?" the old man said testily.

Deon scratched his back and tried to look even more sad.

"Sir, I had this bit of rash this morning and I'm afraid his diagnosis is"—he paused to give it weight—"rubella, sir."

"German measles! Good God!" the professor exploded. "How dare you come near this hospital! There are pregnant women here, you fool!"

"Yes, sir," Deon said contritely. "I'm about to go home to bed, sir."

"Well get out, fellow! Get out!"

His luck had held that time and he had been lucky with his medical case too. But the written exams hadn't gone as well. Medicine particularly. He'd come out of the hall (this hall; although it had looked different then, with the rows of desks and the patroling proctors and the almost palpable air of tension) with his hands clammy and his knees weak. He had gone blindly past the usual group of bright boys who had collected at the top of the steps to compare notes. He didn't want to talk or even think about the paper. All he wanted to do was get the hell out.

It was the fiasco of Trish's pregnancy, he thought bitterly. I simply didn't do enough studying. But how could I concentrate with that sword over my head?

Who was to blame, he asked himself at once. Tell me that, sport, old sport: who was to blame?

He looked across the aisle toward the front of the hall, where that dark head sat very still among rows of short and bright blond hair. Was it Trish? He was almost sure of it.

How was she, these days? He had seen her only once, and then briefly, for a quick snack lunch, since she had been out of the hospital. He felt miserably guilty about it, but there was nothing he could do, for he was working seventeen hours a day, trying to make up lost time. She had been working hard too, for that matter, for her finals were also approaching. He had phoned her once, to suggest they go out somewhere, but she had an art assignment to finish by the end of the week. She had been a bit offhand and he hadn't phoned again. There hadn't been time.

Would he telephone again, now that there was time? Probably not.

A polite burst of applause snatched at his thoughts, and involuntarily he straightened up. The distinguished English academic smiled gratefully and regained his seat with a final flick of the hair. The audience stirred; there was a rustle of paper, of program pages being turned. The important part of the ceremony was about to begin.

The Dean of the Faculty was on his feet, addressing the Chancellor with ritual courtesy. The Chancellor's reply was as dry as the rustling pages.

Doctorates first, in their gowns ablaze with color. Hearty handclapping for each of them; special applause for a Doctor of Medicine who limped to

83

the rostrum on a cane. Would he make it up the steps? Cheers when he did and was duly honored.

Now the common herd, the mere Bachelors. Moving quickly now, a briefer pause between names. Those waiting to be called moved from seat to seat down the rows to retain the alphabetical sequence and avoid delay.

Abrahams, Donald Robert. Adams, Peter McArthur. Bajee, Mohammed (a slight increase in the volume: they were liberal-minded people). Bartlett, Monica Mona.

The Dean paused and looked at the list in his hands. Even his normally pedantic voice had a slight catch as he pronounced the measured phrases: "With distinction in the second, third, and final professional examination and the degree with first-class honors." Again the almost imperceptible pause. Then he said quietly, "Davids, Philip."

Philip was on his feet, moving quickly. The applause rose like thunder behind him. He went up the steps almost at a run and knelt as quickly, and still the storm of handclapping continued. These were restrained people, conventional people, and they would not sing and dance in the aisles or carry him on their hands in triumph. But they approved. My God, yes; they approved. He turned to face them, to receive his hood, and on his face, again, was that expression, so fierce that Deon was almost frightened to see it.

It said: "You cannot beat me down. I cannot be beaten down."

A nudge from his left reminded Deon that he had to shift seats. As he moved he glanced to the back of the hall and saw something that almost caused him to miss the seat in his astonishment.

His father was applauding too.

In the midst of all those Englishmen sat Johan van der Riet, his face hard and unmoved. But, like them, he was clapping his hands. Clapping his hands for Flip Davids, a Coloured boy from "Wamagerskraal."

Five

It was the same familiar gray-stone building. And yet it was quite different.

He stopped halfway across the shrub-covered traffic island that guarded the entrance to the hospital and stared up at the somber, many-windowed façade.

I've worked and studied here for six years, Deon thought. I've learned to know every inch of it. I know where the passages lead and which side stairs to take to wherever I want to be. I know the wards and the labs and the operating blocks and the Administration floor. I know the linen room and the dispensary and even the kosher kitchen. I have seen it and lived in it through every hour of the day and night. I have seen sick people here, and some have lived and some have died. Until now I have been, if not exactly indifferent, at any rate not responsible for their recovery or the manner of their death. So, in fact, I know nothing about this hospital. Now it is all changed. I have to learn to carry the burden. This is where I'm going to start learning. This is where I start medicine.

That's about enough dramatics, he told himself. Anybody would think you're already a specialist. You're a houseman, boy. About as much use to anyone as a fistful of thumbs. A lot less use than a quick and capable staff nurse. As any capable staff nurse will be quick to tell you.

He went past the porter's desk into the foyer, feeling self-conscious in his new starched white coat; lacking the green cuff bands that had marked him as a noncombatant and with a new name badge, brown to proclaim his advanced status.

Last night, on the bed in his allotted room in the housemen's quarters, he had found two handbooks and a mimeographed form announcing a morning meeting of all interns. One book dealt matter-of-factly with hospital routine. The other gave equally humdrum information about the handling of blood, urine, feces, and other specimens destined for special investigations.

He did not really expect much from this morning's meeting either. Probably be no more than a pep talk. At ten minutes to eight, he drifted toward the stairs. No one else seemed to be around. They were, very likely, all recovering from New Year's Eve hangovers.

He saw the porter was looking at him suspiciously over the top of the morning paper. He turned and went up the stairs. When he reached the lecture hall he found, after all, that he was not alone. It was crowded with familiar faces, Robby's among them. And, unexpectedly, next to Robby sat Philip Davids, his look reserved and withdrawn as always.

"I'll be damned," Deon said, moving up to Philip. "What are you doing here?"

Philip smiled slightly and fingered his own brown badge.

"Same as you, I imagine."

"But weren't you going to the Transvaal?"

"I applied here as a first choice." Philip looked at him intently. "But I didn't think I really had a chance."

"Well, for God's sake. Surely they would have grabbed you?"

Philip's glance did not shift, but he changed the subject abruptly.

"You look well. Were you on the farm?"

"Only for a couple of days. We went down to the coast for the holidays. To Knysna." Deon added quickly: "And you?"

"I had a working holiday. They gave me a job in the Path lab."

"Really?" Deon said without great interest. "What were you doing?"

"The same stuff I worked on in the June vacation. The prof is trying to get a new technique underway for studying chromosomes. You know; I told you about it."

"Oh, yes," Deon said, only half aware of what he had been told, for a woman doctor with a thin, vinegary air, whom he knew as one of the deputy superintendents, had come into the room, accompanied by a number of men. At once the lecture hall was tense and quiet, and Deon remembered the time his father had taken him to the traveling circus at Beaufort West when he was small and the feeling of half dread and half frenzy that swept through him when he heard the grunting and heavy movement outside which meant that the lions had been brought up in their wheeled cage, and then the iron gate clanged as a signal that they were about to enter the ring.

The woman doctor welcomed them without warmth and, in a flat monotone, delivered an endless lecture on hospital procedure. It was all from the handbook.

They were expected, she instructed them, to wear their name badges; to write legibly on forms; to fill in infectious diseases certificates, death certificates, operation consent slips, and prescription forms; to take care of equipment and to be polite and kind to the nursing staff.

Deon listened gloomily. His former enthusiasm and sense of wonder were steadily diminishing, driven out of him by that nagging and persistent voice. At primary school there had been a teacher who spoke to new children in exactly that voice.

The woman introduced a gray, stooping man as the head of the Blood Bank. Another lecture. And then another. Finally they were asked to fill in tax, bank, and sports club forms and told to report tomorrow morning. As they filed out Deon turned to Robby. "After all that crap, let's get on to serious matters. Have you cuddled any of the nurses, yet, Doctor?"

Robby laughed. "No, Doctor. But I've been doing a bit of research."

A senior houseman, passing them, warned: "Don't kid yourselves. This is no picnic."

They looked at him in silence, belligerently. He nodded his head.

"It's going to be a long year. Wait and see."

It seemed to him afterward that he had scarcely ever slept, that the days and nights dragged by in a haze of fatigue, that he was constantly on his feet: in the wards, in theater, in outpatients. When he did sleep it was often only fitfully, for an hour or two at a time, dozing off with the certain knowledge that a sepulchral voice on the loudspeaker would soon be whispering: "Doctor van der Riet. Doctor van der Riet."

Yet, perversely, he had never in his life felt so much alive. His senses were almost continuously on the alert, keyed to the finest pitch. Colors seemed bolder and brighter; his hearing was acute and took in everything from the squeak of a nurse's rubber soles down a long corridor in the lonely night to the bubbling sigh of an old man fighting his last battle against the slow-rising tide within him.

He was disturbed by the accuracy of his premonitions. One morning during the surgical round, he met a young woman who had been admitted during the night with a slight hematemesis. A duodenal ulcer had been diagnosed and she had been placed on antacids and booked for a laparotomy the next day. She was thirty or so and attractive. The surgeon had joked with her and she had replied saucily, and then the surgeon and the members of his firm moved on to another bed. Deon, backing so as to get an unobstructed view of the next patient, bumped against the young woman's bed. He leaned over to apologize and smelled the stench of death. He had been unable to adjust his expression quickly enough and the woman caught his stare and frowned.

"Sorry," he said to her softly, and she lay back on her pillows; soft lazy body relaxed in her nightgown with pink roses embroidered around the shoulder straps.

"Clumsy," she whispered back conspiratorially and winked at him.

After the end of the round he looked at her chart, but there was nothing unusual. The vital signs were all stable and the prescribed treatment correct. All he had to go on was a smell, which had most probably never been there, and a feeling of unease. Finally he convinced himself that the three deaths in B–4 yesterday had left him feeling edgy.

During the afternoon the woman felt nauseated and asked a nurse for a bedpan. When it came she retched a few times, leaning over the side of the bed, holding the pan. Abruptly her body was shaken by spasm after spasm and she cried out incoherently and bright blood gushed from her mouth in an uncontrollable stream.

Her neighbor in the ward screamed and only then thought of ringing the bell. A nurse came running and then the two ward sisters. One of them stopped short at the door and, taking it all in at once, spun on her heel to call a doctor.

Two minutes later the woman was dead of a massive hematemesis.

Her name had been West. Maria Johanna West. It was a name he would always remember.

There were other names too, on the debit side of the ledger.

Peter Tait, eleven years old, simple fracture of the left tibia. Cheerful little boy, snub-nosed, freckled, a grin like a terrier's. Broke his leg falling out of a tree. There were already two nurses' autographs on his cast before he had left the O.P.D. His X-rays showed the bone in place. No problems. But Deon, doing a routine examination, noticed that one eardrum was very red. The child had a slight temperature too, so Deon asked the nurse to give him a million units of penicillin. He felt smug about having spotted the minor ailment while everyone else was distracted by the major one.

During the drive home Peter Tait complained of being giddy. His parents thought this might be due to delayed shock. Then his mother noticed that he was having difficulty in breathing. Eventually he was gasping for every breath. His father turned back toward the hospital, driving as fast as he dared through the rush-hour traffic. Peter Tait collapsed while they were still ten minutes away, held up by a line of slow-moving buses. He was dead on arrival: anaphylactic shock due to hypersensitivity to penicillin. Who knew that the life sustainers could kill too? Well, they could, and did. Write down Peter Tait on the debit side.

Write down Willem Ruiters, aged six and a half.

Write down Noni M'vubanjani, eighteen, domestic servant.

Write down Robert Ronald Morton, fifty-two, company director.

These were the names he would remember best, in the lonely middle part of the night. But there were others on the credit side to help balance the books. He had to remember these too, to sustain sanity.

He was in B–1 on the male side that night, changing a drip that had leaked into the tissues of a patient with acute pancreatitis, when he was paged.

Damn! It was still early, hardly ten o'clock, but things had been quiet so far and he had a sneaking hope of being able to get away soon for a couple of hours of unbroken sleep. He was particularly weary. His firm had been on emergency intake last night and the going had been heavy. For some reason the night sister was especially jittery and had kept badgering him with niggling queries. The stupid woman was probably having her period or her menopause or something.

Deon strapped the needle down to the patient's wrist, gave him a brief smile, nodded to the staff nurse, said: "Okay, staffy. Run it at fifty drops a minute for the next two hours, then cut back to twenty a minute," and walked quickly down between the long double row of beds. The young man in the end bed was still awake, still reading, his bedlight on and a book resting against his drawn-up knees. He watched as Deon passed and Deon smiled at him. The boy did not respond in any way, except to follow Deon's progress with his solemn eyes. Then he looked down at his book again.

One for the neurosurgeons, thank God. Cerebral tumor. A bright youngster too. Deon had glanced at the cover of the book during rounds. *Also Sprach Zarathustra.* They had done a biopsy and had him on radiotherapy. They were going to go in again. They weren't very hopeful. They gave him a year at the outside, and he would be a vegetable long before then. The boy knew it too. Nietzsche. Oh, yes, he knew it.

The telephone was in the sister's office. There was an irritating delay before the switchboard came on. He sat perched on the side of the desk, swinging his legs. One of the nurses came in, the pert little one. Rhoda, he had heard the others call her, although they were supposed to use surnames only. She was carrying a tray with two used teacups and a plate on which a few biscuits had been left. He beckoned with a finger and when she approached mock-cautiously he took one of the biscuits. She pretended extreme shock. He grinned at her, munching the biscuit.

"Switchboard," a bored voice told him.

"Van der Riet."

"Casualty wants you, Doctor. Hang on."

"Okay."

A further delay before, finally, the crisp voice of the Casualty officer.

"Deon?"

"Ja. Hello, John."

The Casualty officer did not waste time on greetings. "Look, I'm sending you a kid with a gunshot wound. In the abdomen. He used a .303."

"Lord!"

"Ja. He's bleeding somewhere, so you'll probably have to take him to theater as soon as possible."

"Okay, John. Thanks."

So much for any chance of sleep. He got up, made a play of slapping the nurse on her neatly rounded bottom, and leaned toward the notice board at the door, where the duty roster was posted. Thursday. The registrar on call was Bill du Toit and the surgeon was that Bennett guy.

Deon grunted in exasperation. He disliked scrubbing with Bennett. Sarcastic bastard, with a down on housemen. You'd think he had never been one himself. Inferiority complex, probably. Bill was all right. He even let you do something yourself once in a while, instead of merely standing around, hanging on to a retractor. Bennett, who had spent a couple of years in America, referred to a retractor scathingly as "the idiot stick," and for once he was right. But this didn't make it any easier to bear the feeling of utter uselessness at the table.

Nothing to be done about it. Bennett would be running the show tonight, having his notorious little rows with the theater sister and making his stinging remarks out of the side of his mouth as he worked. It wasn't even as if he were a particularly good worker. In fact, he was a lousy surgeon; one of the slapdash ones. All the same, he was the boss tonight.

Bennett was in the changing room, stripped to his underpants, when Deon came in. He glanced up briefly over his thick horn-rimmed spectacles.

"How much blood has he had?"

Deon opened his jacket, unbuttoned his shirt.

"Three pints, sir. And there's another running."

"He's bleeding a lot. I assume you've ordered more?"

The tone was sharp and needlessly domineering and Deon's temper rose. Did the man think he was dealing with fools?

He nodded as curtly as he could manage.

Bennett hopped on one leg to keep his balance as he pulled on the white linen trousers. He jerked his head toward the door.

"Is Bill ready?"

"He's with the patient," Deon told him.

"How is the kid?"

"He took the blood well. And the peripheral pulses are okay now."

"His blood pressure was a bit low."

"It was ninety-sixty when I left him."

Bennett cleared his throat with a dry cough. He buttoned his fly and pulled on his boots without saying anything further.

It was obviously beneath his dignity to share knowledge. Well, damn you too, Deon thought. He stripped quickly and stepped under the shower, running it cold, delighting in the breath-catching shock of the icy water. He turned off the shower and toweled himself hard. A necessary edge had been restored to his mind. He began to dress.

Bennett was putting his outside clothing tidily away in a locker.

"Shake it up," he said without lifting his head. "We can't wait all night."

Deon suppressed the rude reply which came instantly to his lips. Instead he clamped his teeth firmly together, so that a muscle jumped in his jaw, and said nothing. He stepped past Bennett and gathered vest and pants from the neatly stacked assortment in the wall cupboard.

A head peered apologetically round the door. Behind the distorting lenses of the spectacles eyes blinked in make-believe shyness which was belied by the pointed, inquisitive nose.

"Hello, boys," Professor Snyman said. He opened the door wider and came into the dressing room. He was in evening dress, neat as always, his black bow impeccably tied and set absolutely square.

"Evening, sir," Bennett and Deon said in chorus.

Professor Snyman brushed his hands dismissingly down his body, in a gesture intended to explain and apologize for the formality of his clothing.

"One of those dinners," he said with a small laugh. "Luckily it didn't last very long, so I thought I'd pop in to B–1 to have a look at that gastrectomy from yesterday." He paused before asking in a nonchalant voice which fooled no one: "And what have you got on here tonight, Tim?"

Deon turned away, pulling his vest on over his head and hiding a smile. Everyone knew the old man regarded the theater block as his personal holy possession and was obsessively jealous that others, even if they were his own staff, should also have access to the sanctum. Nevertheless he always went through this elaborate ritual of seeming to ask permission to be there and of being overwhelmingly grateful to the duty surgeon for granting it.

"Bullet wound, sir," said Bennett. "Looks as if it got the liver. And there's probably some spinal damage." After a well-judged interval he said brightly, as if the thought had only just occurred to him: "I wonder if you'd mind giving us your opinion, sir."

Snyman went through his tail-wagging performance and Bennett held the door open for him, smiling. The old man went out, his footfall softened by the green cloth overshoes. Bennett, still holding the door, turned to Deon; he raised his eyebrows and assumed an expression of tolerant resignation.

"I'd be glad if you could arrange to join us sometime tonight, Doctor van der Riet," he said. His voice was pitched just high enough to reach Professor Snyman in the corridor.

Deon felt his face go hot with anger. But again, with very deliberate control, he refused to rise to the bait. He bent to tuck the bottoms of his trousers into the white rubber boots. Just wait, you little sod, he promised Bennet and himself both. The day will come.

Snyman, his trim black-encased body (strange, almost indecent to see black here) bobbing eagerly, and Bennett, his head inclined deferentially toward his chief, were already going into the induction room.

Deon clumped after them, pausing outside the scrub room to get a cap and mask and tie them on, making firm bows behind his head with practiced skill as he continued down the passage.

The patient was on a trolley, gowned for surgery and being anesthetized. Deon glanced at him and, like a card popping up in a filing cabinet, the case history was before him.

Daniel Jacobus Albertus Labuschagne, aged eighteen years. Occupation apprentice motor mechanic. Complaint: gunshot wound in the upper abdomen; self-inflicted; accidental (?).

What the history sheet did not mention was the frantic eyes of the father as he told his stumbling, commonplace story, over and over again, to anyone who cared to listen. He had this old army Lee-Metford, see, and it was kept in the wardrobe, see, he'd had it there for years, didn't have a license for it, but he didn't really use it ever, just kept it in the wardrobe with a box of cartridges and took it out once a year or so to clean and oil it. When Danie was a little boy, oh, about five years old, he had caught the child playing with the gun one time and he'd given him a hiding, a real thrashing to make sure he would never do it again and it had worked, for Danie had never touched the rifle again and tonight he and his wife were sitting in the lounge listening to the radio, they lived in Bellville, see, and they didn't go out very often, they were listening to a play on the radio and they thought Danie was in his room and then they heard the shot.

He had looked helplessly at Bill du Toit and Deon and the ward sister, but had carefully averted his eyes from the still, pale body on the bed between them, and from the foreign tubes that ran into it.

"He's going to be all right, Doctor?" he insisted. "He will be all right?"

Bill had nodded briskly. "We'll do our best."

The man looked at him and had nodded too, but had not believed, had not been comforted.

It was just an old army .303, he told them, and Danie hadn't touched it since he had been a small boy. Danie was a good boy, he was quiet and he had worked hard at school, although he wasn't clever. He never gave them any trouble; didn't smoke or go out with girls or anything like that. It had to be an accident. It was an accident, wasn't it?

Daniel Jacobus Albertus Labuschange, eighteen years old. Why would anyone wanting to commit suicide shoot himself in the belly? Only Daniel Jacobus Albertus knew the answer to that one.

If they wanted any answers from him, ever again, there was no time to mess around. Deon looked up at the anesthetists.

Solly Morris looked Jewish even behind the mask. He had a squat, powerful welterweight boxer's body and curly, very black hair on his arms. Working calmly behind his machine at the head of the trolley, he concentrated solely on what he was doing, as if he were the only person in the room. He hummed softly to himself and, as always, it was Brahms's "Lullaby." It had started as a joke and then became a habit, so that people hardly noticed or commented on it now. Bill du Toit stood at the side of the trolley, his anxious hands continuously on the move. He was looking back over his shoulder at Bennett and answering a question. He gulped as he spoke, so that Deon could catch only snatches of what he was saying. Something about the blood pressure, which was down below sixty again.

The way Bill looked before an operation was enough to put the fear of God into anyone. But his agitation vanished the moment he stepped up to the table. Deon knew him to be a tough and cool surgeon and admired his skill.

Old Snyman was hovering on the outskirts, pretending to be no more than an interested guest, seeming not to notice how carefully everyone kept out of his way. But his eyes were quick.

"What do you think, sir?" Bennett asked.

The professor made a deprecating gesture.

"I'd value your opinion," Bennett insisted.

Snyman discarded his pose of reluctance the way he might have shrugged off a soiled surgical gown. He stepped forward a pace and leaned down to examine the dressings. Solly Morris was securing the intratracheal tube to the boy's nose with a strip of plaster. He was still humming.

Professor Snyman straightened up, pushing a hand into the small of his back as if the movement cost him effort. Now he poked two fingers at his own round belly, neatly concealed under tailored black cloth.

"You say the entry wound is here, between the tenth and eleventh ribs."

"Yes, sir."

Snyman traced a path from left to right over the dinner jacket.

"And the exit wound is here, eh?" He tapped his belly on the right-hand side. "It could have hit the spleen, the stomach, transverse colon, and small bowel. And goodness knows what else."

Bennett shook his head, but still contrived to look deferential.

"I don't think it traveled in a straight line, sir. The kid complained of numbness in his leg. I'm inclined to believe he tried to shoot himself in the heart but the bullet hit the spinal column instead and was deflected upward and to the right."

Professor Snyman propped his right elbow on his left hand and chewed reflectively at the web of skin between fingers and thumb.

"Hmm."

After a moment both hands dropped decisively to his side.

"We're only guessing. You had better go in and see."

The swinging door banged and the floor sister came in, hurrying. She stopped, as if abashed, when Snyman turned to look at her. He nodded in reply to her mumbled greeting.

The sister beckoned to Bennett.

"E–1 is on the phone, Doctor. They've admitted a probable acute appendicitis and they want to know when someone can see the child."

"When we've finished here," Bennett said. Then he held up a hand, frowning weightily. "No. Hang on." Obviously there was a need to impress

94

the professor. His glasses glittered in reflected light and hid his eyes. "Bill, will you see it?" He did not wait for assent. "Then I'll need another pair of hands here. Sister. Who's next on call?"

Snyman gave a little dry, polite cough.

"Wait, sister."

The woman stopped immediately, hand reaching for the door. She remained frozen in that exaggerated pose of instant readiness.

"I'll give you a hand here, Tim," Snyman said to Bennett. "It may take quite a while."

"That's very kind of you, sir." Bennett was doing his own tail wagging now. "There's no need for it, really. We can get another pair of hands up here quickly enough. But if you'd care to . . . I would be honored . . ."

"Good," Snyman said briskly. Convention and courtesy had been duly satisfied. Now he was anxious to get on with the job. He dismissed the nurse with a wave of the hand and turned back to his intent scrutiny of the boy on the table.

"How's he doing, Solly?"

Morris made a small adjustment and watched his dials for a moment. He nodded. "Okay. I'm ready."

Snyman headed for the door. "I'll change," he said to Bennett over his shoulder. "Will you open him up? Upper midline incision."

"Right," Bennett said, all eagerness and action. He barked out machine-gun stutter commands all round the room, most of them unnecessary and ignored.

Deon helped Solly Morris move his machine and the dripstands as the orderlies wheeled the trolley across the corridor and in through the double doors of B theater. He was rewarded with a nod and a wink. Solly never spoke more than he could help.

The nurses began to prepare and drape the still figure, and Deon lingered for a moment to watch. He had seen all this scores of times as a student and participated in it often enough in the last four months, but it never failed to excite him, to quicken his pulse and his breathing. People moved around the operating room, aimlessly it seemed, without seeming to hurry. And yet things were happening; swift and efficient things. The orderlies with their trolley had gone and the patient was on the table. The sterile area around him was being established, marked off by green drapes as forbidden territory. The theater sister was setting out her instrument trays, the swab nurse was chalking something on a blackboard, other nurses were moving in and out with trolleys.

The door to the scrub room opened and the floor sister came through, looking at him reproachfully. Behind her he could see that Bennett was scrubbing. He had better move it now, before the fellow had an excuse to get off some new caustic remark.

They scrubbed side by side in silence. Bennett rinsed the soap off his hands and arms and closed the long swivel tap with an elbow. A nurse was ready to pour spirits over his hands.

Deon used his brush meticulously on his fingernails, waiting for Bennett to finish before he gowned up. The scrub room was small and it was difficult to avoid getting in the way. He wished to avoid further scenes.

Bennett put on his gloves.

"Be so kind as to let us know when we can start," he said with a sarcastic twist of the lip and went through to the operating room.

"Go to hell, you little shit," Deon muttered into his mask.

The nurse heard him and giggled as she offered him a gown at the end of a pair of forceps. He had to show her that he was undaunted, so he held the gown spread out in front of him, then threw it into the air flamboyantly, thrusting his hands adeptly into the sleeve holes as it flared out. The nurse looked startled and he winked at her. She shook her head remonstratingly while she tied the tapes at the back and Deon powdered his hands.

The feel of the gloves as they slipped over his fingers was like a caress. The opening caress of a possible love affair, he thought. The first touch; the first tentative, questioning kiss. It arouses the same feelings: of exhilaration, of drunk-without-wine; of who-knows-what-the-night-may-bring.

He went into the theater, tucking sleeves into the cuffs of the gloves, keeping the skirt of his gown fastidiously from accidental unsterile contact like an elderly lady walking along a slum street. The scrub sister and Bennett were folding out the covering drape with its square opening across the iodine-painted upper abdomen. Deon moved up to the table and the nurse looked at him, lifting her eyebrows slightly; an unspoken criticism of his lateness. He returned her glance with a hard glare, and she blinked in surprise.

At once he felt more light-hearted, for it wasn't often one could put a scrub nurse in her place with a look. This was Rita. She was a bit of a know-it-all, with a tendency to argue back at the junior surgeons. But at least she was quick; not like Margaret, the other one on night duty, who was as slow and fumbling as a cart horse.

"Ready to start, Solly," Bennett said. "How are things at your end?"

The anesthetist was pumping up the blood pressure cuff.

"Okay. The B.P. dropped at induction, but it's coming up nicely. The pulse is a bit fast. About one forty. Cut when you're ready and tell me if he's a bit tight."

Bennett held out his hand and the nurse put the handle of a scalpel into it. He held the knife dramatically posed.

"Right," he said. He waited a moment, as if hoping someone might applaud. He began to cut.

Deon and the sister exchanged another quick glance. The girl's face moved under her mask and her eyes wrinkled at the corners. He smiled back at her, then leaned over the table to swab and cauterize the bleeding points as Bennett went through the skin and subcutaneous fat down to the rectus sheath.

"Old man was as pleased as punch to get in on this," Bennett observed. He thrust an instrument vehemently back at the nurse. "I want something which can cut here, sister, not a blasted wool shears."

She handed him a smaller pair of scissors and he snipped at the peritoneum, pushed the hand with which Deon was holding the retractors roughly aside, said: "For God's sake, Doctor, I can't see to cut with your hands all over the place," and then resumed his usual sneering tones: "He was due to do a laparotomy this morning but the patient ran a temp so he had to put it off. And he isn't happy if he doesn't use the knife once a day."

He looked around to gauge the effect of his observation, but there was no visible reaction from any of the others. The sister had her back turned and was counting dissecting swabs. Solly Morris was making yet another delicate adjustment in the balanced flow of nitrous oxide and oxygen and his lips were pursed in a soundless whistle. Deon pushed the sucker down into the open peritoneal cavity, from which blood was spilling over on to the wound towels. He pretended not to have heard.

Bennett scowled and snatched the sucker nozzle.

"Don't dab, dab, dab at it, man. If you want to clear it, do the job properly, or not at all."

He thrust the nozzle irritably down into the abdomen and the steady slurping sound stopped abruptly. Bennett looked startled, then tried to disguise his consternation behind anger.

"Sister! The blasted sucker has packed up." He whirled round at her, the absolute image of concentrated fury and frustration. "It's the same old story! How do they expect us to work with this rubbish they give us?" He jerked his head. "Don't just stand there! *Do something!*"

The sister examined the rubber tube methodically.

"There's nothing wrong with the suction, sir. It's blocked at your end. The tube has sucked flat."

Solly Morris looked over the screen.

"You'd better stop the hemorrhage. He's losing blood faster than I can put it back."

"I can't do a thing," Bennett yelled at him. "They can't get the blasted sucker to work."

Bright red blood was spilling over the drapes.

"Why can't anybody help me?" Bennett asked in a tight, shrill voice. He groped for the sucker tube with frenzied fingers.

Deon lifted the nozzle from the blood-filled cavity and with it came the piece of greater omentum which had sucked in and blocked the nozzle. He freed it, then held the omentum out of the way with a swab and replaced the sucker. At once the slurping noise restarted.

Bennett had not noticed and he turned now, his expression a comic mixture of relief and incredulity.

"There!" he said to the sister. "I told you there was something wrong with the thing."

Deon winked at her and no one spoke.

The door sighed softly on its hydraulic spring and Professor Snyman came in, jaunty and with eyes bright above his mask, nodding affable greetings here and there. He was proud of his courteous theater manners. Outside he might be irritable and crotchety, but once he was at his place beside the table he was every inch the perfect gentleman. Other surgeons might rant and rave like prima donnas; Professor Snyman seldom raised his voice above a genteel tea-party murmur. Disapproval was seldom vocal, most often indicated by a little frown or a look of pained surprise. Clumsy scrub nurses and slow assistants feared that frown as much as the torrent of abuse they might receive from other doctors. For the courtesy was an act that did not deceive the professor's victims. The old man did not forget or forgive. Retribution would come in time, when they least expected it.

Now he went through the ritual, but his eyes had already hardened and were fixed on the table, swiftly evaluating progress.

"Hello, hello, hello," he said. "What have we got here?"

Bennett changed sides to make room for him. "I haven't had a chance to assess the injuries, sir," he admitted lamely. "We couldn't get the sucker to work properly."

The old man gave him a darting glance from under his eyebrows.

"It appears the patient is bleeding from the spleen," said Bennett.

"Um," said Professor Snyman.

He emptied the peritoneal cavity by lifting out the small bowel and the transverse colon. Bennett covered the protruding intestines with a moist swab, and Snyman, warmth and good cheer again fully restored, thanked him urbanely. He hooked a right-angled retractor under the left rectus muscle.

"Would you kindly come on to my side, Doctor van der Riet? Give me some retraction here, if you please."

Using a swab, he picked up the anterior wall of the stomach and requested Bennett to hold it out of the way in a tone which implied that he would remain forever indebted. Bennett was not fooled.

Snyman had sucked away blood and clots, peering into the opened cavity as he worked. Now it was clear from where all the blood was coming; the bullet had smashed through the spleen, leaving half of it a pulp.

Solly Morris peered at him over the drapes. There was a trace of austere reproof in his voice.

"Blood pressure's still falling."

"We'll have it under control in just a moment, Solly." Snyman bobbed his head politely at the anesthetist. "Don't panic."

Snyman worked deftly and quickly, and in time with him Bennett and Deon retracted and swabbed and sucked. The splenic area was exposed and Snyman burrowed down into the peritoneal cavity like an intent, nimble-fingered pickpocket working silently in a packed crowd. He pulled what was left of the spleen toward him and held out a hand. The sister, leaning forward over the drapes which covered the young man's knees, had been watching intently. The long dissecting scissors were ready in her hand and Snyman took them without looking at her. He cut the attachment between spleen and kidney and pulled it farther forward and up. Out went the hand again.

Forceps . . . forceps . . . scissors . . . cut.

All the vessels from the splenetic artery to the stomach were divided between artery clamps, and the spleen was held only by a pedicle consisting of the splenic vein and artery. Professor Snyman used forceps to clamp them and divided the pedicle. His hand emerged from the hollow of the abdominal cavity, bearing the smashed spleen aloft.

The sister offered a dish and he placed the organ tenderly inside it.

"The hemorrhage is under control now, Solly. Give some blood. I'll stop for a while so that you can get things under control."

He placed a gauze swab on the area he had dissected, then looked across at Bennett. "It seems to me the bullet missed the spinal column. It went through the spleen and through the stomach and hit a few loops of the small bowel. But it missed the spine."

Bennett was obviously reluctant to change his diagnosis. "He definitely complained of numbness in his legs."

Professor Snyman shrugged, not prepared to be drawn into a futile discussion.

"It may have been due to shock. You didn't find any neurological changes, did you?"

He did not wait for a reply, and instead looked over the drape at the anesthetist. "How are things up there, Solly?"

Solly Morris stopped pumping blood for a moment and ducked away out of sight. His voice was muffled behind the drape. "Better. Pressure's up to ninety. You can carry on."

Clearly Bennett had been shaken by the uncharacteristic snub. He was sweating too, in the hard brightness of the overhead lights. Deon could see that the lenses of his spectacles were misting up. Bennett tilted his head backward to try to clear the foggy glasses.

Professor Snyman removed the swab, held up one of the artery clamps, and glanced at Bennett. The man did not respond immediately, so Snyman said with elaborate cordiality: "Hold the clamp, if you please, so I can tie the splenic artery."

Deon saw that Bennett was still having trouble with his glasses and moved to take the clamp. But Bennett pushed his hand away. The sister had already ripped open a packet and handed the suture to Snyman. He tied a loop round the forceps and slipped it down to get it into position round the artery. The loop slipped back on to the clamp. Bennett, struggling to see, tilted the forceps at the wrong angle, pulling and tugging at them.

Even Snyman's patience was wearing thin. "Show me the point of the forceps, if you please," he said sharply.

Bennett jerked the forceps toward him. They slipped off the artery. Instantly blood spurted in one bright red jet into Snyman's face and over his glasses as he bent over the open wound. The sister with discipline instilled by hours of training and repetition turned to whip an artery clamp up from her tray and hold it ready and poised.

But, quick as she was, Deon had been quicker. He had sucked the welling blood from the wound and then had reached down instinctively to catch the pulsating pedicle between unerring fingers. His hands were shaking almost uncontrollably from the tension but he did not let go, would never let go, through eternity.

And Bennett still had not moved.

Then Professor Snyman, glasses cleaned roughly by one of the floor

nurses, snatched the clamp from the sister and, bending over to see through
the smeared film of blood, clamped the artery behind Deon's fingers.

Even after he had caught the artery he held that position, peering down
into the raw wound as if it contained a mystic message, a cypher he had
only now learned to read. He straightened up slowly, still contemplating
the dread import of the revealed message.

And at last he turned to Bennett.

"Fool," he said in a voice which did not carry farther than the tense figures around the table. "You bloody fool."

As Professor Snyman had predicted, the bullet had passed through the
back and front walls of the stomach and through two loops of the small
bowel.

He continued the operation, and all of them tried to the best of their ability to act as if nothing had happened. The holes were stitched and sections
of the small bowel resected and reanastomosed.

Deon was doing most of the assisting now. Once, at the start, he had
fumbled, and had received and borne Professor Snyman's utterly courteous
and cutting comment. But he watched unblinkingly the next time as the
holder with its curved needle found its place on the old man's palm and the
needle went *snick* and Snyman pulled it through and gathered a new section of tissue and the needle went *snick* again and the segments were pulled
together. Snyman tied knots with effortless speed and Deon lifted and held
with the forceps, and the needle and its holder were already moving and
went in again and out and the stubby delicate fingers inside the skintight
gloves advanced the row of stitches with immaculate precision. Now Deon
had found the rhythm and the pace. He was working faster but also more
easily than ever before. He imagined that this was how it felt to play a duet
with a master musician; there was the sense of faultless timing, of movement and response, flow and counterflow. It was all absolutely natural and
controlled, with no wasted movement anywhere.

As Snyman started the posterior layer of the anastomosis he turned to
Bennett. "Would you follow from your side, Doctor?"

The silence in the room was deep and echoing.

Bennett took the forceps and immediately the rhythm became disturbed.
He was inaccurate and inclined to fumble, so that Snyman had to wait for
him time and again. It was like watching intricate tapestry work being
done on an inferior loom; the stitches were placed as beautifully and with
equal skill, but the end result gave a lumpy, overhasty impression. Bennett

was aware that he was bungling and the awareness made his hands more unsteady. Snyman showed no sign of having noticed anything. And Deon, knowing that he should feel pity but hardening his mind against it, was contemptuous (now that he had seen and been in tune with perfection) of anything that was less than perfect.

The tension was gone and the sister gave a small, almost involuntary shrug. It did not go unnoticed; nor did it serve to soothe Bennett's ragged nerves.

Snyman replaced the anastomotic bowel, then pulled the omentum over to protect it. He stooped and examined his work critically.

Deon looked at the dome of the head bowed over the table close in front of him and at the bristly gray tufts of hair which had escaped under the edges of the surgical cap. You're a pompous and opinionated old sod, he told that half-hidden head affectionately. Your juniors fear you and your peers hate you. With good reason, for you're as closed-minded and self-centered as a hawk. But, by God, you're a damn fine surgeon.

"Will you close up?" Snyman said and stood back from the table. He smiled artlessly at each of them in turn, allowed the swab nurse to undo his gown, smiled again, said: "Thank you, gentlemen," and went out, walking with his customary short, swift strides.

Deon and Bennett closed the incision in absolute silence.

They left the theater together, still not speaking, pausing at the outside door of the scrub room to discard masks and caps. Bennett walked away toward the changing room and Deon lingered briefly to peer through the glass partition into A theater. It was empty, so obviously Bill du Toit had finished up the appendectomy without fiddling around. Unlike Bennett.

The poor bastard, Deon thought. He'll never forget that. He'll never be allowed to forget it.

And a good thing, too. He's not made to handle the knife. Let him go somewhere else where he can't do harm.

Don't be sanctimonious, he told himself. Wait till you make your own first serious mistake. Maybe it's by your mistakes that you learn; but keep praying that there's someone there to catch yours in time.

We worked well together, the old man and I. He works fast, and he thinks even faster. He thinks ahead. He doesn't do anything without knowing exactly why he's doing it and what he's going to do next. You only have to watch him to see it. We worked well together.

He tried to relive the excitement and the keen pleasure of those few minutes when their hands had worked perfectly in unison.

Suddenly he was ravenously hungry. He looked at his watch. One thirty.

He had scarcely been aware of time passing. Too late for midnight supper, but there would be coffee and sandwiches in the common room.

Professor Snyman was sprawled in an easy chair at the window, chewing moodily at a chicken sandwich and staring out at the darkness. A half-empty cup of coffee stood on the floor beside him.

He looked up and nodded when Deon came in, but neither of them said anything. Deon poured coffee from the urn. His hands were shaking now, in reaction, and the cup rattled faintly in its saucer. He put the saucer down hurriedly and held the hot cup between his hands, sipping gingerly from it.

Snyman finished his coffee with a slurp and stood up. There was a smear of blood on one of his trouser legs. He stood in front of Deon, feet apart and body braced.

"In my theater," he said, his voice taut and cutting, "I am the surgeon. I will not have interference. When I want an assistant to do anything except assist I will tell him so. Is that quite clear?"

Deon stared at him, at first in wonder, then with growing anger. But Snyman did not look away or change his attitude. He stood there squarely and determinedly, glowering like a miniature bulldog.

"Is that clear?" he demanded again in the same cold voice.

"Yes, sir," Deon said, not troubling to mask his contempt.

"Right," Snyman said. He turned and began to walk away with a quick swagger. But at the door he turned again. "Van der Riet."

Deon watched his face, stared resolutely back at the bulbous eyes. There were still tiny flecks of blood at the edges of the spectacle lenses.

Professor Snyman nodded his head slowly. "Well, well, well," he said aimlessly, as if he had forgotten what he had intended to say.

Then, with a slow smile: "You've got a good pair of hands there, my boy."

AUTUMN

Six

It started off as a quiet day, with only one case on the slate. Deon scrubbed with Bill du Toit on an uncomplicated cholecystectomy. He saw the patient back to the ward and decided to have an early lunch. Maybe he could catch up with some sleep this afternoon. But he had only just started his soup when he was paged.

Two admissions to the female ward. There was no urgency, so he went back to finish lunch. That ended any hope of an afternoon nap, however. Well, he would clerk them as fast as he could and try to leave himself free for tonight.

The first patient was a middle-aged woman with a pleasant face and worried eyes. A nurse was fussing at her bed, being efficient; perhaps too efficient.

Deon waited for the nurse to finish and glanced through the notes. Mrs. Malan. She had first been admitted fifteen months ago and had undergone a radical mastectomy for a schirrous carcinoma of the left breast. At her last visit to the clinic a hard supraclavicular node had been palpated and now she was in for a biopsy. Scrawled at the bottom of the notes was a question mark: "? recurrence of breast cancer." The same question was in the woman's eyes. Probably the clinic doctors had told her reassuringly that this was merely a routine examination. The question was there nevertheless.

Deon smiled and said: "Hello, Mrs. Malan," and was about to add something inane about welcoming her back when she turned her face away and began to weep, quite soundlessly.

So he stood there, patting her shoulder and looking wildly around for the efficient nurse who had now efficiently vanished. At last the sister came and he was able to order sedation and reestablish the calm routine in which pain and fear and suffering had its place, a recognized place, provided it did not go beyond the bounds of propriety.

He decided he would examine the other patient meanwhile and give Mrs. Malan time to settle down; as far as it was possible to be tranquil with that question unanswered.

Nevertheless, he told himself sternly, you have to stick to the routine. If you don't abide by the rules then there are no answers to any of the questions. In fact, even the questions are no longer questions.

"There's a remedy for everything except death." The words came to him abruptly, although he could not remember whether or not the line was a quotation. It was something Trish had said to him once, sitting cross-legged on his bed in that servant's quarters flat. (Who lived there now? he wondered. What student had inherited the sagging bed and the hard mattress and the wardrobe with its bottom drawer that needed a hard kick before it would close properly? Did he have a girl too?)

He turned resolutely to the next bed. This woman, thank God, was in for nothing more than the stripping of varicose veins. To many babies; too constipated, too fat, too vain.

When he had finished filling in the multitude of forms for X-rays, blood examination, biochemistry and preoperative orders he walked down to the duty room. He was depressed, both about Mrs. Malan and by the unexpected memory of Trish that had come to haunt him. What he needed was to get away from the hospital. There was a party at Hamish's place tonight. He had not really intended going, although it was his free night, for he needed sleep more. But perhaps a party would provide the release he sought. And at Hamish Denton's parties you could always be pretty sure of finding whatever it was you were seeking.

In the duty room he found only Philip Davids, sitting at the table and writing a letter.

"Hello," Deon said. "Haven't seen you for ages." He poured coffee, glancing at the headlines of the evening paper, lying open on a chair.

"Hello, Deon. Yes, they keep us occupied, don't they?"

"Ja. Oh, well. Four months gone and eight to come. Have you decided about going overseas yet?"

"Not quite decided. But I probably will go."

"Be a damn fool if you didn't."

Deon went up to the notice board, cup in hand, and examined the duty roster.

"Damn it!"

Philip looked at him in polite inquiry.

"They've got me down here for Casualty. I was on duty last week and I damn well should be off tonight."

"Jerry's away sick so they're one short in Casualty."

Deon looked at the list again. "Ja, I see that. Still," with more than a vestige of irritation and disappointment, "they could have let us know."

"Were you planning something special?"

"Well . . . ja. A party, out at Hout Bay."

Philip considered briefly.

"Look. Go to your party. I'm on wards tonight, but things are pretty quiet. I'll help out in Casualty and call you if I can't manage."

"That's nice of you. Only trouble is I don't know if this chap has a phone. I'll have a look in the book anyway."

He paged rapidly through the directory. Denton, Hamish P., Number 10, Marina. That was Hamish's flat at Clifton. But, surprisingly, he did have a telephone out at the Hout Bay cottage as well.

"I'll write the number down for you. Okay?"

"Good. I won't call you if I can help it."

"Okay, Philip. And thanks."

"Pleasure. Enjoy your party."

The party was well on its way by the time Deon arrived. He could hear the music from inside the old house even before he had stopped his car. He parked in among stunted shore-side bushes, at the end of a row of Triumphs and MGs. The music thumped its monotonous beat, counterpointed by other sounds that rose and fell like waves: the steady hum of conversation; the occasional shriek. It would take some time to catch up with the others. Should he forget it and go back to the hospital?

What the hell. He hadn't driven all the way out here for nothing. He squared his shoulders and went along the well-worn footpath toward the house.

The old woodframe building stood on a little hill of its own, separated from the other cliff-edge cottages by a ravine. He went through the deep shadow of the little valley and climbed the hill on the far side. Ahead of him the hill dropped steeply again toward a dark line of boulders. The sea, beyond, lay still and smooth in the moonlight. He stopped to look. Perhaps it was not entirely because of the parties that Hamish Denton preferred to live here.

A whitewashed splitpole fence had once surrounded the neglected garden, had confined its shaggy growth and kept it from spilling outward.

There had been bonfires at some of the parties, however, and slowly the poles had vanished. Only the gateposts and the superfluous gate remained. There was a sign on the gate. Deon leaned closer to read it in the moonlight: "Cirrhosis-by-the-Sea."

He smiled and walked around the gatepost up to the house. Two pairs of dark bodies lay on the veranda floor, locked in unmoving embrace. Deon stepped carefully over them. In the dark passage was another couple. It was too narrow for him to get by, so the two separated briefly and grudgingly.

The house was little more than a shell: a passage with three doors, each leading into the same room; a kitchen at the end of the passage, too small to be worth breaking into, and an outside bathroom. Hamish slept, when he slept, on a folding stretcher on the veranda.

He was dancing in the half dark now with a small black-haired girl who was unsteady on her feet and whose head rested trustingly on his chest. He waved an amiable greeting, pointed to a corner and shouted something that was inaudible above the general uproar. Deon cocked his ear, but Hamish had already danced past with the drunk dark girl.

Deon stood at the door for a moment, still flinching back from that solid-seeming noise, like a swimmer poised on a diving board, hesitating for a moment, anticipating the sudden shock of the chill water below. There was only one way to immunize himself. He shouldered his way through determinedly to the corner where the liquor stood.

It was one of Hamish's wine parties; there was no beer or hard liquor in sight. Deon, who had retained his student preference for beer, was disappointed. Eventually he poured a tumbler brim full of red wine from a bottle that had lost its label and stood sipping wine and staring at the party.

Plenty of girls anyway. That was the one advantage of the Fast Young Set parties. The men tended to be junior executives or young lawyers at big law firms, but the dollies were plentiful and beautiful. Deon himself liked Hamish's artistic parties, but the girls at those were always a little weird.

Suddenly he caught a glimpse of a girl with long dark-red hair gyrating wildly, and his arms went rigid with shock and wild expectation. He spilled a little of the wine. But it wasn't her. Of course, it couldn't be her.

He had run into one of Trish's old art school friends earlier in the year, outside a shop in Adderley Street. They had stopped to chat briefly. "How's Trish?" he had asked, very nonchalantly. "Seen much of her lately?"

The girl had looked at him assessingly.

"Oh, hadn't you heard? She's gone off to the Continent. To Spain."

"Really? That's interesting. What is she doing?"

"She plans to paint, I believe. She'll be lucky not to starve."

107

The friend had landed a job as an artist with an advertising agency within a week of graduation. She was very pleased with herself. Deon met her later, again by chance, having a meal alone at a cheap lunch counter near the hospital. He took her out a few times, but they didn't really click. She was boring and already talked in advertising jargon, and besides she was a virgin and determined to stay that way. They hadn't mentioned Trish again.

Now he looked at the dancing girl with the hair and he felt momentarily sick at the thought of what he had lost. In the intervening months she had taken on a new shape in his mind; had become part alive, part illusion. He had forgotten her sharpness, her razor-tight mind. He remembered her skill and inventiveness in love-making, her passion and enthusiasm in conversation, her quietness and isolation when she had seemed utterly at peace with herself and he had watched her, not wanting to speak, not daring to shatter that inner stillness.

Would she have found someone else, in Spain?

He imagined her making love with someone else (someone vaguely dark and Latin-looking, with a thin moustache) but immediately tried to banish the thought.

He drank the wine quickly, in a few gulps, unable to repress a small shudder of distaste at the end. Nevertheless, he refilled his glass determinedly and again began to study the party.

A tall blond girl spun away from her partner and was dancing on her own. Deon stared, and she stopped to return his gaze.

"Hullo," she said. "What are you gaping at?"

"I've just arrived."

"You're a stranger here. I've never seen you before."

"That goes for both of us."

"You look new and lost. Or are you bored?"

"No. Not bored. But you've all had a start on me." He lifted his glass and laughed uneasily. "I've got to get in the mood."

"Do you need someone to help you?"

"Yes," he told the girl very seriously. "I think I need help."

Her pupils were unnaturally large, so that the pale blue iris was only a sliver around each pupil. It gave her a fixed, staring look which was disconcerting. Drugged? Deon wondered.

"What's your name?" she asked. She wasn't drunk anyway. There was no slurring about that Old Cape Aristocracy accent.

"Deon. And yours?"

"Me?" As if surprised he didn't know. "I'm Liz."

"Liz who?"

"Just Liz."

"Well you must have a surname."

She shook her head. "Just Liz. Mystery Liz." She grabbed him by the arm and pulled him after her. "Let's dance."

Her former partner, standing behind her, scowled at Deon and moved to intervene, but she pushed him scornfully out of the way.

"Go away, Tony. Get lost."

Conscious of male pride, of having won a victory without needing to fight a battle, Deon put down his glass and danced away with his new-found conquest.

The beat was fast and he was a poor dancer. For the first few moments he was compelled to look down, watching his feet to make sure they were following the rhythm or, at any rate, were not totally out of step. They seemed to be doing roughly the same as all the others around him, so after a time he felt bold enough to be able to look up at his blond partner, smiling.

She was dancing in an attitude of complete abandon, her waist coiling and uncoiling like some lithe snake, her hips grinding in a provocative imitation of the sexual act. His smile became strained. He was not accustomed to this kind of girl.

She raised her arms limply, in a gesture intended to show extreme weariness, but which seemed to him exceedingly lovely, like the studied hand movements of a ballet dancer. I bet that's what she is, he thought. Ballet. Either that or an actress. Something to do with the stage anyway.

The girl danced with her arms half raised, and Deon became aware of another even more provocative possibility: that her breasts were naked under her sweater, which was made of some rough-woven material, like string tightly knotted together.

He watched the movement of her breasts under the garment and she saw where he was looking and smiled faintly, opening her mouth and running her tongue very slowly along the line of even teeth. He suspected she was mocking rather than teasing and lifted his eyebrows with pretended disdain.

Then she stopped abruptly.

"You don't dance very well, do you?"

"No," he admitted. "I haven't had much opportunity to learn."

She shrugged indifferently.

"Doesn't matter. Let's go outside anyway. This is boring."

Deon followed her through the crowd. People called out, "Liz!" "Liz!" but she ignored them.

They went into the passage. The couple who had been there earlier were gone. Deon reached out and took the girl's hand. It was hot, almost feverish. He tried to put an arm round her waist, but she pulled away.

Her voice had a hard edge on it. "I said let's go outside."

Humbly he allowed her to lead him out on to the veranda. He kissed her, expecting at least initial restraint. But she kissed back with devouring passion, making deep "Hmmmm," sounds of contentment. It was he who pulled away first. His body burned with an uncontrolled hunger for this strange girl.

They kissed and his hands were on her, on her hips, and she made no move to disengage them. He ran his fingers slowly up the receptive curve of her back. He moved his cupped hand over her breasts. They were firm with nipples pointing in excited erection.

They kissed again and her mouth opened in full submission.

His breathing was harsh and husky, but he did not care. He strained his body against hers, crushing, wanting to rend resistance, even though none was offered. His desire was mounting to an uncontrollable climax. He pulled away.

Someone was moving at the corner of the house, and they were both as still as the night. The interloper came blundering along. He tripped over something and cursed softly. Deon recognized the girl's former partner. Toby. Tony. Whatever. He stood still and tense, holding the girl.

The man stood in the moonlight, peering at them.

"Liz?" he asked uncertainly.

Then, seemingly able to make them out more clearly, he came closer and said to Deon, his voice surly: "You Doctor van der Riet?"

"Yes," Deon said guardedly.

"Well, you're wanted on the phone."

"I'm wanted . . . how did you know my name?"

"Hamish said . . ." the man started to explain. Then, his voice suddenly high and indignant: "What the hell do you think I am? Your messenger boy?"

"Thanks," Deon said. He turned to the girl. "It must be the hospital. Will you excuse me? I shouldn't be long."

The girl did not reply. Her face was in shadow.

Deon walked quickly into the house, hunting for Hamish Denton. Hamish was not in the multiple living room. There was no sign of a telephone anywhere.

A young man, carrying a bottle of wine, stopped near Deon. He tilted the bottle back and drank straight from it. It did not take long for Hamish's parties to degenerate.

"Excuse me," Deon said, "where's the telephone?"

The other lowered his bottle, then cupped an ear and made a gesture toward the dancers and the source of the drum-thundering noise.

"Phone!" Deon bellowed at him. "Where . . . is . . . phone?"

The young man shrugged and tipped his bottle again.

Deon stared frantically through the half gloom. Where could the blasted thing be?

He found it eventually, predictably enough, in the lean-to toilet outside. The receiver was off the hook, lying on the cistern. It must have been there for five minutes at least. He gave an involuntary snort of laughter at the thought of what the caller must have overheard.

Even out here the noise was overwhelming. He held the receiver against one ear and blocked the other with a finger.

"Hello," he said tersely. "Van der Riet."

After a brief hesitation: "Hello, Deon." Philip's voice, cool and amused. "Sounds like quite a party."

"It is."

"Sorry to have to drag you away, but we've got a bit of a panic in the wards. You'll have to come in."

Damn and damn again.

"Okay. I'll be there as soon as I can."

"Good. Sorry, Deon. 'Bye."

"So long," Deon said automatically. He held the receiver a moment longer, then slammed it irritably down on its cradle. He went around the house now to find Liz. She was gone. So was Toby-Tony. He might have expected it. But when he returned inside in search of Hamish, to apologize for leaving, he saw her dancing. Not with Tony, true. However, this one looked even more repulsive, with a bushy air force moustache and a permanent leer.

He tried to work his way toward her through the dancers, but the press of bodies was too thick. He waited till she came near enough for him to shout.

"I have to go!"

She smiled brilliantly at him, but then shook her head.

"Called out!" he bawled. "Have to go!"

She waved at him still smiling, then danced away with the imitation air ace.

He drove back to the city as fast as the Volkswagen could go.

The Casualty sister met him at the door. She looked haggard, but her face brightened when she saw him.

"Evening, Doctor."

She went on hurriedly, without waiting for him to return the greeting. "Can you give us a hand in the drip room please?"

He nodded, then walked grumpily past the mass of humanity which crowded the corridor. Coloureds and Africans. Women and children. There were infants swaddled in blankets; adults dressed in their best party clothes. Some were patients; others were there because they could not be left alone at home. They waited. They asked for nothing, demanded nothing.

Deon stopped at the entrance to the drip room. Children, many of them babies, lay on long, wooden tables. Bottles hung on overhead rails and thin, plastic tubes dangled like so many coiling snakes. Nurses wove their way deftly through the crowd.

A group of stout African women, sitting in a circle on the floor at the far end of the room, were eating from a common dish as if they were gathered for nothing more than a social occasion in a slightly unconventional setting.

The sister seemed to construe Deon's silence as criticism.

"It's the only way we can manage," she said defensively. "I've only got four nurse's aids to look after this whole business. We've got to keep the mothers here to give us a hand."

Deon knew all this. It was the only way to deal with the multitude of gastroenteritis patients, especially during the summer. What astonished him was the good-natured willingness with which these people stayed, often for days. Here they stayed in this big room with its screaming babies. There were no other facilities for mothers. This room became their bedroom, kitchen, and dining room. In here they shared what they had, even the pain of approaching death and the sorrow of its presence.

Their neglect was partly the cause of their children being here. But, in here, their patience and devotion was absolute. It was a paradox beyond his understanding. He shook his head and turned back to the white-haired sister: "What the hell is going on here?"

She sighed tiredly.

"We've had forty new admissions today, Doctor."

He sighed too. This was not going to be a matter of an hour or two. "Let's get started."

He went into a little cubicle and began scrubbing his hands.

The sister went to the door and called down the corridor, "Here's the doctor, mommies." Then she pointed to a scared-looking young woman at the head of the line: "You're first, mommy. Quickly now. Bring your child."

It was one of her affectations to refer to every woman who went through the drip-room service as "mommy" and to speak to all of them in exactly the same cheerily condescending tone, as if they were unruly and not overbright children. She always spoke in English, which few of them understood anyway. But she was fast and capable and even as she spoke the child was on the examination table, the mother shunted out of the way, and the swaddling cloths removed. She unclipped a safety pin and unfolded the diaper. It was stained watery green.

Deon glanced at the sister's notes. "Baby Manyase, aged seven months. Present weight 7 lb. 8 oz. Birth weight? Rectal temperature 105.8°. Feeding—mother's milk and mealiemeal porridge. History—diarrhea and periodic vomiting for two weeks. Rectal swab sent for examination."

Now, on the table, there lay a dried-out and emaciated human infant. The eyelids were half closed and the sunken eyes turned upward, so that only the whites showed. The anterior fontanel was depressed, leaving a hollow in the middle of the head. The pulse was fluttery and rapid, the lips dry, and the mouth parched. The shape of the skull was clearly discernible under the mummylike skin.

The child's belly was distended and its stick-thin arms and legs waved aimlessly in the air. It looked like some gray-black beetle mischievously turned on to its back and grasping at an invisible straw. Death could be only a few hours, or perhaps even a few minutes away.

The urgency hit him then, with the breath-catching shock of icy water flung into the face. It was late in the day for Baby Manyase.

"Sister, let's get some fluids into this child."

Gastroenteritis. Lay people called it apricot sickness. Deon had never understood the association. In most cases the cause was unknown. If a child was well nourished the disease normally lasted only a few hours. But the poor and the hungry fared less well. Vomiting and diarrhea went on and on, depleting the child of water and salts, progressing rapidly to stupor and circulatory arrest. Gastroenteritis was one of the commonest causes of infant mortality among the Coloureds and Blacks.

"Get the woman to hold the head steady."

About 10 percent dehydrated. He would need 100 milliliters per kilo of half-strength Darrow's in 2.5 percent Dextrose solution. The weight? Three kilos. So that was 300 milliliters to replace the fluids he had already lost.

The sister had shaved the side of the head, leaving a bald patch in the curiously reddish-gray hair. She tapped with her fingers and compressed the skull to bring up the collapsed vein. Deon, hands scrubbed and dried, cleaned the patch while the young African woman watched incuriously. He gripped the little needle with an artery forceps. Getting a scalp vein drip going was an incredibly tricky job. One of the pediatricians was said to be so good he could set up a drip on a billiard ball. Steady hands; that was the secret. And he was uncomfortably aware that he had yet to learn to control the tremor of his own hands.

"Okay, sister. Let's see what we can do."

He sat down next to the baby's head and braced his arm with an elbow on the table. He could not keep it quite still. The vein was as thin as a thread of cotton. He pushed the needle through the skin. The African girl looked away, although her expression did not change. He advanced the tip of the needle along the vein, tilting it slightly backward. Suddenly blue blood ran back into the plastic tube.

He grinned in happy triumph.

"First shot! Sister, let's have the . . ."

She had the drip-set ready and waiting and handed it to him without a word. He connected it.

"Okay. Open it."

Both of them watched the drip chamber. The drops began to fall.

Deon strapped the needle down securely and stood up. "Let him have this one-fifty fast. I'll see him again when it's run in and work out the rest of his fluids."

The mother was still holding the child's head.

"Why did you wait so long before you came here?" he asked.

He did not know what purpose the question could possibly serve. There were many explanations. She had been to a private doctor but her money did not last. She didn't have the busfare. She hadn't realized the child was so sick. She had no one to tell her where to come. And so on.

The girl did not offer any of the explanations. She was humming under her breath, a monotonous, hardly audible lullaby.

He turned to the sister who was already undressing the next baby.

"Has this woman had anything to eat today?" he asked. "Do you think you could get her something? Maybe a cup of tea and some bread? Please?"

"I'm sorry, Doctor. The hospital will not provide food or drink for the mothers. I'm sorry."

"Maybe I should put a drip up on the mother as well," he said, vehemently.

She shook her head. "I know. But those are the rules. I'm sorry."

The night went by, its progress measured not by seconds or minutes or hours but by screaming, vomiting, shitting, and dying babies.

And through it all Deon was constantly and bitterly aware that the real battle lay elsewhere. This was no more than a skirmish, a holding action. The enemy was not gastroenteritis. It was something more tenuous and at the same time more implacable, a system that held people in bond to the color of their skins.

And then, almost startlingly, it was two o'clock in the morning.

They had worked down through the waiting rows, swiftly but without rushing, working as a team, matching and supporting each other. A few additional patients arrived, but the buses had stopped running and soon the stream would dribble to a halt.

Deon realized, with a reassurance of hope and frustrated desire, that it was not too late to return to the party. Unwise, perhaps, for there were early rounds in the morning. But he needed a drink, even if only as an antidote to the rank and fetid smell of excrement.

Would she still be there?

The white-haired sister looked through the door again. "Last one, Doctor," she announced. She sounded relieved. She wasn't so young and this job probably played the devil with her feet.

The last mother was a youngish Coloured woman with a scarf tied around her head. She had the usual driven expression and the usual blanketed bundle in her arms. She dawdled at the door and the sister's lips tightened. "Come along, mommy," she said a little impatiently. "Come on." She began to unwrap the dirty, torn blanket.

The child, a girl eighteen months old, had been asleep against her mother's shoulder. The moment the shielding blanket was removed she woke with a shriek. The sister reached out for her and she drew up her legs and screamed again. The sister took her with a firm, no-nonsense gesture and put her down on the examination table. Immediately the little girl tried to claw her way off it. The nurse looked at Deon in exasperation.

"What's wrong with your child?" he asked.

The woman mumbled something unintelligible.

"What?" he asked sharply.

"She is sick," the woman said. And burst out crying. She sank down on her haunches, shoulders back against the wall, and wailed as if her heart would break.

The child stopped crying.

Deon and the sister exchanged glances. Then the nurse kneeled briskly to prod the woman back on to her feet.

"Come on, mommy. Come on now," she said over and over. It was as if the crisp English phrases, although possibly not understood, served as an incantation, for gradually the woman's sobs grew less, although she would still not look at the white people.

Deon sensed the need to go slowly. "Where do you come from?"

"Worcester, Doctor."

"Worcester!"

Seventy miles away.

"Why did you bring the child here?"

The woman shook her head.

The nurse had been struggling with a large and rusty safety pin. Now she spoke, and there was something in her voice which caused him to look at her at once.

"Doctor."

She was staring at the diaper. Instead of the familiar greenish mess it was stained with blood. Both of them looked at the child. The sister drew in her breath. Deon noted this fact absently and the thought came to him that no matter how hardened you might believe yourself to be there would always be something for which you were unprepared, something that would shock you in spite of your sternest resolve.

He leaned over to examine the bruised and swollen vulva. "What the hell happened to this child?" he asked loudly.

The child pulled away and both she and the mother began to cry again. The sister looked at him reprovingly.

"Come now, mommy. Come on now."

It took them fifteen minutes of patient questioning to extract the story.

Her husband worked for a builder at Worcester, the woman told them. He was a laborer, one of those who mixed the cement. But during the pressing season he worked on the wine farms from Worcester as far as Barrydale. The pay was better on the farms in the pressing time. He had left again last month for Montagu and had sent her a message to tell her she had to come to visit him for the weekend. But the aunty with whom she always left the child was also away for the weekend. She hadn't known

116

what to do, but in the end she had left the child with some other people. They were people she did not know well. This afternoon she had come back from Montagu and had fetched the child. The people told her the child was sick, so she took the child to a doctor in Worcester. The doctor told her to take the child to the big hospital in Cape Town. .

"Did he give you a letter?" Deon asked.

She nodded.

"Let me see it."

The woman fumbled inside a shabby yellow handbag. A few copper coins fell out of the bag. They rolled along the floor. She gave Deon the folded envelope and he read aloud while she scrabbled in a corner after the pennies.

"Casualty Officer. Please admit female baby, aged eighteen months; severe bruising and laceration of vulva and vagina. Query . . ." He stopped reading abruptly.

He looked at the blunt, unequivocal word and then at the child on the examination table.

"My God!" And then to the sister, in his loudest voice: "Get them to call the gynecology registrar. This isn't a case for the drip room."

He lay on his bed in the dark room, fully dressed.

He tried not to think, but then the image of the child's eyes, the black eyes in the restless, ever-seeking head, interposed itself. He got up again in sudden revulsion and crossed to the window.

The black bulk of the mountain stood aloof from the city. In the sky beyond it were faint stars.

Why do you allow it to happen, he asked whatever was beyond the stars. What kind of monsters have you set loose on earth?

Rage possessed him like a physical presence, boiling chokingly up into his throat. What punishment was just for someone who was capable of doing a thing like that? How did he do it? Did he push her down on to a bed, or had he held her up against a wall? How could you even begin to understand the workings of a mind which could contemplate such an act and then go on to perform it?

The registrar, a young, round-faced man with a gentle, almost apologetic air, had come to the drip room and had immediately taken the child away for an examination under anesthetic.

Deon had checked a few drips that were not running well, written up some maintenance fluids, and had then also gone to the gyne theater.

The child lay on the operating table with her tiny legs held up by straps. At least, Deon thought, she was now oblivious to pain and terror.

"Complete tear, as one would expect," the registrar told him as he removed his gloved finger from the vagina. "The posterior wall of the vagina has been torn through into the rectum up to the cervix. There's also a tear in the posterior phornix, through into the peritoneal cavity, but it's been sealed off by loops of small bowel or omentum maybe. The whole thing is grossly infected. I can't repair it tonight. I'll do a colostomy and leave it for a few weeks to let the inflammation subside." He hesitated for a moment: "Have you notified the police?"

"No. I thought . . ."

"Would you do that, please? And make the necessary statements and so on?" He smiled. "That's one thing I learned from my prof. Don't sign affidavits. I've wasted too many days sitting in court."

"But surely," Deon protested vehemently. "You want to see this bastard punished, don't you? Even if it means wasting time in court, it's your duty, isn't it?"

The registrar had looked at him with that kind and apologetic expression. "Duty? As I see it, my duty lies with the child. There are other people whose duty is to seek justice. Or to mete out punishment if you prefer. To seek revenge maybe? I don't know. What I do know is that it is not my business."

And he had turned and walked quietly away.

He's wrong, Deon thought now as he watched the dim and distant stars. There has to be order and justice and retribution, or we would all roam wild like beasts.

He had to speak to someone about it.

Philip. Philip would understand.

The hospital was very quiet now, at three o'clock in the morning. A patient groaned from behind a door as Deon passed it and the sound was startlingly loud in the silence. A nurse passed him in the corridor, moving like a pale phantom on noiseless feet.

Philip was in the doctors' office in C–5. Deon flopped down in a chair opposite him. "You through?"

"Ja. We didn't have to go back to the operating room after all. The hemorrhage stopped spontaneously after the patient got a pint of blood. Sorry I had to bring you back here."

"That's okay."

Philip looked at him attentively. "What brings you here?"

"Jesus, Philip, I saw a terrible thing tonight."

Philip raised his eyebrows slightly, but apart from this he listened to Deon's story without any change of expression.

"If they catch that bastard they should cut off his penis flush with the pubic arch," Deon said and chopped a hand down fiercely into a flattened palm.

Philip's mouth pulled down at the corner. "If you had grown up in District Six as I did, this wouldn't surprise you. It wouldn't even be the worst case you had ever come across. When people live only for food and booze and sex, then the father screws the daughter and the son the mother. What else have they got to live for?"

"An animal in a pigsty wouldn't do a thing like that," Deon said furiously. "That's no excuse for rape."

Philip continued to look at him with that remote, placid expression. Be angry, it seemed to say. Be outraged. But when you come to judge, do so with compassion.

Seven

The party had grown quiet now, for it was almost six o'clock. The line of cars had diminished.

Deon had not really wanted to return. Certainly not for the sake of the party. But he must see the girl again. The uncertainty and possibilities that surrounded her had drawn him away from the certainties and impossibilities of the hospital.

He climbed the hill again, went past the fenceless gate once more. There were many more recumbent bodies now, and no dancers, although the music blared on. Daylight was cruel to the slack, abandoned-looking faces of the sleepers. He was both disappointed and relieved to see that the blond girl was not among them.

Hamish Denton was sitting in the kitchen with a couple of the serious drinkers. They welcomed Deon back with uproarious enthusiasm. He waved away the proffered glass of wine.

"Where the hell have you been? Having a screw somewhere, I bet."

"Who was the tall blonde called Liz?" Deon asked.

"Liz?" Hamish said befuddledly. "Blonde?"

"Yes." Deon was cold sober and impatient.

"Liz? Could it be Liz Richardson? No, she didn't come. Anyway she's not blond." He swayed backward and regained his balance at the last moment. His expression cleared dramatically. "I'll tell you who it was. Liz Metcalfe. Beautiful broad." He turned to a man who was doing a balancing trick with empty wine bottles and glasses, piling them on top of one another in a perilous column. "Peter, have you seen Liz Metcalfe?"

Peter nodded, concentrating on his edifice, and Hamish turned back to

Deon with an elaborate, knowing wink. "That's it. Liz Metcalfe. She's got itchy pants. Boy!"

"Is she still around?"

A bottle fell and Peter caught it neatly. "She's gone," he said disinterestedly. "Probably shacked up with someone."

The remark hurt. There was no reason for it, but it hurt.

"Where does one get hold of her? What does she do?"

"Do? Liz Metcalfe?" Hamish laughed. "She doesn't do anything. Goes to parties."

"Where will I get hold of her?"

Hamish was growing bored with the conversation. "All she does is go to parties. Like this one. Bunch of drunken bums."

And he surveyed his guests fondly.

There were half a dozen Metcalfes in the telephone directory. The last was Metcalfe, P.J., and the address given was in Constantia. It sounded the most likely.

A starchy-sounding man's voice answered almost at once.

"Metcalfe residence."

"Is that Mr. Metcalfe?"

A brief pause, then the voice said, disapprovingly, "Did you desire to speak to Mr. Metcalfe?"

"No," Deon said humbly. "Actually I'm looking for someone called Elizabeth Metcalfe. A girl by the name of Elizabeth Metcalfe," he explained, as if he might not have made himself sufficiently clear.

Another pause. "Miss Elizabeth. Do you wish to speak to her?"

Miss Elizabeth, for heaven's sake. Who was the guy? The butler?

"If you please."

He had prepared a flippant introduction. "Is that Mystery Liz?" he had planned to ask. But the frosty voice had disconcerted him, so he merely said: "Elizabeth?"

She sounded bored. "Yes. Who's that?"

"Deon."

"Who?"

Thoroughly deflated now he said: "Deon. You know. I . . . I met you last night at Hamish Denton's party."

"Oh. Oh, yes." A faint giggle came over the line and put fresh heart into him. "You ran away. Did you get scared?"

"Is that a challenge?"

"Hmm."

"Listen, I'd like to see you again. If you want to see me, that is."

"I guess that might be fun."

She sounded definitely less bored now. He found that he was becoming a little breathless.

"Tomorrow night."

"I can't manage tomorrow. Friday?"

"Oh, hell! This is my weekend on duty. I have to work on Friday night. When will you be free next week?"

"I don't know what I'm doing next week. Ring me again and we'll see."

He had to be content with this casual dismissal. It took two frustrating weeks before he was able to arrange to see her again. This time he planned the seduction with care: dinner with sufficient wine at a new and fashionable restaurant; a few hours at a nightclub; finally Hamish's flat at Clifton. He hoped to hell Hamish hadn't forgotten his promise to leave the key in the mailbox.

But it didn't work out that way at all. For a start, the girl was more than an hour late. She came roaring up the drive in front of the hospital in a Triumph (bright red, predictably), when Deon was already at the point of despair, and made a face when he named the restaurant.

"I've been there. It's grotty. Full of fat faces."

He looked crestfallen and she took pity on him. She held open the door of the sports car. "Don't look so sad. Jump in and we'll drive around."

She drove toward Sea Point and the Atlantic Coast, weaving the little car in and out of the dense traffic, spurting away at traffic lights, driving very fast whenever the road was clear.

He looked sideways at her firm, determined profile and the streaming blond hair, which changed color subtly as they passed from patches of bright light into shadow and into light again.

"Do you pay a lot in traffic fines?" he asked finally.

She laughed and accelerated to beat a ponderous bus into a center lane. "I practically own the traffic court. Why? Am I scaring you off again?"

"Not particularly. It's only that I have this wife and ten children to support."

She laughed again, but looked at him quickly, sidelong. "You're not really married, are you?"

"Me? Good grief, no."

"Just wondered."

He sat considering the implications of the question as they swept through the tight corners beyond Bantry Bay. The Triumph's lights bounded from steep cliff face to night-black rock fall below. They passed the building where Hamish had his flat and Deon looked at it longingly, then decided it would be impolite to suggest that they stop.

"Where are we going?" He had to speak loudly, shout almost, against the thrumming of the wind.

The girl shrugged. "See when we get there."

He resigned himself. Pity about the flat. Pity about the restaurant too, for that matter. He hadn't been able to afford a good meal for a long time and he'd skipped lunch today in order to pay it due justice. Well, too bad. Here he was driving to a mysterious destination with a beautiful blonde and it was a hell of a time to think about mundane things like food.

Suddenly he wanted to touch her. He looked down ruefully at the barrier the bucket seats presented. Certainly not the most romantic invention. With a carefully casual air he twisted in his seat, crossing his legs and draping an arm nonchalantly over her backrest. The Triumph cornered sharply and he dropped the arm forward off the backrest.

She glanced at him, then smiled and pressed back firmly and frankly against his hand. He felt both pleased with success and a trifle ashamed of the obviousness of the ruse and the ease with which she had seen through it.

"I won't run away tonight," he observed brightly. "I'm not even on standby."

Frowning, obviously puzzled, she asked: "Standby for what?"

"You know. At the hospital."

"Oh."

She seemed totally disinterested and he was annoyed. He considered telling her about his work, about the lives and deaths he held in his hand each day. But it would be as crude and transparent as the speculative hand resting lightly against her back.

They swept through Clifton, Camps Bay, Bakoven, and out onto the open Peninsula road. Where the blazes was she planning to go? But he would not ask her again. He contented himself with the slithery feel of her muscles under the silky texture of the blouse.

The swinging headlights caught a narrow gravel verge, gray boulders, and leaning trees. She spun the wheel, drove in under the trees, braked with a lurch and switched off the ignition.

She looked at him.

"Well? Enjoy the drive?"

He laughed.

"Slowest airplane I've ever flown in."

She cut the headlights with an emphatic gesture. Darkness was complete, but after a moment resolved itself comfortingly into familiar degrees and shapes and expanses. He could see the girl's head and shoulders in silhouette against the sky. He leaned across and pulled her nearer. She did not resist, and held back nothing.

At last he sat back, fighting for breath. "I think I love you," he said wonderingly.

She freed herself with determination. "And I suppose you've never met a girl like me and all you're really interested in is my massive intellect. Look, let's skip the soppy stuff. You'd like to sleep with me. Okay. But let's not have any of this 'I love you' crap."

His night vision was still sharpening and he could see that they had stopped on the edge of a long grassy slope. There were trees in small clumps and then a sickle beach, curving away into the night.

"Let's walk," she suggested.

"Okay."

He climbed out and opened the door for her. Almost instinctively they turned toward the slow slope of grass and the crescent beach below it. At the end of the slope there was a slight drop, a rocky cliff. He helped her down with great care, as if the least little jolt might cause her to break.

Then they walked at the edge of the ocean, where the sand was hard and the wavelets made little sucking sounds as they ran forward and retreated, ran forward and retreated.

The girl took off her shoes and forced him to do the same. He looked at her slender feet and ankles. They walked in the ankle-deep shallows and she gave muted, appreciative screams at the coldness of the water.

Obviously her good humor was completely restored; or else, he thought with a touch of pique, she was so indifferent to him that she had never even been upset.

They reached the shadows of the rocks at the far end of the beach and he hesitated, then took her hand. She watched him with that same coolly quizzical look.

Well, what the hell, he thought and kissed her defiantly. She kissed back fervently and when he held her body she moved her hips forward against his. He pushed her down gently on to the sand, ready to stop at the first sign of resistance. She did not resist and they kissed again for a long time, their bodies hungry against each other.

Her breathing was short and sharp. She pushed a leg under his body and pulled him down on top of her.

* * *

To Elizabeth, love-making was unconfused and uncluttered. It was a part of life that was available and enjoyable, and she used it as such. She told him this, often.

She was cheerfully willing to talk about herself, her attitude toward life, toward sex, anything at all. But it was always mere talk. She was determined to take nothing seriously. She did things, she said, "for kicks." It was one of her favorite expressions: "for kicks," and Deon thought it said a lot about her.

He often compared her to Trish. Trish could be wild and abandoned too, but even then there had been a shadow, a deep and abiding sadness, a sense of isolation.

"There's only one thing I can't stand," Elizabeth had said once as they lay together on his bed in the doctors' bungalow. "Fat faces." She had twisted her lips scornfully. "Yech! Fat faces!"

It was another of her phrases and she applied it indiscriminately to all things spurious or pompous and particularly to her family and the way of life into which she had been born. The Metcalfes, as she told it, were business tycoons, landed gentry, cultural leaders and magnanimous squires all rolled into one. They rode to hounds and owned estates and vineyards and went to art galleries and opening nights. She lived with them and on their money because she was too lazy and untalented (she said this herself, without coyness, and waved away his polite protests), but she had stopped doing the things they did.

She had left school at sixteen because it bored her and had cajoled her father into allowing her to go to London to take ballet. She had grown bored with that too and had taken to photographic modeling. "In the nude?" Deon asked, and she looked at him out of her slanting eyes and said firmly: "If they were nice and they asked me nicely." When her family heard of this, a stern uncle had been dispatched to fetch her, to save her from degradation. Now she had an allowance and a car and the run of her father's house, although she and her second stepmother disliked one another. When she turned twenty-one she would inherit money and then she would be free to go off somewhere again. Not London or the Continent, for those were passé. The Far East perhaps.

Meanwhile she did nothing much except go to parties.

Deon had left the Cape early enough, but the Volkswagen gave trouble soon after he had passed the Hex River mountains and he was delayed for more than an hour at Laingsburg while a garage mechanic traced and repaired the fault. Then he had a blowout as he passed the Coloured township on the outskirts of Beaufort West and he had to change the tire, swearing and sweating in the hot sun, while a horde of Coloured children watched with fascinated attention. By the time he reached the church it was past three o'clock and the wedding had already started.

As he slipped quietly and quickly into one of the pews at the rear he thought with relief how fortunate it was that he had been unable to promise to be Boet's best man. He had been able to get only twenty-four hours' leave and had to be back on duty at the hospital at seven the next morning. It would mean leaving the reception early and driving through the night. Still, it would have looked peculiar if he had stayed away from his own brother's wedding.

Boet stood very stiff and upright and awkward-looking in a new dark suit, listening to the dominee with rigid attention. Liselle looked small and fragile beside her big farmer almost-husband. They would probably be happy in their way, Deon thought, watching him. The wool price wasn't too good at the moment, but at least Boet was inheriting one of the best farms in the district. He was a hard worker and he talked about his plans to expand production. All he had to do was persuade his father that he was right, that he could make the farm pay even if wool failed to make a quick recovery. However, he had confessed wryly to Deon in one of his rare letters, his father was not easily persuaded, especially since his schemes would cost money.

Even so, they would be happy. Liselle might be a bit schoolmarmish at first, making snide little remarks about the lack of social graces and cultural outlets. But as the years passed she would slip into the pattern, comfortably, putting on weight with each successive baby, taking less interest in operatic music and more in the women's agricultural association. He guessed it was happiness of a kind. Contentment, rather.

He felt suddenly grimy and out of place, like a tramp in torn clothing at a well-bred party. Strange feeling to have, for he had stopped at a filling station and used the rest room to wash his hands and face and comb his hair and brush the dust off his suit. It was the sense of being out of place, he thought. This is their world, but it is no longer mine. I can come back to it only as an intruder, a visitor from another place. It's sad. But there it is.

He sought for and found his father in the front pew. It is the same, even with him, he thought. He is still my father and I respect him as I respect few men. I know he is honest and firm in believing what he believes. But there is a gulf between us. Even when we both lean forward as far as we can reach, only our fingertips touch.

Something in his father's attitude caught his attention. A difference. Something has changed. Something about his bearing. That's it. He drew in his breath very softly. Johan van der Riet, who normally sat the way he stood, tall and erect, was now bowed at the shoulders.

Age, Deon thought. It creeps up unnoticed and suddenly it's there for all to see. He's lost a lot of weight too.

His mind had sharpened; he was on the alert. He sat, deep in thought, as the service progressed to the ring ceremony and the dominee escorted the bride and groom and the wedding party to the vestry door, everyone smiling and looking happy and Liselle's mother wiping away a conventional tear.

Deon realized that he should probably be in there as well, to witness the signing of the register or whatever. But it would make him conspicuous, coming all the way from the back of the church, so he stayed in his seat.

The "Wedding March" pealed out again and the family emerged from the vestry, now in a vaguely processional order. Boet saw him and winked a greeting and Liselle smiled at him. She looked very pretty and young. She would make a good wife.

Deon's father saw him too, as he stood up to join the procession, and nodded and smiled in welcome. They shook hands and his father's grip was still firm. Deon watched his face sharply and noted its pallor, its new gauntness, and the bruise on the neck. He tried to be rational and professional, as if this were any other patient and he the doctor, looking for signs from which to make his diagnosis. But the fear and sense of confusion grew within him. There's something very wrong here, he thought; he's a sick man.

The reception was at the hotel and there was champagne with the toasts (at least the Coloured waiters called it champagne, but it was a sickening-sweet sparkling wine), for the new dominee was one of the enlightened kind and did not object to moderate drinking at weddings. He, of course, stuck to soda water.

At last the speeches were over and people began to move among the tables, filling their plates.

Deon pulled up a chair beside his father and looking intently at him asked: "How are you?"

"Very well, man. Very well. This is a big day for us. I am pleased you could come." And, in a slightly accusing tone: "You were late."

"I had car trouble," Deon explained tersely. "But how are you really?"

His father looked at him; that old look of ironic amusement.

"Why do you ask?"

"You don't look well to me."

"None of us get any younger."

"Have you seen a doctor?"

"Doctor? Ha!" Something of the fierce spirit returned. "I wouldn't trust these new young doctors to cure a sick donkey."

"You're talking nonsense and you know it. How did you get that bruise on your neck?"

"Old people bruise easily," his father said evasively.

"Have you got other bruises?"

"A few," his father admitted.

When he pulled up his sleeves there were blue-black blotches all over his arms.

A chill of suspicion passed through Deon's body.

"Do you get tired easily?"

"Stop asking all these questions, Doctor. Go along and talk to the people. I am sure some of them would like to tell you their complaints and get free medical advice." And his father stood up with the same look of faint amusement, of hidden laughter at a secret joke no one else would ever understand.

But Deon was not going to be shaken off so easily. Later in the afternoon he was alone with his father in the hotel room where the family had changed for the wedding. "Look," he said circumspectly. "I've got to be off back to Cape Town in ten minutes. Let me have a quick look at you before I go."

His father protested half-heartedly, but eventually he took off his jacket and shirt and lay down on the bed.

No enlarged lymph nodes. The mucous membranes were very pale. Purple marks over the whole upper body.

I wonder how much he knows, Deon thought suddenly. Or has been guessing at. Has he been waiting to tell me, but too proud to confess to weakness, even the inevitable decaying weakness of the body?

"Will you loosen your trousers, please? And pull them down a little so I can examine your stomach."

"You doctors leave a man no dignity," his father grumbled. His eyes wandered away from Deon's face; began to search the ceiling.

No liver enlargement. He could not feel the spleen.

"Take a deep breath."

As his father's chest rose he pressed the tips of his fingers deep in underneath the rib margin.

Something hard moved against his fingers.

He was not even conscious of having held his breath until he felt pressure against his ribs. He breathed out with very deliberate slowness. It was probably the rib margin he had felt. It *had* to be.

"Another deep breath."

This time there was no doubt about it. He could feel the notch of the enlarged spleen.

He straightened up over the bed and his father turned from examining the ceiling.

"Are you finished, Doctor?"

Deon smiled at him. "All finished."

"And what's wrong with me?"

"I don't know if there's anything seriously wrong." Deon forced himself to keep looking steadily at his father, to keep smiling without showing anything. "But I think you should come back to Cape Town with me. I'd like the professor to have a look at you and to do a few blood tests."

"Now? Today?"

"Today."

"Boet's going off on his honeymoon. Who's going to look after the farm?"

"Boet can wait for his honeymoon," Deon said ruthlessly. "Or the farm can look after itself. This is more important."

His father shrugged. "Well, you're the doctor."

As they walked together down the creaking hotel stairs his father chuckled and slapped him lightly on the back. "Cheer up, my boy. What does it say in Job? 'Man that is born of a woman is of few days and full of trouble.'" And he laughed again at the joke of which he alone could see the point.

WINTER

Eight

Telephone, telephone, telephone. Over the months he had grown to hate the infernal instrument. It dictated his life, ruled his movements, broke without apology into his meals and his sleep with a summons for him to drag himself back to the ward or Casualty or the operating room.

"Van der Riet," Deon said with exaggerated exhaustion, hoping to evoke a grain of sympathy.

The bloodless voice of the hospital exchange announced: "Outside call for you, Doctor van der Riet. Hang on."

Deon grunted a response. He had been trying to snatch a few minutes' sleep after dinner. But it was time he went back to the ward anyway. He was worried about the little Janssen boy. It was the third post-op day and there were still no bowel sounds. And tonight the kid had developed a high temperature. Bill du Toit's case. He'd better give Bill a call later on.

The exchange said: "You're through," in a bored way and the girl's voice broke through immediately.

"Deon?"

"Hello?" He pretended surprise. "Oh, hello, honey."

"Hello, stranger," Liz said. "I had to phone to find out whether you're still alive."

"Hey, that's not fair," he protested. "I saw you . . . I saw you . . ."

"Two weeks ago," she completed his sentence for him.

"As long ago as . . . ?" But he could not keep up the pretense of not knowing. "Actually we've had a very busy time here. And my old man has been down again for more treatment."

"How is your father?" Her voice was unusually sympathetic.

He toyed with his stethoscope. "He's better. The blood tests show some improvement anyway."

"I'm glad. He's a nice old man." Again her voice was surprisingly warmer than usual.

"Yes. And I think he's taken a fancy to you," Deon told her. "He asked about you."

"You should have let me know. I liked him too."

That had been surprising too. His father had been in Cape Town a month ago for a course of cytotoxics. He had used this as an excuse to cancel one of his dates with Liz, for he wanted to be with his father. She had accepted the reason, and when he had gone to his father's private ward after the morning round he was puzzled to find a bowl of chrysanthemums on the bedside table.

The thought of someone sending his father flowers was incongruous, to say the least.

"Have you got a girl friend?" he asked. There had been a subtle alteration in their relationship since the chilling diagnosis: acute granulocytic leukemia; Deon was permitted such small liberties now. "Who sent you those?"

His father cleared his throat and put down his book, then removed his reading glasses. "They mixed me up with someone else. I don't know anyone by the name of Elizabeth."

"Elizabeth?"

Deon examined the florist's card. Just the one name. No surname.

"Do you know an Elizabeth?" his father asked. He looked at Deon's face. "Elizabeth, hey?" He put on his glasses again. "It was kind of her to think of an old man," he said firmly. "Say to her thank you from me."

Deon had passed the message on dutifully and Liz had asked: "Do you think he'd mind if I came to visit him? During visiting hours, of course."

"Visit him?" Deon was utterly mystified. She had always shown distaste at the mere mention of disease, and he had learned firmly to suppress temptations to discuss medical or hospital shop. "No," he said a little dubiously. "I don't think he'd mind. If you really want to."

The visit had not been an unqualified success. There was the language barrier as a start: Elizabeth's Afrikaans was so poor as to be almost nonexistent; his father could speak passable English but was self-conscious about not being able to master it perfectly and this made him appear more than usually stiff and formal. There were long silences which Deon tried desperately to fill with meaningless chatter.

Toward the end of the unendurably long half an hour there had been a sudden thaw.

"Can you ride a horse?" his father had asked, for no apparent reason.

The girl had looked at him questioningly. "Yes," she said then.

"Good?" He asked again. "Do you ride good?"

"I was the show-jumping junior champion when I was thirteen," she told him. And then blushed, looking sideways at Deon, who was staring at her. She had talked about many things to him, but never about this.

The old man nodded and leaned back in his pillows, content. "I could see it. It's in the way you sit," he explained. "Farmers don't ride like that, but I haven't got anything against show jumping. Some farmers have a lot to say about show riders. But I think you have to be good, a better rider than a lot of farmers." He smiled at her a little mischievously and said: "You must come to the farm to teach Deon and his brother to ride a horse. They ride like this, like sacks of potatoes." He flopped his shoulders to demonstrate. "Come to the farm and show them you don't ride a horse the way you ride a motor car."

Remembering this now and remembering also how rarely invitations to visit Wamagerskraal were extended, Deon said with conviction: "I know he liked you. He told me you were all right, considering you were an English girl."

She laughed. "When is he due here again?"

"I don't quite know," Deon said guardedly. "It all depends."

"On what?"

"On how long the remission lasts." He was deliberately vague. He did not care to let his mind dwell on the slow spread of death within that spare body. "How are you, anyway?"

"Lousy," she said. "When can I see you again?"

"It's going to be a little difficult," he said lamely. "I'm on call again this week. So I don't know if I can really spend any time out of the hospital."

"Balls!" she said, so sharply that he winced in spite of himself and hoped the switchboard wasn't eavesdropping.

"It's not, you know," he protested.

"Surely you could plan something if you really wanted to. I've taken a flat, you know."

"Really? Where?"

"Near you. In Newlands. Why don't you come round and have a look?"

"Sweetie, I can't. Honestly, I can't."

"If you really wanted to you could."

Was there an element of truth in that? Was he growing tired of her?

They had seen one another practically every day at the beginning. Now? Two weeks had slipped by and he had hardly noticed.

"Honestly, I can't."

She made a sound of exasperation.

"I suppose it'll have to be the bloody bungalow again."

"Well . . ." He had rather hoped she wouldn't insist. He was tired. He hadn't had much sleep for two nights running.

"You're not backing out, are you?"

There was sufficient menace in her voice to cause him to make a hurried denial: "No. No. Of course not. Good Lord, no. I'm only worried that there might be an emergency."

"Well this is an emergency," she declared challengingly.

He thought it wiser not to take up the challenge.

"Okay, I'll leave my door unlocked. I've got a couple of things to do in the ward which'll take me about an hour or so and then I'll be with you if nothing drastic turns up."

"If anything drastic turns up, you turn it right back again." She finished with a terse farewell.

He closed the door behind him, leaving the key in the lock. That girl's starting to act as if she owns me, he thought.

As it turned out love-making that night was not a great success for either of them. Deon was genuinely tired and found it difficult to simulate a passion he did not feel. Elizabeth was jittery and tense and showed it by making constant, irritating demands. Finally she pushed him away and rolled over as far as she was able to on the narrow bed and said crossly, "It's no damn good."

They had a fierce little row then, though they were forced to whisper and hiss their accusations because of the paper-thin walls. They dressed, stiffly, back to back, and went down the corridor to the lounge. Robby Robertson was having a late supper. He had met Liz in the bungalow several times before and he greeted her casually. There was an unwritten, unspoken camaraderie about this: you could try to steal another man's girl outside, but in the bungalow you treated her with reserve and chivalry which would not have shamed a medieval knight. Nor was the signal of a tie hung over a doorknob, showing that the occupant was preoccupied, ever willfully ignored. Now Robby's shrewd eyes moved swiftly from face to face. Then he got to his feet, apparently lazily, moved his supper tray and offered his seat in the armchair by the fire to Elizabeth.

She hesitated. "I was just going, Robby, thanks."

He pretended abject dismay. "Oh, come on, you can't walk out of my life like this. Besides, it's cold outside." He showed her the shoulders of his coat, wet from the fine winter drizzle.

She laughed, although there was still some strain on her face, and sat down obediently, holding hands and feet out toward the flames.

"I had a beauty in Casualty tonight," Robby told Deon.

Elizabeth immediately put her hands to her ears.

"Oh, no, please. You're not going to talk shop again."

"It's not shop, I promise you. It's damn funny. I couldn't keep a straight face for the life of me."

Elizabeth looked at him warningly and he winked back.

"And it's a clean story," he assured her. "Perfectly clean."

"Well, tell us about it, man," Deon said.

"These two cops brought this little chap in to Casualty, see? With a safety pin stuck through the tip of his nose."

"Yech!" Elizabeth said. And, reproachfully, "Robby! You *promised!*"

She gave Robby what Deon recognized as her Sweet Innocence look and he realized that she was flirting a little. Trying to get her own back. Somehow the rather obvious ruse was touching and made him sad rather than jealous. What is happening to us? Deon thought confusedly.

"He was furious with the cops for not being interested in his problem and told them exactly what he thought of the South African Police Force. He's an old 'dronkie,' you see, and he's obviously been on a real bender. For the last week or two he hasn't been able to sleep. He couldn't close an eye because of all the little men."

"Little men?" Liz asked.

"Hallucinations," Deon explained shortly. "Delirium tremens."

"That's right," Robby said. "Well, it was getting out of hand, according to him. The same thing happened every night. He'd get into bed and put out the light and the little men would come pouring in through the crack under the door and climb up the side of his bed. One night it was the Coldstream Guards, led by a full brass band with a drum major and all and they marched on to his chest and drew up in formation and then the colonel drew out his sword and shouted 'Charge!' and there they came, all trying to climb down into his nostrils and his mouth and his ears."

"Robby, you're making this up," the girl said.

Robby kissed two fingers and held them solemnly up into the air. "So help me."

"Anyway, what was the pin in aid of?" Deon asked.

"Wait. I'm coming to that. This little guy tried everything to get rid of the little men. He even painted his body with golden syrup so they would stick to him, but they brought spades and made little roads through the syrup, like you'd shovel snow. So tonight he got a brilliant idea. He showed us, like this . . ." Robby tapped his forehead. "A brilliant idea. He filled a bath with water and made up his bed next to the bath. Then he pretended to go to sleep and waited for the little men. As soon as they were all on top of him he jumped up and into the bath. And all the little men got drowned."

He waited till they had finished laughing.

"All except one, that is. This one must have been a good swimmer because he splashed his way to the tip of this guy's nose, and there he clung. He wouldn't let go, even when the guy got right down under the water."

"And the pin?"

"Well, he couldn't drown the little bastard without drowning himself. So he got a safety pin and shoved it through the little man, and pinned him to his nose. He got dressed and went down to the charge office and made just one simple request to the blockheads there: would they please arrest the little man."

The door opened on their roar of laughter and Philip came in. He looked round good-humoredly, but made no comment.

Deon got up quickly to perform introductions. Philip made a slight, deferential bow toward the girl, but he did not approach her. He hesitated, then went to an armchair in the corner farthest away from the fire. He was carrying a medical journal.

"Why don't you join us?" Deon said before Philip could sit down. Again the Coloured man checked, then retraced his steps. He pulled a straight-backed chair away from the table and sat awkwardly on the edge of the seat, holding the journal on his lap. He looked into the fire and the reflected light danced on his stiff, high-boned face.

"You're taking over from me in the burn ward next week, Deon?" he asked abruptly.

"Ja. That's right."

"I had three more admissions this evening," Philip said. Then, curtly, as if he had planned the words in his head before speaking them: "One is bad. I estimate over thirty percent. So dehydrated I had to do a cut-down." He twisted a lip, as if he somehow blamed himself for failing to get the drip going by merely pushing in a needle.

He stared at the flames again.

135

"I think this formula for working out the fluids for burns is plain guesswork," he said contemplatively. "Especially in the severe cases."

"What do you mean?" Robby asked.

"Look, there are so many factors involved. I don't believe one should work it out based only on the weight and the extent of the burns."

"What other factors?"

"Well, for example, the child's state of nutrition before the burn occurred. The duration of the burn. The treatment already received. And so forth."

"All the same one has to have a working basis. I suppose you've got a better idea?" Robby said, one eyebrow lifted disdainfully.

Philip ignored the sarcasm. "Yes. The venous pressure." His voice was emphatic. "Look, it works this way . . ."

Deon noticed that Elizabeth, who normally was quick to demonstrate her lack of interest when medical talk started, was following the argument closely. Her head swiveled from side to side, like that of a spectator at a tense tennis match, as Philip and Robby wrangled on. He was sure she hardly understood half of what was being said, and certainly none of the implications. Was it a little grande dame study she was putting on to reassure Philip?

The loudspeaker hummed into life and breathed out softly: "Doctor Davids. Doctor Davids."

Philip took the call on the telephone, said, "Yes, yes," impatiently a couple of times, then replaced the receiver and went quickly to the door. He paused there, as if suddenly remembering something, or as if he had been recalled from some place he had already reached.

"Good night," he said to Elizabeth, with another small and formal bow. They heard his light but firm footsteps vanish down the corridor.

"Who's he?" Elizabeth asked.

"The resident genius," Robby said grumpily.

Deon laughed. "You have to admit he knows what he's talking about."

"Trouble is he's always bloody well right. I like a bloke to show a bit of human fallibility now and then."

"But who is he?" Liz asked again.

"Houseman. Same as us. Except he knows twice as much as most consultants. And doesn't mind showing it."

"Come off it, Rob," Deon said.

"Okay, okay. He's a bright boy and we all know it," Robby admitted grudgingly. "Don't think I'm gunning for him because he's a Coloured. It's just that he's so infernally sure of himself."

Deon shook his head. "I don't think he is, you know." Elizabeth had taken out her cigarettes and he got up to light one for her. He struck a match, still looking at Robby. "He's a modest guy really. And he's not all that self-confident, underneath. You have to admit he's never righteous, anyway."

"Maybe."

Elizabeth thanked him with a tight, reluctant nod. She blew a stream of smoke toward the fire.

"Where does he come from?"

"Strangely enough, his mother used to work for us on the farm. But she came to Cape Town long ago, oh, in . . . I don't know . . . even before the war. Then my father helped him to come to university and he turned up in our first-year class, with one jacket and one pair of pants he wore right through the year."

"Did your father help him?" she asked with interest.

"Ja." Aware of Robby's ironic look, he added hastily: "But only for the first couple of years, of course. Old Philip's good. He got scholarships and so on. Last year in the finals he even landed a couple of overseas scholarships."

"Why didn't he go? Especially being Coloured."

"He wanted to do his housemanship here. I imagine he'll go next year. But he's rather secretive about it. He's a strange guy. I used to know him well as a kid, but I still don't know what makes him tick."

"He looks like that kind of person," Elizabeth said. She sat back in her chair, looking at the dying leap of flames.

"Robby, you'd better put more wood on that fire for us."

Two nurses lowered the sides of the iron crib with a metallic clang. The sound was that of a prison door.

In fact, Deon thought, these children *were* prisoners. Some of them were even tied down by their hands and feet.

The line of masked figures, like hooded monks from a gothic fantasy, gathered around the first crib. The child in it, a little girl, started to cry. It was not a cry of pain but of the fear of pain.

The registrar reported to Professor Snyman from behind his mask, but the noise in the ward drowned his words. Deon could make out only something about "twenty percent." He gave up the attempt to overhear the mumbled comments and looked around him again. Last night Philip had taken him round the ward to show him the patients who were now his responsibility. There were fifty-five of them packed into six cubicles. They varied in age from two months to twelve years. They were all burn cases: hot water burns, hot tea burns, fire burns, primus stove burns. Into which category did the baby fit? The baby who had been held up by its mother to screen herself from the oil lamp her husband had thrown at her. Deep burns of the right arm and right leg, so severe that the limbs had to be amputated.

The procession moved on. The next case, a boy of seven, held himself erect at the end of the crib with legs and arms that were bent like those of an old man. He kept saying softly: "I want to go home. Where's my mother?" And again: "I want to go home. Where's my mother?"

Deon looked at the child almost angrily. It's at home that they get burned to hell, but they want to go there. Their mothers sacrifice them for the sake of their own skins, but it's the mother for whom they ask. Are they then ruled by the same urge that attracts the singed moth back to the flame?

What had Philip said once? "If you had grown up as I did this wouldn't surprise you." Bedroom, living room, dining room, kitchen, playroom, nursery were all one room. Seven children in one room. Sex and laughter, hunger and joy, snot, tears—and boiling water—in one room.

The procession moved on. These were interesting cases. You had to concentrate on that. Concentrate on the medicine and forget the rest. Concentrate on curing. Give them plasma, give blood, give electrolyte solution, scrub the burn, clean it, prevent infection, graft skin. Then you sent the child home. Home to one room.

The next cubicle. Clang, clang, clang went the sides of the cribs.

"What the hell is this?" Professor Snyman's voice wavered between horror and outrage.

A small boy, tied down by hands and feet, lay on his back. The front of his chest was covered with large blisters. Some were ruptured and collapsed and there were areas where the skin had shriveled up, leaving raw, red flesh. The whole burn had been smeared with a yellow, sticky-looking fluid.

"Hot tea burn," the registrar said from under his mask. "Admitted last night, sir. The mother tried to treat it by pouring condensed milk over it."

"Why has the burn not been cleansed?" Snyman asked. "I spent a lot of time compiling the notes on burn treatment," he said with ominous emphasis, not looking at anyone.

Deon had read the notes last night: "On admission shock must be treated with plasma, blood and half normal saline in 5 percent dextrose water. The amount of fluids is worked out according to a formula which takes into consideration the body weight and the percentage burn." When the patient's condition became stable he was taken to the operating room where the blisters were opened and the skin snipped away. The burned area was thoroughly scrubbed with a nail brush, liquid soap, and lukewarm water, then dressed with vaseline gauze.

"Why was this child's wound not scrubbed?" Snyman asked again.

There was a shuffling in his entourage. No one looked at him.

The registrar gave a dry cough. "Well, sir . . ." He hesitated. "I intended to talk to you about it and get your advice. But we've been very busy here and I simply didn't have time to talk to you."

Snyman looked at him coldly. "So you've been busier than I have, John? I've had time to talk to you."

"Yes, sir. Sorry, sir." The registrar, who was very tall and thin, bowed his head, as if to show how patiently he bore the rebuke. "But you see we're at the height of the burn season. With this continuous rain, and now the cold spell, we've had fourteen admissions in two days."

He sounds like a Karoo farmer, Deon thought. The nice rains have caused a good lamb season.

The registrar was pointing to one of the unbroken blisters. "You see, when the blister is left like this there is less loss of fluid."

Snyman frowned. "How do you know that?"

"Philip Davids has been doing some research for me." The strip of face above the mask was flushed with enthusiasm. "We made up some cups which we could fix down over blisters and lead the fluid they collected to test tubes. Then we measured the fluid loss from both ruptured and unruptured blisters over twenty-four hours."

"And what did you find?"

"On the average, the loss from a ruptured blister is about three times higher."

"How many studies did you make?"

The registrar peered around him, then shook his head disappointedly. "Unfortunately Davids has left us for the gyne service, sir. But I think he did about thirty cases."

"That sounds pretty conclusive, John. How do you suggest we change our treatment?"

The circle of attendants stirred. The old man's interest had been engaged. There would be no thunder and lightning after all.

"Sir, the point is that scrubbing the wound perpetuates the shock condition. In fact, it increases the shock like hell."

There was a hesitant laugh.

"Sorry," the registrar said. "But it does increase the shock terrifically, and I'm sure we'll reduce our morbidity and our mortality rate if we leave the children with blisters and dead skin."

"And condensed milk?" Snyman asked with raised eyebrows.

"And condensed milk," the registrar said incisively.

Snyman nodded slowly and contemplatively.

Why hasn't anyone thought of it before, Deon wondered. It seems so obvious. He thought admiringly of Professor Snyman; of his ability to grasp a fresh situation and adapt to it, even to the point of discarding long established rules. This was the way a great doctor thought and worked Results: that was what counted.

You had to concentrate on the medicine and forget the rest. Cure the patient; don't think about what brought him here.

"They have such sad eyes," a woman beside him said, her voice itself sad

Deon looked at her, angered at being drawn back to considering aspects beyond the purely medical.

She wore a white coat over a discreet dress. Doctor? He glanced at the name badge on her lapel. Miss D. Lutke. He knew vaguely that there was a social worker at the hospital and that she dealt mainly with the children This was probably the social worker. He examined her covertly. Not really pretty, but she had a nice face. Now, as she contemplated the child in the crib, it wore a brooding look.

Such sad eyes.

He looked at the child too. It looked back mournfully. Its lower lip pouted as it made another futile attempt to scratch its chest, but it did not weep.

Deon thought distractedly of the little Malay girl down at the end of the ward. She was bad too, when she was admitted. However, the grafts had taken nicely and she was always in and out of bed, lively as a cricket in her hospital dressing gown.

Pain is not made for children, he thought suddenly. It is an adult thing Children should not have to bear it, for once they've borne it they cannot be children again.

Now you're being sentimental, he reprimanded himself. Pain doesn't select a victim any more than death does. And who says you can't forget suffering? Isn't the brain made to erase memories of unpleasant experiences?

Is it? Then what is the thing which makes a man sit up in bed suddenly in the middle of the night, pale and sweating and afraid of something in the darkness which has no shape? Will this child become that man?

The group moved on to the next cubicle and Deon fell into step beside the social worker.

"Do you have many problems with these kids?" he asked.

She turned to him antagonistically.

"Problems? Of course there are problems." She had a faint accent which was apparent even under her angry tones.

He was taken aback by her vehemence.

"All right, Miss . . . uh . . . Lutke. You don't have to snap. I was only asking."

Her expression softened. "I'm sorry, Doctor, for, as you say it, snapping. But it sometimes makes me very . . . disheartened, yes? You doctors think only of their"—she made a sketchy gesture with both hands to indicate the outlines of a body—"the exterior. Not of what happens inside." She tapped her forehead with long, expressive fingers.

He said to her stiffly: "As a matter of fact I have been thinking about exactly that. About what goes on inside the minds of these burn cases."

She looked at him with fresh interest. "So? You are interested in that?" She glanced at his own lapel badge. "Doctor van der Riet." She pronounced it so that the name sounded German. "You are the houseman on this ward now, yes?"

The procession moved on. More hot water burns, hot tea burns, fire burns. The registrar repeated his story over and over again. Professor Snyman was unusually quiet, responding only with nods or the occasional terse phrase.

They came to the door of the last cubicle and Snyman stopped sharp, causing the train of followers to telescope awkwardly. The old man waggled a finger at the registrar.

"John, I don't think you should treat all your patients the way you suggest. Come and see me after the round and we'll work out a study program. What worries me is that you'll get a tremendous increase in the sepsis rate if you don't clean the wounds properly."

Snyman looked around challengingly, as if anyone might be disposed to argue with the chief of surgery.

"Right," he said briskly, and went in through the door.

In the crib sat a child, drinking a green fizzy drink with the remnants of his hands and lips. He looked up with interest as the masked figures trooped in.

"Hello, Bobby," Snyman said, smiling at the child. "Why are you back?"

Bobby smiled and held up the bottle of green liquid.

Philip had told Deon about Bobby last night. The child had been pushe
into a Guy Fawkes bonfire by a boisterous playmate and had been admitte
with an extensive fire burn of the face, scalp, neck, and chest. Hospital car
had saved his life and now, two and a half years and twenty-one operation
later, Bobby was almost entirely free of pain. He was the burn ward's favo:
ite patient.

Deon had seen pictures of what the child had looked like when the pla:
tic surgeons had started their almost impossible task of making him loo
like a human being again.

The burned areas had been covered with angry-looking granulation ti:
sues. His eyelids had been burned away, but by some miracle his eyes ha
been spared. Perhaps he would have been better blind. Two black holes fc
a nose. Bare teeth which should have been covered by lips. His ears had nc
been badly burned and at the back of his head there were still bits of scal
with hair. There were no fingers on his right hand and on the left onl
three fingers and badly burned tendons. There were large, deep burns o
his chest.

Still, he had been alive, and the plastic surgeons had accepted th
challenge he represented.

The first task was to heal the raw areas by covering them with split ski
grafts taken from the legs and abdominal wall. This took five operations.

Bobby could not shield his eyeballs and had to sleep with his eyes oper
By now there was scarring and retraction of the remnants of both uppe
and lower eyelids. The upper lids were dissected free and reconstructec
complete with tear ducts. The lower lids were rebuilt with full-thickne:
Wolf grafts taken from the inside of the arm. This took four operations.

He was then sent home. Five months later, when the scarring of the spl
skin grafts had softened, he returned to hospital. The nostrils we:
refashioned from the edges of his ears and a pedical graft from his foreheac
This took six operations.

Eyebrows were made from bits of scalp, implanted with the hair pointin
outward, like real eyebrows. The tissue where his mouth had been was su
gically mobilized and reconstructed with a pedical graft. This took seve
operations.

The left hand was rebuilt into a three-fingered claw. This took thre
operations.

Nothing could be done about the right hand.

Deon looked at the hand, resting on the white coverlet. Once, during
holiday, he and his father had gone for a walk along a beach. His fathe
had picked up a piece of driftwood and used it, half jokingly, as a walkin

142

stick. It was the gnarled root of a tree, brown with white blotches and with a knob at one end.

Bobby's hand reminded Deon of that stick.

Professor Snyman glanced around at the group. "Why is this patient back?"

Bobby stared at him between reconstructed eyelids and continued to smile with reconstructed lips. One of the plastic surgeons pushed forward, looking down at the child, a creator's pride in his eyes.

"Areas of his scalp have broken down again." The surgeon examined three areas the size of postage stamps. "This is a problem we find among the Coloured patients. I think it's due to their curly hair."

Snyman looked at him doubtingly. "How does that work?"

"When there's a deep burn of the scalp, as in this case, most of the hair follicles are destroyed. Those which do recover form new hairs which curl up under the skin. They form little lumps there and these eventually cause breakdown of the skin."

"I dare say it's possible," Professor Snyman said.

"He's much better," the registrar announced. "I think we can send him home."

The ward round was finished. Everyone filed out through the door. Deon, tagging along at the end of the line, beside the social worker, looked back at Bobby. The child was weeping silently, wiping away the tears with his walking-stick hand.

"Why is he crying?" Deon said to the woman.

"He gets terribly upset when he hears he has to go home," Miss Lutke said despondently. "The other children make fun of him. He is an outcast at home."

"But that's terrible," Deon said indignantly.

The woman caught her lower lip between her teeth and looked down at the ground.

"Perhaps. But that's life. And I think that doctor, the surgeon, I think he is wrong with his theory about the hair."

"How do you mean?"

"I honestly think Bobby produces those raw areas himself. He scratches them open so that he can come back to hospital. This is his home. He is our child. We have created him."

She went on down the corridor and Deon turned into the tearoom with the other doctors.

Nine

Elizabeth lay on her side, looking out through the window at the mountain, which was covered by slate-gray cloud, torn into long shrouds by the battering wind. Yet it was warm here, for a pale winter sun was shining over the city.

It was Sunday and they were together in her flat, secure in the knowledge that they had the day to themselves, that there would be no intrusion from the outside world.

"Doesn't it give you a lovely feeling," the girl asked, "to see the wind blowing outside and to be nice and snug behind a window where it can't reach you?"

"Lovely," Deon agreed uneasily. She was provocatively nude in front of the window, and although the flat was on the side of the building, out of sight of prying eyes, the vestiges of a puritan conscience still prickled from time to time. He would have preferred her to be not quite so close to the window.

"It must be grotty to be really poor," she said. "Imagine not being able to get somewhere out of the wind, ever."

She rolled over on her back and Deon's gaze flickered almost involuntarily along the length of her body. She saw him looking at her and flexed herself very slightly, like a cat at rest and content in the warmth of a fire.

"I met your Coloured doctor friend the other day," she said. "You know, Doctor Davids. Did I tell you?"

"Philip? No, you didn't."

"He was waiting for a bus and I gave him a lift." She glanced at him quickly from under lowered lashes. "He must be pretty poor, I guess."

"Well, I . . . Ja, he hasn't got much money. His mother works in a fac tory. And he gets the same miserable salary I do. Even less, maybe. Coloured blokes. I'm not sure if they get the same as whites."

Money talk usually bored her almost as much as medical shoptalk, but she asked: "How much would he get?"

"I get twenty-five pounds a month and he couldn't be getting more than that."

She folded her arms behind her head and the movement lifted and tightened her small, neat breasts. He glanced at her body again, then away. "Twenty-five pounds. How does he survive?"

Deon was slightly nettled. "Hey, what about me? Don't I get any sympathy?"

She made a sweeping, dismissive gesture. "I know your father helps you. He hasn't any father. Has he?"

"No. His father was killed. Way back. Long ago, when they still lived on the farm. But his mother works."

"It must be really grotty to be poor," the girl said again.

"Why this sudden concern? You turning commie now?"

"No." She turned back to the window and when she spoke her voice was muffled.

"You should invite him here. We could have . . . you know . . . a party."

"Who? Philip?"

"Who do you think we've been talking about?"

Deon ran his fingers distractedly through his hair. "Do you think that's such a good idea? In your flat? Anyway, I don't think he'd come."

"Why not?"

"He would think we were trying to . . . well, kind of patronize him."

"I think he'd come. He likes you."

"How do you know?"

"We talked about you. When I gave him a lift."

"Did you now?" The idea made him vaguely uneasy, as well as embarrassed. "And what did you talk about?"

"Oh, nothing much. Only that you'd grown up together. On the farm."

"Well, I told you that anyway."

"Yes."

She was still looking away, at the greasy-looking storm clouds driving against the flank of the mountain. Then she sat up unexpectedly and swung herself off the bed with a swift and athletic jackknife. "What are we doing today?"

Disconcerted, he propped himself up on an elbow. "What?"

"What are we doing today?" She pronounced each syllable with elaborately overstressed clarity.

He pretended not to notice and lay back again. "What's wrong with . . . this?"

She pushed his hand away and began to dress, fastening her bra with a single practiced movement. He was forced, resentfully, to get up too.

"What's got into you? I thought we were going to spend the day here."

She avoided his gaze.

"I want to be outside. I'm stifling in this place."

He rolled his eyes at the dramatic tone and she caught him doing it and gave him a hard look.

"A minute ago you were saying how nice it is to be out of the wind," he grumbled, starting to dress himself. "And now . . ."

She turned her back on him and demanded: "Zip me up."

He obeyed reluctantly.

"Where the hell do you want to go?"

"There's no need for you to come, you know," she told him indifferently.

"Don't be ridiculous. Of course I'm coming. Where do you want to go?"

"I mean it," she said, still with that intensely annoying indifference. "You don't have to come."

He did not reply, keeping his growing anger carefully masked.

They drove in her car to the False Bay coast and walked on a long deserted beach in the wind. He was despondent at first, but after a time he found himself enjoying the struggle against the hard thrust of the wind. The sea was a turmoil of green and white and a handful of gulls soared in the dirty sky like bedraggled kites.

Exhilarated by the wind and the sound of the surf he grabbed her arm and made her run with him. She began to skip instead, her blond hair rising and falling rhythmically as she moved quietly along that barren beach.

On the way back to the flat they had a violent argument which started over something so trivial that Deon could not afterward remember what it had been.

They parted outside the flat, in aggrieved silence, and Deon drove his own car sullenly to the hospital. His day was ruined, and he spent the afternoon in his room, sleeping and reading the Sunday papers.

The next day he was remorseful and tried to telephone her, but there was no reply. Perhaps it was for the best, he thought.

Then the case of the Fowler child came up, and he forgot about Elizabeth.

The mother had noticed the small pinkish growth for the first time three months before, while she was bathing Mary Jane.

She had undressed the child, and when Mary Jane insisted that her doll should share the bath and started to undress it too, the woman looked on with loving patience. She's going to be a heartbreaker one day, she thought, looking at the slimly formed body.

Then she saw it—protruding from the child's vagina like a small bunch of grapes. She bent down to have a closer look.

"What happened here, darling? Did you hurt yourself?"

"No," the child said. She was still fumbling at the big buttons on the doll's dress. "I don't know."

The woman mentioned it to her husband that evening and persuaded him to examine the child too, with some difficulty, for he was a modest man, even when it came to his own child.

"I can't think what caused it, Jack," she said worriedly, watching his face. "Little girls sometimes push things . . . well, you know . . . up there."

He pulled the bedclothes over the sleepy child's shoulder. "Could be that."

"I don't know. I think I should take her to the doctor tomorrow."

He lit a cigarette, quickly, impatiently. "We're still cutting cane down on the river field. We could take her in to town day after tomorrow and see the doc."

She considered this, then shook her head firmly, as if by doing this she could shake off something which had settled there, something which would not go away.

"I'd prefer to go tomorrow. I'll take the pick-up, if you can spare it."

He drew deeply on his cigarette, eyes narrowed against the coiling smoke. His narrow shoulders were slightly hunched. He carried this air of frenzy only barely under control with him in everything he did. They had been married for five years, had known one another for eight; but there were times when she felt she did not know him at all.

"The boys can carry on with the cutting," he decided suddenly. "I'll come up to town with you."

He looked down at the child. Mary Jane had fallen asleep as they stood talking. Jack Fowler watched her for a moment, expressionlessly. He turned abruptly and left the room.

Their doctor in Eshowe also had a daughter aged three. He was a sentimental, good-natured man whom years of general practice had failed to harden or make cynical. When he had finished examining Mary Jane he tugged at his small, trim beard and hoped that he gave the impression everything was under control.

"You can dress her, Mrs. Fowler," he said, and opened the door into the waiting room. "Will you come through, Mr. Fowler?"

The doctor was uncomfortably aware of both parents' tense scrutiny. "I'm sure it's nothing," he said with a vague, all-embracing smile. "Mary Jane, tell sister to give you a sweet." He closed the door behind the child.

"What's wrong with her?" the man asked. His voice was calm, even a little disdainful. But the naked fear and anger were masked only by the need to present an even front to the world.

"Jack," the wife said softly and cautioningly. She put a hand out toward him, resting it on his forearm. He shook it off, not roughly but firmly.

"I'm going to refer her to a gynecologist," the doctor said, addressing the mother by choice. She was fidgety and pale and obviously distressed. But he still preferred to speak to her rather than the father, who showed no emotion at all. "I think that will be the wisest step, Mrs. Fowler. I have a friend in Durban and I'll get on to him right away for an appointment. These chaps are the experts."

"What's wrong with the child?" the man asked again, flatly and without intonation.

The doctor tugged at his beard. "I think it's only a urethral caruncle, but it's best to make certain."

"It's not cancer, Doctor?" The woman stumbled a little over the words.

"Of course not, Mrs. Fowler. You know what a urethra is?" He looked questioningly at both of them. The woman nodded; the man did not.

"The urinary canal from the bladder. The mucous membrane . . . you know, the lining of this canal . . . it prolapses and becomes swollen so that it looks like a bunch of grapes." The doctor smiled steadfastly into the woman's eyes. "But we must be certain, and that's why I want a specialist to see Mary Anne."

"Mary Jane," the woman corrected him quickly, frowning, as if the lapse had been grave.

"Mary Jane, of course. Sorry." He looked down at his notes in embarrassment. "We'll have tests done. A biopsy. So on. To make quite sure. And with any luck . . ." He spread his hands, smiling once more.

When they had gone he made a few more notes, then sat quite still at his desk, looking at the pen with which he had been writing. It was a slim ball-point, rough-finished to simulate gold, with the name of the pharmaceutical firm whose salesman had presented the gift to him tastefully engraved alongside the clip. He stared at the fake gold pen as if it were an instrument of profound significance.

The woman will be all right. She's tougher than she looks. But I don't know about the father. I've seen eyes like that before.

He touched the buzzer of the intercom system which he had recently had installed and with which he still delighted in playing, like a child with a new toy. "Jeanette? Before you send in the next patient. Get me a call to Durban, will you? Doctor Meyerson, the gynecologist."

There was no doubt about it. A malignant tumor of the vagina which for some reason bore no fewer than one hundred and nineteen different names, among them sarcoma botryoides—a tumor presenting like a bunch of grapes. Its Greek flavor and vineyard reference seemed to move the disease into a remote realm, where pure science ruled and names were nothing more than names, with no ability to kill.

Mary Jane Fowler came from the Durban hospital in a small flurry of publicity, for at the last moment the father had insisted that there was no time to waste and that she should be taken to the Cape by air ambulance. An airport reporter picked up a fragment of the story and added embellishments of his own, to which a sub-editor with fixed ideas about the meaning of the word tumor added further confusion (the headline read: AIR MERCY DASH FOR BRAIN DAMAGE GIRL). But there were political rumblings in the air that afternoon and the story was dropped from the later edition, never to appear again.

Deon was on ward duty when the child was admitted, but word had got around and Bill du Toit was present himself to take the history. Deon was relegated to being little more than an interested spectator while the registrar wrote up his notes.

Mary Jane sat up in bed in pyjamas with some kind of furry nursery-tale animal embroidered over the breast. She was tired after the unusual excitement of the journey but her eyes were bright with remembered joy and interest in the strangeness of place and people around her.

"They have such sad eyes," the social worker had said in the burn ward on the other side of the corridor a few weeks ago. There was nothing sad about Mary Jane.

God help us, Deon thought, picturing what they were going to do to her.

The parents stood at the foot of the bed, speaking now and then as Bill du Toit asked questions. The mother did most of the answering, confidently and readily, having clearly replied to much the same series of questions many times before. The father added only the occasional comment. Once his and Deon's eyes met momentarily. Then his gaze slid away, like a dark snake vanishing into dense bush.

Deon found himself obscurely angry, tempted to grab the man and shake him violently. Don't act as if this is an arrow which has selected you as a special victim he thought. It's terrible, but it's life.

Memory flicked like a whip. In their fourth year the senior lecturer in medicine had shown them a bone-marrow smear taken earlier from a boy in the wards. The lecturer had examined it himself through the microscope's low-power lens, briefly, and had then placed a drop of oil on the slide, turned on the oil-immersion lens and studied the slide carefully for several minutes. Finally he had turned away, a little tiredly, and had asked: "What do you think of this, Doctor?" He always called the medical students that, perhaps in the hope that premature promotion would serve as a spur.

The big cells with dark-stained blue nuclei had made little sense to any of them, and finally Dr. Marks had whispered, as if he dreaded to pronounce the diagnosis aloud: "Acute leukemia."

They had been in the ward when the parents were told. The mother had turned on Marks viciously, her eyes dark with the same hatred Deon could sense now in Mary Jane's father.

"You're wrong," she had screamed at him. "You're confusing him with someone else. My doctor said it was nothing more than a cold on the liver."

Marks had explained again, with infinite patience, but she refused to listen. Finally she stormed off, still screaming at them, using obscenities it was astonishing she knew.

"What a hysterical woman!" one of the students said smugly.

Dr. Marks had turned to him and had shown anger for the first time "That, you damn fool, is the mother of a child dying from an incurable disease."

The stinging comment echoed now in Deon's mind. As the examination proceeded he was careful not to look at the father again.

Professor Snyman saw Mary Jane on his evening round. He smiled at her as he picked up her folder.

"Hullo, sweetie."

"Hullo," she said, quite unalarmed. She had grown accustomed to hospitals since the first one she had been to two and a half months before for the biopsy which, to everyone's delight and the surprise of some, had showed no sign of malignancy. But Dr. Meyerson had still been suspicious. The mass in the pelvis could not be explained away by the finding: edematous epithelial cells. Had he taken the biopsy deep enough?

A second biopsy was done, and as the pathologist stared down the barrel of his microscope the round cells, steloid cells, spindle cells, striated muscle cells and mesenchymal cells spelled out the diagnosis. He had clicked his tongue irritably and a girl technician busy slicing wax sections and floating them on to slides in her corner of the laboratory had looked at him with intelligent interest. But he had only shrugged and not spoken.

Professor Snyman continued to smile at Mary Jane, steadily and reassuringly, then paged swiftly through the reports.

"I want a cystoscopy and an intravenous pyelogram," he said and turned to Deon, standing ready with the ward book. "Arrange that with the urologist, please."

He beckoned to Bill du Toit and began to walk away on quick, impatient feet. The registrar caught up with him, following at his elbow, a pace behind. They began to talk in muted, discreet voices. But Deon, ears sharp, caught a few drifting words.

". . . only way . . ." Professor Snyman was saying. "I'll have to . . ." And then they were out of the ward, out of earshot.

Deon had read up the literature again last night and he could quote it almost line by line.

He had sat alone in his room in the bungalow, listlessly paging through a textbook on pediatric surgery. The general excitement about the tumor that was invading Mary Jane's body depressed and sickened him. A senior houseman had stopped him in the corridor the other day to ask: "You're in the kids' ward, aren't you? Have you seen that sarcoma botryoides case? It's going to be a fantastic operation."

Jesus! Fantastic!

Deon stepped out of the way as a floor nurse came past, wheeling a trolley. Best to stand right back against the wall where he wouldn't be a nuisance. He was only an onlooker this morning, one of several, for the news of what old Snyman was going to attempt had spread widely. He had been early, however, accompanying the little girl, who was peacefully sedated, up from the ward. So he had been able to secure a position of vantage, at the head of the table and slightly to one side, where he could see past the theater sister's head.

Snyman was starting to cut now. Instruments went in and out of his hands in a steady flow.

The textbook's succinct and unemotional phrases returned to mind. Sarcoma botryoides. Prognosis: extremely poor. Only a few patients survived five years without recurrence. Strange how five years cropped up, like a magic symbol, in so many accounts of cancer. Why?

Sarcoma botryoides did not respond to radiotherapy alone, so radical surgery was advocated.

A line from somewhere else came into his head. "Full fathom five thy father lies; of his bones are coral made." That went back a long time. *The Tempest* had been a matric setwork book.

Yes, my father is dying. One can see it happening, the degeneration, the slow wasting. But somehow, with an older person, one learns acceptance. It doesn't make it any easier, but you know that you have to make the same journey yourself, some day, and you accept that too.

But Mary Jane Fowler, aged three?

There was a clutter of gear on the floor, along the wall. Deon rocked back on his heels and allowed his body to fall backward till his shoulder touched the tiled walls. He stayed that way, half leaning, half lying, and watched the surgeons working on the child's body.

How did the rest of it go? ". . . a sea-change: Into something rich and strange."

A change *was* taking place. But who could tell what shape would follow?

He hadn't imagined the father would ever give his consent. Not that tight man with the bitter eyes. And yet, who could ever tell? People were strange. Rich and strange.

Both parents had been weeping yesterday morning when they had come with Professor Snyman out of his office and back to the wards. Refusing to go into the ward, they had watched their daughter for a little while, half hidden behind the swinging door. Then they had quietly gone away, and last night during visiting hours only the mother had come.

This morning both of them had visited her, and the father was cold and hard again. But changed all the same. You could not disguise the subtle alteration which took place; you had to suffer that sea change.

What did the old man say to them? What would he, Deon, have said in the same situation?

152

There wasn't really much to say. The choice was brutally uncomplicated and all you could do was put it before them, phrasing it as delicately or as bluntly as your nature dictated. But (and this was the point) did you leave the ultimate decision to them, or did you lead them skillfully along a road you had already chosen?

You could never escape. The final responsibility, or culpability, whichever way you wanted it, rested squarely with you.

It was this that was conferred on you when they put that hood around your neck at the graduation ceremony. It had nothing to do with degrees or honors; it was a noose, a strangling knot that obliged you to make the final choice. Always a simple choice: life or death. And yet the most complicated of them all.

How would I have advised them, he wondered.

Now Snyman was working deep inside the abdominal cavity. Bill du Toit, who was second assistant, was making regular minor alterations to the positioning of the lights. There was little talking today; none of the usual cheerful, semimacabre joking.

Life is the most precious possession. Squander it, or deny it, if you wish. Turn your back on it, wish yourself out of it, go through it without thought. It remains the greatest gift.

But does that mean that anything, any means whatsoever, is permissible in order to preserve life?

It's better to be alive than dead. Surely no reasonable person could argue against that statement?

But was it true?

Is it better to be alive with hydrocephalis, to survive as a vegetable, to drag out your slow life with less awareness than that of an animal? Better to be alive when nothing, no opiate on earth, could ease the utter agony of terminal cancer? Better to be alive after surgical mutilation had left you deformed and grotesque?

Professor Snyman and the surgeon who was first-assisting were conferring in quick, clipped tones. The old man pointed at something, asked a terse question, then wrinkled his nose to push up his slipping spectacles. The sister fumbled in handing him a dissecting forceps and, uncharacteristically, he snapped at her. Her forehead and ears were crimson above her mask when she turned back to her instrument trays.

There was no pleasure in this operating room today.

Who is infallible? Deon thought. Who can give snap verdicts when the accused standing in the dock is life itself? What judge is so wise that he can

153

say unerringly "Yes" or "No" when the facts of the case are so clouded, the motives hidden, and the evidence ambiguous? Nevertheless we have to judge. Just as Snyman had to pronounce verdict three days ago and did so, too, without hesitation.

Oh, the weight of scientific evidence was all on his side; no doubt about that. Anything less and the child would be dead within two years at the most. The authorities were unanimous. There was slim hope of survival at the best of times. What hope remained rested with the surgeon. Even so, few surgeons were willing to do what, it was so widely agreed, was the only thing to do.

And now it was done. One final tidy cut with the scalpel, a suture swiftly and deftly caught and tied. A nod and a signal. A kidney bowl placed in readiness. Out, in one piece, came a great mass of tissue. Their eyes followed it involuntarily. Deon pushed himself upright away from the wall, watching. Even Professor Snyman's hands were still for a moment as he looked at the bowl, overflowing a little, which contained the anus, rectum, vulva, vagina, uterus, urethra, and bladder. His face worked slightly under the mask, but the square of material was large enough to hide his expression, whether of triumph or grief, and his eyes showed nothing. He grunted and held out a hand for an instrument and they were all swiftly recalled to the job at hand.

Total pelvic exenteration, Deon thought. I've seen one done. I hope I never have to see another.

Under those green drapes lay a child named Mary Jane Fowler, aged three, who had been stripped by human hands of many of the organs which made up her being. Hands prompted by the highest motives; no question about it. Hands that worked with love and tenderness and great hard-earned skill. Hands that sought only to heal, which mutilated with sorrow and grave regret because mutilation was the only means of preserving the life under that mound of sterile cloths; a life that would, hopefully, continue to be lived for years to come.

The operation continued.

Now the ureters were to be implanted into a section of the sigmoid colon which was to be brought to the outside of the abdominal wall on the right side of the belly. The end of the sigmoid colon was to form a permanent colostomy on the left side.

For as long as she lived the child would wear a belt, fitted with plastic bags to collect her urine and feces. She would never know sexual love, or motherhood. The ovaries had been conserved, so the hormonal drive would remain, but there would never be means of gratifying it. Would her mind come to terms with her deformities, eventually?

That August, when Johan van der Riet came to the Cape for treatment, Boet and Liselle accompanied him. Deon had not seen them since the wedding. His brother had thickened a little in the few months and he walked with a slight roll, with self-conscious dignity. Liselle had put on weight as well. They looked prosperous, although a little uncomfortable in city clothes. Boet had a new way of looking at things, evaluatingly, with deliberate movements of the head. The new master of "Wamagerskraal," Deon thought, not without envy.

They stayed at a quiet hotel in Rondebosch, but drove in to the city almost every day in their new Chrysler with its shark fins over the taillights. Liselle did a lot of shopping in and around Adderley Street.

Deon did not see much of them during the week they were in the Cape. But he spent as much time as he was able with his father. The old man had shrunk. His long bones would once have filled, or even spilled over the edges of a hospital bed. Now, when Deon came to him in his ward while he was asleep, it was difficult to be sure that there was a human form at all, under the blankets. He breathed shallowly, like a bird, and the nurses were very polite to him, and very gentle.

On the last night before Boet and Liselle left to return to the farm Deon had dinner with them at their hotel. Conversation was awkward. They spoke of the coldness and wetness of Cape winters, the rudeness of shop assistants and their reluctance to speak Afrikaans, a childhood friend who had gotten married, and another who had had a son.

They had coffee in the lounge. The Indian headwaiter served them himself, and Deon was amused to see that he and Boet were on casual, cordial terms. The Indian spoke good Afrikaans and was careful to say "Baas," but he and Boet had sly private jokes and eventually Boet gave him a generous tip. When Liselle made her excuses and left, Boet ordered more coffee and liqueur brandies for both of them, firmly overriding Deon's protests.

"How's the doctoring going?" he asked. Was there a trace of condescension? If so, Deon was determined not to notice it.

"Fine. Four more months, that's all."

"Good. Good. And then are you coming to practice in the town? We could do with a bright young doctor."

"I don't know. I haven't quite made up my mind."

155

"You must, man. You must. We need you there. And anyway you have to start standing on your own feet now. The farm can't carry you forever." He had had a couple of brandies before dinner and wine with the meal. His speech was not altogether distinct and his expression was belligerent.

Hold on, Deon cautioned himself. He tried to keep his voice level. "Whatever I choose to do, I'll make sure the income is adequate."

"Good."

Boet had obviously sensed Deon's anger. He sipped at his brandy, then leaned forward repentantly over the wickerwork table with its round glass top.

"Man," he said, looking earnestly at Deon, asking for sympathy and understanding, "you can't imagine what it's like, with this drought, trying to keep the farm going."

"We all have our problems," Deon said, not placated.

"Do you think this is just the usual farmer's grumbling?" Boet's voice was bitter. "Do you think I'm getting the farm as a present? I'll tell you what, I wouldn't mind swapping it for your nice safe salary."

"I have to work for it."

"So do I, my boy. Do you know that we've lost nearly two hundred sheep so far this winter? And we worked to try to save each one of them. But you wouldn't know any of that. Not you, in your nice town job."

"Don't forget I grew up on a farm," Deon said coldly.

Boet was immediately contrite. "Sorry, Boetie," he said, using the old, the very oldest nickname, which had once expressed their brotherhood. "I didn't mean that, man." He turned his face away and smashed a fist into a flattened palm. "God, I'll tell you, it's hard to take, with the animals dying round you like flies."

"I can imagine," Deon said, moved to sympathy.

"It's hard to take," Boet said. He swirled the dark gold liquid in the glass, then sat up erect, suddenly cheerful. He had always been impulsive, and nothing had ever bothered him for very long. "What the hell! We're not dead yet." The glasses had left wet rings on the tabletop and he began to draw patterns with one thick forefinger.

"I'll tell you, the wool price is bad. But I know how to get the farm back on its feet again. The Old Master," self-consciously using the respectful name by which the laborers addressed their father, "hasn't been able to really keep a hand on things the last couple of months. But I'll tell you what I've been thinking of doing."

He spun out his plans, his cobweb of dreams, drawing earnest diagrams on the glass tabletop to illustrate them, while Deon listened and watched him fondly and a little wistfully for a brotherhood and a companionship which had vanished.

"Capital," Boet said finally, despondent again. "That's the problem. Where to find the capital."

"If you're so sure of things, why don't you mortgage the farm?"

Boet gave him a derisive look. "Do you think the Old Master would sit still while I do that? Anyway you'd be surprised to know what kind of load we're carrying already."

"Look, if things are really so bad, you must forget about the allowance I'm getting this year. I guess I could manage without it."

Boet held up an imperious hand.

"Never! That's part of your birthright. No one is going to take that away."

Clearly he was not open to argument, in this suddenly magnanimous mood, so Deon did not try to argue. Besides, he was already calculating the awkward necessity of making do on his hospital salary. It wouldn't have been easy.

Boet beckoned to him mysteriously. "Look, you know all about the city. City life, and so on."

Deon looked at his brother, uncertain what to make of the change of subject.

"You've been here six, seven years almost. You must know how some things are done in the city."

"Uh-huh," Deon said, still watching his brother's slightly liquor-flushed face. Was it possible that Boet, staid, belly-thickening, four-months-married Boet, was going to ask him to find a girl?

"Well, what would you do if you had a parcel? How would you go about getting rid of it?"

Blankly: "A parcel?"

"Yes, man." A momentary flush of irritation. "Diamonds, man. A parcel of diamonds."

"I see." Deon thought for a moment. "Well, I'll tell you how I would get rid of them," he said then. "I'd get in my car and drive out to Sea Point."

"Yes?" Boet asked eagerly.

"Then I'd stop somewhere where no one could see me and I'd throw those diamonds as far out to sea as I could. You don't want to get mixed up in that kind of business."

"Don't you lecture me!" Boet said, really angry now. He had raised his voice and the Indian waiter looked at them with curiosity.

Boet hesitated, then held up two fingers to order more brandy. This time Deon did not protest. He was curious despite himself.

"You don't understand, man," Boet said when the Indian was again safely out of hearing distance. His temper, never long-lasting, was under control and his voice appropriately hushed. "You're not a businessman. You don't understand about money."

"I understand enough not to monkey around with illicit diamond buying."

Boet waved a hand dismissingly. "You just don't understand about money," he said again, vaguely. "If you play it carefully, there's no risk."

Was there a shade of doubt in that breezy voice? Was he trying to bolster his own courage?

"Where's this parcel supposed to come from?"

Boet's eyes sharpened at once. "Look, you mustn't talk about this."

"Do you think I'm a fool?"

"Of course not. But even a hint, just a wrong word somewhere . . ."

"I don't talk about things which don't concern me," Deon pushed his chair back. "I must be going. Say good-bye to Liselle for me."

Boet caught at his arm. "Wait, man. Wait. Don't get in a huff. I didn't mean anything. Sit down. You haven't even finished your brandy."

It was clear that, secretly, he wanted to tell; wanted to confide. It was a game to him, an exciting adult version of cops and robbers. Reluctantly, Deon pulled his chair up to the table again.

Boet began to speak in a low monotone, now and then looking over his shoulder at the waiter or at people at other tables. "You know Manie van Schalkwyk, don't you?"

Deon shook his head and his brother looked disappointed.

"You sure you don't know him? Big man with red hair. A little moustache like this." He scratched at his upper lip.

"No. I don't know him."

"Then he must have come since your time. He's rented Senegal. You know, old Jan Grobler's place. He used to work on the railways, but now he's hired grazing. He's a good friend of mine."

There was a time, Deon thought briefly, when a van der Riet would not have been close friends with men who used to work for the railways and grazed on other people's land. Well, times change. And who am I to judge?

"Manie bought some sheep from me at the end of the summer for three hundred pounds. He was going to pay me in June, after he got his wool check, but, well"—with an understanding shrug—"the price was bad this season and he couldn't make it." A quick look, searching for sympathy for another farmer's predicament.

"Yes?"

"Anyway I had to go to him last month and sort of remind him about the three hundred and see if we couldn't come to an arrangement. You know, paying it off or something."

"Three hundred pounds," Deon said.

Boet caught the hint of disdain, but this time did not take offense.

"Three hundred is three hundred," he said defensively.

"So what happened?"

"It was a bit difficult, with the bad season and so on. But he had a business proposition for me. He knows these Coloureds from the Vaal diggings who have diamonds, you know, a parcel every now and then. It's big money. Manie himself made two thousand, just like that." He snapped his fingers. "Two thousand in a couple of days."

"Look, you'd be a fool to get mixed up in this. For a miserable couple of pounds. You'd be a fool."

"Maybe." Boet's expression was guarded again. "There's a lot of money to be made out of those things." He looked toward the waiter. "Would you like another brandy?"

Deon rose quickly. "Thanks, Boet, no. I've got to be on duty early in the morning."

Boet stood up too. "All right. Well, look after yourself, man."

They parted amicably; brothers again, almost friends.

Driving back to the hospital Deon thought about how his brother had used that almost-forgotten nickname in the moment of pleading. He was reminded suddenly of the fact that when he had been very young Boet's own nickname had been Ouboet—Old Brother—but that it had been shortened to Boet over the years. Who had been responsible for the abbreviation? Their father? And, if so, for what reason? Was the old man disappointed that this one, *this*, was the elder brother; the heir? Or was he merely imagining things? His father had never favored one over the other. It was even possible that he himself had been responsible for the abbreviation, through verbal laziness. Or because he was reluctant to admit, even to himself, that anyone could be his elder brother and, by implication, his superior.

The whole thing was complicated. And hardly worth bothering about.

But I hope he doesn't go and do something stupid.

SPRING

Ten

She was a capable girl, a senior nurse, due to take her finals in a month or so. Trained to be impassive, even when all her instincts urged her to avert her face, to shrink away and withdraw within herself.

She was dressing Mary Jane Fowler. She put on the belt which held the two plastic bags and fastened it in place around the child's waist. Then she slipped a gay, flowery dress over Mary Jane's head and pulled it down to cover the belt and bags. The little girl was excited and chattered without cease. The nurse was quiet.

She stood silently aside when Professor Snyman came to Mary Jane's bed with Deon.

"What's this I hear?" Professor Snyman asked with pretended indignation. "They tell me you're leaving us today."

The child smiled and nodded. Then, with sudden concentration, she bit her lip and recited what was obviously a rehearsed speech: "Thank you very much, Professor, for what you did for me," she said.

The nurse burst into tears. Training and discipline flung to the wind, she ran from the ward.

Professor Snyman turned round, pushing back his glasses, then pressing a hand against his back in the familiar gesture, wincing slightly, as if he was in pain.

"Well," he said. And, quietly: "What was all that about?"

Mary Jane had lost interest and was looking in her locker for clothes to dress her doll.

"Tell the girl to come back and help the child," Snyman told Deon. "I'll be in the office."

He smiled at Mary Jane, pushing at the curtains which had been drawn

160

around the bed, momentarily unable to find the opening between them, pushing at the blanketing folds of cloth.

On the way from the duty room, where he had calmed the sobbing nurse, Deon passed the social worker, Miss Lutke. She was talking to a child whose left leg had been amputated at the hip because of a cancer of the femur. The boy, resting on his crutches, listened to her as quietly and attentively as always. As Deon watched he saw the woman lift a hand and allow it to rest, very briefly, very lightly, on the boy's head. Then she took her hand away.

And it broke inside him like a damn wall broached, a flood unimpeded.

Professor Snyman was holding the yellow pathology report: which he had picked up from the desk in the doctors' office. He showed it to Deon. "The lymphatic glands showed no evidence of tumor involvement. I think that means we've cured her."

"Of what?" Deon muttered.

He had not spoken loudly, but Snyman looked at him sharply. "Of the cancer, of course. If the glands are not involved, we were obviously able to remove the cancer in toto."

"That's not what I meant, sir."

"Then what do you mean?" Eyebrows raised in polite, surprised inquiry. But with a frosty look about the eyes.

"How can you really say that she's been cured?" Deon plunged on recklessly. "She's young, so her body has healed quickly. Practically all that shows is a scar or two. And the openings of the colostomy and the bladder. She's young, so she's even adapted to those too. But what of her future? Is she going to withdraw from life? Shouldn't we have asked that too? All we've been able to achieve with our so-called surgical skills has been to destroy her as a woman. The dice were loaded against her from the beginning. Is it right and fair to perpetuate misery?"

"Misery? That child you've just left? She's miserable?"

"In the future," Deon said stubbornly. "When she comes to realize."

"You ask for fairness," Snyman told him coldly. "Then you're asking too much of life. You talk of loading the dice. But it's not a game, you know, with each player getting so many chips. It's not a . . ." The old man hesitated, then moved around the desk and crossed to the window. "Come here. Look out there. What do you see?"

Deon stared into the distance. Mountains, far away. City buildings. Moving traffic. He turned with a puzzled frown.

"No!" Snyman said impatiently. "Here! Here! Look in front of you. Across the road."

"Oh. I see. The graveyard, sir."

"Right." The old man grinned with sardonic relish. "Every now and again there's a palaver about the fact that the hospital overlooks a cemetery. People say it's not a good advertisement. But if you ask me it's a salutary reminder for the doctors. We need it from time to time."

He leaned against the desk.

"One thing I've learned, my boy," he said then, his voice unexpectedly gentle, "is that there's no great ethic of life and death. You have to scratch up the little knowledge and cunning and intuition you've managed to acquire and try to make the right decisions. The best you can do is try. And finally you have to hope that you weren't wrong. Do you see that?"

"Yes, sir."

Professor Snyman sighed. "And of course you don't see it at all. You think I'm just another prattling old fool and that medicine is an exact science and someday it'll all be absolutely exact and absolutely perfect. Well, I'm sorry. This won't happen before life becomes absolutely perfect, and so it'll never happen at all."

He was no longer looking at Deon; he might have been speaking to himself.

"The one truth we are prone to forget is that medicine is no more than an extension of life. And life is a dark place. We're doing no more than to fumble in the dark. The best you can hope to do is to strike a match here and there as you go along. You can only try."

The old man was silent for so long that Deon thought the conversation had ended. He fidgeted, wanting to go away.

Then Snyman spoke again, more briskly. "You're concerned about what we had to do to the Fowler child. But consider this: if we had not operated, she would have faced a slow, painful death from invasion of the bladder and the rectum. With infection, hemorrhage, ulceration, and eventual intestinal obstruction and inability to pass urine. No, my boy. Our duty as doctors was crystal clear. To preserve life and make it as tolerable as possible."

"Yes, sir," Deon said. And then, blurting out compulsively, though he was afraid of being misunderstood: "What can I do, sir?"

"Hm?" Snyman looked puzzled, so perhaps he had misunderstood after all. Then he said: "Do? You want to know what to do? That's not a question to ask me, my boy. Only you have got the answer to that."

"Yes, sir," Deon said humbly. "I'd like to do surgery, sir."

The old man smiled broadly. "I thought it would come to that. Well, you've got a good pair of hands."

"But I don't want to be a destructive surgeon. Cutting off and cutting out doesn't appeal to me. I think it's defeatist."

"Hm." The frosty look reappeared momentarily.

"I want to do only repair work. To me that's real surgery."

"I see." Snyman took off his glasses, breathed on the lenses and polished them vigorously. Without them his eyes appeared abnormally large. He gave Deon a squinting, myopic stare.

"Where do you find that kind of surgery?"

"Cardiac work, sir."

The old man replaced his glasses and nodded, then clapped Deon on the shoulder, having to reach up slightly to do so.

"Well, go on, my boy. Go away and learn to be a heart surgeon. Then we'll see."

Was it the right decision? It meant years more of study; years of comparative poverty. And at the end of the road a question mark: could he make it? How could he be sure it was the right choice? He was too close to it, had been living too near the core of it for too long, in a state of unnatural tension and exhilaration. He needed to stand away a little, to examine things from a new angle. It would be fine to go to the farm now, to spend a few days in the veld, to go hunting perhaps. But there wasn't time.

On the spur of the moment he decided to telephone Elizabeth Metcalfe.

He thought, as he listened to the ringing tone, that Liz had changed. Ever since that Sunday when they had quarreled on the way back from the beach. Curious. He still could not recall what idiotic little thing had started the row. They had patched it up eventually and gone out together again a couple of times, but a new sense of hurt and restraint had grown between them. Or perhaps it had been there all the time and he simply hadn't noticed.

He tried to persuade himself that this was what he secretly wanted; that her moodiness and unaccountable enthusiasms had become a bore.

He reached out to depress the receiver button and cut the connection. At the last moment he hesitated, fingers suspended over the instrument.

Why are you phoning her? Why can't you simply stop and allow her to fade out of your life? There are plenty of women around. Any number of the nurses would be only too eager to go to bed with you. And variety is the spice of life, isn't it?

163

But the thought of Liz undressing before other eyes and being touched by other hands made him angry.

Was it merely that? No more than jealousy? Like a dog growling over a dead bone? I don't want it, but you're not going to have it either?

"Hello?"

Elizabeth's voice was eager, but it went flat when she recognized his, as if she had expected another caller.

"I had nothing much to do, so I thought I'd give you a call."

She ignored the sarcasm and merely said, vaguely: "Oh, yes?" At once he felt intensely ashamed of the infantile remark.

"Been busy lately?" He tried to sound casual.

"Busy enough."

"So have I. You know. Tied up with the work, and there's been a real run of parties and so on."

"Uh huh."

He was surprised to find her quite so cool. "Look, are you doing anything tonight?" Perhaps he had sounded too eager. He tried to feign nonchalance. "I have a night free, if you'd care to have a meal or go to a show or something."

She hesitated, then agreed abruptly. "All right. I want to talk to you in any case. I'll pick you up at the bungalow. In about an hour."

He put down the receiver with a sudden numbing knowledge of how sad he would have been had she refused.

He watched through a window till Elizabeth drove recklessly up to the entrance to the bungalow and swung into a vacant parking place. Then he went to his room and waited for her to come to the door. He forced himself to wait awhile before calling out: "Who's there?"

Elizabeth opened the door without answering.

Deon could not remember ever having recognized so clearly that she was beautiful.

"Shall we go?" Her expression was aloof. "We'll use my car if you don't mind."

He agreed, determined to sidestep a clash of wills tonight. Besides, he had a habit of allowing his thoughts to wander when he should be concentrating on traffic.

They drove to a favorite restaurant, a tiny place off the beachfront, where empty wine bottles dangled from the ceiling and candles crusted with stalactites of wax stood on each white tablecloth. The fat Italian owner waited cheerfully on his customers and, at some time in the evening,

Mamma would be persuaded to come from her kitchen and shyly accept compliments on her cooking.

They both ordered grilled crayfish. Calculating ahead, Deon decided not to ask for the garlic butter sauce.

Elizabeth was moody and preoccupied and Deon was careful not to force the conversation. He was relieved when, after a few glasses of chilled white Cinzano, she cheered up a little. His news would not keep.

"I've decided to carry on and do surgery," he confided and was proud that he could say it with composure.

"Good," she said with equal coolness.

He swallowed his disappointment. By now he should have known this wouldn't impress her.

They finished the meal and the wine. Mamma was duly praised and they sat talking companionably over coffee and cigarettes. But after a while Elizabeth's observations and replies became sketchy and more and more distracted.

Finally Deon leaned back in his chair and grinned at her. "All right, Liz. You're thinking about how to start what you want to say to me. Let's have it."

"It's not really important."

"Now look. I know you well enough to tell."

She looked at him, her expression searching. He maintained the reassuring grin.

"Deon, I've decided I'm not going to see you again."

His grin became a little more fixed, but he persevered with it. "May I ask why not? What have I done?"

"I doubt whether you're really interested, but I've fallen for someone else."

"Did you fall on your back?"

She looked defiant. "Not yet. A bit later, maybe."

He was ashamed of the self-conscious crudity of the question, but determined not to let her know of it. He had tipped his chair backward and was rocking it gently to and fro.

"You'll never change," he mocked. "The same old Liz."

"And neither will you, my love." She looked at him, and he was dismayed to see active dislike on her face. "Deon, when we were kids we used to take oranges and kneel on them till they were soft. Then we'd poke a hole in the skin and suck out the juice. Then we'd throw away the sucked-out orange. Well, that's how you treat people. But this time you can find yourself another orange to suck. Get yourself another tit to suck."

He nearly lost his balance and had to grab at the table to save himself knocking over a coffee cup in the process. He straightened up grumpily aware of loss of dignity and her small smile. He pushed back his chair and rose. "We had better go. This isn't getting us anywhere."

Elizabeth, face averted, collected her handbag and coat and walked stiffly ahead of him to the door. She was effusively sweet toward the fat little Italian. Deon left a tip and received a bow and a smile of gratitude and then, when Elizabeth looked away, a swift shrug of commiseration.

The gesture of male sympathy amused him and he felt almost light hearted again as he walked behind Elizabeth to her car. She started it and pulled away with such violent acceleration that his half-closed door slammed against his leg. His temper rose in response to hers, but he re pressed it with determination.

"Liz," he said finally, choosing the conciliatory words with care, "I'm sorry that happened. The last thing I wanted was to insult you."

She said nothing. Her face, presented to him in profile, was hard and expressionless.

To hell with you, little bitch. Why should I run after you? He was about to say this, to express the hurried thought in equally hurried and irrevo cable words. But a fragment of hope and the memory of good times spent together restrained him.

"Come on," he said, as charming and warm as he was capable of being "Let's stop this. It's so futile. The only reason I've been trying to hurt you is because"—and he lowered his voice—"because I've come to realize that I re ally do love you."

He knew that it sounded false. And yet, he meant what he was saying Would she recognize this?

She had been driving at high speed in the right-hand lane and now she swung without warning to the left, causing an outbreak of angered hooting at the rear. She ignored this and cut into the side of the street, squeezing the little red car into a parking place.

"Let's walk," she said, and opened her door before he could say anything She was already yards ahead, crossing the lawns toward the seafront prome nade before he managed to catch up with her.

"So you want me to run after you," he said with a breathless laugh.

"No, Deon. Neither of us need run after the other. I used to run after you. Even after you had already started running in the opposite direction But that's finished. You don't have to run anymore."

"So you mean it's finished? All done?"

166

She was looking at the sea. "I think so. Don't you? And anyway there's
. . . this other person."

Something in her tone made him wonder for the first time. Was it a ruse
on her part too? A bit of play-acting?

"Who is this guy?"

"It doesn't matter."

"Is there really such a guy?"

"What do you mean?"

"Does he really exist?"

She gave him a cool look. "He exists."

"When did you meet him?"

"Long ago."

"How can you be so sure you're in love with him?"

"I'm sure."

"Who is he, anyway?"

She made a gesture of impatience. "All this interrogation is a bit pointless. Wouldn't you say so?"

"Well, you've got to know your opponent if you want to beat him."

"You haven't any opponent, Deon. Forget it. You're not even in a fight.
Go back to your hospital."

"What do you mean?"

"You told me often enough that your patients were your first responsibility, didn't you? Well, now you've got all the time in the world for
them."

Could he conceivably ever have used work as an excuse for not seeing
her? Yes (with a mournful and disbelieving shake of the head), he had.

"You're not very fair to me," he said.

"Fair?"

"Well, I am a doctor, after all. I do have responsibilities toward those patients."

"Oh, Deon." She sighed helplessly. "Please, let's not try to bluff ourselves. Not at this stage."

"I'm not bluffing."

"Please. I'm not altogether blind, you know."

They reached a gap in the sea wall where steps went down to the windswept beach below. The waves broke with a long drumsound and surged
over and around the scraggy rocks.

Deon remembered another time and another beach where they had
taken off their shoes and walked through the ice-cold water. She was a

lovely girl and they had shared marvelous times. He would not let her go without a struggle.

"Look. Please believe me. I love you."

She turned to face him frankly. The wind blew her hair forward around her face.

"Do I have to spell it out to you? It's futile. It's pointless. Can't you see that?"

"I love you," he said, stubbornly insistent, as if the phrase were enough to set all to rights again, an incantation that would shield him from the perilous and unknowable future.

The taillights flickered at the corner of the hospital building and vanished around it. He heard the deep note of the red car's engine, then that too was lost in the larger sound of distant traffic.

Elizabeth was gone.

The wind blew around the corner with a mournful hoot that exactly suited his mood. But it was chilly too, so he turned and went inside the warm, well-lit doctors' bungalow.

He needed company, suddenly, and was disappointed to find the lounge deserted. Obviously people had been here a moment ago, for the chairs were disarrayed, the fire was burning, and an opened book lay on the carpet. But now they had gone and taken the presence of their bodies and the sound of their voices with them.

Quick footsteps in the corridor behind him. Philip, rubbing his hands together vigorously against the cold.

"Hello," Deon said. "Bitter, isn't it?"

"Freezing." Philip went up to the fire and held his hands out toward it, sitting on his haunches. He looked round at Deon. "You alone here?"

"Ja. Don't know where everyone's gone. I've just got in."

"Pity. I was looking for a volunteer."

"What for?"

To Deon's astonishment Philip imitated the Dracula voice and look which was one of Robby's party pieces.

"Blood!" Philip said ghoulishly. "I'm looking for blood."

Deon could not remember ever having seen him so gay.

"Blood? At this time of night? What on earth for?"

Philip had turned his back to the fire now and was bouncing up and down on the balls of his feet as if he could not keep still. "Man, it's tremendous. I've at last got that technique taped."

"Technique? What are you talking about?"

"You know. The new technique to study chromosomes. The thing I've been working at."

"For God's sake! Chromosomes! You expect me to get all worked up about chromosomes?"

Philip gave a defensive shrug and held his hands out to the fire again. "Well, anyway, it's quite important to me."

He looked crestfallen and a little lost, and at once Deon was remorseful.

"You said you wanted a volunteer. Will I do?"

Philip's face brightened. "Would you do that? Would you mind?"

"No. Sure. It's all in aid of science, isn't it?"

"That's right. What's your blood group?"

"O."

"That's great. Mine is O as well and I've been looking for some more for comparison. The karyotypes I've managed to arrange are all from my own blood."

"What do you do?" Deon asked, curious in spite of his divided attention.

"Come down to the lab and I'll show you."

Grudgingly, Deon went out into the wind and the cold again while Philip, walking with eager strides beside him, talked on about the improved method of preparing chromosomes that he had at last managed to apply.

A light was burning in a small side laboratory in the pathology block.

Philip went directly up to the microscope bench, without waiting for Deon. He stooped over the instrument, peered down the eyepiece and focused with an adjustment screw. He signaled to Deon without lifting his head.

"Come and have a look here."

It was warm inside the little cramped room, and Philip's enthusiasm was infectious. Deon sat down obediently in front of the microscope. He recognized the strandlike structure under the lens from pictures out of last year's textbooks. They varied in size and shape: some were like lopsided X's; others resembled U's joined together at the bends.

"Uh-huh," he said noncommittally.

"Can you see?" Philip was at his shoulder patting him on the back as if to transmit his feverish excitement.

"Ja." Deon was embarrassed by the other man's emotion as much as puzzled by it.

"That's a perfect example of the forty-six chromosomes of a human white blood cell. Locked up in there are all the hereditary factors. One could even say that you're looking at the complete man."

Deon looked up to interrupt, but Philip went on speaking. "What I do now is photograph them, then cut each individually from the photograph, arrange them in pairs in decreasing order of size and add the two sex chromosomes. Then I've got what we call a karyotype."

"And then?"

"Then? My God, Deon, this is the thing of the future. You know that some diseases are associated with chromosome abnormalities. Well, what we've got to do is find out why, and learn how to prevent it, if possible."

"Tall order."

"Maybe. But who knows? Do you remember your Bible? 'For I, the Lord thy God, am a jealous God visiting the iniquities of the father upon the children unto the fourth and fifth generation.'" Philip glanced at Deon. "I've always thought that unfair," he said.

Deon gestured vaguely. "Well . . ."

Philip waited, head inclined politely, for him to finish speaking, and, when it was clear that he was not going to continue, pointed at the microscope.

"In there is the secret of why your skin is white and mine is brown. Why I can't drink in your bars or eat in your restaurants or swim from your beaches. Just because of a variation in the arrangement of probably one molecule among the hundreds of thousands in those chromosomes. Just because of that."

Deon eyed him briefly, then dropped his glance. "It's stupid," he said.

He was a little alarmed by Philip's sudden passion. He could not remember any previous direct reference by the Coloured man to his race, could not remember that the bitterness had ever before been so apparent.

Philip laughed briefly, harshly. "Sorry. I didn't bring you here to listen to a speech. Do you mind if I take some blood?"

"Help yourself." Deon took off his jacket, squeezed the right bicep, and balled his right fist to bring up the veins. Philip was ready with a syringe.

"Just a little prick," he said.

"That's what the bishop said to the actress," Deon said, and they both laughed.

Deon watched the dark blood rising in the syringe. "What are your plans for when you finish here at the hospital?" he asked with new curiosity. "I take it you're definitely going overseas?"

Philip pulled the needle out deftly and pressed a cotton-wool tuft down on the pinprick wound, motioning to Deon to bend his elbow. His expression, as he started to inject the blood into a culture bottle, was tense and guarded. "There's no future here."

"No. I guess not."

"No future and no hope."

Deon made a fuss about examining the needle mark in the crook of his arm, making sure that it had ceased to bleed. He did not want to be drawn into argument or even into discussion tonight. He wanted to be left alone. But the trifling wound was not enough to distract Philip.

"I'm surprised they even allow me to look at white people's cells," he said, and smiled thinly. "You know Doctor Rajan?"

"The Indian guy in pathology?"

"Yes. Senior registrar. Well, he was showing me how he does frozen sections the other day when they brought him a lump which had been taken from a white woman's breast. The surgeons were waiting in the operating room for his decision. In other words it depended on him whether or not they went ahead and removed her breast and pectoral muscles. This decision was his, but he wouldn't be allowed to go to the ward and palpate that breast lump."

Deon shook his head and looked away. "Ja. It's stupid."

He could think of nothing else to say. The wrath was righteous enough, but did it help? Could you achieve anything against prejudice by talking about it? Perhaps. What had caused Philip to let go tonight?

He smiled suddenly. "Do you remember when we used to palpate breasts together?"

"What?"

"Do you remember that old loft? The loft above the shearing shed?"

Philip's expression of stony withdrawal vanished and he gave an answering smile of recognition. "I'll grant you that point. I'd forgotten about that."

They smiled together, a little shyly, a little shamefully, at the memory.

Deon couldn't quite place the time. It must have been after he had started school, however, and before Philip's father, Piet Davids, was killed when a truck loaded with wool bales overturned while he was driving it to the station at Beaufort West. It must have been before this, because immediately after the accident Philip and his mother had packed up and left the farm and moved to Cape Town. Anyway, he was perhaps eight then, or nine, and Philip about ten. And it was Philip's job to round up the little Coloured girls from the rows of shanties behind the quince avenue, where the farm laborers lived, and lure them up to the loft in the shearing shed.

They came there, giggling in anticipation, and were made to remove their tattered shirts and sit in a row while Deon and Philip, in the role of doctors, examined them thoroughly one by one.

The examination couch was an old packing case, and Philip had made a make-believe stethoscope out of a boot-polish tin and a length of electric wire. They had surgical knives too, borrowed from the cutlery drawer in the kitchen, but the girls always ran away when they produced the knives.

In Deon's mind that smell of dust and the greasiness of sheared wool and sheep manure and hessian bags and the sweat of unwashed bodies would always be associated with furtive, youthful sex.

They knew what they were doing, he thought now, remembering half-developed brown breasts in the gloom inside the loft and his own white hands exploring the mysteries. And yet they hadn't really known. It was wrong in some way. They knew that, or they would not have played the game in the secrecy of the loft. But they did not understand the curious excitement there was about playing it.

In any case, the doctor game had ended abruptly one day when his father had come into the shearing shed to fetch something and had heard the faint giggles coming from above and had quietly climbed the steps to investigate. He thought that was probably the most severe beating his father had ever given him. And Philip had received a double beating—from Deon's father with a leather belt up in the loft and from his own father that night in the shack behind the quince avenue.

"You're a bad bugger, you know that?" Philip said now, shaking his head in mock disapproval.

"You're no little angel yourself."

"Do you know something?" Philip said, suddenly serious again. "I don't think I've ever told you, but that business in the shed, that doctor business you started . . ."

"Just a moment. I seem to remember it was your idea."

"Anyway, whoever thought of it first, it was really that which gave me the idea of becoming a doctor. I kept that tin-can stethoscope, you know. I kept that thing for a long time."

"Even after the beating my father gave us?"

Philip pulled a wry face. "He could use that belt of his. But even after that I wanted to be a real doctor. I remembered that time your mother was sick and the doctor from town . . . what was his name?"

"Steyn, I think."

"That's right. Doctor Steyn. I remembered he came to the farm, and even your father was very polite to him. Doctor Steyn this, and Doctor Steyn that. Anyway," he said quickly and in some embarrassment now, "I thought it would be nice if people like your father had to call me Doctor Davids. What made you decide to take medicine?"

Deon shrugged. "Don't really know. At high school I was good at science and math and I think the principal suggested medicine. He spoke to my father, and since Boet was at agricultural college and would take over the farm, the old man agreed. Only, he would have preferred me going to Pretoria."

Philip smiled slightly. "Yes. I dare say he would."

They were silent, each with his own thoughts.

Deon's first fear was for his father. The thought was with him constantly: thank God that he, at least, is safely out of the way, here at the hospital. Thank God he wasn't on the farm. If he hears about it, it will kill him.

Like pain, the thought stayed with him from the moment he received Liselle's tearful telephone call. The call came at ten o'clock that night. Liselle was half hysterical and at first he was under the impression that Boet had been in an accident. Finally, he calmed her and was able to drag out the story: his brother had been locked up in a police cell, and his father must never know. He extorted compassionate leave from the perplexed hospital superintendent and drove home through the night.

Boet's appearance in the morning, as he came shambling into the dock among the drunks and the knife wielders and the dagga-smokers, was a fresh shock. He had a fugitive's look, as if constantly on the watch for unsuspected blows, and there was a constant half smile on his lips. He was apologizing for being there, for breathing, for casting a shadow, for his very existence. I am nothing, his cringing attitude declared. Nothing at all. Ignore me.

Deon had awakened the local attorney at half past five this morning, and ever since, the man had worn a harried expression, as if he were being swept along to the destination he did not wish to reach. He rose and mumbled his formula and then he and the young, aggressive prosecutor wrangled interminably about the amount of bail.

"It's a very serious charge, your worship," the prosecutor kept saying. "Illicit diamond buying." He pronounced the phrase with relish. "Unlawful possession of uncut diamonds. It's a very serious charge."

But at last Deon was allowed to sign the bail bond and the attorney produced the cash and Boet was free to go.

He and Deon walked together out of the courthouse into the bright sunshine on the street. Neither of them said anything. Liselle was waiting in the car, parked in the shade opposite the court. Deon held the passenger-side door open for his brother and Boet nodded stiffly and climbed into the car. Liselle started the motor and they drove out of town in silence.

They rode along the dusty road over the stony veld, and the silence hung between them like the curtain of dust raised by the passage of the speeding car. The dust was orange in color and went dry and burning into the throat and the lungs.

Then Boet spoke. "They treated me like a Hot-not," he announced in an ordinary, but somewhat flattened voice.

Liselle glanced into the driving mirror and caught Deon's eye. He gave a faint, warning shake of the head.

"Did they ill-treat you?" Deon asked, his own voice tight and angry.

Boet turned in his seat to frown bemusedly. "Ill-treat?" he said finally. He appeared to consider. "No, not really. But I begged them not to lock me up. I promised I would not run away if they allowed me to sit on the bench in the charge office. They said it was the law, they had to put me in a cell for the night. Later, they brought me tea in a Coca-Cola bottle. It's the way the Coloureds drink tea in jail." Then, in the same expressionless voice: "They could have given me a cup!"

"How did it happen?" Deon asked. He was concerned about this obsession with the trivial. Perhaps having to tell the story again would serve as catharsis.

"What?" Boet asked. His voice went high and aggrieved.

"What happened? Why did they arrest you?"

There had been two of them. There were always two of them, and this alone should have alarmed him.

But it had happened in such an ordinary, even orderly way that he had not been alarmed until it was too late. He had been to town that morning to see the accountant and returned in time for lunch. They ate and then had coffee on the stoep, Liselle talking and he making absent-minded replies. She wanted them to build a new house at a distance away from the old one, among the weeping willows and near the dam. It would be a modern house with a big tiled kitchen and modern bathroom and many large windows; she had even cut out a number of plans from those English and American magazines on interior decorating. The old house was very dark and inconvenient, she said, and too small for their needs, especially now with Pappa van der Riet so ill. He had listened with half an ear and made perfunctory replies and finished his coffee. Then he had gone back to the farm office and the accounts with which he had been struggling for days.

The price of wool was low and all the farmers were living on their reserves or on what they could squeeze out of the bank manager. Whenever he met up with other farmers at the tennis club on Saturday afternoons or at auction sales, or in the cooperative store, everyone talked about how serious things were and what steps the government should take to alleviate the hardships of the farmers. But until this year, when his father had become sick, Boet had never really related any of this to Wamagerskraal. That had always been there, solid and secure as his father was, its camps stretching, it seemed, into infinity across the gray plains. Now, for the first time, he had a taste of insecurity, and it frightened him.

He was astonished by the size of the bank overdraft. Where did it all go? On fodder for the dry months, but even with feeding, they had lost a lot of sheep this winter. It couldn't go on like this. And Liselle, who had been a teacher, and whose father owned a not-very-profitable grocer shop in town, seemed to think that once you had married a wool farmer you could pick money off the Karoo bushes.

With all this, how was he going to afford the improvements he had planned? More boreholes, for one. And that meant more camps . . . He stared unseeingly at the unwieldy ledger, thinking of the matter-of-fact way in which the teachers at agricultural school spoke about proper farm planning. They made it sound so easy. No one ever bothered about the money. Another bond was out of the question, and even the Land Bank was sticky these days. What it boiled down to was capital. You couldn't farm progressively without capital behind you.

There was a tap on the door and he looked up from his father's old-fashioned roll-top desk with its many small pigeonholes and said crossly: "Ja?"

Old Jantjie's gray peppercorn head peeped cautiously round the door.

"What do you want?"

"Two people, little boss. They say they want to talk to you."

"What do they want?"

A shrug. The old man's mute face made it clear that he regarded the question as idiotic. Why should he ask people for what reason they wanted to speak to a white man? "They did not say."

Boet shoved his papers away irritably and pushed the chair back.

"Where are they?"

"Outside, little boss."

The two Coloured men stood quietly and deferentially alongside the sheep-loading ramp. One was dressed a little too well in slacks and a sports-coat; the other wore the usual broken shirt and stained khaki trousers of a farm worker.

"Yes? What do you want?"

"Morning boss," the well-dressed man said.

"Yes. Morning. I haven't got work for you."

"We're looking for money, master."

"Well, I told you there isn't any work. I've got too many boys. They'll still eat up the farm. They're worse than locusts."

Both the men chuckled at the white man's joke.

Then the one in the sports-coat said knowingly, confidingly: "We want to do business with the boss."

Boet took a threatening step toward him. "What do you mean, you bloody . . ."

Sports-coat fell back rapidly and put up restraining, pleading hands. "Please, boss." His voice was urgent. "I know how the boss can make a lot of money."

For the first time Boet noticed the old brown round-backed Chevy parked alongside the road, drawn up next to the farm gate. Then he understood. These were the Coloureds Manie van Schalkwyk had talked about.

He had been to see Manie a fortnight ago, about the three hundred pounds which were still owing. Manie had given him a sly wink and had talked about unimportant things till his wife left the porch to fetch fresh coffee from the kitchen. Then he had hunched forward, leaning elbows on knees, and spoken quickly.

"Those people from . . . you know," he said in a side-of-the-mouth mutter. When Boet stared at him uncomprehendingly he jerked his head. "You know. Those people I told you about. I had a message yesterday to say they're coming this way soon. I'll send them to you."

Boet reminded him again that he knew nothing about diamonds. He didn't have any idea of how much to pay for them or how to get rid of them again.

Manie assured him that he would look after his old friend. All Boet had to do was contact him as soon as he had the diamonds. He would help him to make lots of . . . he had rubbed thumb and forefinger together with a significant look.

Boet had wanted to ask questions, but Manie's wife returned from the kitchen then and Manie sat up and began to speak of the drought. When Boet raised the subject of the three hundred pounds again Manie had given him another wink and pretended not to understand.

"Is that your car?" Boet asked the Coloured men Manie van Schalkwyk had sent to him.

"Yes, boss," Sports-coat said eagerly.

"What do you want here, man?"

Sports-coat lowered his voice. "To talk business, boss."

"What kind of business?"

Sports-coat nodded at his companion. "Show the boss, you!"

The other man fumbled in a pocket of his ragged, much-patched trousers and produced an old drawstring tobacco bag. It was so stained that Boet could not make out the trademark it once had borne. Sports-coat took the bag from his companion and opened it. Inside was an even dirtier cloth, folded and tied at the corners. The Coloured man untied it and held it in his palm for Boet to see. Two roughly square objects a little smaller than the nail of his little finger lay in the middle of the rag.

"What's that?" he asked, pretending indifference. "Bits of old glass?"

Both the men chuckled again, as if at a profound witticism.

"Stones, boss," Sports-coat said. "Little stones."

"Little bits of glass, you mean."

The one with the ragged clothes shook his head and hid laughter behind a hand. Sports-coat smiled broadly. Neither of them said anything.

"How do I know they're not pieces of glass?" Boet asked.

Sports-coat looked around and spotted an old wooden window frame, with some of the panes still in place, which was leaning against the end of the loading ramp. He beckoned and walked toward it. He kneeled quickly and there was a scraping sound and he showed Boet the fresh scratch mark on the dusty pane of glass.

"Does boss see that? Only a stone can do that. Only a shiny stone."

"Did Baas Manie send you?" he asked.

The Coloured men exchanged glances.

"Baas Manie van Schalkwyk," Boet prompted.

"It's better if the boss does not ask questions," Sports-coat said, very earnestly, so as not to give offense.

Boet shrugged. He could understand the need for caution. "How much?" he asked casually.

"Five hundred, boss."

Boet whistled. "Too much. Three fifty."

"Four fifty, boss."

"All right. Make it four hundred."

"Four hundred, boss."

Boet considered. He was sure they were worth more than four hundred pounds. Still, he needed time to get Manie's advice.

"I'll think about it," he promised vaguely. "I don't know whether I want to do this kind of business. You'll have to come back. Come back on"— What was it today? Wednesday—"on Saturday. Saturday afternoon about three o'clock." Liselle would be off at tennis and he would make an excuse not to go. By three all the farm laborers would be out of the way too; the fewer witnesses the better. "Three o'clock on Saturday."

He watched them drive away in the Chevy. Warrenton plates on the old car. If they had come from Kimberley he might have become suspicious, for city people were dangerous. But Warrenton was a small town. It was close to the Vaal River diggings where, obviously, the diamonds had been stolen.

Stolen. It was an ugly word. Steal. Thief. He knew what his father would say to the mere suggestion that a son of his could become involved in stealing. He tried to put the thought firmly out of his mind.

The next two and a half days he tried in vain to contact Manie van Schalkwyk. This made him nervous. He'd heard that you went to jail without the option. For a long time: two, three years. It wasn't damn fair. People who beat their wives and children half to death got off without a warning. And what was so evil about buying diamonds? It was only illegal so as to protect the interests of a couple of diamond magnates who already had money to burn.

He went to town again on Friday morning and added four hundred pounds to the monthly wages check. The teller lifted his eyebrows slightly when he saw the size of the check, and for a moment Boet thought the young man was going to query it with the bank accountant.

But the youngster stamped the check and asked politely: "How do you want it, Mr. van der Riet?"

On the way back to the farm, however, his mood changed again, and he became sickeningly apprehensive. As a result he was tense and snappy and he and Liselle had a bitter row which ended with her slamming the bedroom door in his face and locking it, so that he had to sleep in a spare room. He was angry and ashamed about being locked out of his own bedroom by his own wife and was relieved that his father was again away in Cape Town for treatment and had therefore not been a witness to his shame. Perhaps, however, his father would have understood and sympathized, for Liselle had developed a very sarcastic way with him too, lately, ever since he had become weak. His father was unexpectedly mild and tolerant about it, even when she was unduly sharp. Once or twice Boet had seen those dark brows draw together and a look of gray stone had come into the tired eyes. He had held his breath, expecting the outbreak of one of those cold rages which were a hundred times worse and more frightening than any ranting and screaming he had ever witnessed. But the old man had controlled himself and had gone on reading the newspaper or mending some small object by the light of the table lamp in the big, warm kitchen, and the storm clouds had never produced anything more than distant lightning and a soft rumble of thunder.

Saturday morning Liselle would not speak to him. She went off to tennis in her own car, which secretly relieved him, for it meant he did not have to make excuses for staying away today.

But for her sudden silence he might still have backed out of the diamond transaction. He had slept badly in the spare room and had been awake half the night, thinking about the dangers. When she went off like that without a word, without even greeting him, he thought: damn you; I'll show you.

So he bought the two diamonds from the men in the brown Chevy and gave them the four hundred pounds, which Sports-coat put away carefully in an old wallet. The two of them greeted him, although not with quite the same amount of respect as before, then went off in the Chevy, pulling away in a cloud of dust.

Now he would have to contact Manie to come over as soon as possible.

The detectives came in the late afternoon, shortly after Liselle had returned from tennis. She had been willing to talk to him again, although still waspish. He was excited about the diamonds, so he didn't really mind her manner. He was getting them a drink (they had become accustomed to a drink or two before dinner in the evenings, whenever his father was away) when she called out: "There's a car stopped at the gate. Are you going out?"

It was a big car with Kimberley license plates. As he walked toward the garden gate two men climbed out. Both wore gray suits, but they had something in their bearing, a heaviness, a squareness, which told him at once what they were. He wanted to run, but there was nowhere to run to, so he continued to walk stiffly toward the gate, as if his joints had suddenly started to ache.

The men met him at the gate, unsmiling, both bulky-shouldered under their gray jackets. In the back of the car sat the two Coloured men, Sports-coat and his friend of the patched khaki clothes.

"Evening," Boet said. He was surprised to find his voice quite steady.

Eleven

Once, a long time ago, Deon had woken from a dream of death.

He had been a small boy then, sleeping in the porch room at Wamagerskraal. It must have been during the holidays, for the first thing he heard, on waking with a gasp of fear, was the reassuring sound of Boet's deep and even breathing, interspersed with an occasional snore.

He could not remember what had caused the dream. Was it a casually overheard phrase or hellfire-promising preacher, or merely too much fatty mutton the night before? He did recall vividly the terror in which he had woken, hands clutching the top of the blanket, trying to pull it up over his face. And then the limp relief with which he recognized that he had been dreaming. ("It was only a dream," a soothing woman's voice said out of very long ago, out of childhood, out of his rocking cradle, and the cradle soothed too, and echoed: ". . . only a dream . . .") He lay in the dark, listening to his brother's breathing and trying to piece together the fragments.

He had been in a long passage. It was dark with drab-colored walls and patterned linoleum underfoot. He walked down the passage, occasionally passing a door set into the walls on either side, but he did not try to open them.

All at once someone was with him in the gloomy corridor. He was not being followed or pursued. But there was a presence. A Stranger had joined him.

He turned slowly, to try to catch the other unawares, but the Stranger was always just out of sight. He could only see a grayness. Nothing more. A hovering grayness which he associated with the look of congealed fat.

The Stranger had come to take him away.

He had woken with this knowledge and had not dared to close his eyes again for a long time, in case he should find himself back in the long dark passage. But he had never again dreamed that dream, not even after death had become a familiar enemy, a natural phenomenon which you could sometimes beat, or trick, or delay, but to which you had to concede defeat in the end.

Now the Stranger was back in the room.

His father coughed weakly, and Deon looked at once at the long frame tucked in so neat and orderly a fashion into undersheets and bedcovers, all severely squared off. Hospital routine was unvarying; two brisk young nurses had come to tidy the patient and his bed only minutes before. Even imminent death could not be allowed to disrupt the routine.

Deon stood up and walked around the bed to check that the drip was still running. No problems. He could almost wish that something small would crop up, so that there could at least be a job to do, a mechanical interruption to the unwanted flow of thought.

His father did not stir. The effort of letting the nurses settle him had made him tired and his eyes were closed. Perhaps he had fallen asleep.

Deon looked at the limp hand and the bony wrist to which the I.V. needle was strapped. The skin between the blue black bruises was pale, almost translucent. It had been a rough hand, hardened by work. Now the calluses showed only as faintly yellow blotches at the root of each finger.

The door latch clicked softly and he turned suspiciously, prepared to shoo away any unnecessary intruder. What was the sense of continuing to force him to do leg and breathing exercises when his last defenses had been overrun? Couldn't they leave him alone?

Philip Davids came in quietly. He glanced at Deon, then at the motionless figure on the bed, and finally turned back to Deon with a questioning look. Deon rose and they went into the corridor. Philip stood to one side of the door, whether out of sympathy or deference it was hard to determine.

"How is he?"

A shrug. "Looks pretty hopeless."

"Ja."

"The last dose of radiation knocked out practically all the white cells. Now they think he's developed septicemia."

A long silence while they stood awkwardly opposite one another, eyes not quite meeting. An African cleaner in hospital khaki, the initials CPA for Cape Provincial Administration stenciled on his back, worked his way toward them with mop and buckets. Both of them turned to watch him, as if there were relief to be found in the sight.

A nurse, carrying a tray, came briskly round the corner, followed by one of the senior housemen, a small, sandy-haired man who checked slightly in his stride when he saw Deon and Philip, then came on down the corridor toward them, rubbing one hand worriedly up and down the lapel of his white coat.

"Hello, Deon," he said. "How's your old man?"

"He's sleeping," Deon said flatly.

"Oh." The sandy-haired doctor looked at him helplessly, then pulled back a cuff to examine his watch. "Well, I'm sorry but the lab says they want to do a blood count. I'll try not to wake him."

Deon grimaced. "If you have to."

"Yes . . . well . . ." The other man pulled at his matching sandy moustache. "Maybe the white cells are up this time," he said with forced cheerfulness. "Come on, Staffy."

Deon wanted to go back into the ward after the sandy-haired doctor left to console his father for the little indignity, the extra pinprick. And Philip waited with him.

The sandy doctor emerged, carrying the test tube of blood triumphantly aloft, like a banner. He gave Deon a brief, reassuring smile.

"Didn't wake him."

He held the test tube out to the nurse.

"Tell the porter to take this to the lab."

"I'll take it," Philip volunteered unexpectedly.

All of them stared at him.

"I was going to the hematology lab anyway," he told them. He took the test tube and looked at the label: J.P. van der Riet and the ward designation. "I'll take it along right now." He turned and began to walk away, then stopped.

"Give my regards to him," he said to Deon.

"Thank you. I'll do that," Deon said.

He left the nurse and the other doctor abruptly, without greetings, and went into his father's room. The old man's eyes were still closed, but his breathing was quicker. There was crusted blood on his lips.

In the beginning chemotherapy and blood transfusions had helped. But, inevitably, the periods of remission had grown shorter, and then there had been a relapse which had reduced his white cells to a dangerous level. And now he had developed blood poisoning.

Deon stood watching the wasted body under the sheets. Why do I find this so distasteful? he asked himself. Why do I want to run away; hide; get drunk?

Granted: he is my father and the family bond can never be discounted. But we were never close. There was always a degree of privacy about him, a natural reserve which kept people at a distance. I have it too, I suppose. There was a barrier between us, as invisible and yet as impenetrable as this wall which separates us because he is dying and I am not.

Then why do I want to run away?

Perhaps because he has always been *there*. Once he is gone nothing can be permanent again. Once he has gone disillusion starts. Once he is gone I shall be alone in that passage with the gray Stranger.

He sat down on the stiff-backed, white-painted chair beside the bed and it creaked a little under him. His father's eyes opened and regarded him quizzically.

"How are you?" Deon was obliged to ask.

A flickering smile which showed bloody gums. "Fine. Fine."

Deon stood up again, walked to the front of the bed, pretending to examine the pulse and temperature chart.

"There was someone here," his father said after a while.

"A doctor and a nurse came to take a little blood," Deon told him reassuringly. "For a blood test."

The old man shook his head irritably and the gesture seemed to tire him, for he closed his eyes again and lay slack.

"Earlier."

"Oh. Of course. It was Philip."

"Philip?"

"Flip," Deon amended. "Flip Davids. From the farm, remember? Old Mieta Davids' son."

"Flip," his father said, eyes still closed.

"He sent you his good wishes."

His father nodded, but did not comment. Presently he fell asleep again. Or, if he did not sleep, at any rate he was silent.

Deon looked at his watch. Fifteen minutes before he'd be on call. It was fortunate that he had been placed with a surgical firm for the last quarter of the year; they were kept busy enough, but unless the slate went far over the scheduled time he could usually manage to snatch a couple of minutes here and there to spend with his father. This week he had been mainly on night duty and, amazingly for October, the theater had been comparatively quiet.

Nevertheless—and here he felt a sudden surge of resentment—he should not have had to shoulder the burden alone. Then he reminded himself that Boet and Liselle were alone too. Boet in a prison cell starting a three-year sentence. And Liselle alone on the farm, trying her best to make a success of it. Her parents came to visit her every weekend and that couldn't help but make it worse.

He had gained respect for Liselle in the months after Boet's arrest and trial. Her father was a fat and pompous town grocer and her mother was a sharp-tongued bitch, but somewhere far back in her ancestry Liselle had acquired steel. She had never wavered. If she had wept, she wept alone. She had never showed any trace of self-pity. Nor did she seek or welcome sympathy. She had sat in court beside her father throughout the long ordeal of the trial in the circuit court.

Deon looked at the motionless body in the bed. Yes, you poor old bastard; they didn't even spare you that. They didn't keep you from having to see your eldest son, a van der Riet of Wamagerskraal, go off to jail in a police van with bars on the windows.

Deon had tried his best to prevent it. He had connived with Liselle and his father's doctor to keep the old man in hospital, during the examination in the magistrate's court, and the trial itself.

But one afternoon while Deon and Liselle were both visiting Johan van der Riet he had asked, unexpectedly: "Where is Boet?"

Liselle's face told the whole story.

So he had insisted on sitting through the trial, in the front row of the hard and uncomfortable public benches, his hands folded on top of the knob of his walking stick and his chin resting on his hands. He listened impassively to the evidence, the argument by counsel, the judge's summing-up, and the verdict. His eyes had rested always on whoever was talking: witnesses, judge, barrister, or even the court orderly commanding: "Silence in court!"

Seldom had he looked at the man in the dock: his son. From the public benches, in any case, one could not see Boet's face, only the rounded, hunched shoulders that had already admitted defeat.

The judge, passing sentence, was stern about the seriousness of the offense and insistent about the need to protect society from people like Boet. He was forced to send him to prison, he explained, for it was clear from the evidence that the motive for Boet's crime had been his financial difficulties. He would therefore not have money to pay a fine. It had been said that the father of the prisoner was prepared to pay, but this would not be justice; it would be punishing the father instead of the son. (As if sending Boet to jail would not be punishing his father anyway.)

So, if Boet were a rich man he could have escaped a jail sentence, Deon thought. That was justice.

The judge had stared at Boet from under sparse gray eyebrows and said coldly: "The sentence of this court is three years' imprisonment."

The night they took Boet to jail, Deon had gone out to look for Boet's friend, Manie van Schalkwyk, who, one of the detectives had admitted under cross-examination, was a paid police agent. He had once been arrested for diamond dealing and freed on condition that he serve as an informer and agent provocateur.

Deon did not find the man at home, nor in any of the bars in Beaufort West. Which was perhaps as well, for, from the moment he had seen his father's face as he watched his eldest son being taken off to jail, he had been prepared to kill.

Time to go. He rose and the chair creaked again, but this time his father did not stir. Deon regarded the familiar and yet strange face for a moment longer. Quietly he left the room.

He and Bill du Toit were drinking coffee and waiting to start scrubbing on the strangulated hernia which had been admitted earlier in the evening when the call came.

Deon knew. He knew before he had even picked up the telephone, before he had heard the sympathetic voice of the night sister from the medical wards.

"Your father, Doctor van der Riet. I'm afraid . . ."

"Is he . . . ?"

"No, but he has become unconscious."

"I see." For a moment he could think of nothing to say. "Have you called Doctor Boonzaier?"

"Yes, Doctor." She resented being reminded of the obvious. "Fortunately he was still in the hospital. He's coming over at once."

"I'll be there as soon as I can."

Bill du Toit took one look at his stricken face. "Your old man?"

Deon nodded. He did not trust his voice.

Bill waved a hand which held a cheese-and-tomato sandwich at him.

"Go on. Push off. I'll get the sister to help me."

Deon hesitated.

"Don't mess around," Bill said angrily. "Push off. I don't want to see you again tonight."

"Thanks, Bill."

"Don't be bloody stupid." The registrar gulped down the sandwich, brushed crumbs off his scrub suit and resolutely avoided Deon's eyes.

His father's doctor was already in the ward when Deon arrived. Dr. Boonzaier was only middle-aged, but he dressed with the fastidious care of an older man. A morning coat and striped trousers would not have looked out of place on him. He had a large and flourishing practice to prove that attention to detail was not unimportant.

Be fair, Deon thought. He's a damn good doctor too, even if he is a bit of a pain.

The physician leaned over the motionless man on the bed. His hair was thin on top, but he grew it long on the sides and combed it over his crown. Vain as well, Deon thought. Doctors imagine they learn a lot about their patients. They should realize patients learn a lot about doctors too.

Now Boonzaier straightened up and tugged at the front of his immaculately laundered coat. "He seems to have lost consciousness," he announced to no one in particular. "But the pulse is strong."

Deon forced out the words. "What does it look like, Doctor?"

The physician made a soft, sucking sound, as if he had detected a strand of some foreign matter between his teeth and disapproved. "Shall we go outside?" he said.

The corridor was very quiet. Two nurses crossed at the far end, moving noiselessly. Their uniforms showed briefly under the dimmed lights, so that they appeared like great white birds flitting from tree to tree.

"What do you think?" Deon asked.

Boonzaier's professional aloofness diminished a little. "I don't know, my boy. He's unconscious." He lifted a hand limply. "It could be the end. In spite of the blood we've given, the white cell count is only six hundred. And, of course, there's the septicemia."

"But can't we do something? Something to . . ." Deon was aware of a quality of desperation in his voice, a surfeit of emotion which he had thought he could suppress.

Boonzaier regarded him briefly, not unsympathetically. "We could," he admitted. "More blood. You know the rest. But why?" He waited, to let the question sink in, then continued, his voice kindly but implacable: "You would be doing him no favor. He's unconscious, he's not in pain, he's slipping away. So why not simply let him . . . go?"

All Deon's instincts and all his training told him that death was an enemy, that to surrender tamely was a basic betrayal. The rational mind could accept its inevitability, but some dim recess, perhaps the voiceless spokesman for the cells which made up the body, which groped instinctively toward life, argued differently; cried: "No!"

Then suddenly he remembered his father saying as he walked down a flight of old creaking stairs in a small-town hotel: "Man that is born of a woman is of few days, and full of trouble."

And then his father had laughed at an inner, self-directed joke.

"I don't know," Deon mumbled. "I suppose you're right."

"All right, my boy. Are you going to stay on here for a bit?"

"Yes."

"Good. I've got a couple of calls to make yet. Old friend of mine had a coronary playing golf this afternoon." He sucked at the invisible object between his teeth again, then gave Deon a calculating glance. "Sure you'll be all right?"

"I'll be all right."

"Good. As I say, I'll be around for a while yet. And after that I'll be at home. You can call me at any time."

"Thank you. Thank you, Doctor."

Boonzaier touched him lightly on the shoulder, nodded and went away.

Now he was alone and had to face it.

He must have dozed off early in the morning, for he woke with a start and sat up erect to find his father's eyes open, contemplating him. The dim lamp harshly accentuated the shadows of the sunken cheeks, so that the head seemed already a skull. But the eyes lived and moved with bright intensity. Deon rose at once and went hurriedly to the bed. How long had his father been conscious? How long had he been the object of that silent, unwavering scrutiny?

He bent over. "Are you all right?"

The lips parted, the deep voice said, with difficulty: "Water."

Deon poured from the decanter into a glass and helped his father to drink.

Van der Riet lay back on his pillows, and sighed, and closed his eyes. For a moment Deon believed he had lapsed into unconsciousness again.

But then the voice, stronger, said: "Deon."

"Yes, Father."

After a while: "Johan?"

Boet had the same names as his father.

Deon hesitated.

"He is . . . Boet is on the farm, Father."

The eyes opened and his father gave him the dry look with which he had always greeted evidence of folly or stupidity.

187

"Boet is in jail," he said very distinctly. "Is he all right?"

Chastened, Deon said: "Yes, Father."

The old man nodded, seemingly satisfied. Then he said, as if speaking to himself: "Johan is his mother's child." A pause for a labored breath. Then again: "Innocent. He was innocent."

Humor him at the last.

"Yes, Father."

"Like his mother. Not worldly. They don't understand. So anyone can pull the wool over their eyes." He added, approvingly: "She had spirit. But not enough. It broke her back in the end."

Puzzled, Deon asked: "Who? Liselle?"

"Who is Liselle? I am talking about your mother."

His mind was wandering a little after all.

"I see," Deon said.

After a while his father spoke again. "The dominee came to visit me. When was it? Yesterday?"

"The day before. It's past midnight now."

"What is the time?"

Deon looked. "Half past three."

"In the morning? The night is long, oh, God. But our sins shall be forgiven us."

"You mustn't tire yourself," Deon said in embarrassment and wondered whether he should ask for something to put the old man back to sleep.

But after this his father was silent for a long time and once again Deon believed that he was asleep or unconscious. He himself was feeling drowsy.

"That boy," the voice said out of the half dark. It came out as a croak and his father asked for more water.

"That boy," he repeated then. "That Flip. He came to visit me as well?"

"Yes, Father."

"He's turned out to be a good boy. Call him for me."

"You want me to call Flip Davids?" Deon asked in astonishment.

"Yes. Call him."

Doubtfully: "It's very late, Father."

The gaunt head jerked irritably. "Don't you understand, Deon? I want to speak to Flip, my son."

The voice was testy, and Deon thought it best to obey. Obviously there were moments when the old man was quite lucid, other times when his mind was not under control. In any case, he deserved to be humored.

Philip was on obstetrics. But tonight proved to be his night off. He had left an emergency call number, however, and the sister was able to give this to Deon.

He thought about it for a time, holding the telephone receiver and listening to the b-r-r-r of the dialing tone. Your night off was a precious thing; the one night when you were fairly certain of being able to sleep undisturbed. He remembered the night Philip had doubled up his duty in order to salvage his own night off.

On the other hand, possibly Philip felt he owed something. It had been the old man who had helped him through university, after all. And it was true that he had come, wanting to pay his respects, this afternoon. Yesterday afternoon.

He made the decision and began to dial.

It was only when he had spun through the first two digits, still looking at the number scrawled in the sister's handwriting on a prescription pad in front of him, that he recognized something familiar about it. He stared at the pad for a moment longer, the tip of his forefinger still on the dial. Then he quietly replaced the receiver on its hook.

The number the sister had given him was the number of the telephone in Elizabeth's flat.

The woman looked inquiringly at him. "Changed my mind," he said. He bared his teeth at her in a semblance of a smile. "Not fair to disturb him at this time of the night."

She nodded her agreement and he went into the corridor. But he could not go back into his father's room.

Philip.

The bastard.

He leaned against the green-painted wall, feeling the cold slickness of many layers of paint beneath his fingertips.

Finally he went back into his father's room, thinking out an excuse for not being able to reach Philip Davids.

The excuse was unnecessary. Van der Riet had become unconscious again. He went into a deep coma soon afterward and died shortly before dawn on what promised to be a perfect Cape spring morning.

Deon drove around aimlessly at first, circling toward the city and the seafront beyond. Then, as the first thin scattering of early morning citybound traffic appeared on the roads, he turned back, heading toward the False Bay coast.

But after he had passed the hospital he turned off toward Newlands. Philip and Elizabeth. It seemed impossible. He couldn't really imagine it. And then he discovered that he *could* imagine it, very vividly indeed. He tormented himself with the vision of them making love, brown limbs and white inextricably mingled.

He stopped a block away from the flat, lit a cigarette distractedly with the lighter on the dashboard, and was shocked again by the thought he had vigorously suppressed for almost two hours.

My father is dead.

Everything else was an evasion.

He stubbed out the half-smoked cigarette and climbed out of the car, slamming the door behind him. As he walked round the Volkswagen, two middle-aged women, passing on the way to a bus stop, broke off in mid-conversation to stare at him, and he realized that he was still dressed in his operating clothes: singlet, cap, and white trousers with their bottoms tucked into white rubber boots. The curious, half-apprehensive stares neither amused nor concerned him.

My father is dead.

It was the first thing he said when Elizabeth opened the door of the flat for him.

She was pale. Was it the effect of the stark announcement? Thinner too, since last he had seen her. How long ago had that been? He could not remember.

A hand was at her throat. "Your father . . ."

"Dead," he said angrily. And then: "Where is Philip?"

Philip was there, dressed in black. In anticipation of mourning? He was frowning; he looked anxious.

"My father is dead," he told Philip earnestly.

He saw Philip and the girl look at one another. They have secrets, he thought, and was immediately enraged again. They can't keep things hidden from me. I know all about them. There's nothing secret anymore.

It occurred to him that they were both dressed, in conventional city dress, although it was still very early in the morning.

"Come in," Elizabeth said. "Come in here. You look absolutely . . ."

Shuffling clumsily in the surgical boots, he went past Philip into the familiar room beyond. The studio-couch still stood in front of the window.

He should not be here. He had to be alone. Loneliness was the only condition which he could bear.

He turned away, headed back into the hall, out of the flat. But Philip grabbed him firmly by the arm.

"Here," he said. "Take it easy."

All at once Deon calmed down.

Philip and Elizabeth.

No. That was wrong.

Philip and Deon.

Or Philip versus Deon, for they had always been rivals, and it was foolish to pretend differently. All the things that separated the son of a wealthy white farmer from the son of a Coloured servant kept them apart. But the one thing that was a bond, an enduring bond, was the fact of their rivalry. That was beyond race or class. It had started in childhood and had resumed the instant they found one another again. And now it had come to a head for the classic yet most banal cause of all. A woman.

"What are you doing here?" he asked Philip. "This is no place for you."

Philip did not answer, however, and it was Elizabeth who asked: "What do you mean?"

"Why do you have him here?" he asked her accusingly.

"That's my concern." But her fingers were clasped together and she stared into the hollow of her cupped hands as if she hoped to read the answer to a riddle.

"Tell him to get out."

The girl's face became paler, more drawn. Her voice was like stone. "I love him. Can you understand that?"

"Love?" He laughed scornfully. "Love . . . him?"

He had expected loathing and contempt, but she did not stir. Philip stood in the doorway, still as a figure carved in wood.

"Love him?" he went on. "You're crazy. Where do you think it's going to get you? It's crazy, Liz. Can't you see that?"

She shook her head wearily. "I don't know."

It was a sign of weakness, of impending surrender, and he seized at it. "Liz, I love you. Believe me, I love you." Did he mean it?

She did not react, but merely repeated, "I don't know."

"I don't think you understand," Philip said with polite patience.

Deon turned on him, coiled like a snake about to strike. "I understand all right," he said. "I can see what's going on all right. Flip, the son of Outa Piet and Aia Mieta, my father's Hottentot servants, thinks he can run around with white girls. This smart boy, this Hotnot boy, is too good for Coloured girls now."

A fleck of color came to Philip's cheeks and his mouth thinned. He made a curious little half-bow toward Deon. "I am very sorry to hear about your father," he said.

Deon made a hacking sound of contempt and whirled around to face the girl again. "Choose!" he shouted wildly at her. "Choose now! Him or me."

Her eyes remained lowered and he tried to will her to look at him. Obstinately, she would not.

"Choose!" he told her, his voice harsh.

It was Philip who spoke again. "You don't understand. There is no choice."

Deon set his body to strike a blow and Philip's hands rose, covering his chest. He shook his head. "Fighting me won't serve any purpose, you know. Everything is already settled."

"Why don't you get the hell out of here? Can't you see when you're not wanted?"

Philip smiled, but kept his hands up. "I was about to leave when you came."

"Well, don't let me detain you."

"You apparently feel this is no place for me." Philip's voice was light and mocking. "You will undoubtedly be glad to know that Elizabeth and I have come to the same conclusion."

Whether the mockery was intended to conceal a deeper sadness Deon could not tell. He said: "Why don't you shut up and get the hell out of here?"

"We were saying good-bye," Philip told him.

"Why don't you get out?"

"Shortly, my friend. Shortly. As I've said, we have said good-bye, because we recognize that there is no future for us. Not in this country, anyway. As you so kindly pointed out to us. And, probably, not anywhere else."

He said the words crisply, matter-of-factly, giving no hint of torment or struggle.

Philip put a hand on the doorknob. "Good-bye," he said to Elizabeth, very courteously.

When he turned back to Deon, his face wore an old familiar mixture of affection, challenge, and aloofness. But now there was something else: a look of infinite compassion.

"I am very sorry indeed," he said, "about Father."

He closed the door behind him.

Deon had been thinking of the time they had fought behind the dam wall over the ownership of an ox made of clay with a pair of needle-sharp white thorns for its horns. Philip was older and heavier and had knocked him to the ground and then stood over him with exactly that expression.

Then it occurred to him that Philip had said: "Father."

Not: "Your father."

"Father."

Our father.

My father.

He looked at Elizabeth for confirmation, but she had, perhaps, not even heard.

My father. I am sorry about my father.

I'll smash him, he thought. I'll smash his face and his black lying lips and I'll break his teeth and his jaw and I'll . . .

My father.

"Bastard," he said softly. Then again, more loudly: "Bastard." And again: "Bastard."

He wrenched open the door and screamed his rage and frustration and humiliation shrilly down the empty stairs.

"You ba-a-A-A-A-stard!"

He ran then, stumbling down the steps in the gum-boots, nearly tripping on the stone-finish paving of the hall floor.

The street outside was empty.

He ran to the Volkswagen and the two women, still waiting for their bus, stepped off the sidewalk as he went lumbering past. A postman at the end of the block stared and a dog barked tentatively from behind a garden wall.

Deon started the car and swung it wildly around the first corner. Another length of empty street. A second turn. Nothing except an elderly man in an old Morris, chugging sedately down the middle of the road. Where has the yellow bastard run to?

My father.

Other jumbled images began to appear from the haze of the past, mystifying at first until suddenly they matched. A pattern was taking shape.

A vision from years ago: his father's terrible anger when he caught them up in the shearing loft with the little Coloured girls.

His mother sitting at the end of his bed, looking into a lost world and saying: "Yes," and again: "Yes."

Mieta Davids climbing the steps, on her son's arm, and Johan van der Riet looking past her, at the blue of the mountains.

Later that day his father saying: "That's enough. You are brothers."

The sight of his father clapping as Philip walked up the aisle at graduation.

A student cafeteria, and the astounding information that his father had paid for Philip's education.

His father again, dying lips apart. What he said was not: "I want to speak to Flip, my son."

But: "I want to speak to Flip. My son."

BOOK
II
SUMMER

One

The house stood high up against the mountain. A well-proportioned and comfortable building in a setting of great natural beauty, surrounded by gardens the landscaping expert had, sensibly, left relatively unchanged.

This evening the garden was little more than a gray-green shadow, broken regularly by the deeper shadows of trees. So eyes turned naturally the other way, to look down the mountain at the lights of the city and the harbor beyond.

Deon heard Philip, at his side, let out his breath in a long sigh, so he stopped the car for a moment at the entrance to the paved driveway. Philip was still looking at the lights, from Signal Hill on the one side to miles beyond Devil's Peak on the other. He did not say anything, so Deon said it for him.

"Beautiful to come back to, isn't it?"

"The fairest Cape," Philip said at last.

Deon was negotiating the tricky bit just in front of the left-hand garage (his wife's station-wagon, with the surfboard carriers clamped to the roof, stood on the right, where she had a clear run to the street) and could not determine whether the comment had been made sarcastically. He decided to ignore it anyway and brought the Jaguar to a smooth, gliding halt.

"Here we are," he said. He opened the door on his side and the interior light came on, illuminating Philip's dark, serious face and the contrasting gray hair.

Someone inside had switched lights on over the steps and terrace at the moment Deon had driven into the garage. He stood aside and indicated with a hand gesture that Philip should lead the way.

Philip paused at the top of the steps, gazing again at the city below, then, turning, at the dark bulk of the mountain. A light shone in the cableway station. It might have been a particularly bright star.

"Beautiful," Philip said. "Quite beautiful."

"There are worse places to live."

"Oh, yes."

"They tell me Canada is a great country to live in too," Deon said. "The winter hunting . . ."

"You've never been there, have you?"

"No. It's always been the States, somehow. Never Canada."

"That's why we never met up with one another again. However, I've followed your career with interest."

"And I yours," Deon assured him with a smile. "One of old Snyman's boys took a job at McGill University and he's kept us posted."

He opened the front door and stood aside for his guest.

Philip paused in the hall, briefly, to examine the big unframed painting on the wall. The artist had been enormously clever in welding together blobs of muddy browns and grays and patches of ochre with concise black strokes into a clear yet troubling representation of a slum township in the early morning. Philip looked at the painting, then through the floor-to-ceiling glass wall at the inner courtyard where a fountain, subtly illuminated by hidden lights, played among shade plants.

He was smiling faintly when he turned to greet Elizabeth van der Riet, coming toward him over a great expanse of tiled floor, her long-skirted dress flowing so gracefully from her waist that she appeared to glide rather than walk.

"Welcome home, Philip," she said in tones of great sincerity.

There was a hint of theatricality, of the planned gesture, about her greeting, but neither of them appeared to detect it.

"Good evening, Elizabeth," Philip said solemnly, with exactly the right mixture of warmth and respect. "Thank you."

Elizabeth turned a cheek to allow her husband to kiss her. When she drew away she looked archly at both of them. She laughed too, and Philip noted that the bubbling warmth had persisted through the years, although it was now muted and more shallow, as if the spring of recklessness that had fed it was drying up at last.

She was still beautiful. She had grown her hair fashionably long and it hung, thick and golden-smooth as ever, to below her shoulders. There were fine lines in the corners of her eyes and around her lips when she smiled, but her body was trim and supple.

As she walked ahead into the living-room, her hips swayed a little, bringing back another memory of long ago.

"Drinks," Deon said cheerfully. He slapped his hands together and busied himself at a discreet cabinet below a bookcase filled with new bestsellers. "Darling?"

"I'll . . . a sherry, I think." She turned back to Philip, her bright social smile carefully in place. "I got in some Canadian rye when Deon phoned to say you were coming. But anything else, if you prefer."

"Rye will be fine, thank you." He would have preferred a lighter drink.

"Ice?" Deon asked. "Water?"

"On the rocks."

They sipped at their drinks and were silent. The awkward moment had come.

"I enjoyed your lecture," Deon said finally. "The parts I could understand, anyway." He was aware of being a shade breathless and spoke more slowly, so that the conventional words gained unusual weight and substance. "Everyone was very impressed." He gave a light laugh. "I'm a bit worried that one of these days we surgeons will be out of a job."

Elizabeth laughed too and said, with an air of exaggerated bewilderment: "I looked up your subject in the encyclopedia this afternoon, Philip, so that I wouldn't sound too stupid. But about all I learned was that fruit flies breed at a fantastic rate."

"We won't go beyond the fruit flies," Philip promised. This time they all laughed and settled into their seats a little, as if they felt easier in one another's company.

Soon Deon poured fresh drinks, a little heavy-handedly, and they continued to make practiced conversation. After a time Elizabeth left them to supervise the final preparation of their meal. Philip refused a third drink, but Deon poured himself a stiff whisky, almost absent-mindedly, and returned to the other end of the room. He did not sit down but, glass in hand, leaned casually against the mantelpiece and looked down at Philip with a slight smile.

"Well, Professor," he said finally.

"Well, Professor," Philip echoed in the same gently mocking tone, and ease was almost restored.

"Who would have thought it, eh? Would you have thought it, forty years ago, when we were brats on the farm? And now, as the story goes, both of us are famous and rich. Are you rich, Philip?"

"No."

Deon laughed. "Neither am I."

"You could have fooled me." Philip looked round pointedly at the superbly furnished room.

"Elizabeth," Deon said. "She's a genius at picking up things before they become fashionable." He sipped at his whisky. "You were married, weren't you?"

"Yes."

"An actress, wasn't she?" Deon persisted in the face of Philip's obvious reluctance.

"A model."

Deon finished his drink and walked to the liquor cabinet to get another. Halfway there he changed his mind and returned to the fireplace. He put his empty glass down carefully on the mantelpiece. "Was she Canadian?"

"French. Not French-Canadian. French. She was born in Marseilles."

"But you met her in Canada?"

"Yes. She went there because it was next door to the States, and that was where she really wanted to be. Hollywood. She had her eyes set on Hollywood, and Canada was just a stepping stone. So was I."

The meal was splendid: a crayfish bisque followed by thin wafers of sautéed veal and ham, served with asparagus and ratatouille. They drank wine sparingly and talked of the comparative merits of South African and Continental wines. They discovered similar tastes in food and restaurants and cities and disregarded the few points of disagreement. The maid, schooled by Elizabeth during the afternoon, showed no surprise at having to serve someone of her own race.

They returned to the living room for coffee. At the door Deon hesitated. Then he turned away toward the hall telephone. "I must phone the hospital about that child. Won't you please carry on?"

Elizabeth preceded Philip into the room. Their eyes met briefly as she bent over the coffee tray.

"Black or white?"

"Black, if you please."

They could hear Deon in the hallway, dialing, then banging down the receiver and dialing again.

"What are your plans?" she asked.

There was a fragrance of freshly made coffee.

"I'm not altogether sure," he said. "My mother is dying, you know. When she's gone there will be nothing to keep me here. Then I suppose I'll go back to Canada."

Deon was still dialing and mumbling to himself.

"I'm sorry to hear that," Elizabeth said softly.

"I know what you won't miss once you're out of this bloody country," Deon shouted from the hall.

Philip and Elizabeth looked around together.

"You won't miss our fantastic telephone service. I've now tried about half a dozen times to get through to the hospital. Twice I've been connected to a very irritable old dame and otherwise all I get are engaged signals. I wonder how much time is wasted every day with busy lines, crossed lines and wrong numbers."

Elizabeth turned back to Philip, raising her eyebrows. Neither of them spoke until Deon came back to the living room and poured himself a cognac.

Philip declined brandy and glanced surreptitiously at his watch. And so the evening would have ended, at a quarter past ten, a good time to end a pleasant social evening with nothing much said. Three adults had enjoyed one another's company, an obligation had been fulfilled, and now they could part, most probably never to meet again. Except that Deon leaned forward and swirled the amber liquid in its glass and lifted it to his nose and said: "My father wanted to see you before he died. I never told you that. It was the last thing he said before he died."

At first Philip said nothing, scarcely showed that he had heard. He sat upright, hands resting lightly on his knees, staring at the empty grate (late summer still; no evening chill to cause a need for fires; the cold still months ahead in the future) as if watching the play of invisible flames.

"I imagine you know the reason," Deon said.

Philip considered. "Yes."

Their eyes brushed, then slid aside.

"I've thought about it often over the years," Deon said. "How long had you known?"

Philip frowned. "Thinking back now, my mother said things which should have made me suspicious. She'd say things like 'You don't have to struggle like this' or 'If you had your rights you wouldn't have to wear these old clothes.' That sort of thing. You know."

"Yes."

"She never said anything outright. It was only when I examined your blood that the penny dropped."

"What do you mean, examined my blood?"

"It was at the time of the so-called chromosome breakthrough. The professor asked me to have a go at perfecting the technique to obtain high quality karyotypes."

"What on earth is that?" Elizabeth asked.

Philip pulled at his ear lobe and looked at her. "Well, essentially it is just a photograph of chromosomes as seen through a high-powered microscope."

She smiled slightly. "I see."

"Well, as you can imagine, I had to start from scratch as nobody in the laboratory knew much about it. I did trial runs on blood taken from laboratory staff and when there were no volunteers, my own blood. At first I was only interested in getting the technique taped. After that I began to study the results more closely, and that's when I noticed something wrong with one of my chromosomes. It had an unusually long arm."

"Did you compare it with others?" Deon asked.

"Yes, and I really got worried when the professor could not explain the abnormality. As I have said, in those days no one in the department knew much about the whole thing. Anyhow, he sent the picture to a friend in Oxford for an opinion. I spent three weeks in a cold sweat thinking I had inherited something terrible, and then the reply came. Nothing to worry about."

"What was it?"

"It was a normal congenital variant. Naturally, I was enormously relieved and forgot about it till the day I had a look at your blood."

"When was that?" Deon asked in surprise.

"Don't you remember? It was one night when I bumped into you at the bungalow and we went down to the lab where I used to work and took some of your blood."

The memory returned as if a shutter had sprung open.

"Of course," Deon said. "That's quite right. One evening. After . . ." He hesitated, then glanced at Elizabeth. "It was the evening after we . . . the evening . . ." He shrugged and turned back to Philip. "And I suppose you found the same long-armed chromosome in my blood?"

"Yes, Deon."

"And in my . . ." Again Deon checked. He looked fully and frankly at Philip. "In our father's blood too? While he was in hospital?"

"Yes, I could not rest until I knew the truth."

"The long arm of coincidence, you might call it." Deon laughed aloud at the sheer inanity of the phrase. Then he shook his head wonderingly. "It still seems . . . so incredible. Anyway, at least he tried to make amends at the end."

Philip was silent, looking away. Then he said quietly: "I was never bitter about it. Although I felt the unfairness. It's hard not to be recognized. But you learn to accept it in a way. I suppose." He turned to contemplate one of the paintings on the wall, in which much had been made of the blue shadows on dark skin.

They were silent for a long time.

"Nevertheless," Philip said eventually, "those were good days."

Deon, sharing the need to change the subject, but unwilling to let it go altogether, said eagerly: "They were marvelous days on the farm. All this didn't matter then. It doesn't make any difference to children."

Philip was still examining the painting.

"Perhaps not. Although you have to be on the other side to see it fully, you know. But that wasn't really what I meant. I was thinking especially of that first year in the hospital. The year we were housemen."

"Yes. You met Robby again today. Do you remember Robby and the carol singers?"

Philip laughed. "Yes."

"Carol singers?" Elizabeth asked.

"The time he joined them," Deon told her.

"I've never heard about that."

"Well, you know what Robby was like, what he still is like. The responsibilities of being a doctor have never exactly overawed him."

"Robby's a clown," she said firmly. "Sometimes he's not as funny as he thinks he is."

"Do you want to hear the story?"

"Yes, go on."

Deon's smile was strained. "The nurses have carol singing each Christmas Eve," he said. "All of them who're off-duty—and probably those who don't have a date—dress in their uniforms and they carry candles like a lot of Florence Nightingales and they go round the wards singing Christmas carols. Usually a couple of sisters go with them. Well, Robby bet he could join the procession without being spotted. And he would sing too."

They all laughed. Deon continued, more animatedly. "So Robby prepared himself for the performance. He got hold of a wig, a nurse's uniform, cape, shoes, cap, the works. Even false eyelashes. So on Christmas Eve he dressed and made up his face and fortified himself with a couple of brandies and then he sneaked up to the sluice room and waited there among the bedpans."

"I can imagine," Elizabeth said. She was smiling and the tight, over-controlled look had gone from her eyes.

"The singers were just waking up the patients for the umpteenth time with 'Silent Night' when Robby slipped out of the sluice room and joined them. He got a couple of odd looks, but some of the girls were in on the joke and they masked him from the others."

"And did he sing?" Elizabeth asked.

"I think he decided not to push his luck too far. He just moved his lips in time with the music. Mimed it."

"And then there was that business in the chapel," Philip said.

"That's right. That wasn't the end of it," Deon told Elizabeth. "When they'd gone right through the hospital all the little angels went on to the chapel for the midnight service. That year there happened to be a young Catholic priest and Robby got a seat right under his eyes. Halfway through the service Robby gave the priest a wink."

Elizabeth's smiled broadened.

"Well, the priest couldn't believe his eyes, and he looked away. But Robby could see that he was watching out of the corner of his eye. So he fluttered his eyelashes and licked his lips in a sexy sort of way and pushed out his falsies and the poor priest went just about incoherent. I don't think he knew whether he was with Genesis or Revelation. And he just couldn't look away."

"Apparently he was absolutely hypnotized," Philip said. "Like a bird with a snake."

"And finally Robby started showing a bit of leg," Deon said. "Whenever it looked as if the priest might be gaining control of himself old Robby would hitch his skirt just a bit more. And the sermon ended just there."

After a momentary hesitation Elizabeth joined in the laughter.

"Poor chap," she said.

"Yes," Philip said.

They were briefly, reflectively silent.

"Anyway, those were good days," Philip said.

Deon was anxious to keep the joke going. "Do you remember the notice board in the Nurses' Home? The things the guys used to stick on it! What was that one about the virgins?"

"I can't quite remember."

"Oh, yes, something like this: 'There will be a meeting of all the virgins —in the telephone booth tonight.' "

Philip smiled and then there was an awkward pause which Deon felt compelled to break.

"How long do you expect to be in South Africa?"

Philip shrugged. "I have six months from my university. But it all depends on . . . well, you know."

"Yes. I should have gone to see your mother long ago." Deon knew that he was trying too hard to be properly sympathetic, and was conscious of clumsiness. "It's funny that both your mother and my . . . my father had to . . ."

"It's not funny, really."

"I don't mean funny in that sense. I meant . . ."

"I know what you meant. But it's no coincidence. Old people. You know."

"When do you think they'll find a cure for cancer?" Deon asked, to fill the void. "There is so much research going on but they don't seem to get anywhere."

Philip pursed his lips. "I wouldn't say that. We are learning more and more all the time, especially about the pathogenesis."

"Pathogenesis, what's that?" Elizabeth asked with sharp interest.

"Well, literally translated it means: genesis—the beginning; and patho—disease. The beginning of the disease. For example, it has been shown that certain viruses play an important part in tumor formation, at least in animals."

"Really? Do you think they will develop a vaccine against cancer, like we have for smallpox?"

Philip gave a small, dry laugh. "It's possible, once we can isolate the virus."

"How do you think the virus affects the cell?" Deon asked.

"Let's start at the beginning. What is a cancer? It is uncontrolled growth, that's all," Philip explained with patience. "And, what is a virus? It is either a piece of DNA or RNA. The same chemical material that controls division and growth of normal cells. These so-called nucleic acids have the plan for the construction of the next cell, in other words. Do you follow?"

"I think so," Deon said. Elizabeth was silent.

"Presumably what happens where a virus causes a tumor is that it enters and links up with the genetic information of that cell. This, in turn, interferes with the control of cell division. The cell growth now goes haywire. And there you have a cancer."

"Isn't that an oversimplification?" Deon asked.

"Maybe. But, you know there's a lot of evidence to support the virus theory. It has been known for a long time that in the fowl and mouse, leukemia can be transferred from one animal to another by viral particles. There is also reason to believe that abnormal chromosomes are in some ways associated with leukemia. I don't know whether you have read about the Philadelphia chromosome?"

"Just in passing. I don't recall the data clearly."

"They found an abnormal chromosome in ninety percent of the patients suffering from a certain type of leukemia. What is more, mongols and people who have been exposed to irradiation, as you know, run an increased risk of developing leukemia, and they have abnormal chromosomes. So you see, the evidence is building up."

"That's interesting," Deon said and then he thought for a while. "Father died of leukemia, and we all three have abnormal chromosomes!"

The outside door banged and all three of them were silent and turned to look. For a moment there was no further sound. Then a woman laughed.

Philip, startled, caught the swift glance which passed between the other two. He had been listening attentively to the exchanges between husband and wife, noting the lack of ease and wondering whether his own presence was the sole cause. Until now, however, neither of them had made him feel like an outsider.

As Elizabeth crossed to the door, the woman outside laughed again and, a moment later, came down the shallow flight of steps from the hallway.

The first impression was of hair: a tangled, streaky-blond, uncombed and, clearly, unwashed mass of it. Defiant brown eyes glared at them briefly from under it. Then the girl looked away with a shrug and once more uttered that laugh which was simultaneously scornful and vacuous.

"My daughter," Deon said tightly.

"Come and meet Professor Davids," Elizabeth told the girl. Her voice was gentle, but Philip could detect apprehension.

The girl continued to stand at the head of the steps. She wore a long, loose-fitting dress of dark material with much-stained embroidery at the breast. There were fringes on the skirt and on her shawl. Philip had seen the type in enclaves of the young and reckless in cities all over the world. He had not thought to see it here, in this house.

"This is Lisa, Philip," Elizabeth said, turning. Her smile was firmly in place.

"Hello, Lisa," he said gently.

The girl focused on him finally and her eyes widened in glad astonishment.

"Wow, man, like brown, man!"

Elizabeth bit her lip and Deon made an awkward, groping movement.

But the girl's tone had been so disarming, so spontaneous and genuine, that Philip was moved.

"I'm brown," he said, and smiled at her.

She bent forward at the waist, leaning over the guard rail toward him.

"I dig brown, man," she told him with passion.

"Do you?"

"Yes, man. It's like . . ." She reached both hands toward the ceiling and looked upward. ". . . like the sun." An anxious expression came to her face. "Do you dig the sun?"

"Lisa," Elizabeth said quietly.

"I like the sun," Philip told the girl.

She gave him a flashing, fervent smile and tossed the wild hair backward; then she was gone. He heard the slap of her bare feet on the tiles in the hall.

Elizabeth returned to her seat. Deon was fussing with the cognac bottle. There was a long, uncomfortable silence.

"You have other children?" Philip asked at last. "A son, not so?"

"Etienne," Deon said. His voice was raw and he coughed to clear his throat, then added: "He's away at present."

"He's younger than Lisa?"

"Yes. He's fifteen."

Philip thought the girl had been seventeen or eighteen, and did the calculation quickly: so Deon had been about twenty-seven when she was born. They hadn't waited long before getting married. Soon after he himself had . . . left. Young to marry, for a would-be surgeon. He looked at his watch again.

"It's very late. Would you call a taxi for me, please?"

"Good heavens, no. I'll take you home," Deon offered.

Philip was adamant. "My mother is right out on the Cape Flats. It'll take you hours there and back. And you have to operate tomorrow."

Despite Deon's protests he could not be dissuaded. Elizabeth served more coffee and they drank it and made desultory conversation while they waited for the taxi. At last headlights flashed on the window as the vehicle made its turn down in the street. The driver honked impatiently and they made hurried farewells on the terrace. Deon escorted Philip to the bottom gate. They shook hands, somewhat formally, then Philip went across to the waiting taxi, raising an arm in final greeting.

Deon saw the driver lean over his seat to open the back door. Philip hunched his shoulders, preparatory to climbing into the car. But the driver said something to him and he stopped, straightening up slowly. He stepped up to the driver's window. The taxi man flung his hands upward and outward in a decisive, dismissive gesture.

Frowning, Deon approached.

"What's wrong?"

Philip's voice was cool and toneless.

"This . . . gentleman . . . tells me he is not allowed to convey me. His taxi is reserved for Whites only."

Deon saw the illuminated sign on the taxi roof proclaiming this fact.

"This is absurd," he said angrily. He stooped to glare at the driver. "What kind of nonsense is this?"

The taxi driver was a young, tough-looking man in a leather jacket with steel studs along the seams. Despite his tough exterior he seemed embarrassed. He repeated that abrupt, responsibility-avoiding gesture.

"You shoulda said you wanted a non-White taxi," he said plaintively. "They only allow me to drive Whites."

Somehow the apologetic tone made Deon even angrier than if the man had been insolent.

"Do you know who I am?"

"Yes, Doctor," the driver said. He would not meet Deon's eyes.

"This is Professor Davids, who is a world-famous doctor from Canada."

"I can't help it, Doctor," the man said with weak stubbornness. "You shoulda said it was for a non-White. They'll take away my license." He fumbled awkwardly with the ignition key, then added, in great earnestness: "It's the law, man. I mean, Doctor."

"Damn the bloody law!"

"Deon," Philip said, still in that cool, untroubled voice.

Deon turned to him helplessly. "Jesus, Philip. I don't know what to say."

"Oh, well." In the half dark it was still impossible to make out anything of Philip's expression. "As he says, it's the law."

The young man in the leather jacket coughed. "Sixty-five cents," he said. "What?"

"Sixty-five cents for the call." The taxi driver sounded slightly aggressive now. "I had to come all the way up here from the rank for nothing."

Deon pulled some money out of a pocket and flung it through the open window. He still felt guilty. He should have remembered the rules about taxi apartheid and insisted on taking Philip home. But the gesture was somehow cathartic.

"Would you telephone for another taxi?" Philip asked him. And, with lightly ironic emphasis: "One with the right color."

"No," Deon said brusquely. He walked up the slope of the driveway. "I'm taking you home. No arguments."

Philip hesitated, then submitted with a shrug.

When they climbed into the Jaguar the inside light came on once more. Deon glanced quickly at Philip. But if the incident had disturbed the other man, he showed no sign of it. Perhaps his mask had slipped, in the dark. Now it was in place again.

Two

Deon's measure of a patient's state of health was the number and timing of the telephone calls he received while away from the hospital. The most dreaded summons of all was the relentless cricket-chirp of the phone beside his bed in the early hours of the morning. His night staff called him only in a real emergency.

There had been no calls last night so, presumably, the mitral annuloplasty was recovering well. Nevertheless he was tense. He looked in at the Intensive Care Unit, just in case, but there were no problems. Trying to suppress the nagging feeling of doubt and unease he crossed to the operating block and turned into the dressing room.

As he was changing one of the heart-lung technicians came to the toilet.

"Morning, Prof."

Deon turned.

"Hello, Martin. How far have they got?"

The technician had his hand on the toilet door handle, as if he was in a hurry.

"They're still opening up."

"For God's sake! It's past ten. What are they doing? It keeps getting later and later."

The technician glanced at him apprehensively. "They had trouble putting up an arterial line. Doctor Moorhead had to cut down on the radial artery." He ducked into the toilet to avoid further interrogation.

Inside the operating room Peter Moorhead was cutting the sternum with a pair of broad-bladed scissors. Deon peered over the sterile barrier between the anesthetist and surgeon.

"Why're you using scissors?" he asked sharply.

Peter's quick glance was a duplicate of the technician's. "The saw has packed up again." He pointed at the sternotomy saw with its blood-stained blades lying uselessly in a basin.

Deon glared at the theater sister, who turned away to fiddle with the instruments on her trolley. Her back was rigid.

"I suppose it's the same old story, sister," he said loudly. "It came back from the workshop only this morning and you tested it and of course it worked perfectly."

The woman swung round resentfully. "It's not my fault, Professor. We put in a requisition for a new saw months ago. But it has to go to tender."

Deon could feel the beating of his heart. "Next time this happens I am not going to continue with the operation. I'll close up the skin incision and send him back to the ward. I'll tell the parents I can't operate on their child because it takes a year to get an instrument costing four hundred rand."

The threat was empty and everyone knew it. But still none of them dared to meet his eyes.

Under Deon's critical gaze Peter Moorhead began to dissect away the thymus gland from the base of the heart sac, holding it up with dissecting forceps. Clearly Peter was upset as well. His hands were not functioning with their usual dexterity. Once he cut dangerously close to the left innominate vein, and Deon was about to make a sarcastic remark. But he saw Peter's eyes above the mask and controlled himself with an effort. It was better to get out of here now. He went through the scrub room to the adjoining theater where Robby was doing a patent ductus.

He had divided the ductus between two clamps and was closing the cut ends with a running 4-o silk suture. His assistant was holding the clamp incorrectly.

"Have you ever seen one of those clamps slip, Guido?" Deon asked.

The little Italian registrar looked up slowly, his eyebrows gathering in a puzzled frown. He shook his head.

"Well, pray that you never do," Deon said ominously. He snapped at the Italian: "Hold the blades of the clamps parallel, man! Look at the way the tips point toward each other."

Guido corrected the error hastily and Robby paused momentarily in his stitching. He did not look up, however.

After watching for a time Deon turned away. He could do nothing here. Robby had the situation well in hand. He went out, throwing down his mask and going down the corridor with long, purposeful strides, although he did not really know where he was going.

Presumably Peter Moorhead was having matrimonial trouble again. If that blasted woman wasn't careful she was going to ruin a fine career.

It was difficult not to carry your domestic problems to work with you. You couldn't just close the front door in the morning and leave them behind. He knew it only too well himself.

Still, he would have to speak to Peter. Perhaps there was something he could do to help. He disliked meddling, but if things went on like this Peter would be forced to resign. That would be a tragedy, for he was really a cool and competent surgeon.

Well, Deon thought in sudden anger, I'm damned if I'm going to lose a good man just because of the impossible woman he happened to marry. Why had he married her anyway? Anyone could see she was crazy.

He remembered one time when he had seen her in action. It was at a party he and Elizabeth had arranged for the heart team. Gillian Moorhead was obviously in a vixenish mood even before she arrived, for she had left her husband at once and attached herself firmly to Robby Robertson, the only bachelor in the room.

Robby had attempted a few uneasy jokes, but when they failed he began feeding her whisky. She downed it, neat except for ice and a few drops of water. When she spotted her husband on the opposite side of the room, talking to Colleen Blake, the senior theater sister, she thrust her drink into Robby's bewildered hands and stalked through the crowd like a bird of prey. She stopped beside her husband, said something to the nurse, and, as the girl began to turn, Gillian Moorhead slapped her across the face.

It should have been clear to anyone with eyes in his head that poor Colleen, with her square body, close-cropped hair, and gruff voice, was a lesbian. She was a superb scrub nurse, the best in the whole unit, and the staff respected her for this and tried as best they could to ignore her long-standing affair with one of the junior sisters at the main hospital. Colleen would no more flirt with a man than go into the theater without a mask.

Deon felt a sudden rush of pride for his unit. He had started it, moulded it; it was his creation. Most of the technicians, registrars, and surgeons had trained under him. He had seen them grow and develop. Some had learned quickly; others not. But they had all grown.

They were his team and he would always defend them, even if it meant falling out of favor with the hierarchy. He knew that this made him unpopular, but his standard reply was: "I'll start to worry when my patients start to complain about the way they are treated."

That was what it was all about, wasn't it? Strange how easily people forgot. They became entangled in their jealousies and obsessions and ambitions and forgot that everything about the hospital and everyone who worked in it, from the man who heaved coal into the boilers to the surgeon cutting into a living brain, existed solely because of the patients.

He thought bitterly about the latest bit of bureaucratic arrogance. He had been engaged in a prolonged battle to get two more technicians for the heart-lung machine. His technicians did not work by the clock. In emergencies they were called out at any hour.

He had fought with the administration to have his people paid better salaries than technicians who worked regular hours—or at least paid overtime. Some official had turned down this idea and suggested instead that the technicians be given extra days off. Obviously no one had troubled to look at the overloaded operating schedule.

He made a request to an ad hoc committee for additional staff. Two months had gone by and three reminders had been ignored. Yesterday the reply had come. There was no need for extra technicians. What was needed was better organization of the cardiac department.

He reached the end of the corridor and turned distractedly into the dressing room. He thought of how he would reply. He was only human, he would say. He realized he had failings. He was delighted to learn that someone in the administration was better qualified to run a cardiac unit. Would they please send this person along to show him how it should be done? The sooner the better.

He thought he would make a note of the letter before he forgot and opened his locker to get out a diary. As he did so a framed text that hung on the wall beside the window caught his eye. He had seen it there two or three times a week for months and years now, aware of it, yet hardly noticing. It had been a long time since last he had read the words and he stood beside the locker now, a hand still in the inside jacket pocket of his suit, and read them slowly to himself.

The text was a quotation from *The Surgeon and the Child* by Willis Potts. It read: "If this infant (on whom you are about to operate) could speak, it would beg imploringly of the surgeon: 'Please exercise the greatest gentleness with my miniature tissues and try to correct the deformity at the first operation. Give me blood and the proper amount of fluid and electrolytes; add plenty of oxygen to the anesthesia and I will show you that I can tolerate a terrific amount of surgery. You will be surprised at the speed of my recovery and I shall always be grateful to you.'"

He read it again, carefully, from beginning to end, then replaced the jacket inside the locker, closed its door and left the changing room.

The source of his nervous irritability was clear to him. In fact he had known it all along, but had refused to face it; had resolutely closed his mind to the thought.

He had told Philip about it the night before as they drove through quiet streets. They had been talking about Pamela Daley and her tragic, needless death. He had blamed himself for missing that extra defect and felt a dim need to justify himself, for he remembered saying angrily: "The guys who really get me are the nine-to-five doctors. All those guys who think disease takes a holiday outside working hours and at weekends. Surgeons are a different breed anyway."

"Do you think so?" Philip asked quietly. He had looked out at the dark avenue of trees that hid the golf course they were passing. "That's the Royal Cape, isn't it? I used to caddy there, after school."

Deon was silent, uncertain how he should respond. He remembered with discomfort that he had an appointment to play golf at the Royal Cape on Sunday, and that Philip, no matter what his status and merits, would still be welcome at the course only as a caddy.

Philip saved him by returning to the original subject.

"Why are you a different breed?" He laughed. "Always remembering that I am a bit of a nine-to-five doctor myself."

"Well, you're in another category," Deon said quickly. "Experimental work. That's something else altogether. When last did you see a patient?"

He sensed rather than saw Philip turn to look at him. Then the other man laughed again, brusquely. "Not for quite a few years. All right. Point taken."

"I think surgeons are more directly involved. They feel more personal responsibility for the patient's condition. Take the patient who's seen by a physician. He might be in a diabetic coma . . . well, his doctor will make the diagnosis and treat him, and if he dies, well that's tough. He tried his best, but no one can blame him for causing the disease."

"There are some pretty cold-blooded surgeons around too, you know."

"You don't see the point. The surgeon's approach is more urgent, because if he loses a patient he has himself to blame."

"Or maybe his ego is bigger."

Deon waved the remark aside. "Let me make my point. Take my own position. Let's say I'm going to do even a relatively simple operation. A V.S.D., say. Now before the op a child with a V.S.D. is usually in a reasonable condition. It can run around and play and so forth. So I operate and close the hole. It has to be done, else the child will run into trouble in later life. Nevertheless, immediately after surgery he is going to be damn sick and could even die. And I can't help knowing that I am personally responsible. I did it. With my own hands."

After a moment Philip said: "Yes. Yes, I can see that." He added thoughtfully: "It must be difficult to avoid getting emotional about these kids."

"I try to avoid it, but it crops up all the same. All the time."

"How do you avoid it?"

"I try to have as little contact with them as possible beforehand. The heart clinic does all the preliminary work and I hardly ever know what's coming up until the surgery meeting. The first time I see a child is on the day before the op. Even then I keep my examination as brief as I can."

Philip nodded, then pointed ahead as they approached an intersection. "You know the way?"

"Ja." Deon spun the wheel and the Jaguar slipped easily round the corner. For a while he concentrated on driving. Then he said: "But it doesn't always work."

"Not?"

"I'm afraid not. I'm doing a V.S.D. tomorrow; that's probably what reminded me. Well, this kid said something to me which really got me."

"What did she say?" Philip had asked.

A nurse, big-eyed above her mask, touched Deon's arm diffidently. He jerked round and she took a couple of involuntary steps away from him.

"Doctor Moorhead, Professor."

He tried to control himself, but his voice was still rough.

"What about him?"

"He says he is almost ready for you, Professor."

He nodded and then walked out ahead of her, back to the operating room.

The anesthetist silently made place for him and he looked down at the table again, at the steadily pulsing heart. And again he remembered what the child had said to him.

Her name was Marietjie and she was eight years old. As usual he had avoided seeing her until the previous afternoon, and even then everything had gone as normal. Regular pulse. No unusual pulsation of the veins or arteries of the neck. She had red hair and freckles and a snub nose and she submitted impassively to the examination.

The bulge on the left of the chest, indicating that the heart was enlarged, was clearly visible, as was a persistent right ventricular thrust.

He smiled encouragingly at the little girl and put a hand on her chest, then glanced at Peter Moorhead on the far side of the bed and lifted his eyebrows slightly.

He had left his stethoscope behind and there was a quick rush to present him with one. A houseman managed to win the race and smiled embarrassedly when Deon thanked him with a quick nod.

Very distinct blowing murmur during each systole. He could hear it best just to the left of the sternum and in the fourth intercostal space. Farther up, in the pulmonary area, he could hear the splitting of the second heart sound, with a very loud second component.

Pretty straightforward. The murmur, of course, was caused by the shunting of blood through the hole between the two ventricles. Besides receiving their normal supply of blood the lungs were overfilled by the shunted blood. This caused the loud pulmonary valve sound.

An assistant fumbled with the X-ray viewer, hunting for its switch on the wrong side, and finally Deon took the plate from him irritably and held it up against the window light. He traced the enlarged outline of the heart with a finger.

"Blood okay?" he asked the ward doctor.

"All normal, Professor. The urine results are okay too."

"Fine."

Deon looked directly at the child's face for the first time. Shrewd green eyes had been watching him intently. She wasn't as impassive as she looked.

How much did she know?

He winked, to reassure her. At once her eyes softened.

"You're Doctor van der Riet," she announced.

"That's right. And you're Marietjie."

"Yes," she agreed solemnly. Suddenly she smiled and lifted herself onto her elbows and told him, as if sharing a fascinating secret: "I've got a broken heart."

"She said to me: 'I've got a broken heart,' " Deon told Philip.

Philip made a grunting sound of understanding.

"It really got me," Deon said. "I've got an uneasy feeling about that op tomorrow."

They passed under a streetlight and Philip turned to look at him quizzically. "Why? Are there problems? Complications?"

"No. Nothing wrong. I've done . . . well, heck . . . probably two hundred or more V.S.D.'s in the last couple of years. It's just that . . . oh, I'm probably just a bit on edge. Losing that child last night." Deon hesitated. Then, facing stiffly ahead, he added: "And Lisa doesn't make it any easier for us."

Philip's reply was unhurried. "I think you have a very sweet daughter."

Deon searched the words for hidden meanings then, finding none, became more easy.

"Perhaps. I suppose so. I suppose she is quite a sweet child, really. But this hippie business. And I'm pretty sure she's using drugs too. What the hell can you do? Argument is no good. There's no reasoning with these kids. She simply refuses to discuss it. So what do you do? Lock her up? Hand her over to the police? God knows."

"It's difficult."

Deon smiled tightly. "Difficult is about the right word for it."

They were silent for a time, looking ahead to where the headlights shone briefly and repetitively on high fences and tall hedges which hid houses and gardens. This was a cloistered, guarded suburb for moderately wealthy whites. The Coloured townships started close beyond its border, and this, perhaps, was the reason for its almost paranoic air of closeness and secrecy.

"Thank God we still have Etienne, anyway," Deon said then, "Even if he isn't our own child."

"Not your own . . . ?"

"He's adopted."

"I see."

"And it's sad to have to say this about one's own child, but he is everything Lisa is not."

Philip watched him without speaking.

"Everything," Deon said again, emphatically. "He's good at school. Brilliant, actually. That's why he's away. He's in Johannesburg taking part in a mathematics olympiad. He's gifted at languages and he's good at sports. Not fantastic, but good. He was head boy at his primary school. He gets on with people and he knows how to lead them. He's a thoroughly decent boy. Lisa is a drop-out."

He shook his head wearily. "It's only by a sheer miracle that Etienne is alive, you know. He was premature, born at just over seven months after an attempted abortion."

"What!"

"Incredible, isn't it? A G.P. I got to know when I was surgical registrar handled the business. Apparently this young woman and her boyfriend went to him, asking him to do it. But she was already at thirty-two weeks, so naturally he refused. A couple of days later she was back, in strong labor. Obviously she'd attempted the abortion herself. At that stage the fetal heart was not audible and he told her that the child was dead. She was relieved. Anyway, this doctor delivered the infant and to his dismay it made weak attempts to breathe. He thought it would die soon, so he wrapped the baby in an old sweater and left it in his consulting rooms overnight."

"Good lord!"

"Yes, indeed. Well, it wouldn't die. The next day it was still alive and he got panicky and gave me a call. He knew Liz and I were looking for a boy to adopt. You see, after Lisa was born, Liz just could not get pregnant again. So, eventually the gynecologist suggested we should adopt a child, maybe that would help. Anyway, Liz brought the baby home while I went to town to try and get the adoption arranged. When I got home that evening, she said she was worried about the baby and showed him to me. At first I thought he was dead. He was ice cold, blue, and hardly breathing, and I told her: "You haven't got a baby there; you've got a corpse." We rushed the child to the Children's Hospital and got it on intravenous feeding and into an incubator. It was touch and go, but he survived. Liz tended the child herself for a whole month. She slept right next to that incubator. We took him home at three months and even then he only weighed four and a half pounds."

"But that's absolutely unbelievable."

"Isn't it?"

The barricading fences were behind them now and the houses alongside the road were smaller. They passed an occasional fruit stall with a board above it proclaiming its Malay ownership, or small shops with heavy steel-mesh burglar grates over their display windows.

"How is your mother taking it?" Deon asked. "Does she know?"

"She knows. But she's always been . . . well, fatalistic about things. That's her attitude to life. And, of course, she's very happy to have me at home."

"Yes. After all these years.

"Is she fairly active anyway?" Deon asked.

Philip gave a grudging laugh.

"Far too much so. I wanted to get her a servant, someone to help her just while I'm here. But no. Flat refusal. If she can't run her own house, she might as well die tomorrow."

"My mother has . . . had that way of thinking too. But of course, with the stroke . . ." Deon pulled up his shoulders.

Philip sat erect, peering ahead through the windscreen. "Next street to the left," he said. "And then left again at the end of the block."

They drew up at the house he indicated. It was small, like the others, and basically similar in design. There was a streetlight directly outside, shining on a cheerful and tidily kept garden beyond a neat brick wall.

"Thank you once again," Philip said. "And for bringing me. It was kind of you." He pulled open the door catch, then hesitated. "Would you like to come in for a moment? My mother would like to see you."

Deon was caught unaware. "Well, I . . . well, it's probably a bit late for her, isn't it? And I have a heavy day tomorrow."

Philip's face showed neither regret nor relief. "Of course," he said easily. He opened the door. "Good." He smiled briefly at Deon. "I hope everything goes well tomorrow."

He stood at the garden gate until the Jaguar pulled away, and Deon, glancing into the rear view mirror, saw him open the gate, then vanish behind a row of shrubs.

Deon felt instant regret at having refused what, after a moment's consideration, had clearly been a genuine invitation. Damn fool, he told himself. Think how the man must feel. Aren't you the big-hearted liberal hero, asking a Coloured to your house for dinner. And then when he asks you to his house in return, it's not good enough for you.

He took the corner too fast, so that the tires squealed on the asphalt.

It wasn't really a question of race, he decided. It had been a long and difficult day: a child dying and the bitter discovery of what had caused her death; a long operation this morning; the lecture this afternoon; the dinner party with its own tensions. And yet. He should not have refused.

He was afraid to face a woman (an old woman now; but the fact that he was afraid remained) who had once been his father's mistress and who had borne his child.

Suddenly a detailed image of his own mother's face rose up in his mind. Her hair was beyond grayness now. Pure white and sparse, as if her scalp were covered with a fine layer of cotton wool. The stroke had left her right side paralyzed, so that her mouth was lopsided and her speech dragged. Yet her eyes followed wherever you moved.

I'll go to see her this weekend, he promised himself. And even as he made the vow he felt a twinge of repugnance he was unable to suppress.

How bitter to sit out the end of your life and face rejection, he thought. Take your place in that long queue, mother.

Take your place among the unwanted.

Her placid and undemanding face remained in his mind as he remembered exactly how it had been a year ago, when that telephone call came from his near-forgotten uncle.

He had been puzzled when his secretary announced a trunk call from a Mr. De Jager of Lichtenburg. Only when they had completed the ritual of greeting and counter-greeting, of: "How are you?" and "Fine, and how are you?" had he been able to place the gravelly, hesitant voice.

"Man, I hope you don't mind me telephoning," his uncle had said.

"No, of course not. Not at all," Deon had said with as much warmth and sincerity as he was able to muster.

"I know how busy you are," the old man insisted. "I read about you in the papers. Always operating and so on. Always traveling. I know how busy you are."

Deon tried gently to put an end to the rambling apology. "Was it about my mother, Uncle Pieter?"

"Your mother? Man, yes, it's about Magriet. Your mother. She's in hospital. I had to bring her in to Lichtenburg, to hospital."

"Hospital!" Deon was concerned and ashamed. Perhaps there had been more sting in the old man's apology than he had perceived. When had he last seen his mother? Three or four years ago when she was visiting relatives in Pretoria and he happened to be in that city for a medical congress. And before that? A couple of years as well. He had visited her at his uncle's small Western Transvaal farm only once, to make the half-hearted suggestion that she should move to the Cape to make her home with him and Elizabeth. He had expressed conventional regret when she refused. But perhaps it was best that way. She would not really fit into the lives he and Elizabeth had made for themselves. So he had given her a check for a hundred rand and left her with her brother.

She had asked to see her granddaughter, however. Lisa had just started school at the time, so they had waited for the winter holidays and then Elizabeth had taken the child to the farm. The visit had not been a success. Elizabeth had been bored and the old people spoiled the child and finally Lisa became bored too, for there was little to do on the farm with its dilapidated little trading store where Africans from the neighboring asbestos mine came to buy blankets and pipe tobacco and cheap sweets. The following year they went to America. They had never returned to the farm.

"Why is she in hospital?"

"Man, she had a stroke last night. We were just sitting down at table when she complained about this headache, and then it got worse so we thought she'd better go and lie down and . . ."

"Yes, yes," Deon interrupted impatiently. "But how is she?"

"Man, she's in hospital, but the doctor doesn't really say anything. She's lame on the one side. She can hardly talk, but she asked for you."

"I'll come up to Lichtenburg right away," Deon promised.

He had managed to get a seat on the Boeing to Jan Smuts that afternoon and had been met at the airport by a girl from the car rental service and had driven over the rolling Transvaal hills in the yellow light of early evening. He reached the town after dark and drove directly to the hospital. His mother was awake, although she had been sedated. She was waiting for him. She had waited for him all day.

Elizabeth had driven up on her own in the station wagon two days later. Quite clearly the old woman could not return to the farm. She had suffered a moderately severe cerebral thrombosis and the prognosis was uncertain, according to the harassed country G.P. (slightly nervous, face to face with an internationally known surgeon). He would not advise her being moved at this stage, but in any event she would probably need intensive care for a while after being discharged. Deon's uncle was not far short of eighty and his wife only a year or two younger. They could not be expected to shoulder the burden of an invalid.

Deon had telephoned Boet, who was then selling agricultural machinery in the Eastern Province. He proposed that they should share the responsibility; that their mother should spend half a year with each of them in turn.

The conversation did not go well. His brother was reluctant to become involved. He could not come up to Lichtenburg right now, he said aloofly. He was working on a big sale of tractors and he couldn't just drop things. Nor did he really know if he could offer the old lady a home. He and Liselle had been talking of giving up the house anyway. A flat would be more sensible, seeing that he was out of town most of the week.

"Well, then I'll take her," Deon said at last, angrily.

"I think that would be best," Boet said, unperturbed. He added, with ill-disguised envy: "You're the doctor and you have got that nice big house, so it won't be any trouble for you."

Elizabeth had been amazingly good about it all. She had stayed on in Lichtenburg after Deon had to return to the Cape and had visited the pale, shriveled old woman at the hospital twice a day, every day. Three weeks later Deon had returned and they had driven his mother home to Cape Town.

In fact Elizabeth had been marvelous throughout the whole thing. Probably they felt guilty about having neglected the old woman for so long and for what had been done to her years before. They both felt guilt, but it was Elizabeth who had been obliged to work at atonement for sins they never discussed.

It had not been easy. His mother was not a demanding patient, but even so there was little she could do to help herself. She was installed in the spare bedroom, where there was morning sun and a view of the harbor and the sea. She had to be dressed and bathed and fed. They installed an electric bell for her, but there were occasions when Elizabeth or the servant did not hear it ringing, or when it failed, and then the old woman would soil her bedclothes and lie there, gray-faced and ashamed, until someone came to change her linen.

Deon had seen what it was doing to Elizabeth; had noticed her flinch when the imperious bell shrilled twice in one hour; had seen the new haggard look on her face; had been concerned about her short way with Etienne, fourteen then, and with adolescent problems of his own. He had tried once to discuss it, but she had been blunt and bitter. It had been a long time since they had really talked about anything and perhaps they had lost the ability to do so. This was sad, when you came to think about it. But they did not bother about it unduly, for they were both busy people who lived crowded lives. So there it was.

Then his mother solved the issue herself by falling out of bed while reaching for the Bible at her bedside. When they helped her up she complained that her hip was hurting.

Deon had waited with the Casualty officer while the radiographer developed the X-ray, pacing impatiently to the window and back, turning each time to the motionless figure on the trolley, to give his mother a comforting smile or a little pat on the shoulder. The girl came in with the plate still wet and smelling of fixer and he examined it and saw the fracture at the neck of the femur. He realized with horror and self-disgust that he had hoped to find it there, for then his mother would have to be admitted to the wards.

As punishment he forced himself to stay with her the whole night. The next day he was tense and irritable in the theater and that night Elizabeth and he had a row about nothing in particular. But two days later they went out to a restaurant and later when they were home they made love tenderly and with real fondness for the first time in months.

Afterward they lay with only the sheet covering them, bodies contentedly touching, and he said: "I think we'll have to try to get my mother into a home."

"I think that would be wise," Elizabeth had said.

Even then it was not easy. He mentioned the subject to his mother, in elaborately casual tones, a week before she was due to return home.

"I went out to the place myself yesterday," he told her. "It's beautiful. Lovely and sunny. You'll make lots of friends there."

"Yes," she had agreed mildly. Then she started to weep, soundlessly, and turned her face away so that he should not see her weeping.

On his next visit she reported with excited triumph that she had been able to move the fingers of her right hand that morning, and insisted on demonstrating.

"One of these days you'll be quite all right again," he said to humor her.

"Yes. Then you can get rid of that maid and I'll do the housework."

He laughed and she watched his face eagerly. But something had shown on his face, for the eagerness faded and her eyes seemed to film over, like those of the newly dead.

She made no further protest, and when the day came for her to leave the hospital she let the nurse wheel her outside to the car quite docilely. Deon had her handful of possessions in a suitcase in the back and she wanted a knitted shawl round her shoulders against the cold, although it was a warm day. The nurse and he helped her into the car and he folded her wheelchair and stored it in the trunk. As he turned onto the freeway toward the old-age home, he felt as if he were driving a hearse.

He became aware that Peter Moorhead was staring at him, waiting for some word.

He looked down at the opened chest again, within its neat square of drapes. Beating inside the opening was the right ventricle, in which he would presently make an incision and start to patch Marietjie's broken heart.

It's simply another surgical problem, he reminded himself. You've done this many times before. Don't get yourself worked up. Forget about trusting eyes of whatever kind or age. Forget white hair and a claw-stiff right hand working with slow perseverance to make itself supple and thus prove, without real hope, that it may still serve. Forget your mother. Forget a freckled, snub-nosed face and the unknowing, uncaring faith of youth. Forget Marietjie.

"Okay," he said. "Carry on. I'll scrub now."

Three

He moved, almost mechanically, to his customary basin on the far left. He always scrubbed at the same basin, just as he always took the same road from home on operating days and always said a brief prayer as he drove toward the hospital. (He imagined that his father would have approved of the praying while at the same time appreciating the irony: that his son, the cold scientist who had dismissed religion as self-deluding nonsense, should turn to it for solace during his work in the cause of science.) Once at the hospital, he always parked in the same space; went in through the non-White entrance; turned to the left at the elevators and went up the stairs on the "Whites Only" side. He followed this unvarying routine not so much from superstition—although, to be frank, there was an element of it; he was afraid of what might happen if, some morning, he should forget and take an unlucky road by mistake—as to build his confidence.

He turned on the swivel taps and mixed the water till it ran warm. He soaked his hands and forearms, enjoying the feel of the water against his skin. Then he reached for a brush in the bin next to him. He soaped his hands and arms and began to scrub his left palm. Something was different, but he was thinking about the operation to come and did not take it in at first.

He thought briefly that this must be how a boxer felt before the fight, bouncing on his toes in the dressing room, working his shoulder muscles and thinking about his opponent, about his strengths and weaknesses. He, too, knew the tactics that might be used against him: hemorrhage, heart block, ventricular fibrillation, and so on. Each blow, if not promptly countered, could bring about defeat.

With long strokes he began to scrub the inside of his left forearm. Then it registered. He stopped scrubbing and stared at the brush. He rinsed it under the running water and stared at it again. It was a new type, with a wooden backing instead of the plastic handle to which he was accustomed. He ran a soapy finger across the bristles. They were stiff and hard.

A junior nurse stood at his shoulder, holding a bottle of disinfectant, ready to pour it over his hands. He swung around toward her. "What the devil is this?"

She backed away, startled. He waved the wooden brush with its hard white bristles at her.

"These things aren't nail brushes! They're damned scrubbing brushes!"

"Yes, Professor." She was biting her lower lip. "I'm sorry, Professor."

"Where's sister?"

The little nurse put down the plastic bottle and scuttled out. Deon threw down the brush and went on soaping his hands and arms.

The theater supervisor was a tall, fattish woman with a look of permanent despair. As he had learned before, she was also completely unflappable.

"Can I help you, Professor?"

Deon was already feeling annoyed at himself for bellowing at the nurse, so he kept his voice deliberately mild. "These things are impossible, sister. They've got bristles like porcupine quills." He picked up another brush and showed her the angry red marks it left on his skin. "They're fine for scrubbing floors, I'd say. But I don't know who the devil put them here."

She sighed. "I told them they wouldn't do, Professor. This is what Supplies have sent us. I said they were no good. Shall I get the Super for you on the phone?"

He shook his head. "I have to go in. Never mind." He turned back to the basin, where the water was still running. "I'll take it up later, sister."

He finished scrubbing and then, trying hard not to show his anxiety, went through to the operating room. There was the faint smell of burning flesh from the bleeding points which had been cauterized. His arms were smarting from the scrubbing and the disinfectant. A nurse helped him into a gown and tied the tabs behind his back. He hardly noticed, for all his attention was with the patient on the table. The high-pitched beep . . . beep of the cardiac monitor was regular. About ninety a minute. The manometer showed that the mean arterial pressure was in the region of seventy. There was no undue activity, which was always a favorable sign.

"How's she, Tom?"

The anesthetist, crouching, was writing a note on the operation flow sheet. He nodded, without looking up. "Okay. No problems."

Why are you so wound up? It's only a ventricular septal defect. Including tetralogies, you must have done a couple of hundred of them. Even the registrars are doing them these days. It would only be tricky if it turned out to be one of those with holes like a Swiss cheese. But the ventriculogram had shown a single, high defect. Then why so jittery? Because of a child's chance remark? Don't be a fool.

He washed the powder off his gloves and took his place on the left. Peter changed round to take the first assistant's position on the right, and the young Frenchman (he had joined the team as a registrar only two weeks ago, too recently for admission to familiarity, so that everyone still called him Dr. Carrére) crossed to stand next to Deon.

The pericardium was open and the heart beat in perfect sinus rhythm, like a rock'n'roll dancer so adept that his timing was almost instinctive. Each atrial contraction was followed a fraction of a second later by the ventricular response.

The dilated right ventricle and pulmonary artery bulged forward. Deon placed a forefinger gently on the heart. He could feel the vibration as, with each contraction, blood squirted through the hole in the septum. Now he had to close that hole.

But first of all he had to reach it. Without looking up he held both hands out toward the scrub sister.

"Dissecting forceps and scissors, please."

The nurse was overeager. She put the scissors in his left hand and the forceps in his right. Keeping his eyes on the heart he put down the instruments, held out his hands again and said coldly: "Dissecting forceps and scissors, please."

She colored, realizing her mistake, and whipped up the instruments again to change them over. Then she rolled her eyes slightly.

Deon noticed, and could almost read the thought going through her mind. "One of *those* days." The knowledge that others were aware of his tension did not help to diminish it. He gave her a hard look. "Let's hand out the arterial line and suckers, Peter. Martin, you can recirculate in the meantime."

Peter lifted the half-inch Mayon tubing from the sterile tray, uncoiled it and clamped it to the drapes, then handed the other end to the heart-lung technician. The sister handed out the sucker and vent which would keep the heart clear of blood still seeping in after the heart-lung machine had taken over.

They prepared to connect the heart to the machine.

A cotton tape around the superior vena cava. Careful with the

O'Shaugnessy clamp with its curved end. Easy to start a hemorrhage by making a hole in this big vein that carried blood from the upper body. Must feel that the tip is all the way around before cutting. Watch out beneath it, for now you were close to the artery that led to the right lung.

"Snip the tissue in front of the forceps, Peter. Doctor Carrére, would you kindly hold the atrial appendage out of the way." There. "Tape, please."

Got it. Now the inferior vena cava, the vessel which brought blood from the lower body. Careful with the Sems. Left atrium is enlarged from overload. Go wide before pushing through the point of the forceps.

"Tape. Snare."

He noticed the tremor in his hands. But the shake was no worse than usual and his fingers inside the parchment-thin gloves were performing their delicate duty with certainty.

Confidence began to return. "Heparin, please, Tom."

Now to get the catheter into each of those veins so that, when the tapes were tightened, the blood to the heart would be short-circuited away to the machine. Purse-string suture around the base of the atrial appendage. Needle holder, forceps, and scissors flowed between the sister's hand and Peter's and his own. One advantage of having them realize that it was a bad day, he thought with grim humor. It keeps them on their toes.

Atrial clamp on the base of the appendage. Incision with scissors. Suck. A little too small. Snip again. Should do now.

Peter moved the clamp and blood welled up as he pushed the venous catheters into the right atrium, guiding them first into the top, then into the bottom vein. He was slow in tightening the suture and blood spilled over into the pericardial sac.

Deon glared at him. "Tighten the snare and suck," he said harshly.

"Pressure coming down," the anesthetist warned.

"We're obstructing the venous return," Deon told him. He flashed a bitter look at Peter Moorhead. "It'll come up in a minute."

Peter flushed and emptied the pericardial sac with the sucker.

"Finished recirculating, Martin?"

"Yes, Prof."

"Have you a clamp on the venous side?"

"Ye . . . uh . . . y—es, Prof," the technician said, and reached hastily for a clamp.

"Divide the line here, Peter. Hold it up, Doctor Carrére, so that the blood doesn't run out."

Both Peter and the registrar obeyed in silence.

The venous system was connected to the oxygenator. Now to link up the arterial system. First a catheter in the large artery through which the heart fed the body.

Purse-string suture in the ascending aorta. Stab wound with a stiletto-blade knife in the isolated portion. Blood squirted out. He controlled the bleeding quickly with a forefinger. Release pressure. Peter placed the 22 Bardic arterial catheter with the accuracy of a picador placing his lance in the bullring and driving it home with his weight over the side of the leaning, gut-shattered horse.

Why had that image occurred? Spain. Trees laden with small, sweet oranges hanging over a dusty road and the smell of oranges and dust and heat. Elizabeth and he eating prawns on the terrace of a Valencia hotel with Spanish friends they had met that morning. Trying to drink wine from a wineskin and getting it over the front of his shirt, but persevering, and the Spaniards applauding with much laughter when he at last succeeded. The corrida on a Sunday in Madrid, which had sickened him, but which he watched through to its appointed end.

Why had that image come to him? No time to think of it now. Connect the arterial line.

"Ready to go on bypass, Martin?"

"Ready, Prof."

"Start the machine."

"Pump on."

The whirring of the pumps joined the symphony of other sounds: the metronome beep . . . beep of the monitor, the *sshhss sshhss sshhss* of the respirator.

The heart began to shrink as the venous blood was carried away to the bubble oxygenators.

"Everything okay, Martin?"

"Yes, Prof. I'm on full flow."

"Okay. I'm tightening the venae caval tapes." He glanced up at the anesthetist. "Stop ventilation."

The blowing of the respirator ceased. The lungs stopped moving and the heart, now emptied, looked small and exhausted in the chest.

"Start cooling. Take it to about twenty-eight degrees."

"Cooling on," the technician said.

Cold water began to circulate through the jacket of the heat exchanger. The heart beat slowed.

Everything was going well. The machine had taken over the work of the heart and lungs. The cooling would protect heart, brain, and other vital organs from any lack of oxygen. It was an additional safeguard. Belt and braces.

Now he had to open the right ventricle in order to reach the hole.

"Knife."

A careful incision about an inch long between and parallel to two branches of the right coronary artery which ran across the front wall of the ventricle.

"Bottom sucker on, please."

Peter worked the nozzle of the sucker through the incision and cleared the ventricular chamber of the blood which was still seeping in.

"Eyelet retractors. Hold this one here, Peter. And you, Doctor, this one. Like this. Jesus! Hold it in the position I give it to you, can't you!"

Deon peered into the ventricle, which was now held open by the two retractors. "Where's the bloody light shining? I can't see a thing." Irritation rose again like water in a well. He *must* control himself.

The anesthetist moved the overhead operating light. "Is that better?"

"Can't you see it's shining right behind my head?" He was aware that his voice had almost been a shout.

"*That* better?" Tom Morton-Brown asked softly. He was a small, pert man whose accent in moments of stress slipped betrayingly toward Cockney, despite the double-barreled name. "All right?" he asked.

"It's not right, but leave it like that, for God's sake."

Deon heard the anesthetist sniff sharply, twice, but ignored it. He was picking up one of the flaps of the tricuspid valve, which connected the right atrium and ventricle.

"There it is," Peter said.

Deon grunted. It was a characteristic defect in the membraneous area of the septum, although it extended a little lower than usual, into the muscular portion of the septum next to the tricuspid valve.

"Small eyelet retractor."

The sister's hand reached across.

"Haven't you got one with a longer handle?"

"No, sir. This is the only one we have."

He tightened his lips under the mask.

"Hold it, Peter. Pull upward, so that I can see the bottom edge of the hole."

Blood gushed into the heart, obscuring his view.

"Not so much, Peter! You're making the aortic valve leak now."

Peter relaxed the retractor. The sucker slurped and the blood vanished.

"Aortic clamp."

He would cross-clamp the aorta just above the valve. This would prevent blood leaking past the valve and would also stop the flow into the coronary arteries. The heart would relax, the beat would slow and eventually it would cease to beat.

"Aortic clamp on," he called.

The anesthetist would time the period during which the heart muscle was without oxygen and would warn him every five minutes. If oxygen was withheld for too long, the muscle would be damaged.

He could see the beat gradually slowing. His practiced ear would continue to register, without him having to think about it. Any change in the beat would set off an alarm signal inside his head.

Now he could clearly see the boundaries of the hole. It was too big to close by simply suturing the edges together. He would have to use a patch. The sister put a needle holder into his outstretched palm. She held on to the second needle, at the other end of the suture, to prevent it hooking on to something.

Three mattress stitches through the rim of the tricuspid valve.

Beep . . . beep . . . beep went the monitor.

Peter tagged each stitch with a small artery clamp.

Four stitches in the rim made by the ring of the aortic valve. Don't pick up the edge of the cusp or the valve will leak.

Beep . . . beep . . . beep.

The clamp had been on for seven minutes.

"Don't pull so hard on the retractor . . . uh . . . you." He gave Carrère a darting, sideways look. "This is a heart, remember. Not a stomach."

He swung round toward the heart-lung console. "More suction, Martin! Damn it, man, I can't see through blood."

He began to stitch along the muscular septum next to the tricuspid ring. Stay away from the edge; pick up only half the septum. Stay away from the nerve bundle.

The heart beat stopped.

An invisible bell shrilled in his mind as he stared at the heart, lying flabby and unresponding within the chest.

"Relax with your retractor," he shouted at the Frenchman.

Was the sudden break in the beat due to lack of oxygen, or had there been an interruption of the impulses because of damage caused by the last stitch?

Beep . . . went the monitor again.

"Was that a conducted beat, Tom?" he asked pleadingly.

The anesthetist shook his head slightly. "Can't say, Deon. The interval between atrial activity and ventricular response is pretty long. It's hard to say for sure."

Deon continued to stare at the heart, while questions whirled through his mind. Should he cut out the stitch? Release the aortic clamp and re-warm the heart? Or should he simply carry on?

"There's ventricular fibrillation now," Morton-Brown said, looking at him over the top of the drapes.

"You're cooling too much," Deon shouted accusingly at the heart-lung operator. But he knew this was not the cause, for blood had not flowed through the heart muscle for at least ten minutes.

Calm down, he told himself. The standstill was caused by anoxia. Everything will be fine. You'll see. It's okay. Isn't it? Everything is okay. Relax and get on with the job.

He picked up the needle holder and put in the rest of the stitches into the muscular border of the defect. "Teflon felt, please." To the anesthetist he said: "I'm releasing the aortic clamp now."

"Twelve minutes," Morton-Brown said tersely.

The heart picked up and became tense. The fibrillation became more vigorous. Deon cut the plastic patch to the size and shape of the hole, then passed each stitch through it in turn, cutting the needles and tagging them again. Then, as Peter held the web of sutures up tightly for him, he guided the patch down to where it would cover the gap between the two chambers of the heart, as neatly and firmly as a new patch on a pair of worn trousers.

"Rewarm," he called.

"Warming on," the technician replied promptly.

He tied the sutures firmly enough to hold the patch down securely but not so tight as to risk them tearing out or breaking. Three knots each.

"I'm going to aspirate the air from the left heart. Needle and syringe, sister."

She was slow and he waggled his hand impatiently, waiting for the instrument.

"Tip up the apex, Peter."

He put the needle through the apex into the left ventricular cavity and drew out the froth of blood and bubbles. In a moment the blood was clear of air. He squirted it into the pericardial sac and Peter sucked it back to the heart-lung machine.

He closed up the ventriculotomy, sewing with painful care so that he could disguise and partly control the trembling of his hands. "What's the heart temperature?"

Morton-Brown glanced at his apparatus. "Normal now."

230

"What's normal?" Deon snapped at him.

The anesthetist sighed with an air of weary patience. "Thirty-seven Centigrade. Would you like it in Fahrenheit too?"

Deon ignored the retort. The incision was closed and the heart was fibrillating vigorously, but had not taken up a sinus rhythm on its own, as happened sometimes. He would have to defibrillate with an electric shock.

"Let's have the paddles."

They were shoved hurriedly into his hands and the anesthetist connected the leads. "What shock do you want?" he asked. "Thirty watts okay?"

"We'll start with thirty."

"Okay. Charging."

Deon slipped the one paddle in behind the heart and put the other in front of the right ventricle. He held the heart between the cupped metal blades. "Okay, Tom."

The child's body jerked. The heart convulsed and then lay quiet for a moment as if uncertain. Then it contracted. Beep. Another—beep. All eyes turned to the oscilloscope and its jagged dancing pattern. Beep . . . beep . . . beep.

Deon's ear had already told him the disastrous news. The rate was too slow.

He looked down at the heart and could see the atria racing away and the slow, regular beat of the ventricles. Maybe it's a three-to-one or a two-to-one block. Maybe some of the beats are being conducted. Maybe the pathway is partially clear.

"Is there a constant PR interval, Tom?"

"I'm not quite sure."

"Well take a tracing and *make* sure," Deon told him.

Morton-Brown turned a switch and the long strip of paper on which the stylus had duplicated that lightning-stroke pattern on the screen came rolling out of his machine. He tore off a section and examined it.

"No. There's complete atrio-ventricular disassociation."

It was confirmation of what he already knew. But he had continued to hope it was not so.

Complete heart block.

The ventricles had stopped responding to the stimulus from the atria and had taken up their own rhythm. It was like a duet with two obstinate musicians, each determined to keep to his own timing.

"What's the rate?"

The anesthetist counted the moving numbers on the scope. "Forty-five."

Deon looked up at the screen, not knowing what he hoped to see.

The P waves were much faster than the QRS complexes and there was no relation between them.

Complete heart block.

That stitch must have caught the nerve bundle. Why hadn't he taken the damned thing out? He thought he could take the chance. You damn fool, it's the patient, not the doctor, who takes the chance. But it was impossible. He had taken so much care. Surely to God he could not have caught both bundles?

The slow, insistent beep . . . beep of the monitor seemed to grow louder and more shrill, its clamor blocking off all his ability to think.

Something had to be done. But he could think of nothing. He had managed to repair Marietjie's broken heart, but in the process had left her with a far more serious disability. Heart block could end in sudden and rapid death.

He felt as if he had been given a child's precious toy to admire and had allowed it to slip and fall and shatter.

Should he open the heart, cut out the patch, and do the whole thing again? But how could he be certain that further stitches would not do more damage? Perhaps he should cut it out and leave it; leave the hole open again.

"Give me a knife," he told the sister.

But, with scalpel already poised, he hesitated.

Be sensible, he told himself. Don't let anxiety drive you into making an overhasty and unintelligent decision. Draw on past experience.

What would be the sensible thing to do? Wait and see. And, in the meantime, put the child on a pacemaker.

"Pacemaker electrodes, sister."

"Permanent or temporary?"

"Let's have the . . ." He thought for a moment. "The temporary ones."

He began to sew the small electrodes onto the front of the right ventricle. His hands were shaking and he could hardly control his movements. Peter held the first electrode down on the heart with a pair of forceps while he tied the stitch. It tore out of the heart muscle.

"Hold the bloody thing still, can't you!" he said between fiercely clenched teeth. "Look what you've made me do." He turned to Carrére. "Doctor, be so kind as to hold those forceps for me, if Doctor Moorhead finds it too difficult."

What he was doing was preposterous and unworthy, he knew. But he could not help himself. His conviction of failure, of having botched every-

232

thing, seeped through the theater as if it were a physical presence, a dark and evil-smelling tide which would rise higher and eventually engulf them all.

Peter was agitated and uncertain. The Frenchman stood there like a dummy, too nervous even to risk touching the forceps. The scrub nurse, who was one of the good ones, fumbled as she handed him a needle holder, and almost dropped it. He swore at her and the floor nurses stood shocked and motionless. The heart-lung technicians stared in frozen fear from behind their machine.

Everything was going to hell. He was going to lose this child too.

"Forty," the anesthetist's inexorable voice said. "Forty-two. Forty-four. Forty-five. Forty-two."

It was all Deon could do not to scream.

"Shut up, will you? I can hear for myself."

Another horrified silence.

He linked the wire from the electrodes to the long lead and gave the other end to the anesthetist. "Connect it. Set the pacemaker at one twenty."

The atria were still racing away, as if determined to pass their message on to the sluggish ventricles. Nothing happened. Beep . . . beep. Too slow.

"Okay, Tom. Switch on."

There was no change in the sound from the monitor.

"Is the pacemaker on?" Deon asked agitatedly.

"It's on," Morton-Brown said. He alone seemed unshaken by the frenzy of the last fifteen minutes.

"Then turn up the strength of the stimulus."

"Okay. One. One five. Two. Two five."

At last responding to the electrical impulse from the pacemaker the heart jumped abruptly from forty-five to a hundred-and-twenty beats a minute.

"Okay. Leave it at that."

Deon felt the last reserves of strength drain out of him.

Nevertheless he completed the operation, as he had to do: stopping the heart-lung machine; checking the heart function; having pressures measured and remeasured; removing the catheters from the veins and the aorta and closing the incisions; sewing in drains inside the pericardial sac and the mediastinum. But he did all this almost mechanically. Skill returned to his hands, but this caused him no joy, no exhilaration.

Burning in his memory like a brand which would never be eradicated, a scar which would endure no matter how thickly the healing skin grew over it, was that moment of physical agony when he had stood over the child and had been unable to decide what to do to save her life.

He left Peter and the young registrar to finish closing up, discarded his gown and gloves, went out into the corridor, mechanically pulled off mask and cap and threw them into the bin. He wandered into the doctor's room. Guido Perino was alone in there. The wall clock said a quarter to one. Presumably Robby had finished long ago and had left.

Guido began to talk excitedly about the patent ductus arteriosus division he and Robby had done. Deon answered in monosyllables.

He remembered that he had an appointment at the office. But he did not want to leave the hospital before he had seen the child again. He wished he could avoid seeing Trish. He was numbed. The thought of more people, more emotions, was like a crushing load on his chest.

He poured himself coffee. It was cold. A plate of sandwiches stood on the table. It was lunchtime and he should have something to eat. But he had no appetite.

He nodded a greeting to Guido, aware of the young man's curious stare, and went back into the corridor, intending to return to theater and watch the final stages of the closing up.

The supervisor appeared in her office door. "Professor," she called.

He turned to her with a puzzled frown.

"I spoke to the Superintendent about the brushes."

"The brushes?" It was an effort to recall what she was talking about. "Oh, yes. The brushes."

"He says there's nothing to be done about it."

"Nothing to be done about it," he echoed her vaguely.

She seemed nonplussed by the tameness of his reaction. "Head Office bought those because it was the lowest price."

"The old story." A little of his earlier annoyance began to return. "One would think Head Office could at least have consulted the doctors who have to use the damn things."

"I quite agree, Professor. But I'm afraid we'll just have to carry on using them. They ordered forty thousand."

"Forty thou— You must be joking."

She could obviously see no reason for humor.

"They really are awful, but we'll have to use them up."

"But forty thousand. It's unbelievable." He began to laugh. "Forty thousand."

The woman stared at him, still puzzled by his laughter.

"Let's say you autoclave them only an average of twenty times each," he calculated. "They're rubbish, so they probably won't take more than that. Even so that's eight hundred thousand scrubs. We'll still be using the things next century." He could not stop laughing. Everything was so sad that laughter was the only antidote. Laughter, the cure-all, he thought. If only we had enough comics, the doctors could close up shop. Laugh, while everything went to pieces around you. Laugh at pain and all the other indignities creatures have to bear. Laugh at death and it will go away. Laugh at petty rules and obtuse officialdom. Cleanse the world's corruption with the acid of laughter. Laugh; for sure as hell weeping won't get you anywhere.

"Well, thank you, sister," he said.

Peter and the registrar came out of the theater together. They had finished, and soon Marietjie would be wheeled out to the recovery room.

"Thank you, sister," he said. "I'll speak to the Super about it. It's not very urgent, is it?"

He left the hospital at half past two. He had stayed in the recovery room with Marietjie, silently praying that her own pacemaker would take over. She woke and managed to smile weakly at him. Her circulation was good and there was little blood through the drains. He switched off the pacemaker several times, hoping to see the P waves on the monitor screen followed regularly by the steep rise and fall of the QRS. But there was still complete block. Worse still, the last time he had turned it off there were only P waves. The ventricles had come to a standstill. He had seen the child wince and realized her brain was being starved of blood. He had hurriedly switched on the pacemaker. Her life now depended solely on those little wires to the heart. He hoped the electrodes would hold firm and that the leads would not come adrift.

There was probably some edema around the bundle and this was making things worse. He thought hopefully that this would probably only be temporary.

He ordered a spare pacemaker on standby, in case the one driving her heart failed. And after that there was little more that he could do for Marietjie.

His car was like an oven inside. He opened the windows to let what breeze there was blow through. It hardly helped. He sat in the hot car, looking blankly at the ignition key. Maybe he should cancel his appointments for the rest of the day. He couldn't concentrate on other things when he was worrying about a patient. Maybe he should go home early. Or, better still, drive down to the beachfront, totally beyond duty's call, or to the harbor to walk slowly among the trains and look up the steep sides of cargo ships with the names of improbable ports painted on their sterns and watch the slim-winged gulls swooping and quarreling over floating bits of garbage on the silk-green water.

With a sigh he turned the key and reversed out of his parking space. Tempting. But he could not do it.

He drove the Jaguar into the grounds of the medical school. His reserved parking space was occupied by a car with Provincial Administration plates. In the wave of fury and frustration which overwhelmed him he was almost tempted to drive straight into the back of it, to exorcise himself in that mad moment when metal would crumple and glass shatter. He took a deep breath and drove past.

Another PA car pulled up as he drove into a space farther down the row. The driver climbed out, collected a single test tube of blood from the rear seat and disappeared into the building housing the blood grouping laboratories.

Unbelievable, Deon thought. This sort of thing happens all day long. If they were to use one car fewer and spend an extra quarter cent on a brush for the scrub room . . . Oh, to hell with it.

He walked up the stairs and went through to his office with its paneled walls, bookcases and the African witch-doctor's mask under the window. A portrait of Elizabeth hung on the wall facing his desk. It had been painted soon after they were married and the artist had caught that look of caprice.

It's not there anymore, he thought. It hasn't been there for a long time. Well—nothing lasts forever.

He sat down behind the desk, a little heavily, as his secretary came in through the interleading door with her file. She hesitated when she saw his face.

"Afternoon, Prof. How did it go?"

"Hello, Jenny." He grimaced. "She developed heart block."

"Oh. I'm sorry." She looked shyly away. "Would you like some tea?" she asked gently.

"No thanks. Any calls?"

"Only one. Professor Davids. You were to ring him if you could."

"Get him for me, please."

"He was only going to be there till one o'clock, Prof. And again from half past five."

"All right. I'll ring him when I get home. Anything else?"

"A couple of letters. Nothing very important. The travel agents sent your itinerary for the Australian trip."

"That all?"

236

"And you've got Mrs. Sedara coming to see you at three." She looked at the clock. "That's in a quarter of an hour."

"I know."

"That's all, Prof."

"Thanks."

Jenny had turned on the air-conditioner, but he still felt hot. He rose and turned the control as far as it would go, then settled at his desk again. But he did not start working at once. Instead he played with a crudely forged and beaten brass dagger which Elizabeth had bought him to use as a paper cutter.

Trish. What would she be like after all these years? How many years precisely? He had qualified in 'fifty-three and they had not met or communicated again after that. A lot of years, by any reckoning.

Was he even sure what she had looked like? That marvelous thick, red hair, yes. Her free, swinging walk. But had her eyes been blue or gray? And what exactly did her face look like, feature by feature? Her voice he had heard again on the telephone yesterday. Deeper than that of most women. Almost husky.

Memory was a traitor. You believed you would never forget. And then you forgot all the same.

Sedara. What kind of name was that? Carrére was French. Sedara. Could it be Spanish? Had she married a Spaniard after all? They kept their women pretty much in their place and secluded, didn't they? Trish, with her wild desire to be free; would she have been content with kitchen and babies and church and a duenna? Didn't they have to go around with a duenna? Or was that only for unmarried girls?

He knew little about Spain, although he had visited it with Elizabeth. Then suddenly the memory that had come to him at the operating table this morning, of the bullfight in the languid Madrid afternoon, returned and was explicable.

The whole time they were in Spain, he and Elizabeth, he had been watching, watching. Once he had seen a woman at a distance with that thick, dark hair and prowling walk and had made some hastily concocted excuse to leave Elizabeth and go closer to her, only to find she was a stranger.

Resolutely he turned to the work before him on the desk.

Jenny, quiet and apologetic as always, tapped at the door.

"Excuse me, Prof. Mrs. Sedara. Shall I show her in?"

237

"Please."

He straightened his tie as he got up, then walked round the desk, smoothing his hair with one hand.

Jenny stood aside for a dark-haired woman and the small boy she led by the hand. Deon went forward, smiling. Her face was strange, and yet at the same time as familiar as his own. But after the first searching glance it was the child's face that held his attention.

The Oriental slant to the eyes. The sparse hair. The head rather flat and a little smaller than average. The tongue which appeared too big for the mouth. Down's Syndrome. The child was a mongol.

Deon erased the instinctive expression of surprise and pity, forcing himself to appear as if he had noticed nothing amiss. "Trish!" he said warmly. "How good to see you. Do sit down."

He held a chair ready for the child, who looked at him with those uptilted, unresponding eyes. Trish picked up the little boy quickly and put him down in the chair. The child continued to stare at Deon.

Deon returned to his seat, grateful for the barrier the desk placed between him and them.

"It was quite a surprise. To get your phone call."

"It was very kind of you to see us at such short notice."

"It was the least I could do."

And at once he wished the words unsaid. But she did not appear to have noticed. She was looking at the child. "This is Giovanni," she said. "My son."

Dear God. Poor Trish.

She continued, without faltering. "As you see, he is a mongol. But he also has a heart defect, and that is why I've come to you."

Deon glanced sharply at the boy. Yes, there was a bluish tinge to the lips and fingertips. He was briefly annoyed at having missed these signs through concentrating on the obvious.

She looked at him expectantly. He began to toy with the paper cutter again.

"Can you help Giovanni?"

He coughed, bringing up his hand to hide his mouth. "Well, we'll see," he said evasively. "Tell me, has he been investigated? His condition, I mean. Has any other doctor seen him?"

"Oh, yes. They did all kinds of tests in Italy."

"Italy?"

"Yes. That's where I live now. Near Naples."

"Not Spain?"

"I did live in Spain, but then I went to Italy."

"And your husband? Is he with you?"

"My husband is dead," she said flatly.

He was startled and scrambled through his mind for the appropriate words of sympathy. But she made an impatient, dismissive gesture which he also remembered from long ago. "The important point is whether you think you can do something for Giovanni."

"Let's not be in too much of a hurry. What did the Italian doctors tell you?"

"They said he had a tetralogy of Fallot."

"I see. Yes, that's quite likely. It's not uncommon among children with Down's Syndrome."

"So they told me."

"Why did you bring him here, Trish? There are a lot of good heart clinics in Europe."

"They wouldn't operate when he was small, because of his age. And now, even though he's five, they advise against operating at all. They said he could never be normal, and it was better to let him die. So I brought him to you."

She looked at him frankly, without guile. He understood.

And mingled with his dismay was a wry sense of appreciation. This was Trish. She could make even blackmail appear rational and honest.

The child distracted her for a moment by climbing off his chair. While she had been talking he had stared fixedly at the witch-doctor's mask behind Deon's shoulder. Now he walked up to it with his rolling, disjointed gait and touched it and turned to smile rapturously at his mother.

"Giovanni," she said in a quiet voice of warning.

The boy withdrew his hand at once, but the smile of pure joy remained.

"Don't worry," Deon reassured her. "He can't harm it."

She turned back to him. "You will do it, won't you?"

"We'll see," he said again.

He was utterly confused. It was never an easy decision. Now least of all. He had loved her once, and did love ever vanish completely? He had abandoned her once, and would he abandon her now again? Their child, the child he had forced her to have destroyed, would it have been normal? Almost certainly: Yes.

"Did you bring the results of those tests with you? The X-rays and electrocardiogram and so forth?"

"No. I'm afraid I didn't." She looked concerned.

"Never mind. We'll have to repeat them in any case."

He pressed a button on the intercom and Jenny answered at once.

"Get me the cardiac clinic, please."

He leaned toward Trish again, resting an elbow on the desk. "We can't really tell what we can do for Giovanni till we know exactly what the problem is."

"They told me it was a tretralogy," she said quickly.

"That's probably correct, but we have to be sure. That's not the only cause of a blue baby, you see."

The intercom buzzed.

"Cardiac clinic," Jenny announced. "Doctor Schoeman."

"Excuse me," Deon said. He picked up the receiver. "Johan? Deon here. When can you see a boy, aged five, with a probable tetralogy of Fallot?" He listened for a moment, then spoke again. "Let's have a look at him first. Then we can decide if he needs to be catheterized or not."

Trish had got up and was studying the pictures and certificates around the room. She turned to look at him.

"Fine. I'll ask the mother." He put a hand over the mouthpiece. "Will four o'clock this afternoon suit you?" When she nodded gratefully he put the receiver back to his ear. "The child's name is Giovanni Sedara. Yes, Italian. Please don't let them wait in the corridor. Thanks, Johan."

Trish was studying the portrait of Elizabeth. Without turning she said: "Thank you, Deon. Is this your wife?"

"Yes." There was little else he could say.

"She's very beautiful."

"It was painted quite a time ago, of course. But she is still beautiful."

Trish sat down again. The child had followed her around and now he too shuffled back to his chair. He climbed into it and sat there quite still, his eyes remote, his short legs dangling motionlessly over the seat.

"When the cardiologists have worked things out we can talk again," Deon said. He checked the time. "Do you have anything to do before four o'clock? It's just over quarter past three. Do you have a car here?"

She tossed her hair. It was cut short now, but the gesture was familiar from the time when it had hung round her face, heavy and long. It touched Deon's heart to see.

"Wait," he said. "Have tea with me. I'll run you up to the hospital when it's time."

She sat up straight at once.

"No! Really! I can't waste your . . ."

"Nobody's wasting anything," he said firmly. "Would Giovanni like a cold drink?"

"It's sweet of you, but really it's not necessary."

"I insist."

She looked at him and smiled slightly, then sat back in her chair while he spoke to Jenny on the intercom.

Trish looked round at the modern and functional luxury of his room.

"You've made a great name for yourself. You're even mentioned in the Italian papers every now and then."

He started to make the customary modest disclaimers, then stopped himself. They would make no impression on Trish.

"It wasn't quite what I expected of life," he admitted.

"Things seldom are."

"Still, it has its compensations."

"I dare say."

He leaned back. "And you? Tell me all about it. Tell me of everything that's happened to you."

She needed drawing out at first, and the phrases were hesitant, as if she had difficulty in expressing herself. But as she talked she gained both confidence and fluency. Her face and voice became animated and small mannerisms—a way of gesturing with an open palm; a crooked, wistful smile; a particular set of the head—all these returned to remind him of an earlier Trish. A Trish he remembered (and was it with pleasure or alarm?) he had once loved.

He had built a picture in his mind's eye—of her painting in a garret studio in Spain, never changing, never growing older, never losing the freedom she had seized. This was the image he had treasured through the years and he was absurdly, childishly delighted to find that parts of it had been right.

For six months after reaching Spain she had lived in Barcelona. But then it became too expensive because, thanks to the travel writers, the tourists were starting to discover the Costa Brava. She had moved to Malaga, which was hotter and therefore less fashionable, and there she met Robert, an American busy writing a book about American expatriates.

"Robert," Deon said.

"Yes," she said, but ignored the further, unspoken question. "I lived in Spain for three years altogether. Then I went to Italy. To Rome."

He was still thinking about the American. Had he been her lover? Yes. He was convinced of it.

"What did you do in Spain?" he asked.

"I painted, mostly." She was indifferent. But was she hiding something? He grew more and more convinced.

241

"And when you weren't painting?"

"Well, strangely, then I gave English lessons."

Languages had always come easily to her. There were many other young people who painted and liked living in Spain because it was warm and cheap and adventurous, somehow. It wasn't easy to make a living from painting, so she had taught English to Spaniards. After three years, when she left Spain for Italy, she found that Italian came easily too, so she had continued to teach. One of her pupils in Rome was an industrialist from Naples, Riccardo Sedara. He had been appointed to a United Nations economic advisory committee shortly before and was anxious to improve his English.

She had liked him, although he was considerably older, already in his mid-forties. He owned several small factories, but confessed blithely that he knew nothing at all about economics. Neither did any of the other members of the committee, so that was no problem. However, he was very conscientious about attending meetings. One day he hoped he would learn all there was to learn.

He was gentle and thoughtful and scrupulously correct toward her. She gave him lessons three times a week for six months and in all that time he did not even try to touch her hand.

There was something a little mysterious about him, however, a demarcated area that he closed off from outside intrusion. She had, incuriously, put it down to the differences between them of age, language and background.

And one afternoon he came to her apartment for his lesson and found her crying over a letter.

"It was a letter from Rob," she told Deon.

"The American?"

"Yes."

"Why were you crying?"

"It isn't important. I was telling you about Riccardo."

Riccardo had sat down stiffly in a hard chair in that small Rome apartment and had talked to her. For the first time she was allowed into that shadow world within him. He told her about his wife. She had taken her own life when the young German mechanic who always worked on her car and with whom she had gone off deserted her in turn. She had gassed herself in the same car. They had had no children.

Trish and he talked throughout the afternoon and when evening came they went out and walked through the streets. It was a summer evening, hot and heavy with thunder. They found a table in a pavement cafe overlooking the Piazza Navona and sat there talking, telling one another everything.

"Did you . . . uh . . . tell him about me?" Deon asked.

"Yes."

Deon rubbed his jaw thoughtfully, looking down at the leatherbound desk blotter in front of him.

"It's strange," she said. "There we had been meeting three times a week and holding long conversations. And yet we had never talked."

Now they could not stop talking, and could not bear to part. They spent five days together in Rome. Then they went to Naples and were married.

They had been happy. Riccardo was gentle and patient with her.

"He had sympathy, as they say. He helped me to start painting again."

"Oh. Had you stopped?"

"For a time in Rome I couldn't paint."

"I see."

"I had been very confused for a long time. I still was when I married him, I'm afraid. But he helped me. And after a time things got better and I was able to work again."

He had backed exhibitions of her work in Rome, and later in other cities. He was enormously proud of everything she did. The only shadow in their lives was her apparent inability to have children. But then, shortly after her thirty-eighth birthday, she became pregnant and Riccardo was ecstatic. Nine months later she was a widow and the mother of a mongoloid son.

"He was killed in a motor accident just two weeks before Giovanni was born. He had been to Rome for a meeting of his committee." She smiled. "He was chairman of that economic advisory committee by then, although he used to say that he still hadn't learned a thing about economics. He was coming home from the meeting to be with me. And then he was killed."

"I'm sorry."

"Yes." Her gaze wandered away from his face. "I wanted to die too, those first few days. But I was carrying his child, so I had to endure. And then Giovanni was born."

The infant did not respond normally. He appeared slightly blue and was very quiet. The doctor called in a pediatrician.

"I knew nothing about it. I lay all night dreaming about my son. I woke up three times and each time I tried to persuade the nurse to let me see him. In the morning the doctors came to my room and told me. Giovanni was a mongol. They advised me against taking him home. They said it would be wrong to become attached to him. He would be a burden and all

243

I could expect would be heartache after heartache. As if anything could add to the burden I already had."

Deon could not look at her. He wanted her to stop talking.

"Deon, you don't start loving a child after its birth. You love it from the moment you know it is there. My child is a special person. Some of us have less and some have more. I accepted Giovanni with his limitations. Now, within those limits, I must do all I can to help him attain a full life."

She was silent. Had she finished? Could he get her out of his office now?

The intercom buzzed discreetly and he stabbed a finger gratefully at the button.

"Yes?"

"Sorry to interrupt, Prof," Jenny said. "Your wife is on the line."

Four

"Deon?" Elizabeth's voice was shrill. "Deon?"

"Yes. Hullo," he said.

"Please come home."

"Hullo?"

"Come home."

"Home?" He was uncomfortably aware of Trish's presence. He held the receiver tightly against his ear. "What's wrong?"

"Just come home, please. Immediately."

"But what's the matter?" He had been caught unaware and was conscious of the reluctance which must be apparent in his voice. "What's wrong?"

"I can't tell you on the phone."

"Oh, for God's sake! Do you think anybody would . . ." He caught himself in time.

"What?"

"Nothing," he mumbled. "Now, just tell me what the problem is."

"Isn't it enough that I should ask you to come home when I need you? Can't you do that, just for once?"

Her anger rubbed off abrasively against his own. He held back with an effort. No arguments, please. Not today, of all days.

"Look, I can't make it right away. I have a patient here with me and then I have to go back to the children's hospital to see about . . ."

He heard her draw a savage, rasping breath.

"Patients! Hospitals! Operations! Children! That's all we ever get from you. Has it occurred to you that you have children of your own?"

245

"Elizabeth, please calm down. If it's urgent, obviously I'll come. But . . ."

"Yes. It's always 'but,' isn't it? Well, you can have your patients and your nurses and your stinking hospital."

"Look, dear," he said with fraying patience. "You're obviously upset. Will you please tell me exactly what has happened?"

"Go to hell!"

The line went dead.

Deon held the receiver at arm's length and looked at it ruefully. Then he looked at Trish and attempted a smile. "That was my wife."

She came quickly to her feet. "I think I should leave now."

He put out a hand. "No. Please. I . . ."

She was insistent. "I must go. In any case, it's almost twenty to four. I don't want to be late."

"All right. I'll drive you to the hospital." To forestall refusal he added hastily: "I have to pass there anyway."

They said little during the brief drive. He was thinking, a little uneasily, about Elizabeth's call. What the devil was it all about? Nothing very serious, surely, or she would have told him. He comforted himself with the thought that Elizabeth was inclined to be overdramatic anyway. Probably it was nothing more serious than a row with the servant. Or with Lisa. Yes, that was the most likely. She'd had a bit of a row with Lisa.

He offered to escort Trish to the cardiac clinic but she shook her head firmly. He was relieved to see her go.

"The cardiologists should have an answer for us by tomorrow," he told her. "So perhaps you could come round to my office again tomorrow afternoon. About the same time."

She thanked him gravely.

He looked into the rearview mirror as he drove off. He could see Trish and her son standing in front of the hospital entrance. They had their backs toward him.

The afternoon traffic was thickening and it was past four when he reached the children's hospital.

Moolman was the registrar on duty in the Intensive Care Unit. He was a tall, shabby young man with glasses, the earpieces of which had been mended none too neatly with adhesive plaster. His big hands drooped at the wrists and he wore a constant air of mild apology. He was not a figure to inspire absolute confidence.

"How are things?" Deon asked. His eyes were already moving quickly from oscilloscope to drainage bottles to urine bag to wall chart. He sifted the information his eyes recorded; analyzed; came to conclusions.

"She was a little restless," Moolman said, "so I gave her five milligrams of Pethidine. That settled her nicely."

Marietjie lay with closed eyes. Her nose and mouth were covered by a plastic oxygen mask and a thin tube led from one nostril. Deon moved to the foot of the bed and felt her feet. Warm, with good pulses. No circulation problems anyway. A nurse was measuring the urine that had drained into a clear plastic bag hooked on to the bed frame. Deon looked questioningly at her.

"The output is very good, sir. Two-fifty cc's in the last hour."

He turned back to Moolman.

"You haven't given her any Lasix yet?"

"No, Prof." The registrar was watching the column of red fluid in the venous manometer.

On the chart the heart rate was recorded as a straight line: a steady one hundred and twenty-two beats per minute. The mechanical pacemaker was unable to vary its rate in response to the body's needs. Deon was tempted to turn the thing off again, just to see what might happen. But he knew there was no sense in doing it.

"Okay. I'm going home. Is everything all right in the wards?"

"The Manyani baby, sir."

"Manyani?" Deon frowned at the registrar, thinking. Yes. Of course. An African child from the Transkei. Tetralogy. He had operated last week to do a shunt and the infant had picked up well. He had seen him on rounds this morning, and there had been a continuous murmur high up on the left chest, which showed that the shunt was functioning well.

"Yes, I know the baby. What about him?"

"Well, the ward sister called me half an hour ago, sir. The child was very restless and she wanted to know whether she should give him some morphine."

"Yes? Yes?" Deon always told his doctors to be precise and concise. Moolman had obviously not paid close attention to the latter part of these instructions.

"So I thought I'd better take a look," the registrar stumbled on. "And I found that the respiratory rate had been going up steadily during the day. The circulation wasn't as good as this morning and the child was wet only twice today."

Deon was growing tired of this long-winded case history. He turned away while Moolman was still speaking. "Let's go and see the kid," he said from the doorway.

The Manyani baby was clearly in trouble. Breathing was sixty a minute, pulse one hundred and sixty. The child was cold and much more blue than this morning. Deon borrowed Moolman's stethoscope and examined the lungs. There was a large area of dullness and bronchial breathing at the base of the right lung. Half the lung must be solid.

"I think the child has collapsed the middle and lower lobes." He gave incisive commands. "Get him back to Intensive Care. Get an X-ray of his chest and put up a drip. We'll get a tube down to suck the lungs out properly, then leave him on bubbles for the night. I'll be at home. Phone me as soon as you've seen the X-ray."

He turned away, but stopped after a couple of paces. "And you'd better get an Astrup too."

He could feel the urgency, like a physical constriction, a slow-mounting rise of tension within him. He recognized and welcomed it, for it had become a familiar friend. It had to be there, that tide of excitement, of intense awareness that sharpened thought and reaction. He felt its steady awakening and was content that it had come, so that he would now be able to forget about it too.

The oxygen content of the blood must be very low, especially with half the right lung out of action. Probably the infant had not been receiving adequate physiotherapy. The non-White wards were always crammed, even with extra beds at times, and yet they were always understaffed. The best place for that baby was back in Intensive Care. Children gave you only one chance. And if you let it slip you were in trouble.

It reminded him of when he had been a young boy on the farm. His father grew vegetables at the side of the dam and it had been his duty, once a day, in the cool of the evening, to lead water from the dam to the vegetable beds. They were separated by furrows and shallow walls of earth. Sometimes he would need to water one bed but not the one next to it where, perhaps, beans had been planted but the seedlings had not yet pushed through. If you allowed water into that bed, the soil would dry rock-hard and the plants would not grow. Usually the watering was easy enough to control, but if he had been daydreaming and hadn't noticed that a protective wall was breaking away until it was too late, the ominous flood would already have spread past the gap. He would run with the spade to mend the breach and the earth would turn to mud even as he slapped spadesful of it down over the hole in the wall. And as he was repairing one breach another would start somewhere else, clods melting before the slow, persistent pressure of water, seeming to vanish right before his eyes. Rushing frantically from one gap to another, digging and filling in slapdash haste while the flood threatened at any moment to overwhelm him, his mind was filled with one sickening thought: what would his father say when he found out that water had got into the bean bed?

He had experienced the same hollow-stomach feeling here on a couple of occasions when some condition had been allowed to go too far, and each time he was forced back on to another line of defense, he discovered that it had already been weakened and would also, inevitably, be overrun. Finally there was nothing more you could do. Finally all the walls crumbled before the implacable advance of the flood. You went on fighting, of course, to the end. But there was always a time when you knew that no matter how hard you fought the floodwaters would wash away this life for which you were fighting.

Elizabeth was in their bedroom and the curtains were drawn. She was lying in the half dark with her eyes wide open, staring at the ceiling.

He tried to ignore the danger signs and to appear nonchalant.

"Hi." He pulled off his jacket and hung it in the wardrobe. "Lord, did I have a day of it today. Everything went wrong."

Her voice was small and still. "I *do* feel *so* sorry for you."

He turned, still undoing his tie, and examined her for a moment.

"There's no need to be sarcastic, you know."

"Sarcastic! You wouldn't know when I was being sarcastic. You wouldn't even know whether or not I happened to be speaking to you. You simply don't hear me anymore."

"Look, what is all this about?"

She pushed herself up on to one elbow. "It might interest you to know that your daughter had to be brought home by the police."

"The police?"

"Yes. But of course you're too involved with other things to be bothered about what's happening to your own children."

"Why did they bring her home?"

"They found her in the city. On Greenmarket Square, dancing and singing to herself."

"They didn't charge her with anything?"

"I suppose you would have liked that, wouldn't you?"

"Don't be childish. Did they charge her?"

"Some sergeant felt sorry for her and got her to show him where she lived."

"Thank God for that anyway. Had she been . . . ? Was she drugged?"

"Obviously."

He fingered the half-knotted tie. "I simply can't understand what's wrong with the child."

"You know damn well what's wrong with her."

"What do you mean?"

She gave him a scornful look and lay back on the bed.

He moistened his lips, which had gone suddenly dry. "What precisely do you mean?" he asked.

The telephone on his bedside table began to *chirrup*. He looked at it, startled, then crossed quickly to the bed and snatched up the receiver.

"Yes?"

"Professor van der Riet?"

"Yes. Yes."

"Moolman, sir. I'm sorry to worry you, sir."

"All right, man. What is it?"

"You did say for me to phone you once I'd seen the X-ray, sir." The registrar sounded pained.

"I know. What did they find?"

"The plate shows about two-thirds of the right lung is consolidated. The radiologist says it's a collapse of the lower and middle lobes."

"Okay. I told you what to do. Have you got the kid in Intensive Care?"

The young man gave a dry, nervous cough. "The sister says she can't take the child into the unit, sir."

"The sister says *what?*"

"She says she can't take a Bantu child because there's a white child in there," Moolman told him unhappily. "I've got a drip up, sir. I guess we'll have to go ahead with the intubation in the ward."

"The hell we . . . Was that the only reason she gave? Only that there was a white child in the unit?"

"Yes, sir." Moolman hesitated. "But I don't think it was the sister's decision. The matron told her she couldn't take the baby."

"How did the matron come into it?"

"The sister phoned about the new admission and the matron told her not to allow the baby in there."

"What right has the matron got to tell me where I have to treat my patients?"

"I think it was on instruction from the Superintendent, sir."

"But for God's sake! I've . . . Never mind. Now, listen. You go up to that ward and you pick up that baby in your arms and you carry him down to the unit. And God help anybody who tries to stop you. And get hold of Tom."

"I already have, sir. He's on his way."

"Good man. How's Marietjie?"

"She's fine. It's only the block."

"Okay. Now you do as I say. I'll be right over."

Deon put down the receiver.

"Where's Lisa?" he asked.

"In her room," Elizabeth said.

"All right. Let her stay there. I have to go back to the hospital, but it shouldn't take me very long."

She did not reply.

As he did up his tie once more he thought angrily about the hospital Superintendent's interference. Hadn't he and van Rhyn sorted out that particular problem, at least? When he had started to operate at the children's hospital there had been room for only one Intensive Care Unit. Naturally the race question had soon arisen, as it inevitably did everywhere in this sad, bigoted and confused land. He had promised to operate only on white children one week and only on Coloured and black the next. In practice, of course, it was impossible. Disease did not respect the color bar. Often a child of the wrong color would be too ill to be moved back to the ward at the end of the week. Or there would be a Black emergency during the White week.

He had explained the problem to the Superintendent as tactfully as possible. "It's not working and it's never going to. In the future I'm not going to bother my head about the patient's color. I'm going to operate and nurse the children together, and to hell with it."

Dr. van Rhyn could see the problem but was afraid to commit himself. "That's all very well, Deon. But we've got to obey the law of the country. You know."

"Well, if you want to be so stern about the law then I shouldn't be allowed to use the same operating room and the same anesthetic machine and the same instruments and the same theater staff on both white and black patients. The whole thing is a farce. The same business cropped up at the main hospital the other day. They allow non-white sisters in the operating room for white patients, but those same sisters can't nurse the same patients in the ward. You know what the matron said when I queried it? 'Oh, in the operating room the patient is asleep.' Have you ever come across such crap?"

Dr. van Rhyn had spread his hands. "Deon, I'm here to see that the hospital is run according to the rules."

"Well, damn the rules. You know they're wrong. In future I'm not going to waste my time following rules."

The Superintendent had sighed and had looked out of his window. "You must do as you think best. I won't report you. But sooner or later someone, some white parent, is going to kick up hell."

"I'll tell you what I'll do. I'll send the white child back to the ward. And I'll make damn sure that the parents understand that their prejudice has resulted in their child getting inferior treatment."

Dr. van Rhyn had sighed once more.

The medical Superintendent was talking to the matron outside the Intensive Care room. Deon was derisively amused to find van Rhyn still at the hospital at a quarter to six, well past the end of the official working day. A confrontation was coming; that was quite certain. Let it come.

He gave them a brief nod and went past.

"Professor van der Riet," van Rhyn called.

Deon stopped at the glass-paneled door into Intensive Care. He turned.

"May I speak to you for a moment?" van Rhyn said.

Perhaps he should attack without waiting, while his temper was still aroused. Perhaps he should say all the things he had been planning to say. But there were priorities.

"In a moment." He put a hand on the door handle. "Would you wait a moment, please? I have to see my patients."

The hydraulic door sighed behind him as he went in.

Moolman, Tom Morton-Brown, and a sister were working at a corner bed. The anesthetist had intubated the Manyani baby and was sucking down the tube with a thin rubber catheter. He looked up briefly as Deon stopped beside him.

Moolman looked up too. He tried to keep his face blank, but Deon could read the entreaty. This youngster had defied the rules and he needed support.

"Nice work," Deon said.

Moolman's gawky limbs moved galvanically, like those of a puppet in the hands of an inexpert controller. He risked a smile.

Morton-Brown pulled out the catheter. "Here's the problem," he said. He showed them the tip. A large mucous blob was stuck to the end of it.

"Was that it?" Deon asked him.

The black baby stared around him in terror, squirming and straining against the sister's firm grip. Tom fixed a mask over the end of the tube.

"Was that obstructing the bronchus?"

"Well, I can't be sure," the anesthetist said. "But in any case it wasn't doing much good down there in the windpipes. I'll give it another suck in a minute, once he's had some oxygen."

Already the child's color was improving.

Deon nodded. "Okay Tom. Help Moolman connect the kid to the bubbles, will you? I'll be back in a couple of minutes."

He stopped at Marietjie's bed. She was lying quietly, undisturbed by the activity around the other bed. Of everyone here, he thought, she's probably least concerned about having a black child share a room with her.

The Superintendent was alone outside. He walked away from Deon, pointing at the landing between the wards, where they would be out of earshot.

The careful scene-setting annoyed Deon. "What's the problem?" he asked testily. "I've got lots on my hands, in case you haven't noticed."

Van Rhyn shook his head.

"Really, Deon. You shouldn't have done it."

"What are you talking about?"

"Dumping that black baby in here. That wasn't playing the game, man. You're undermining my authority, doing that sort of thing."

Bitter anger rose. This man, this office-hour doctor—when last had he treated a patient? He was an administrator, a super-clerk. What did he know or understand of what it felt like to have saved a life and then to see it slip away?

"In the first place, how did you come to hear of it?" he asked. His voice sounded strange in his own ears, thin and shallow, as if in fact he were struggling to make himself heard above an all-surrounding clamor.

"I have to know what goes on in my hospital," van Rhyn said defensively.

"The sisters in the cardiac recovery room . . . *my* cardiac recovery room" —with as much vicious sarcasm as he could get into the word—"were under instruction to keep the matron informed about who I chose to admit. Is that right? And the matron, in turn, kept you informed. Correct?"

A muscle had started to jump at the side of van Rhyn's jaw. Deon watched its spasmodic play coolly and analytically. This argument could end only one way: with him walking out of this hospital forever. And at this moment he did not care if he brought everything crashing in ruins around him.

"Don't you see it was for your own good?" van Rhyn asked pleadingly. "You know how headstrong you can be. I had to be sure there wasn't trouble for no reason at all. Can't you see that?"

"Thank you so much."

The twitching muscle on the other man's jaw fascinated Deon. What was the cause of nervous tics? A line from a textbook came out of the remote past: "Eventually these movements are carried out automatically in a purposeless fashion when the stimuli no longer are present."

And suddenly he was tired. In the long run, the movements were purposeless. The textbook had been perfectly right. You made the movements, but you no longer knew the reasons why. What did it matter anyway?

He began to turn away, to go back to his unit. A question occurred to him and he turned again.

"Just tell me this. I've been using this unit for blacks and whites indiscriminately for a couple of years now. You knew this. We agreed that I would take responsibility for any trouble. Then why did you choose today, particularly, to intervene?"

"But surely you knew?"

"Knew what?"

"The child you operated on today. The little girl. Don't you know whose daughter she is?"

"Marietjie Joubert. She was referred here from Swellendam. That's all I know."

The Superintendent shook his head slowly, bewildered by such frank and enormous ignorance.

"And you don't even know who Joubert is?"

"No. Nor do I very much care."

"But don't you see, man. That's why I had to do it. For your own good. He's P. J. Joubert. You know, Piet Joubert. The M.P. He's a firebrand Nationalist. He'll be in the Cabinet one of these days. And can you imagine what he will say if he finds his child sleeping in the same room as a black baby?"

"Now I'll tell you something," Deon said. "Either the Manyani baby stays in Intensive Care or you give the order yourself to send him back to the ward. And in that case you also take the responsibility. Send him back," he told the Superintendent. "But then you treat him. And God help you if anything happens to the child."

The Superintendent turned on his heel and went away, stalking stiff-backed through the corridors of his hospital.

Was it worth it? Van Rhyn was a decent man really; a bit pompous and too conscious of the dignity of his office, but kind-hearted and prepared to be helpful when he wasn't snarled up in the tangles of red tape.

A pity. But there it is.

When he left the hospital he vowed he would quit before the place was able to destroy him. Why should he eat his heart out day by day? All bureaucracy cared about was that a cardiac surgery unit existed. Whether it was good, bad, or indifferent was immaterial.

The southeast wind had come up in the late afternoon and was blowing strongly, buffeting his car from the side as it climbed the exposed slope of the mountain. He drove home, utterly weary, to face whatever he might find there. Little enough, God knew.

Lisa was still in her room and did not appear for dinner. Elizabeth and he finished the meal in chilly silence. Finally he pushed back his chair. "Did you keep food for Lisa? I'll take it to her."

"In the warmer. I doubt whether she'll eat it." Elizabeth did not look up from her coffee cup.

At first there was no response to his knock. Then Lisa's muffled voice called: "It's not locked."

She sat up on the bed when he came in, tucking her legs in tailor-fashion. She wore only a pair of panties.

"Are you feeling better?" He tried to show nothing except solicitude.

"I've never felt bad, Daddy."

Deon thought of Elizabeth walking round her flat, completely naked. How old had she been then? The same age her daughter was now.

"Lisa, why do you do this sort of thing?"

She did not pretend ignorance. "Because I like to, Daddy." She put the plate of food down on her pillow.

"That's not a very sound reason for doing something wrong, is it?" Her frankness had caught him off balance.

"It seems like a sound reason to me. A better reason than *not* to do it because *you* don't like it." She picked up a fork, then looked at him. "Why do you drink?"

Would he have to say: "Because I like to"?

"That's different."

"It's different all right," she flared, and he was again reminded of Elizabeth. "But the difference is that one kind of drug is legal and the other isn't." The hazel eyes were level, the chin firmly tilted. "You drink because you want to relax. I smoke pot because it's an escape. Only thing is you wake up with a hangover and I don't. You poison your body, your liver and . . . well, you're the doctor. You know what you poison with liquor. Pot doesn't do that."

"Don't be too sure about—"

"And let me tell you some of the other differences," she interrupted with passion. "A drunk simply becomes dull, but someone on pot becomes more perceptive. The music sounds better and the colors look brighter and the world becomes a big laugh. But it's illegal. Liquor is advertised and you can buy it round every corner and the more they sell the more money the government makes. But if I want to smoke I have to be on my guard, because both the salesman and I could land in jail."

He felt a sudden unexpected pride in his daughter. Perhaps she knew what it was she wanted.

"Well, you seem to have thought out your argument," he said in deliberately measured tones. "But tell me why you, with your pot, dropped out of school and then out of technical college? You've not really achieved anything with the eighteen years of your life, have you? I, with my liquor, have made a success of my life. How do you explain that?"

Lisa looked away too, through the window at the city lights below. After a while she asked softly: "Have you, Daddy? Have you?"

He looked down at her for a moment. Then he stooped and kissed her on the cheek. He left her bedroom.

The light in his own bedroom was off, so he undressed in the dark. Elizabeth lay motionless, curled up on her side, and he could not be sure whether she was asleep. He put a pillow over his eyes, hoping for sleep, but his mind was working too fast. His thoughts whirled from one image, one problem, to the next. The V.S.D. with heart block. The baby with a collapsed lung. Lisa and the police.

Lisa. Lisa. Lisa. He had expected so much from her. Was that the root of the trouble? Had he expected too much?

He slept, eventually, and was awakened by the sound he hated most of all: a telephone ringing in the night. He groped for the receiver.

"Moolman, Professor."

Oh, God. "What is it?"

"Sir, Marietjie's heart has suddenly become irregular. Very irregular. Her B.P. is down too. From seventy-five to sixty-five."

In the background, behind Moolman's voice, Deon could hear the familiar beep beep of the monitor. It sounded even more shrill over the telephone. He could distinguish clearly that extra beats were coming through.

"Did it happen very suddenly?" He was trying to collect his thoughts.

"Yes, Prof. One moment it was fine and regular at a hundred and twenty-two. The next it was completely irregular. Will you come and see her, Prof?"

"Okay. But first do one thing for me. I'll hold on here and you turn off the pacemaker and we'll see what happens."

"You want me to do *what?*"

"Turn off the pacemaker," he said firmly. "I'll hang on here."

Moolman had obviously dropped the receiver, for there was a bang and a period of loud crackling which made Deon jerk his head away. Then he could hear a rhythmic pounding as the instrument swung to and fro on its cord. But above this he could still make out the sound of the monitor, as clearly as if he himself were there in the ward. Beep. Beep. Beep-beep. Beep. Beep. Beep-beep. And then, abruptly and wonderfully, it became regular. Beep. Beep. Beep. Beep. Beep. He counted. A steady hundred-and-thirty a minute. Then he picked up Moolman's hurried footsteps.

The young registrar was nearly incoherent. "Prof! She's back in sinus rhythm! Beautiful sinus rhythm!"

Deon listened to Moolman's ecstatic voice and to the monitor in the background.

"That's great, my boy," he said at last. "Now, listen. Put the monitor on demand at a hundred a minute and switch it on again in case she reverts into block. But I think she's going to be all right now. How's the baby?"

"A lot better, Prof. I've just seen the last X-ray and the lung is nearly fully expanded now."

"Good. Call me if you're worried about anything. Good night."

There would be no sleep for Dr. Moolman, and for Deon, too, it would be a long time coming. Life was marvelous. Life was carrying on, no matter what. Life was triumph in the face of disaster. He felt a need to share his joy.

The southeaster had hardened during the night and was blowing a gale outside. He could hear its slamming force against the side wall and the eaves. He lay awake, listening to the wind. In a quixotic moment he wished he could be out in it now, sailing a small boat in the gale, fighting with a tiller and rock-hard sheets. He burrowed a little deeper into the bedclothes.

There was a crash and then a wild swoop of air inside the room as an insecurely fastened window latch gave way before the pressure of the wind. Deon leaped out of bed, struggling through the billowing curtains to reach the window before it banged itself to pieces. He caught and closed it.

The noise had awakened Elizabeth. A warm, silky leg touched his as he climbed back into bed. They lay side by side, listening to the storm outside. After a while he reached a tentative hand toward her. She did not resist. Their bodies touched. They went through a storm of their own.

Peter Moorhead called early in the morning, as they sat down to breakfast. Elizabeth sighed dramatically as Deon put down the receiver.

"Dear lord. Can't they ever leave you alone?"

"Peter has a problem over at the main hospital," he explained patiently. "And I don't think his judgment is all that good just at present."

She looked at him shrewdly. "Wife trouble again?"

He nodded. "So I suspect."

"Poor man. That one's a real harridan. Did I tell you what she said to Molly Brennan?"

He listened with enforced forbearance to a scandalously scathing description of Peter's sexual inadequacy. He laughed, despite himself. Poor Peter. How must it be to be tied to a woman who was prepared to say something like that about you?

"I wouldn't spread that around," Deon said. "Molly talks too much anyway."

He looked at his watch. "Look, I'd better skip breakfast. I must see Peter's patient and then I've got to get to the children's hospital. I'm operating this morning."

"I wish that damned hospital would burn to the ground."

"Never mind, darling," he said. "There's the Australian trip coming up next month. By the end of it you'll be heartily sick of me."

She sniffed. "Fine thing. You'll be at the damn congress all the time. And Sydney isn't my favorite city."

"Perhaps I can take an extra week," he suggested. "We could go up to the north, to the Barrier Reef."

She was immediately eager. "That would be nice. We've never been there."

"No." He was committed now. He couldn't really spare the time, but clearly she needed the break. He'd have to find time somehow. "All right. I'll fix it."

They parted as friends. While he was driving carefully round the steep, twisting turns he thought about his wife and his marriage. It hadn't turned out as expected. Why not? Certainly not the fault of his in-laws, for he

258

rarely saw them. Old Metcalfe was overseas again and Elizabeth only knew because she had seen it in the papers. The family met once a year, for the ritual of Christmas, and that was that. Then what was to blame? What exactly had gone wrong, and when had it happened? If, in fact, anything had gone wrong.

He shook his head and concentrated on the road.

The Superintendent of the children's hospital was in the Intensive Care Unit with a middle-aged couple. The three of them stood at Marietjie's bedside with the awkward air of strangers. Deon greeted them with a nod. The parents, obviously. Strange that they had never wanted to meet the man who would be operating on their child. It was typical of Afrikaaners not to show emotion. He often wondered whether they were really grateful.

Piet Joubert, the red-hot racist. "The Cape Lion" the chairman of a political meeting had once incautiously called him. And the Opposition newspapers had at once gleefully seized onto the fact that the Cape Lion had been extinct for hundreds of years. Thin, aggressive face and a gaunt neck. He's going to be the problem, Deon thought. The mother looked like a more pleasant person: plump and quick to smile, even if the smile was uncertain. Both watched every move Deon made. Van Rhyn, however, did not look at him at all.

"Could you wait outside for a few minutes? You can come back as soon as I've examined my patients." He was surprised to find his voice reasonably pleasant, although he had put a slight emphasis on those last two words. "I'll only be a minute or two."

They moved toward the door. Marietjie clung to her mother's hand. Deon went to her bed, smiling. The child looked at him and let go of her mother. They were allies, he and she. They had fought side by side, and won.

"Doctor Moorhead did an early round, Prof," Moolman said. "He went on to the main hospital."

"I know," Deon said. "I've just been with him."

Moolman looked worn-out. He was unshaven, an oversight Deon was usually very strict about. But the young man was having to do double duty and he'd had an exhausting night. Deon decided to make an exception, this once.

He examined Marietjie and studied her chart. She was well, considering she'd had an operation only yesterday. She had remained in sinus rhythm all night.

"Things look fine. What was the last venous pressure? Twelve? Give her five milligrams Lasix intramuscularly and watch the potassium when she starts passing urine. Leave her on the pacemaker for another day or two."

He went on to the other bed. The Manyani baby was fast asleep. The bubbles gurgled as he breathed. During the night there had been a steady fall in the respiratory rate as the lung expanded and began functioning again. The crisis was over.

Will you ever know what we did for you? he thought. Will you ever realize with what determination we fought so that you should live? And if you do, will you curse us for it eventually? For forcing you to stay alive: a black child in a white man's land?

"What's he on? Fifty percent oxygen?"

"Yes, Prof."

"You can start reducing the pressure slowly. Later in the day you can ask Tom to extubate him. I think we should keep him here till tomorrow morning."

"Yes, Prof."

"Robby's ductus. Is she okay?"

"Yes. We took her back to the ward."

"Okay. I'm going to speak to Marietjie's parents and then we can have a look at the wards."

Van Rhyn had left and the man and his wife were huddled together next to the window. Joubert turned as Deon came out.

Here it comes, Deon thought. Last night he would have relished the opportunity. But today it was all changed. The black baby was out of danger and Marietjie was well on the way to recovery. This morning there was no anger left in him.

"Doctor van der Riet," the man said.

Deon waited.

"Thank you for what you did for our child," the Nationalist M.P. and prospective Cabinet minister said humbly. "Will she be all right?"

"She's doing fine," Deon told him and smiled and was surprised to find it cost no effort. "She had a bit of a problem at first. We had to drive her heart with a pacemaker for a while. But her own heart has taken over now."

The man stared at him, obviously making his own assessment. There was a sharp intelligence behind that thin face.

"Do you know what she told me?" Deon said. "She told me she had a broken heart."

"That's how her mother explained it to her. To explain what was wrong with her heart and why she had to come here."

"I thought so. Well, we've mended that broken heart."

"Will she be normal now?"

"She'll be a bit off color for a few days and then there'll be no stopping her."

"We'll always be grateful to you."

The woman had not spoken, but she was smiling.

Joubert cleared his throat. "That black child inside with Marietjie."

Deon felt his chest go tight. No. God help us. Here it comes after all.

"Did he also have a hole in the heart?"

"He still has a hole in the heart," Deon told him tersely. "He is what we call a blue baby and he's too young for us to correct everything. We've done a small operation on the outside of the heart to help him till later on. Then we'll do a complete correction."

Joubert's next question caught Deon unawares. "Is he from here? From the Cape?"

"Why, no. He is from the Transkei."

"What part of the Transkei?" the other persisted.

"I really couldn't tell you. He was referred to us from the hospital in Umtata. But I have no idea where his home is."

"Are his parents here?"

The conversation was taking a strange turn, one which Deon could not quite fathom. But for some reason or other it seemed important to the M.P. so he answered this question too.

"I'm afraid not. He was sent down by train, with an escort." He was tempted to add: "They traveled third class," but suppressed the comment.

Piet Joubert picked up a parcel, wrapped in gay paper, which had been lying on the window sill. "Will you give this to that baby? We bought it for Marietjie, but my wife and I would like the baby to have it."

Deon took the soft parcel and thanked the man. He walked back into the Intensive Care room and unwrapped the paper. Inside was a fluffy white rabbit. He put it down beside the sleeping black baby and went out through the far door.

He stayed in the theater block that morning after he had finished operating. He was worried. It had been a mucky valve.

He had taken great care removing all the bits and pieces and had washed and sucked out the ventricular cavity several times, but he was still uneasy. You could never be quite certain some tiny piece had not fallen into the chamber and got stuck behind a muscle band. As soon as the blood flow to the heart was restored the bit of tissue would be dislodged and pumped into the circulation. It needed only a piece the size of a pinhead to block one of the arteries in the brain and the child could end up as a vegetable.

Once the little boy had come round from the anesthetic he would be able to assess brain function.

He has had a lot of bad luck already, Deon thought. Some patients just seem to have no luck at all.

It had started when the parents got home from a party late one night. The baby-sitter had gone home and they found their son of seven crawling on the floor of his room in agony. He was flushed and complained of a throbbing pain in his right knee. The father phoned the family doctor, but he was strictly a daylight practitioner and he prescribed two aspirin.

The next morning the child was unable to get out of bed, so the father had phoned the G.P. again. The doctor arrived eventually and decided that the boy had injured his knee, although the child was adamant that he had not hurt himself. The doctor prescribed more pain-killing tablets. Only the following morning, when the child still was no better, did he suggest an X-ray.

The little boy arrived at the hospital at noon, desperately ill. He was found to be suffering from acute osteitis of the lower end of the femur, combined with blood poisoning. The knee was operated on and he was put on intensive antibiotic treatment. But the aortic valve had been infected and now, two weeks later, one of its pockets had been destroyed. The valve had started to leak severely. Early this morning, in the medical ward, the child had gone into heart failure.

Robby had taken over the operation Deon was scheduled to do and he had tackled the leaking aortic valve as an emergency. He had found one cusp almost chewed away and an abscess in the heart wall below the valve. He had carefully cut away the dead tissue and sewn in an artificial valve. Now they were waiting for the anesthetic to wear off.

The child opened his eyes and looked round the operating room in wonder. Tom Morton-Brown removed the oxygen mask. A nurse leaned toward the little boy.

"Did I have an operation, sister?" he asked her.

"Yes, old son," Morton-Brown said. "You had an operation and now it's done."

The child noticed the anesthetist for the first time. His expression became apprehensive. "Are you going to give me an injection, Doctor?" he asked.

Deon walked away. His eyes were smarting, and he blinked angrily. Thank God there was nothing wrong with the brain, anyway.

As he changed out of his operating clothes he thought murderously about that general practitioner who used the telephone as a substitute for his own hands and eyes. He hadn't even bothered to get off his ass to see the child and was too disinterested the next day to do a proper examination.

He left the operating block, still angry and with a black weight on his mind. Someone hurrying past the other way stopped abruptly.

"Hey, Deon."

One of the cardiologists. Johan Schoeman.

"Why the hell did you send me a mongol?"

"What?"

"If I'd known you were sending me a mongol I wouldn't have canceled my squash game."

Deon's lips grew thin and his breathing quickened. "Listen. Get something clear, Johan. I send my patients to you for an opinion on their hearts, which you're qualified to give. Not on their brains, for which you aren't qualified."

Schoeman was clearly taken aback by the viciousness of the attack. He gave a wan smile. "Boy, you're in a foul mood. I was only pulling your leg."

"I'm not particularly amused."

"Okay. Okay. Anyway, I sent you my report this morning. It's not a Tet. It's a tricuspid atresia. You can't do anything for the kid in any case." He walked away and said to himself, just loudly enough for Deon to hear: "Probably it's just as well."

Deon went down the stairs and out of the hospital building, into the sunshine. Tricuspid atresia.

How was he going to tell Trish?

Schoeman's report was on his desk. He picked it up with reluctance and began to read, still standing. He skipped the history. The physical findings were typical of a tetralogy: cyanosis, a systolic murmur, a single second pulmonary sound. But the electrocardiogram gave the secret away. Left ventricular hypertrophy, instead of on the right, as it would have been in the case of a Fallot's.

He switched on the viewer next to the bookcase, shook the chest X-rays out of their package, selected an AP view of the chest and flipped it under the clips. He took a pace backward. His eyes narrowed in concentration. Heart enlarged to the left. But it wasn't the boot shape of a Tet. It was more like a rounded bulge, probably formed by the enlarged left ventricle. To the right was another bulge: the right atrium. The main pulmonary trunk was unidentifiable and the lung fields were starved of blood.

He flicked the switch and the picture of Giovanni's heart became opaque.

He picked up the report again and looked at the cardiologist's conclusions. There was no doubt that it was a tricuspid atresia with a large interatrial communication and a probable small ventricular defect. The main pulmonary artery was narrow and the branches were fed by collateral vessels. Schoeman asked for a cardiac catheterization to confirm his diagnosis.

Deon leaned across the desk, putting his weight on his elbow-locked arms and rocking slowly forward and backward, forward and backward.

It was a relief. No doubt about that. He'd been let off the hook. He wouldn't have to make that impossible choice. The choice had been made for him, long ago.

There's nothing to be done for this little tot, he told himself in an attempt to lessen the paralyzing sense of guilt. Nothing anyone in the world can do. All one can offer is a shunt, which will get a little more blood into the lungs.

Trish looked at him with expressionless eyes.

"Deon, you can't help me. Am I right?"

"No. No." He tried to smile. "Sit down and I'll tell you what they found."

It was always a terrible thing, no matter how often you had done it before; no matter how you steeled yourself with the reminder that death was the one certainty.

"Trish. I'm sorry. The Italian doctors were wrong. It's not a tetralogy of Fallot but a tricuspid atresia."

She continued to look at him with those masked eyes. "What does that mean?"

"Well, briefly, the tricuspid valve connects the two right-hand chambers of the heart. It has never developed properly and so blood can't flow through it to the lower chamber and as a result this hasn't developed either. The reason Giovanni is alive is because there's an opening between the two upper chambers and because . . ."

"Deon, please!" the woman said in a voice of desperation, although her expression still had not changed.

After a trembling-tense silence she said: "I'm sorry. But could you rather explain it all to me later? Could you just tell me what it means? Please?"

He could not bear to look at her any longer. "It's a very serious condition," he said finally.

"And you can't operate? Is that it?"

"We can do a palliative operation. It will help, but not greatly."

"But . . ."

He shook his head slowly. "Trish. I *am* sorry. But basically there's nothing to be done."

AUTUMN

Five

There was something familiar about the broad shoulder of the man walking ahead of Deon. He wore a hat and his overcoat collar was turned up against the chill of the gusty morning. Despite the obscuring bulk of the coat Deon was convinced that he had seen that determined, forward-thrusting stride somewhere before.

He followed, puzzled, running mentally through a long list of friends and acquaintances. The man had come up level with a parked cream-colored Volkswagen. He walked around the back of it and put a hand into his coat pocket. The key for which he was obviously searching was not in the coat and he unbuttoned it laboriously. As Deon drew level the other man found his key and turned toward the car door, glancing up over the roof as he did so.

With a slight shock Deon recognized Philip Davids. At once he remembered guiltily that he had never returned Philip's telephone call.

It had been a hectic time those few days before the Australian trip. On the Tuesday he had taken the son of a doctor from Pretoria back to the theater twice to stop the bleeding (things always seemed to go wrong when you operated on a colleague or his family). And there had been trouble with Lisa too.

Nevertheless he should not have forgotten to ring Philip. It was the sort of discourtesy that might seem like a slight.

He smiled now, with warmth that was slightly forced, in overcompensation, and said: "Why, hello, Philip. How are you?"

Philip's look of recognition had also been startled and perhaps a little reserved at first. But he smiled in return, said: "Hello, Deon. I'm fine. I'm very well, thank you," and walked back around the car.

They shook hands.

"Haven't seen you for ages," Deon was forced to say.

"What brings you here?" Philip asked. He looked round at the seedy shopfronts and high grimy walls on both sides of the street.

"I brought my car to be serviced. The shop is just around the corner. They didn't have a driver to take me back, so I thought I might as well catch a bus."

"Going toward the hospital? Can I offer you a lift?"

Deon hesitated. "Are you sure? Won't it inconvenience you?"

Philip unlocked the passenger's door and held it open. "I'm going there myself."

Deon got in gratefully and leaned across to lift the latch on the driver's door.

"Thanks," he said as Philip started the engine and revved it, watching in his mirror for a gap in the traffic. "It's not the most pleasant day for a walk."

Philip swung out into the stream of cars and heavy trucks.

"No," he said.

They traveled for a while in silence.

"How is your mother?" Deon asked.

Philip shrugged. "She's dying slowly, but fortunately the hormonal treatment stopped the bone pain she was getting from the secondaries."

Silence again, while Deon tried to think of something friendly to say. Finally he said: "I've only just remembered your phone call. Must be a long time ago. I really am sorry I didn't call you back."

Philip glanced at him. "Phone call? I don't think it was anything very important. I wanted to thank you for a pleasant evening, that's all."

"My secretary gave me the message, but I had so many problems to cope with I completely forgot to return your call. Do you remember Trish?"

"Trish?"

"Trish Coulter. She was in the art school when I . . . when we were in our final year. I took her out for a bit in our fifth and sixth years. Patricia Coulter."

"Girl with long dark hair?"

"That's right. Sort of dark red hair."

"I remember her vaguely. Remember seeing you together, anyway."

"Well, she turned up suddenly from Italy. She lives there now. Married to an Italian. Was married, rather. He died in a car crash."

He summarized Trish's story and her present predicament.

"That's tough," Philip said at the end of it, real sympathy in his usually unemotional voice. "Some people seem to have more than their fair share of bad luck."

A traffic signal ahead of them changed to amber and he speeded up, then changed his mind and touched the brake instead. The little car halted smoothly at the red light.

"What makes it a greater tragedy is that it could have been prevented," he said then.

"You mean by chromosomal study of the fetus?"

"Yes. Amniocentesis has become common practice these days." Philip glanced sideways. "You know. Aspirating fluid containing fetal cells from the uterus of the mother in early pregnancy."

"I know," Deon said quickly. "Pity it was not done in her case."

"I would certainly have suggested it. She must have been in her late thirties when she became pregnant?"

"Thirty-eight."

"Yes. She was getting to the age where the risk of having a mongol child is high."

"If you had found that extra chromosome, would you have advised termination of the pregnancy?"

"Yes," Philip said without hesitation.

Deon gave a little laugh. "I seem to remember you had other ideas in the old days."

The lights changed and Philip let out his clutch. "The old days?"

"Don't you remember that argument we once had about abortions?"

"Of course. I do remember now." Philip was silent while he shifted gear and overtook a lumbering truck which was occupying more than its share of the road. Then, with the way ahead clear once more, he continued: "I'm still against it when it's merely for the sake of getting rid of an unwanted pregnancy. But when an abortion prevents the birth of a child with an incurable disease I'm all for it. Mental hospitals are already overcrowded. The money spent on looking after mongols, mentally retarded children, those with cerebral palsy and other mentally defective children can be much better used. In this country certainly it could be spent on fighting malnutrition among the Coloured and black children."

A little nettled by the implied criticism Deon said: "You sound rather mercenary. We can't afford them, so we mustn't allow them."

Philip raised his eyebrows. He did not reply.

"You see," Deon said, "to Trish this isn't just another mongol. It's her only child. It has a name. Giovanni. She loves him and he loves her in return. If that pregnancy had ended she would have had nothing."

"From what you've told me she has enough money to look after him. But what if she hadn't? If apart from being a half-human he was also a great financial burden on the family?"

"I don't see that it makes any difference."

"In fact, it should not. It shouldn't alter the principle. Look, you know yourself that nature has ways of keeping the mongol population down. They die from infection and other associated fatal abnormalities and so on. Nature weeds them out. But we, with antibiotics and surgery and what have you, are upsetting the balance."

"Surely you don't suggest we withhold drugs and surgery from them?"

"Why not? No one can force you to maintain a useless life. Each of us has to make his own decision."

"I guess that's true." Deon put a hand to his chin, spreading thumb and forefinger on either side of the jaw and nibbling gently at the web of skin between the stretched fingers. "I guess it's true."

Philip noticed the gesture and laughed. "You don't seem altogether convinced."

"It's not really a question of conviction. I have been asking myself these questions." Deon paused, trying to find exactly the right words. "What you are saying makes a lot of sense in theory. Medicine has allowed genetic mistakes to survive. That's true. But you can't lay all the blame at the door of medicine. The whole of modern technology has contributed. You might as well argue that if someone has had half his brain destroyed in an accident it would be wrong to use a telephone to call a doctor, or wrong to take him to hospital by ambulance. You should carry him, for then he might die on the way."

"Maybe we'll be forced to do that one day," Philip said shortly. "What did you advise her? Trish."

Deon sensed a desire to change the conversation and thus perhaps avoid open argument. Just as well. He too tried to return to a level of composed and tolerant conversation.

"What could I advise her? He's got tricuspid atresia."

"So there's nothing you can do?"

"Nothing." Deon twisted his mouth sourly.

"Has she gone back to Italy with the child?"

"I think so. She was supposed to go back, anyway."

Philip regarded him briefly, and Deon, conscious of being faintly on the defensive, as if somehow he had let Trish down on two counts—being unable to operate on her child and now even uncertain of her whereabouts—explained: "I've been away, you see. Out of the country."

"Of course. I saw the papers. Australia, was it?"

"Yes."

"You're looking very well. Obviously Australia was good for you."

"Oh, we've been back quite a while. More than a month now."

"You have a healthy-looking tan, anyway."

Deon smiled. "I've had a couple of weekends sailing on the bay. But the tan won't last if we get much of this kind of weather."

"No. Strangely, I feel the cold far more acutely here than in Canada."

"Different kind of cold, I suppose."

"I guess it is."

They spent the rest of the journey making conventional conversation. Philip turned off the main highway on to the approach to the hospital.

"You can drop me anywhere here," Deon said.

"It's okay. I have to pass your offices anyway. I'm going next door."

They turned into the narrow street in front of the medical school. It was packed with parked cars.

"The students are back, as you can see," Deon said. "I'll tell you what. I've got a reserved space at the back. Go round and pull in there, if you like."

"It isn't necessary. I have a place too, over at the end."

"Really?" Deon looked wonderingly at the Coloured man. "How come?"

"I work here."

"I meant to ask what you'd been doing, but somehow I took it for granted that . . . well, you mentioned once that you were going to do some writing."

"It didn't take as much time as I expected. So I decided to take up Professor Gleave's offer. I told you he offered me a job in his cytogenetics lab, didn't I?"

"I remember you mentioning it."

"Anyway, that's where I am."

"When did you start?"

"Oh, six weeks ago. In April."

"You're practically next door and for six weeks I hadn't even known you were here."

"A lot of people work in these buildings," Philip remarked.

And Deon, grateful for the excuse being held out to him, agreed hurriedly. "Yes. There must be hundreds of them I've never even laid eyes on."

* * *

The building was brand new, but the doors fitted badly and the wind made a thin, keening sound through the gaps. The foyer was cold and Philip kept his overcoat on while he waited for the elevator.

An arrow flashed and the doors slid open. Two young women came out of the elevator, talking animatedly, and Philip stood aside for them to pass. They went by without a glance.

He got into the elevator and pressed the button for the fourth floor. As he did so the swinging doors burst open directly in front of the two girls, causing them to jump aside with squeaks of dismay. A burly red-faced man came charging through and ran toward the closing elevator doors. The girls turned and glared at him.

Philip sought in vain for the button that would halt the doors as they glided together. He found it, but by this time the big man, with a last convulsive leap, had thrust his shoulders into the closing gap. The doors stopped and banged, then began to open again.

The newcomer forced them apart.

"Couldn't you keep the bloody thing open?" he asked Philip roughly, in Afrikaans.

Philip's brows drew together, but he kept his voice level.

"Sorry." He held a finger ready over the array of buttons. "What floor?"

"Five."

They stood in silence as the doors banged shut again and the lift jerked into motion.

"Are you the elevator man?" the big man asked then, menacingly.

Philip drew in his breath slowly, held it, then let it out in a long, expiring sigh. He did not look at the other. "No," he said finally.

"Isn't there a separate elevator for Coloureds?"

Did you allow them to get away with it every time?

Philip turned toward the red face and small, piggy eyes.

"This building is not part of the hospital. It is on the university campus. I am a professor and I work here."

"I've got an appointment," the man mumbled. He was clearly taken aback and no longer so sure of himself.

The elevator stopped and Philip got out. As the doors closed again the big man muttered: "Bloody Hottentot."

Philip turned sharply, but the doors were already shut. The stairs were next to the elevator. He could reach the fifth floor within seconds.

But what was the use? What could you achieve by fighting them? Even if you beat them, even if you broke their heads and smashed in their smug faces, you didn't change anything. All you could do was to clamp your teeth together, swallow back the bitter taste, like bile, and try to pretend to yourself that it didn't matter.

He squared his shoulders and then, back as straight as a guardsman's, he marched down the corridor to the doorway on which an unobtrusive sign proclaimed: Department of Human Genetics.

The door opened on to a narrow passage with the main laboratory on one side and offices on the other. He went into the laboratory. The two women technicians were working at the big central bench. They looked up from their microscopes and greeted him, smiling. They were always friendly, and he knew that they had accepted him.

Williams was another matter altogether. Unlike the girls he already had a bachelor's degree in biology, and before Philip had arrived had been un-disputed master of the laboratory. Professor Gleave was too involved with clinical work and meetings to maintain more than token control. Now, however, Philip was in charge.

The senior technician had been in the incubator room at the back of the laboratory. He came out and closed the door behind him, then leaned casually against the doorpost. He called to the women technicians.

"None of those last four cultures have taken." His tone was laconic, even careless.

Philip was unsure whether Williams had noticed him. He moved to make his presence known.

"Are you sure, Mr. Williams? No growth at all?"

Williams wore a permanently aggrieved look. He added to this and sur-veyed Philip from under half-closed eyelids. "I'm sure," he drawled. Only then did he take his hand away from the doorpost and slowly, reluctantly, straighten up.

"I'm sure," he repeated. A brief, defiant pause. Then: "Professor."

Philip turned impatiently. The girls went back to their microscopes with a display of intense concentration.

"How long have they been incubating? Six days?"

Williams nodded stiffly.

"The cultures aren't infected, are they?"

"No, there's nothing wrong with my technique."

"All right. Then we'll have to get new samples. Let me have the folder numbers so I can trace the patients."

He walked across the laboratory and the girls continued to apply them-selves assiduously to their tasks. They did not look up at him. He wondered whose side they were on. Did they secretly side with Williams? Were the whites drawing together instinctively; closing ranks against the others? Did they hate him, really, when he gave them instructions?

Nonsense, he told himself firmly. The one thing you mustn't allow yourself is a persecution complex. It's a way of giving in, of surrendering to pressure. You can't achieve anything by fighting them, but you've got to keep fighting just the same.

Probably the girls were merely embarrassed by Williams' surliness.

He crossed the passage to his office. Gleave had been especially good about providing accommodation. He had given up his own office, with the small laboratory adjoining it, and had insisted that Philip take it. All protests had been overridden.

"You'll want to do some work of your own," Gleave had said. "This lab isn't fully fitted. If you need more equipment we'll see what we can arrange. I never manage to make use of the place anyway. I've become a sort of glorified office supervisor, and that I can do in any hole in the wall."

The room was spacious and carpeted and the desk was definitely Academic Order Grade A. Having a private laboratory as well was a real luxury. But, in his new mood of suspicion, Philip wondered: had he been put in here to keep him away from the whites in the main laboratory?

Nonsense, he thought again, and shoved the nagging doubt away.

He settled in behind the wide desk and moved the "In" tray closer to hand.

It was a nuisance that the cultures hadn't grown. Fortunately they had been blood samples. It would have been more serious if they were samples of amniotic fluid. A repeat would have meant another amniocentesis and a further fortnight before the karyotype was ready for study. For a technician, interested only in the scientific findings, the wait was nothing much. But for the woman, waking each morning with the dread that her unborn child was abnormal, it was an eternity.

There must be some way of ensuring that the specimen contained viable cells. Maybe I should do a vital stain on some of the cells before putting the rest up for culture. He thought about the problem for a moment and then the earlier conversation with Deon came to mind.

I hadn't expected him to feel so strongly about abortion, he thought. Frankly, I didn't really think he felt strongly about anything except cardiac surgery. Strange man. I don't really feel at ease with him. I did once. Well, at times anyway. That's because we react in the same way to a lot of things. Only natural.

He smiled derisively.

273

We inherited that hard outside core and the brusque manner from our father. My father. Strange how difficult it still is to think of him like that. The Old Master. Baas Johan. Somehow it sits easier on the mind, hate it how you will.

What caused him to prefer a Coloured woman, a servant in his own kitchen, to the wife he had promised, by the sacred vows of his own savagely unbending, unyielding religion, to love and keep and cherish and honor? What darkness was there in his mind; what corner where no light was allowed to fall? I'll never know now. Do I particularly want to know?

Was it mere lust? He was a strong man, even in old age, and my mother was young then: eighteen, nineteen.

What made her give in to him, for that matter?

But the question raised a specter which he had long ago given decent burial, so he hurriedly avoided the thought and considered instead how strange it was that Johan van der Riet had allowed him, a bastard son, to grow up on the farm. Had even arranged that Mieta should be married properly, by the missionary, although she was already big with child. Then, when the foster father was dead, he had continued to care, no matter how offhandedly, for his one-time mistress and her wrong-side-of-the-blanket child.

The question could never be answered. And meanwhile there was work to do and he was wasting time. He picked the top file out of the basket, glancing at the name on the cover as he did so. Mrs. Edwards. Amniocentesis report. A check to determine whether Mrs. Edwards, aged forty-three years, is harboring a mongol inside her uterus.

He thought about his and Deon's earlier discussion. Strange man, he thought again. I think I remember that girl. Trish.

He flipped open the file and looked at the pink slips, in triplicate, and then the form, written in Williams' fussily tidy handwriting, on which the typed report was based.

Negative. Good.

It was a sad story, really. He had seen the woman in Gleave's office when she came in for the first consultation. A pale, washed-out little woman with round, thin-rimmed glasses and pale hair drawn back against her skull. Spinster, you thought at once. School teacher or librarian. In fact she had worked in a cigarette kiosk near the station for nearly twenty years, and then Mr. Edwards, widower and printer's reader, a daily customer for the previous three years, had finally proposed.

Forty-one and fifty-eight. An autumn marriage. The subject for jokes and a certain amount of prurient curiosity. At fifty-eight, after all . . .

Mr. Edwards had dispelled all doubt about the matter, for Mrs. Edwards had become pregnant within the year. And the child was a mongol.

It *was* Trish, wasn't it? Yes. He was sure he remembered her: a dark-haired girl, pretty in a serious kind of way. Quite the opposite of Elizabeth, who had always believed life was for living. There had been something in the air, that evening he had spent with them. . . . Well, it was none of his business. This Trish was fortunate in a way. She could obviously afford to keep her child and tend to his demands.

Mr. and Mrs. Edwards, in their tiny suburban flat, could not. Their child was in an institution and they visited her once a month with gifts of candy and toys.

Two and a half months ago, in cold dread, Mrs. Edwards had discovered that she was pregnant again. She had kept it a secret from her husband, but fortunately she'd had the good sense to see a gynecologist, who had referred her to the genetic clinic.

This time the news was good. Philip examined the karyotype with its photographic images of the paired chromosomes. No problems. The normal pair of Number 21 chromosomes was present and the third, which formed the condition known as Trisomy 21, the cause of mongolism, mercifully absent.

He studied the karyotype for a moment longer. Not only would Mrs. Edwards be able to be assured that her child was going to be normal but she could even be told well in advance that she was going to have a boy this time.

Lucky Mrs. Edwards. Philip initialed the report and picked up the next file.

"Dodman" was the name on the cover. This one wasn't so easy.

Philip left the file unopened on his desk and got up to walk slowly and thoughtfully toward the window. He had no need to study the report and correspondence, for he knew it all already.

He stood by the window and looked down at the windy street. Early lectures had obviously ended in a free period, for groups of students, their white coats billowing around them, heads down against the press of the wind, were streaming down from the hospital. He watched them for a while. Among them, somewhere was young Dodman.

Twenty-two years old, fourth year, a bright boy, according to his professors. And he was faced, for the next two or three decades of his life, with an agonizing prospect.

The disease was Huntington's chorea, carried and transmitted by descendants of the Cornish miners who had emigrated in the mid-nineteenth century when the old tin mines became uneconomic. From his lectures in pathology and neurology Dodman was aware of the insidious beginnings and progressive course of this disease. He had gone home for the summer vacation and had been startled and puzzled by changes he had found in his father. The father was sales manager for a motor company and had always, in his son's experience, been a breezy extrovert. He had become moody and obstinate about trifles that he would have ignored six months ago.

The members of the family were all excellent tennis players. Dodman senior had once played for his province and Dodman himself had reached the finals of the interschool championships. Once he left school and went on to university he had little time for practice, however, so he and his father had remained well matched. During the holidays he had coaxed his father into a match. He had won in straight sets, with ridiculous ease. It was like playing against a beginner. His father stumbled around after the ball, double faulted his service, put easy forehands into the net, and argued irascibly about line calls. They left the court, silent and embarrassed, and did not play tennis again.

Dodman had always known his father as hardworking and ambitious. Now, his mother told him worriedly, his father seemed to have lost all interest in his job. Sales figures in his area had slipped badly and the directors had asked for an explanation. He had not yet got around to drafting the report. He was only forty-four. There had been every chance of his being appointed to the board and becoming managing director by the time he was fifty.

Dodman became suspicious. He began to make seemingly casual inquiries about his father's family. There had always been a mystery about his grandfather's early death. A hunting accident, it was said. In fact, Dodman discovered, it had been a bullet through the brain from a revolver at point-blank range. His great-grandfather had been in an asylum. The Dodman family, he found, had come from Redruth in Cornwall in the 1860s.

He had returned to university in a state of acute anxiety, and had read all the literature he could lay his hands on in the medical library on Huntington's chorea.

The illness was transmitted as an autosomal dominant. Neurological symptoms developed during the fourth decade of life. Minor symptoms such as clumsiness were often the first to appear. These were followed by an impairment of attention and judgment and a growing lack of initiative, then the onset of involuntary spasmodic movements, first of the face and arms, eventually of the whole body. The disease was progressive and incurable, ending in paralysis and insanity. The average duration of life after the start of the disease was fifteen years.

Dodman had lingered on after one of Professor Gleave's lectures to ask for advice. Gleave had gratefully dumped the problem into Philip's lap.

Philip turned away from his long contemplation of the lines of white-coated youngsters struggling against the wind.

The trouble was that there was so little to say.

"Listen," he would have to tell Dodman. "We really don't know. At this stage of the game there's no way of telling."

There was no way at present of determining whether Dodman, at the age of twenty-two, had inherited the gene that would make him blind and mad in twenty years' time. He could tell him that if he was a carrier and got married there would be an even chance of passing the disease on to his children.

"Should I marry?" he would ask. "Can I take the risk of leaving my own children with this fatal legacy? Will they have a fifty-fifty chance too?"

What could you say? Marry if you must, but be prepared for a short life, and an unmerry one. Have yourself sterilized, just in case.

And the best of luck to you too.

I shouldn't be here, Philip thought. A good social worker would be more useful in this spot. It's essential and it's a very human and valuable service, but it's not for me. My job is in the laboratory, determining what it is about the infinitely complex structure of the genetic code that scrambles itself and produces such oddities and abnormalities as Huntington's chorea.

And yet. Deon had asked him, during that night-time drive home after dinner: "When did you last see a patient?" and it had hurt like a scourge. It had been an accusation, although thrown out without thought. And he himself had asked: "Yes, when?" to himself.

Was the laboratory a refuge? People frightened him, with their demands, and their clumsy lives. His wife had frightened him and had driven him into chill remoteness, which she had interpreted as disdain. Elizabeth, once, had wanted, wanted, wanted, and how could he answer such passionate needs when he had to hide his own needs behind a mask of correctitude and control?

I should be back in my own lab, he thought.

But how can I go, with my mother ill and dying? It's a terrible thing to think, but her death will be a double release. For her: from the pain of living. For me: from the last links with this, the land of my birth. Once she is dead I can go and I need never come back again.

He thought about a long airmail letter he had received from Jorgensen, who was temporarily in charge of his laboratory in Toronto. Jorgensen was a keen and capable research worker, but sometimes prone to jump to overhasty conclusions. This was a fatal flaw in a research scientist. All he needed was experience and guidance, but this was missing now, at a vital stage. Judging from the report, Jorgensen had misinterpreted some of his findings and was on the wrong track. The costly and time-consuming work of months might have to be repeated.

He was itching to be back there himself. He had reached an exciting stage in the project and felt like a detective searching for the final clue that would solve the mystery.

The thought came to him at once, and it was so obvious and yet so startling that he found himself drawing in his breath.

Could he do some of the work? Here?

He crossed the carpeted floor and opened the farther door, which led to the small laboratory. Roomy enough, however, for the kind of work he would be doing. There were a few pieces of dust-covered equipment standing around, but there was a lot more he would need.

That was the problem. It would cost a considerable amount to buy and install all the stuff, if it could be obtained in this country. Gleave had promised to help, but his small budget would certainly not take care of an electron microscope, which, for the work he was thinking about, would be one of the first priorities. No. It was just an idle notion. No point in spending that much money for a couple of months' work.

Tempting, however. And, of course, the equipment would stay here after he'd left. But where would he find the money? Impossible.

He closed the laboratory door, regretfully, and returned to his desk.

Another report on a sample of amniotic fluid. This time to determine the sex of the fetus. And according to the test the embryo was male. What had been the reason for doing an amniocentesis in the first place? He paged through the papers in the file.

A three-page gynecologist's report explained it. This was another sad and problematical case. The woman's married name was Marais, and she had been a Miss Turner. Her brother was a hemophiliac and her elder sister, who was married too, had given birth to a son who was also a bleeder. The little boy had spent most of his life in hospital.

Mrs. Marais, née Turner, was now pregnant too, and the Barr body test had shown she was carrying a son. What were the chances he would suffer from hemophilia too?

How the devil could you advise?

Blood tests had shown that she was a carrier, so her unborn boy had an even chance of inheriting the disease. Those were the odds. So the decision had to be theirs.

But wasn't that evading the issue? You knew the risks involved. Wasn't this precisely why you had been trained to be a doctor? "When did you last see a patient?" The words came back like a distant echo. Wasn't it your responsibility to guide them into making the right decision?

He reached for a writing pad and scribbled his finding and recommendation: "Fetus is male. Under the circumstance I advise termination of pregnancy."

He signed his name, clipped the slip of paper to the file cover, and shifted it to the left-hand basket.

Deon, he thought suddenly. He'll help me. He knows a lot of influential people. He'll be able to think of a way of finding money for the stuff I need.

Would asking for help seem too much like cringing? Baas Johan. Baas Deon. Thank you my master, my king.

He hesitated, hand on the telephone receiver. How would Deon react? Wouldn't it appear as if he were placing too much reliance on a special relationship?

To hell with that, he told himself. It took me years in another country to come to terms with myself, to learn to accept the fact of my race and color and the circumstances of my birth. Four months back in this bloody country and I'm destroyed; I want to crawl again.

Come to think of it, I have a genetic disorder too, and it's worse than mongolism or Huntington's chorea or hemophilia. Its name is race and there's no cure for it, for the sickness is outside myself, in the minds of others.

He picked up the receiver and began to dial. There was the whine of a busy signal. He replaced the instrument. He would try again in a moment.

"This is Miss Arensen," the prissy telephone voice informed Deon. "Professor wants to speak to you."

Deon recognized the ploy. My secretary speaks to your secretary and then my secretary has to speak to you before I deign to speak. It all served to establish relative importance and degree of activity and who was who on the pecking order. And he was sick of it.

"Deon," Snyman's high, querulous voice said in his ear.

"Morning, sir."

"Morning." Snyman sounded busy and bustling. Today, Deon realized, he was playing his forceful role. "The Teaching Hospitals Central Advisory Committee discussed your letter recommending Robertson's promotion, yesterday afternoon."

"Oh, yes," Deon said. Robby, although his deputy, had still not been appointed a senior surgeon. "It's been fixed up now, I hope."

"Although I was for it, the majority of the committee was against his promotion at this stage," the old man said.

Deon's grip on the receiver tightened. "But why on earth not?"

"They do not feel that the position warrants a senior post."

"But for God's sake. Robby runs this department when I'm away."

"I told them that. But they still decided against it."

It was clearly a low blow, aimed not at Robby but at himself. At his independence, his scorn for the hospital bureaucracy.

"Well, the damn Teaching Hospitals Central Advisory Committee isn't the final arbiter," he said loudly. "I'll take the matter over their heads to Province."

Snyman's voice was cold. "You will land yourself in a lot of trouble if you do that."

"That's my *indaba*," Deon shouted. "Good-bye, sir."

He replaced the receiver.

Almost immediately the telephone began to ring again.

Six

It had turned out to be a fine, crisp day after all, despite this morning's cold wind. Deon and Philip sat side by side on a park bench near the top of The Avenue. Yellow and bronze leaves from the great oaks drifted, side-slipping, to the paved walks. It was a fine day, but they were grateful for the sun on their backs.

"It's going to be a long winter," Deon said.

"Looks like it," Philip said.

They had met at lunchtime outside the medical school. Deon, still puzzled about the reason the other man had telephoned him so soon after their chance meeting, had unthinkingly proposed that they have lunch together and Philip had accepted.

Only as he was driving along the flank of the mountain toward the city center did it occur to Deon that he knew of no restaurant where the two of them, men of different colour, could have a meal together. Certainly not in the hotels (unless, of course, he had remembered to apply for government permission; in quadruplicate, presumably,) or in any of the better dining places he knew. He suspected, although he was not quite sure, that they would not even be able to get service at one of the drive-in restaurants with their soggy food and plastic plates and throwaway cutlery. Unless, possibly, he climbed into the back seat and Philip posed as his chauffeur.

He slacked off speed and moved over to the slower left lane while he considered the problem. Perhaps Vittorio would arrange a private corner at the Florenzia. It would be a bit obvious, however, for they would probably have to use the kitchen entrance in case some other patron made a fuss. What the devil could he do? He should have suggested dining at the university, or had a meal sent in to his office. But it was too late for that now. It would mean turning back, away from the city, and would be as obvious as going into a restaurant by way of the kitchen door. Home, then? At least they were heading in the right direction. But Elizabeth was at a bridge luncheon somewhere in Constantia. It was the maid's afternoon off and his own culinary abilities extended no further than bacon and eggs.

Perhaps Philip sensed his predicament then, for he said, as they reached the end of the freeway: "You know, I don't usually bother much about lunch. Shall we buy a snack and find somewhere quiet to eat it?"

"Good idea," Deon had said gratefully. "I seldom have lunch myself."

They had gone into a snack bar and ordered two toasted cheese and tomato sandwiches and two small cartons of milk, complete with built-in plastic straws. Philip had solemnly allowed Deon to pay the bill and they had carried their paper bags through the streets and along The Avenue, past the Parliamentary buildings and their private gardens (a solitary, portly man in a dark suit had been strolling, head down, hands clasped behind his back, among the formal flower beds) to this bench among the oak trees.

They had eaten, not speaking much, and had thrown breadcrusts to the quick, gray squirrels which leaped, bushy tails flicking, up and down the tree trunks.

"I guess you've been wondering why I wanted to see you," Philip said at last.

"Frankly, I have."

"I want money," Philip said baldly.

Deon blinked and stared at him. A flush of fear came instantly. Blackmail? He discarded the thought as unworthy, but still did not feel altogether comfortable.

"Well, of course. I . . . you have only to ask . . ."

Philip laughed, a trifle harshly. "Sorry. I put that badly. I don't want it for myself. It's for a research project I want to get under way. I thought you were probably the best man to advise me about raising funds for it."

Deon felt both relieved and ashamed. "Of course. With pleasure. How much do you want and what's it for?"

"I've told you about the research I've been doing in Canada, haven't I? I think I also mentioned the possible dangers of handling genetic material."

"Yes, we did talk about it," Deon hedged.

"There's some of this work I feel I could do here. But the problem is to get the equipment."

"How much money do you need?"

Philip paused to watch an old gray-haired Coloured man coming slowly down the path toward him. He was blind and wore dark glasses and carried a white stick. A small boy led him by the hand. The boy was watching the squirrels and the old man followed his tugging hand obediently, like some large and clumsy and patient breed of dog. The boy saw the white man and the Coloured man together on the bench, turned off the path, and approached. The old man came unresistingly behind. The child stopped and the man did also, shuffling to a halt, his stick probing at the ground ahead of him.

The little boy held out a tin with a roughly cut slot in the lid and rattled the coins inside.

"Blind, please, sir," he said confidently.

Without hesitation Philip reached into a pocket, took out a small coin and dropped it into the proffered tin. The child turned to Deon and after a moment's thought he dug out a coin as well.

The boy turned away without thanking them and tugged at the old man's hand. At once the old man followed him. They went off down the long lane of oaks, protector and protected, and did not once look back.

"Probably a bit of a racket," Deon said. "The old guy probably gets a pension anyway. If he even is blind."

Philip watched the two figures, becoming small at the end of The Avenue, where the city began.

"Perhaps. But a pension doesn't go far, you know."

"It would go further if they didn't spend half of it on booze," Deon said obstinately.

Philip followed the dying flight of an oak leaf. When the leaf settled on the ground he said: "Deon, I wonder if you can even imagine the feeling of having absolutely nothing to live for."

Deon looked at the Coloured man uncomfortably and said nothing.

"I'd almost forgotten what it can be like," Philip said. "Until the moment I stepped back into this country."

"Oh, I know, I know," Deon said hurriedly. "It's terrible. The things the government . . ."

Philip interrupted him with a raised hand. "Wait. Let me finish. It's not only the government. It's not only the laws and decrees. It's in the attitude of people. A kind of assumption of being right because you're white. And a converse feeling of diminishment because you're not. After a while you almost start to believe they *are* right."

Deon had been watching him as he talked. There was a difference between this man and the Philip of three months ago. He himself had used the word "diminished" and it was the right word. That calm and that

283

confidence had been diminished, had eroded. Is it really that bad? he wondered confusedly. Are we so evil that we can do this to a man like this?

Philip's hand was still lifted. Now he flung it outward in a gesture of despair. "What the hell anyway. I was telling you about the work I'd like to do."

"Yes," Deon said anxiously. "In a minute. But just one point. Just one. You must remember that the whites are running scared. So naturally they try to appear confident. At the same time, anyone who might seem to challenge their assurance is a danger. You understand that? Do you understand?"

Philip smiled thinly. "In theory. In practice it's somewhat . . . but what the hell use is it? Do you think you could advise me about raising the money I need?"

Deon nodded, still reluctant to change the subject. "Of course. I'll do my best anyway. What exactly are you doing?"

"Well, the basis of it is the danger that in handling genetic material outside the body, I mean placing it in test tubes and culture dishes, you might change the information it's transmitting. That's what we want to find out."

"How do you go about it?"

"We've got some fairly sophisticated projects going on in Toronto. But what I was thinking of doing here would be much more straightforward. It would simply be the fertilization in the test tube of the experimental animal's egg by the animal's sperm and the subsequent laboratory culture of the young embryo."

"Yes, I follow. And then you examine the young embryo for developmental abnormalities?"

"Yes. In some of the experiments we will study them early while they are still growing in culture media. In others, we will transfer the young embryo to the uterus of a pseudo-pregnant animal and check the fetus at later stages of development."

"Boy! I can see there's a helluva lot of work in it. How much money will you need?"

"Not so much, apart from the problem of getting an electron microscope. They cost thousands, as you probably know. I don't think we can buy one, but even if we could get the use of one it would help."

"I know they've just installed a new one for the Department of Pathology. You've met Professor Martyn. I'm sure he'll help. What else do you need?"

"I've got to find space to keep the animals. And there'll be a lot of other odds and ends."

Deon slapped his hands emphatically down on his knees and got up. He felt newly resolute and confident. The slight dissension with Professor Snyman this morning still rankled, but he would not allow it to distract him from his purpose.

"Listen," he said. "You make out a list of what you need and let us have an estimate. I'll get that money for you."

There was a call for Deon at the office. Robby was having trouble. The "Mustard" he had done this morning was bleeding.

He left Jenny with a few hurried instructions and drove to the hospital as fast as the Jaguar could take him. By the time he reached there, however, things were again well under control. Robby had given the child extra protamine and calcium intravenously and the bleeding had stopped. Robby was telling stories to the recovery room nurse that would have had her blushing furiously if she had not long been inured to both Robby and his particular brand of humor.

Deon stood around for a while, making suggestions, but clearly his presence was not required and after a while he left.

For the first time in a long while he was at loose ends. Jenny would have handled things at the office. There were no patients to be seen urgently. Elizabeth would not yet be home from her lunch. Etienne was playing in a rugby match at school, and would not be in till after six. The house would be a lonely place.

Briefly he considered driving out to visit his mother. But she would not be expecting him today, he told himself. The change in routine would unsettle her. And, frankly, the place upset him.

Then he would go to watch Etienne's rugby match. That was a good idea. It was seldom he was able to share in his son's life, either at home or at school. He had been forced to leave most of the care of the children to Elizabeth, who, give her her due, had never complained about the extra responsibility.

He drove out to the suburb where the school stood: an elegant ivy-shrouded collection of stone buildings among acres of green playing fields and athletic tracks and tennis courts, all speaking of quiet and respectable wealth.

It's a long way from *my* schooldays, he thought, remembering the gravel-surfaced rugby ground on the outskirts of town and the reluctance with which you went into a tackle, facing the certainty of grazed knees and elbows. Still, I guess the kids today have to contend with more than a few grazes. They know forces and pressures we would have regarded as unthinkable.

The match was being played on the main field, in front of the squat, gray clock tower. Deon had always thought the whole image of the school a little farcical; too much a creaking copy of near-extinct English public school traditions. But Elizabeth's father and uncles and brothers had gone to school here, so Etienne had come here too.

He thought, with amusement and tolerance, how strange it was that, as his wife grew older, she reverted more and more to the customs of the family she had once rejected.

Am I going that way too? he wondered. Some of the things my father believed in I could never accept. But others? I wonder.

He parked among the oaks and turned down the front windows. Young, cheerful voices rang out. There was a solid thump of a boot against leather and lazy applause for a good line kick. The forwards formed two straggly rows near him; the home side in maroon and gray, the visitors in scarlet jerseys. They were puffed and muddy, for it had rained the day before and the ground was wet.

Deon found his son's tousled hair among the three-quarters. Etienne stood with his hands on his knees, watching the line-out.

The ball arched through the air and there was a surge of maroon-and-gray- and scarlet-clad bodies. A neat heel from the loose and a maroon-and-gray was there to send the ball away like a bullet. The flyhalf shaped for a kick and the opposing three-quarters fell away a little. Instead the youngster flicked the ball suddenly toward Etienne, at inside center. The shouts of the spectators rose sharply, only to change at once into a groan. Etienne had fumbled in taking the pass and the referee's whistle shrilled.

Deon had sat up in quick excitement, but now he leaned back in the padded seat. Pity. If the boy had held onto the ball he would have found a gap in the opposition line.

He watched idly as play continued. This was the under-sixteen team, wasn't it? That's right. Etienne had turned fifteen at the end of last year. Fifteen. Hell, time went by quickly. You felt your life had hardly started and here you were with a son of fifteen.

Memory pricked like a touch of a needle to a nerve. How old would he have been now? he thought guiltily. That other one, my own son?

Twenty-one years old. A man. He could have had a child of his own by this time.

His thoughts drifted as he watched the milling, multicolored young bodies charging from side to side and from one end of the green field to the other. What would he have been like? Blond and tall, as I am? Or dark and still and intent like his mother?

The stabbing needle of guilt again. Could that have caused it? A late abortion and its resultant trauma. Could that have set in motion a subtle genetic mutation which ended in a mongol birth?

Oh balls! he told himself angrily. You don't have to chase ghosts out of empty graves. The mother was thirty-eight at conception and the risk of a genetic disorder had increased in direct proportion to her age. The Italian obstetrician should have advised an analysis of the amniotic fluid.

It was this morning's talk with Philip that had brought Trish to mind. Had she really returned to Italy? He imagined so. But it was quite possible that her parents were still alive and still living in South Africa. Both had been relatively young when he had known them. Old man Coulter would be in his late sixties now; Trish's mother a little younger. Might Trish have decided to stay with them for a couple of months?

He wanted to see her again.

He recognized the desire almost with shock, but with a degree of relief as well. It had been there, deeply buried, covered over by the years, blunted by the abrasive passage of time and the effect of events and things. Life drifted by, as apparently casual and half observed as the autumn leaves from the oaks in The Avenue. Till, abruptly, you discovered that the trees were bare, that winter had come and that the things you regretted were the things you had failed to do.

I want to see her again, he thought, and remembered that dark and vibrant mind, the animal tension that was offset by her coldly rational judgment. I want to see her again. But dare I?

She probably hadn't even remained in the country, he told himself in order to curb the rising excitement. Perhaps she stayed for a week or two, to visit her parents; then went home to Italy with her Giovanni.

Poor little boy. He would die and he would never have known what it is to live.

There was not much one could do. For the problem, of course, lay in the fact that there was no chamber to pump blood to the lungs.

A cheer and a blast on the referee's whistle diverted his attention briefly. Maroon-and-gray and scarlet jerseys were disentangling on a distant tryline. Maroon-and-gray had scored and come running back jubilantly. Scarlet formed a disconsolate little group around the goal posts, waiting for the conversion kick.

What if you accepted the situation as you found it? Accepted it and made use of it.

The germ of the idea was there. He sat forward, gripping the steering wheel with both hands, and his mind did not even register the cheer following the kick that sent the ball soaring high and true through the center of the posts.

He forced his thoughts to return to the beginning, to the basic anatomy of the heart. It was nothing more than a muscular pump with four chambers. The two upper chambers received blood and the two lower chambers pumped it. But in Giovanni's case the valve between the right-hand receiving and pumping chambers was blocked. This pumping chamber had never functioned properly, so it had never developed.

Deon sat back for a moment, unseeing eyes fixed on the ceaseless ebb and flow of movement on the rugby field, and again checked back over the essential facts, ticking them off item by item to be sure he had left out nothing.

Blood returned to Giovanni's heart through the major veins, the superior and inferior venae cavae, and flowed normally into the right atrium. But only a trickle passed through the narrowed tricuspid valve into the right ventricle. Most of it went through the hole in the atrial wall by-passing the obstruction and the lungs. The low oxygen content of this blood when mixed with the small quantity of blood that had passed through the lungs when pumped back to the body by the left ventricle, resulted in cyanosis.

Everyone accepted that the condition was irreparable because of the malfunction of the right ventricle.

Then why not short-circuit the obstruction, but not the lungs.

The more he thought about it the more he could see exactly how it should be done.

The blood from the superior vena cava you could divert directly into the right lung. All you had to do was sever the superior vena cava from the heart and link it directly to the artery leading to the right lung. That took care of the blood from the upper body.

Unfortunately the inferior vena cava was quite a distance from the artery to the left lung. This made direct anastomosis impossible, but he could solve this problem by allowing the blood from the lower part of the body to flow first into the right atrium. Right! What you did now was to link the right atrium to the left pulmonary artery by means of a graft. He had on several occasions used an aortic homograft from right atrium to pulmonary artery to bridge an underdeveloped area of the outflow of the right ventricle. No one had ever thought of using it for a tricuspid atresia, but there was no reason why it shouldn't work. The valve end of the aorta would

288

open from the right atrium, so that this chamber would then take over the pumping function of the right ventricle.

Close up the defect between the two atria and there you had it: a heart that would function, if not normally, at least well enough.

He had kept his mind deliberately cold and controlled, working out the details step by step, as unemotional as an engineer making calculations with slide rule and tables of weights and stresses. Now he allowed triumph to well up inside him, like warmth rising from a new-lit fire.

He slammed his hands palms down against the steering wheel. "By God, I've got it!"

The rejection problem would be negligible. The aortic graft, although from another body, would be dead tissue, sterilized by radiation.

There might, however, be another problem. The right atrium was not built to perform its new task. It was a receiving chamber not a pumping chamber. It would be dealing with only approximately half the inflow of venous blood, but nevertheless pressure inside would probably increase. Too high a pressure would dam blood up in the inferior vena cava.

He considered this obstacle for a moment. It needed thought, but it could be solved. The point was that he had managed to leap over the barrier which, until now, had brought everyone down: that weak right ventricle. And it was going to work. He was convinced of it.

In a rush of impatience he wanted to set everything into motion all at once. It couldn't wait. It had to be done now, now, now.

His hand was already on its way to the ignition switch when he restrained himself.

"Hamba kahle," he said aloud inside the car.

Right. The Xhosas had the phrase for it. Walk gently.

There would be a lot of preliminary work. Robby and he would have to sit down to one of their brain-storming sessions and think up every possible complication and then work out a technique for coping with each of them. They would have to do the procedure over and over in the animal lab to perfect it.

There was a sustained blast on the whistle and a fresh burst of cheering. Maroon-and-gray and scarlet came pouring off the field, opponents ceremoniously shaking one another by the hand. The match was finished.

Etienne had spotted the Jaguar under the trees and come trotting over. His face was flushed, but he was grinning widely.

"Hi, Dad."

"Hello, son. Who won?"

289

"What? Oh, we did. We licked them, twenty-three to eight. Did you see me score?"

Deon, who had not noticed, nodded at once.

"Ja. Pretty good."

"I sold that chap a dummy a yard wide," Etienne said boisterously and boastfully. Then, obviously remembering that he was no longer a small boy, and therefore under certain adult obligations of modesty, he added: "But they weren't really a match for us." And, with scorn: "They even lost against Rondebosch, for flip's sake."

"Want a lift home?"

"Ja. Thanks." Etienne looked over his shoulder. "I have to shower first."

"Okay. Shake a leg."

Groups of boys in gray flannels and maroon-and-gray striped blazers came strolling past. Some of them recognized him and stared curiously. Van der Riet's old man. The heart surgeon. Stares no longer bothered him, however, so he looked straight ahead and thought of the work he would have to do on this tricuspid repair. Which of the registrars would he put on to it? Young Moolman was doing well. He was still at the children's hospital, but he could be transferred. And he needed some research credit. He had confided his plans to go to America in a year or two, and some time spent in the lab would help him find a good job.

Etienne was back, in flannels and striped blazer like the rest. Two other boys had followed him from the dressing rooms, but were hanging behind a little, togbags dangling over their shoulders.

"Dad, can we give Bob and David a lift?" Etienne asked. "It's on our way."

"Sure."

The two boys climbed into the back seat. Etienne sat in front beside Deon, twisting around in his seat to talk to the others. As Deon started up the car he caught the nostalgic smell of young bodies and sharp soap and the acrid sweatiness of their rugby garments inside the togbags.

He listened idly to the conversation, which centered round the just-completed match and the rough justice meted out to a flank forward on the opposing side after he had been guilty of some elaborate bit of dirty play. A reference to some master mysteriously known as "Marbles" set all three of them laughing and then they discussed (very ambiguously and with sly, sidelong glances at Deon) the girls at a party they had all attended.

Deon stopped listening. How was he going to create an atresia of the tricuspid valve in an experimental animal?

He would find a way. But Professor Snyman would have to give him back some of the facilities in the animal lab. He wondered whether the professor would help him. Certainly not willingly.

He had to admit the old man had never interfered with his activities. But he liked working behind the scenes, making it more difficult for Deon to continue his research. Just the other day a grant which had been coming to cardiac surgery for years had been switched to another department. He was backing a new horse now.

Why was he so petty and suspicious? Surely Snyman knew that Deon didn't want to become head of the division of surgery?

They had been good friends once, and he admired Snyman for what he was—a brilliant surgeon with an endless capacity for work. In many ways he had learned a lot from him, and he still liked the old man.

Well, there'd been bad blood between them for years. That business with the dog was probably how it had started.

It had been in the year when he had been Snyman's senior registrar. He and Robby had been studying the advantages of cooling the body in conjunction with the heart-lung machine in open heart surgery. They had spent long, weary hours on their feet in the laboratory, checking on what cooling did to metabolism, kidney function, and blood clotting. They had experimented with different kinds of heat exchangers, rapid cooling and slow cooling, circulatory arrest and high flows; jubilant when their ideas worked and depressed when they failed, but determined to make them work the next time.

Often when he drank coffee, even now, he thought of those months, for the cups of coffee had come in endless succession as they sat at a bare, scrubbed table in a tiny room off the laboratory, where a naked bulb hung from the high ceiling and they talked and wrangled about the next experiment.

Snyman had backed him up in everything, supplying equipment and extorting money from the university when it was needed. He had been as elated as they were when Deon was able to report progress, and he had goaded and driven them when he felt they were not going fast enough.

That night they had completed a successful series of experiments to evaluate the ability of low temperatures to prevent anoxic damage to the brain. Deon was a little drunk with triumph and weariness as he drained the last cup of coffee. Robby had looked at his watch.

"Hell, it's late. Ten past eleven. And we have to be in the theater tomorrow, buddy."

"What the hell!" Deon said expansively. "Do you realize you're looking at a miracle?"

The African laboratory assistant was leading the two mongrel dogs back into their cages. Deon made a sweeping gesture toward them.

"Look at them. Dead for an hour. No heart beat, respiration, respiratory movements, circulation or detectable brain activity. Dead by all ordinary standards for a whole hour. And there they are. Walking!"

Robby grinned at him.

"I'll tell you something," Deon said. "We'll be using this technique to do brain transplants one day."

"You can transplant mine right away," Robby said with mock gloom. "You've picked it to pieces anyway."

But Deon barely heard. He stood up slowly, coffee cup still clutched between his fingers, staring at the two dogs with new alertness. He bit his lower lip between his teeth and his eyes narrowed.

Robby, who knew the symptoms, sighed. "Now what?" he asked plaintively.

"I'll tell you how we can do a brain transplant," Deon said. His voice was urgent. "I'll tell you how. I know how to do it. It's just a matter of working out the details."

"That's what the bishop said to the actress."

"Shut up and listen. We're going to transplant the head of one dog to the body of another."

Robby looked at him curiously. "Are you serious?"

"I'm telling you. We're going to do it."

"You're crazy," Robby said flatly. "Okay, so hypothermia can protect the brain. But what about all the nerves you have to connect? Once you've severed the spinal cord . . ."

"You don't understand. I'm not going to cut off both heads. Only one. Then I'll graft it on to the other body, with a common circulation."

Robby pondered. "I see. Yes, I guess it's feasible. A two-headed dog. But you can hardly call it a brain transplant."

"Maybe not," Deon conceded. "The second head won't control any part of the body, of course. But if we manage to protect the brain, the cranial nerves will keep functioning, so if the brain works the head will work too. And it'll show what hypothermia can do."

Robby squashed out a cigarette in his saucer. "Go home and sleep on it," he said.

Deon had gone home, but had hardly slept. He had lain awake until long into the early morning alongside Elizabeth's warm and pliant body while his racing brain faced and conquered problem after problem.

It shouldn't be too difficult. The most important thing, of course, was to ensure that both brains were protected while the blood supply was cut off. He imagined an operating table with the two dogs strapped side by side: donor on the right, recipient on the left. Both circulations could be taken over by the same heart-lung machine. He would drain the venous blood from both dogs into the same oxygenator and then use two arterial pumps to push the blood back. While they were cooling he would do a collar incision at the base of the donor's neck and expose the common carotid arteries and jugular veins. Robby would do the same for the recipient.

He would drop both temperatures to ten degrees Centigrade, then stop the arterial pump to the donor and allow all his blood to drain to the machine. He must remember to tell the technicians to use an extra well for storage. Then he'd divide the four vessels between two clamps and sever the donor head, swinging it round so that the two were face to face. Anastomose the vessels end-to-side to those of the recipient. Release the clamps and while rewarming close the end of the spinal canal with a muscle flap so the spinal fluid won't leak. There would be no muscle support for the head, so he'd have to splint it with a plaster cast.

He moved closer to Elizabeth's radiating heat and she moved away and mumbled something in her sleep. At last he dozed off, and when he woke she was getting up to feed the baby and the sunlight was bright on their bedroom window.

They performed the operation a week later and it worked. The grafted head opened its eyes, blinked in response to a sharp light and showed every sign of normal reactions.

As soon as he was sure the operation was a success Deon set off for Professor Snyman's office, at a fast walk which he only just managed to prevent becoming a trot. Snyman's secretary, in her usual fussy way, tried to head him off, protesting that her professor was busy and he had appointments and he was occupied with vital correspondence and anyway why hadn't Dr. van der Riet telephoned if it was so important? Finally Deon managed to push past her into the old man's office.

Snyman looked at him a little frostily over his glasses. "What's all this about?"

Behind Deon, Miss Arensen was still making noises of disapproval, but he ignored her. "Can you spare me a little time? Only ten minutes. There's something I want to show you in the animal lab."

"What is it?"

"Just something we've done. A new test. But I think you'll be interested to see it."

Snyman rose and took the white coat without which he never took a step outside his office from its hanger behind the door.

Miss Arensen clucked at him agitatedly, but he made his usual gesture of dismissal and shrugged his shoulders into the coat.

"Let's go."

His expression, when he saw the dog with its two heads, face to face, still strapped to the operating table, was a curious mixture of awe and horror.

Deon demonstrated how the grafted head reacted to stimuli and explained how he had linked the circulations. Snyman listened in silence, never once taking his eyes off the animal on the table.

"I'll tell you what you've done," he said at last, when Deon had finished his explanation. "You have created a monster."

And he turned on his heel and left the laboratory.

But a few days later, meeting Deon in the corridor, he stopped and asked with pretended nonchalance: "What did you boys do about that two-headed dog?"

"Oh, we took the grafted head off again. You were right. It was a bit gruesome. And it didn't really prove anything."

Professor Snyman took off his glasses and wiped them on a spotless handkerchief. "I don't know about that. You proved that an organ as delicate as the brain can be protected during grafting. Why not try it again? But put the heads facing the same way, boy. Then they'll look a bit better." He turned away, then added, as if the thought had only just occurred to him: "Oh, and let me know when you do it, will you? I'll come along and give you a hand."

Deon repeated the experiment three days later, but this time joined the arteries in such a way that the transplanted head faced forward. Professor Snyman served as his first assistant to begin with, but once the link-up of the severed head had started he began, almost imperceptibly, to take control of the operation. Deon, with a wry grin of resignation, allowed him to do it. The old boy found it hard to play second fiddle to anyone, and there was no sense in antagonizing him.

They secured the head, facing the right way this time, and waited impatiently for the freshly pumping blood to warm the dormant brain. Once again, as soon as the anesthetic was stopped, both heads came to life.

Snyman was nearly beside himself with excitement.

"Pictures!" he shouted. "We must get pictures of this. Someone call the hospital photographer. And tell him to bring a movie camera too. We'll make a film of this thing."

The dog recovered quickly from the effect of the anesthetic. Robby picked it up off the table and it walked unsteadily around the laboratory floor. Someone brought a saucer of milk from the coffee room and put it down. Both heads lapped at the milk.

"Take a picture of that!" Professor Snyman commanded the photographer urgently. He clapped Deon on the shoulder and laughed with delight. "What a thing, eh? Boy, that's quite something. Did you take notes on that first op?"

"Yes."

"Let me have them some time, will you? I'd like to go through them."

At the end of the week he called Deon to his office. He seemed distracted and kept playing with the furnishings of his desk, pushing calendar and pen holder and dictating machine around; squaring off his blotter pad, first this way, then that.

"That two-headed dog. Is it still alive?"

"Yes, Professor. We've been using it for tests and obviously the cerebral and cranial functions are absolutely normal."

"I see. Good." Snyman rearranged the blotter once more. "Unfortunately the newspapers have got wind of this somehow. They've been badgering me all morning. There was even a call from New York."

Oh, hell, Deon thought quickly. "They'll try to sneak pictures of it. We'll have to lock it away. Put a guard on it. I'll tell the lab assistants to watch out for anyone with a camera."

"I think we'll have to give them the story," Snyman said.

Deon looked at him doubtfully. "Do you think that's wise, sir? They may take it up the wrong way."

Snyman silenced him with an imperious hand. "I've thought hard about it. Better the full story, the true story, than a lot of sensational fabricated nonsense."

"I suppose there's sense in that."

"That's the best attitude toward the press." The old man peered at Deon over his glasses, almost slyly now. "I'm calling a press conference for this afternoon. Three o'clock, here in my office. I want you to be here, of course," he added hastily, with a chuckle. "But I think you had better leave me to handle the reporters. I've had a bit of experience with them, you know."

"Of course." Deon found himself wondering, disloyally, just how the story *had* leaked to the newspapers.

"All right. Three o'clock."

Snyman had been in an expansive mood with the reporters, making little jokes, smiling at the photographers who asked him to turn this way and that while their flashbulbs popped. His voice had been solemnly pontifical as he made the announcement, and he nodded with satisfaction at the excited buzz which followed it.

"Yes, gentlemen," he said. "I think I can risk saying that medical history has been made at this hospital."

Deon and Robby were introduced, but only cursorily, leaving a very distinct impression that they had been only minor bystanders. It was never directly stated, but somehow the inference was easily understood: Professor Tertius Snyman had devised the technique of grafting one dog's head on to another dog's body and then had put his theory to the test in the only arena which really counted—the operating theater.

He sat there, basking in the flattering approval, and Deon watched the proceedings sourly and said nothing.

Professor Snyman and his two-headed dog had received world-wide publicity. Antivivisectionists everywhere had written stinging letters to the newspapers. Editorial writers had reflected earnestly on the moral, ethical, and scientific implications. A medical journal had hailed the experiment as the forerunner of the day when human beings could achieve a kind of immortality on earth.

Well, I guess it happens all over the world, Deon thought. Chiefs take credit for the work their juniors have done. I know it is a hell of a temptation.

Seven

Moolman telephoned that Saturday morning to tell the same depressing story.

"Sorry, Professor. The dog we operated on yesterday has died too." He gulped audibly. "Everything was fine when I left it last night. But when I got to the lab this morning I found him dead in his cage."

They had a bad connection and the receiver crackled in Deon's ear. But even through the electronic uproar he could detect the glum note in the young registrar's voice.

"What? Again? We might just as well give up! What went wrong? The lungs again?"

"I've only just arrived, sir. I haven't done a post-mortem. But it was breathing well last night when I left. I even removed the chest drain. There wasn't any bleeding."

At the start of their experiments on a method to repair tricuspid atresia they had run into a number of technical problems. How to position the graft from the right atrium to the pulmonary artery so that it would not kink or be compressed by the chest wall? Where to incise the atrium to avoid arrhythmias? Deon had decided to prevent any back pressure into the lower part of the body by sewing a one-way valve into the opening of the inferior vena cava. They had struggled for a long time to devise a way of measuring the vein's mouth in order to select a valve of the correct size.

They had slowly mastered all these problems. But still they could not get a dog to survive longer than a couple of hours.

"Are you going to do the P.M. now?"

"Right away, sir. I'll let you have the findings as soon as I'm finished."

"Yes . . . well." Deon hesitated. Nothing much he could do now. He banged the receiver irritably against his desk. The crackling did not improve. "Damn this thing!"

"Sir?"

"This phone line. I can hardly hear you."

"Oh." The young man sounded relieved, as if he had feared himself to be the object of wrath.

"Okay. I've got a meeting at the cardiac clinic this morning, so I'll be leaving the office soon. But we'll discuss things on Monday. Don't plan any further experiments till I let you know."

"Yes, sir."

He swiveled round in his chair and tipped it back so that it rested against the edge of the desk. He stared thoughtfully out through the window. It was a heart-breaking business. They had got the dog off the table yesterday with a beautiful circulation and blood pressure. Everything was fine. Except that the dog had died.

The witch-doctor mask against the wall between the windows caught his eye and he remembered Giovanni's inquiring hand reaching to touch it. Poor little guy. Would he still be alive? Patients with tricuspid atresia sometimes survive for years. Survive. His condition had not yet gone very far. But death was stalking him all the same, as implacably as a hunter with a rifle, creeping up on an animal which stood all unawares in the sun.

He had thought about Trish often while he and Moolman had worked on the experiments. What would she say if she knew he was trying to develop a technique that might enable her son to live? Would that pensive face light up with joy?

On sudden impulse, he picked up the city telephone directory.

B, C, Ca, Co, Coleman, Compton . . . Here it was. Coulter. Coulter's Pharmacy, at an address in Rondebosch. He looked farther down the column, but there was no home address. He remembered that Trish's parents had lived in Newlands. Had they moved away? Died?

He buzzed for Jenny on the intercom.

"Get me this number, will you?" He read it to her from the phone book. "And try to get a better line this time. The last one was damn awful."

"Sorry, Prof," in tones of sweet reasonableness.

A moment later she rang through. "Coulter's Pharmacy on the line, Prof."

A woman, repeating: "Coulter's Pharmacy. Good morning."

"Morning. Could I speak to Mr. Coulter, please?"

A momentary pause. Then: "I'm sorry, we don't have a Mr. Coulter here."

"But isn't that Coulter's Pharmacy?"

"Yes, but it's just the . . . it's the name. Only the name. The manager is Mr. Sloan. Would you like to speak to him?"

"Please."

A clipped, aseptic-sounding voice said: "Sloan. Can I help you?"

"Well, look, I'm trying to find Mr. Coulter."

"Mr. Coulter." Another reflective silence. "Sorry. I can't help you, sir. I've only been here for six months and I didn't know Mr. Coulter."

"Perhaps the previous owner . . ."

"The shop belongs to a pharmaceutical chain, sir. We retained the name for business . . . well, it's a big chain, you see. There have probably been a dozen managers here since Mr. Coulter sold out."

"I see."

Was it so easy to vanish into anonymity? Could you simply be erased from life's book, as easily as from a telephone directory, so that all that remained was a name which no one recognized anymore, which was not more than a formal cypher on a stranger's lips?

Someday someone would say: "Sorry. Deon van der Riet doesn't live here anymore."

"Your staff," he persisted. "Perhaps one of the older staff might remember."

The brisk voice was starting to sound a little irritated. "I regret not, sir. There's no one who has worked here for more than a year."

"Oh. Well, then . . ."

The voice changed. "Wait a minute. I wonder. The . . . Will you hang on a moment please?"

"Right."

A few minutes went by, then there was the sound of the receiver at the other end being picked up.

"Are you there? I remembered that the boy, the old Coloured man who makes the deliveries, he's been here a long time. Anyway, he says he's not sure but he thinks Mr. Coulter moved to Hermanus when he sold the shop."

"Hermanus? Good. Thank you very much."

There was no Coulter listed in Hermanus.

He spun the chair round again fiercely, so that it faced the right way. He pulled back a jacket cuff. A quarter to ten. A combined meeting with the cardiac clinic at ten o'clock. Then, apart from ward rounds tomorrow morning, he was free for the weekend. Provided there were no emergencies. He had a golf date for this afternoon so he'd have lunch out at the golf club.

He looked at his watch again, although barely a minute had gone by. It took exactly seven minutes to walk to the hospital; another minute-and-a-half to get to the conference room. But he might as well leave now. He did not like to be late, for it set a bad example.

And yet he lingered.

For God's sake! Get yourself together! You're not a moon-struck youth. You're an adult, with an adult's responsibilities. Forget it now. Forget her. Right now.

His face was carefully composed as he went through to Jenny's office, gave her last instructions, and wished her a pleasant weekend. Then, without hurrying but walking rapidly nevertheless, he left the office.

Most of the others were already in the conference room. He exchanged greetings here and there, then took a seat on the front bench, crossing his legs, frowning down at a bit of mud which he had somehow collected on the gleaming toe of one shoe during the walk up here.

A child was sitting beside Peter Moorhead on the cross-benches. Dark-haired and dark-eyed, with an oddly pale face, as if she seldom saw the sun. She sat very still, hands and knees pressed together.

Deon lifted his eyebrows and looked a question at Peter.

Peter's expression was apologetic. "This is Kathleen Jennis, Professor. You'll remember. The child from Ireland I spoke to you about last month. She's related to my wife. She's Gillian's niece, actually."

At the mention of her name the child had looked up. She gazed attentively at Deon. Her eyes were dark as coals in that white face and the hollows above her cheekbones were faintly dark as well, as if someone had brushed them with a sooty finger.

"They think Kathleen has a single atrium with anomalous pulmonary venous drainage," Peter said. "She's from Kilkenney and she's been examined in Dublin and in London, but the doctors there were not prepared to tackle the defect. So Gillian's sister wrote to us and we suggested that Kathleen should come out to South Africa. You said you'd have a look at her. She has been recatheterized here at the cardiac clinic and they're going to present the data this morning."

Peter sat back, gasping slightly and obviously relieved that his carefully prepared speech was at an end.

"I remember," Deon said, although his recollection was vague. He added, reprimandingly: "I don't know if it was absolutely necessary for us to see her here today."

Peter flushed and looked flustered. "I'm sorry, Professor. It was Gillian's idea. She insisted that Kathleen should come, so that you could see her," he said unhappily.

Deon raised his eyebrows again in silent comment on a husband who could not restrain his wife's more absurd whims. Peter bit his lip and looked away. The child continued to examine Deon's face with her quiet eyes.

One of the cardiologists switched on the wall-high X-ray viewer. Its fluorescent tubes flickered, then glowed steadily. He prodded with a pointer at the X-rays which were clipped to the screen.

"First case. Lucas Vilikazi. African male, aged twenty-three. Coarctation of the aorta."

He ran briefly through the characteristic symptoms. "A very typical case. Any questions?"

There were a few assenting grunts, but no one made any comment. The condition was clear-cut and the surgical correction straightforward.

"Let's carry on," Deon said.

The cardiologist nodded and pushed a button which caused the row of X-rays to slide out of sight and another series to come into view.

"Dennis van Rooyen. European. Age . . ." He glanced at his notes. "Thirty. Now this case is not so straightforward . . ."

Deon listened to the ensuing discussion and made his own observations. He grinned at a joking remark from Robby at his expense. He scraped the bit of mud off his shoe onto the side of the bench and was constantly and uncomfortably aware of the child's close scrutiny. Even when one of the assistants walked up to hand Deon a folder and came between him and the little girl she leaned forward to look around the other man.

Why the hell had Peter brought the child here? His irritation with both Peter and his half-mad wife grew steadily.

A new set of X-rays rose on the screen.

"Kathleen Jennis," the cardiologist announced with no change in the even level of his voice. "White female, aged ten." He went through the symptoms, signs, electrocardiographic and catheter findings, and diagnosis. "Single atrium with abnormal drainage of the left pulmonary veins on the right of the atrium. There's also leaking of both the mitral and tricuspid valves."

The child was still looking at Deon. He leaned against the hard back of the bench and stretched out his legs, crossing them at the ankles. He studied the X-rays but did not take part in the discussion. He was frowning and once caught himself nibbling at the end of a thumb, a frequent habit when he was in doubt. He put his hands quickly into his trouser pockets.

"Let me see the angios again."

The cardiologist switched off the viewer and bustled importantly to the movie projector. He selected a roll of film and called loudly: "Lights," then set the machine going. A square of light sprang to life on the small wall screen. It began to flicker, then the black and white outlines of the cinéangiograph flashed across the screen. The cardiologist handled the projector with showmanlike skill, speeding up or slowing down to demonstrate a particular stage, stopping it or reversing at times to point out something someone may have missed.

Deon leaned back, hands in his pockets, and watched the filmed recording of a beating heart.

There appeared to be no doubt about the diagnosis. You could trace the flow of blood through the heart. First, the injection of radio-opaque dye into what should be the right atrium, then the white blotch rapidly spreading to fill the single atrial chamber, and then the two ventricles. Ventricular contraction was followed by simultaneous opacification of aorta and pulmonary arteries. There was something about the appearance of the ventricles which troubled him but it was probably due to the faulty valves. Anyway the point was that he had tackled a few of these cases before and the results were quite good. There should be no problem.

The cardiologist stopped the projector and the room lights came on. Everyone was looking at him. Peter Moorhead leaned tensely forward in his seat. The child sat motionless beside him.

Deon nodded. "Put her on the slate for Tuesday. There should be no problem."

At once the tension was gone. One of the junior registrars began to whisper to a girl from the X-ray department. A secretary made notes. Robby checked his watch. The cardiologist set up the next plates.

And Deon turned to look at the little dark-eyed girl, smiling at her for the first time. She looked back at him and then smiled too.

The conference ended and they trooped out of the room. A houseman jostled Deon and apologized breathlessly. Peter Moorhead, leading the child by the hand, appeared at his elbow to pour out embarrassed thanks. Deon nodded abruptly and turned away. He did not want to talk or think about it now.

Why don't those damn dogs live, he thought instead. He considered briefly going down to the animal laboratory himself to see what Moolman had found at the post-mortem. But he would probably have finished and the place would be locked up. Anyway he would have kept the heart and lungs in the refrigerator, so they could study them together on Monday morning.

Forget it. Relax. You can hit the hell out of a golf ball this afternoon.

He would be playing in his usual foursome. He hoped he drew Abe as a partner. Abe wasn't a brilliant golfer but steady as a rock and therefore a sound support for his own more erratic game.

He came out of the hospital into wintry sunshine. It wasn't exactly cold, but there was a bite in the air. A good day for golf. He would have a light meal at the bar, possibly with a beer to accompany it. Then a brisk round and another couple of drinks to end off the afternoon. An excellent antidote to melancholia.

He locked his hands and cocked his wrists to raise an imaginary club. He played the shot with a smooth, unhurried swing, but not so vigorously that some chance watcher might notice and wonder.

But by the time he reached the golf club he had changed his mind once more. He sat in the car, trying to work up enthusiasm for the coming match. Some early starters were driving off the tenth tee. One player sliced badly into thick rough, but the other three managed respectable drives down the middle. They moved off, caddies trailing behind, laughing at something. The man who had sliced his drive turned crossly and motioned to the caddy to run ahead and look for his ball.

Deon remembered Philip telling him about caddying at the Royal Cape. He wondered how Philip's work was progressing. Might he need further assistance, or would the grant they had managed to secure carry him through? Guiltily he remembered that he had intended to telephone to find out, long ago. Again the months had slipped by, almost unnoticed.

He went through to the locker room and began to change. But it was no good. He could not play golf today. Quickly, before he should waver again, he put on his suit jacket, tightened his tie and turned the key in the locker door.

He found Abe Lax sitting broadly on a stool in the bar. Abe waved a greeting.

"Hi."

"Hello, Abe. Look, I'm sorry about this, but I won't be able to make the game today."

There was no need to concoct an alibi. They would all assume it was something to do with the hospital.

Abe looked disappointed, then shrugged.

"Ah, I'm sorry too, man. But don't worry. We'll pick up a fourth. No trouble. Time for a drink before you go?"

"Thanks, Abe. Another time."

"Okay. No trouble. We'll fix up another game, eh?"

"We'll do that."

"Okay. See you."

Deon drove out past the club house and down the drive alongside one of the fairways. Two players were making their approach shots to the green. He passed them without looking. He had not thought about where he was going, but when he drove through the gate he turned almost automatically to the right, into the road which would lead him on to the freeway to the east, out of the city. Elizabeth would not expect him home until the evening. He had the entire afternoon to himself. He was free.

He looked at the dashboard clock. Five past one. It would take a bit more than an hour over the mountain; another forty minutes or so to Hermanus.

Hermanus? he asked himself mockingly. Is that where you're going?

Well, why not? It's as good a place to go for a drive on a sunny Saturday afternoon as any other.

He reached the outskirts of Hermanus sooner than he had expected. He drove slowly through the village, looking at the white-painted bungalows with their thatched roofs and the names outside garden gates. "Summer Place." "Casa del Sol." "Knot-4-Sail." It took him a moment to work that out.

He drew up on a grassy patch at the top of a cliff overlooking the fishing harbor. A little breeze had come up and there were white tops to the waves far out at sea. Among the gray boulders below him the surf rushed urgently and endlessly.

He drove to the business center, parked and went along past the shops. Most of them were closed, for it was Saturday afternoon. He found a coffee-bar open, but the young, bearded owner did not know any Mr. and Mrs. Coulter. Nor did anyone at the fish and chips shop, which smelled of stale oil.

The man behind the cigarette counter of a cafe frowned when Deon mentioned the name.

"Coulter," he repeated. He had a broad Lancashire accent. "I dunno." He scratched the back of his head. Flakes of dandruff drifted down onto the shoulders of his dark jacket. "That name's . . . Coulter. Mr. Coulter. He a thin old chappie? Skinny like? With gray hair?"

"Could be."

"Always walks with a stick, though he doesn't need it. Just waves it about, like." He gave an imitation of someone swinging a walking stick.

"It might be him."

"Always comes in here for the Sunday papers," the man with the dandruff said with satisfaction. "And one packet of twenty Gold Flake. Like clockwork every Sunday morning."

Deon tried to hide his eagerness. "Do you know where he lives?"

The cafe owner scratched his head again. "Well, I don't rightly know. But it's one of the places up on the hill." He pointed. "That's Hill Street over there. I seen him walking up there a couple of times. You try along it."

Deon thanked him and returned to the car. He drove slowly up Hill Street. The corner house at the top had no name, but on its gate, in small and neat lettering, was the street number and the name J. M. Coulter.

The bell jangled somewhere deep inside the house and Deon looked at his watch in sudden dismay. A quarter past three. Perhaps the old people would be having an afternoon nap. However, quick steps sounded behind the door. A moment later Mr. Coulter, grown more spare and much grayer than Deon had remembered him, stood on the threshold, his expression politely inquiring.

"Good afternoon," Deon said. "I don't know if you remember me, Mr. Coulter . . ."

The old man stared at him. He held himself very straight, with the air of some quick, chirpy bird: a sparrow, or a wagtail. Recognition came and he smiled wonderingly.

"Of course. Deon. Deon van der Riet. Well, this is a surprise."

"I happened to be in town, so I thought I'd just . . ." Deon started lamely. But fortunately the old man was not interested in explanations.

"Well, come in. Come in for goodness' sake." He stood aside. "It's been quite a time since I saw you last. Of course I've read all about the marvels you've been doing. And Patricia so hoped you would be able to do something about . . . Oh, well. It's sad, but it's life."

He ushered Deon into a comfortable although slightly fussy lounge. The house was built high, with a fine sea view through the windows. The old man's expression changed to one of self-satisfaction when Deon commented on this.

"Yes. I bought it, bought the stand, more than fifteen years ago, and had the place built. I saw the way things were going. I wouldn't have been able to afford it now," he admitted frankly. "Not with today's prices."

"Land is terribly expensive," Deon agreed.

What the hell are you doing here? he asked himself in desperation. Making meaningless conversation with a man you hardly know. How are you going to wiggle out of this?

His eyes caught photographs on the mantelpiece, over the small brick fireplace. Trish; more or less at the time he had known her. Long hair, darker-looking in the photographs, over her shoulders. A mysterious half smile on her face. Her eyes rounded and brows arched quizzically. In another picture, caught in profile, she sat contemplatively on the banks of a canal, with barges and foreign-looking buildings in the background.

Deon looked hurriedly away. "And Mrs. Coulter. How is she?"

The old man gaped blankly for one brief moment. Then he rubbed his temples in a gesture of sudden weariness.

"My wife has died," he said. "A month ago, next Tuesday."

"Oh, I'm sorry. I hadn't . . . I didn't know. I'm very sorry to hear that."

And although the phrase was conventional, it was sincerely meant. He was sorry to know that Trish, who had so much to bear, had to take on the burden of more grief, even if it was the inevitability of the death of a parent.

"I am sorry," he said. "I tried to telephone you, but . . ."

The old man's lips tightened and he nodded with a show of spirit. "Never had one of the infernal things installed," he said smugly. "I had to be at its beck and call for all those years in the shop. Decided when I retired I'd have some peace and quiet."

Deon laughed. "I know how you feel. I might even follow your example one day."

Mr. Coulter nodded again. "When I need something I use my legs. Aren't many places they can't still take me."

He's obviously gotten a bit cranky in old age, Deon reflected. Although one has to admit he looks astonishingly fit. He could probably walk me into the ground.

To change the subject he asked: "What news do you have of Trish? Patricia, I mean."

"Why should I have?" Suspiciously and a little belligerently. "She took the kiddie to the beach . . ." He looked at the miniature grandfather clock around which the photographs on the mantelpiece were grouped. ". . . only half an hour ago."

"Do you mean she's here?"

"Yes, of course." The suspicion vanished. "Didn't you know she was here? I see. No wonder . . ." The old man laughed, then grew serious once more. "She came out to be with me when Mary . . . her mother, died."

Deon nodded quickly and understandingly. "Of course."

"And you didn't know? She didn't let you know how the child is doing?"

"No. But I'd like to see her anyway."

A shrewd glance very reminiscent of the daughter. "That shouldn't be difficult," the old man said drily. "She always goes to Grotto Beach. That's the one at the end of the village."

There was time to turn back. Or at least to stop and think. What did he want, after all? What did he hope to accomplish?

He found them playing in the sand below the line of driftwood and seaweed and bits of plastic junk that marked the high tide level. Trish was making sand pies with an up-ended beach bucket and the child, gurgling with delight, was destroying them one by one.

She saw him approaching and stood up slowly, brushing the sand off her skirt with a slow, shy gesture. She watched his face steadily as he came across the dunes, stumbling through the soft sand in his city shoes.

The child looked up too and looked quickly at his mother for reassurance. She smiled at him and he went on with his game.

Deon came up to her and for a moment neither of them spoke. On her face was the precise replica of the expression, gently mocking and secretive at the same time, which he had seen on the photograph in her father's house. He realized that it had not been posed specially for the photographer; that it was habitual. Yet he did not remember it from the old days.

"Hello, Trish," he said uncertainly.

"Hello."

"How are you?"

"Very well."

"Good."

They sat down side by side and watched the little boy at his game.

"And Giovanni?"

"No better. But not much worse either, fortunately. At least, that's what they told me when I took him for a checkup."

"When was that?"

"Six weeks ago. My mother died, you see. That's why I'm here."

"I know. I'm sorry."

She did not question the source of his knowledge; merely thanked him with grace and composure.

"What did they say? The doctors who saw Giovanni. In Italy, I assume?"

"No. As a matter of fact I went to England. I saw someone in London."

"Oh." He became slightly withdrawn. Had she doubted his word?

She sensed his feeling at once, but was indifferent to vanity in herself or in others.

"I had to make sure. While there was a chance."

307

"What did he say? This London doctor?"

"Exactly what you said. A narrowing of the tricuspid valve and a faulty right ventricle. They also suggested a shunt operation. But I told them it wasn't good enough."

He came close to telling her then. "I am working on something better for your child." But he restrained himself. What would it gain either of them, if the whole thing were to prove impractical after all?

"How long are you planning to stay?" he asked.

"Another month, I think. Perhaps six weeks. My father is strong-minded and he has taken it well. But it's still not easy for him. He's nearly seventy."

A month, at any rate.

"I'd like to see you again," he said frankly. "Before you go."

"Would that be wise?"

"I think so."

She scooped dry sand into a palm and sifted it through her fingers.

"I don't know."

Doggedly: "Well, I do. I'm sure."

A sideways glance, not entirely devoid of flirtation.

"You always were very sure, weren't you?"

They began to talk casually of that past. Then, unexpectedly, she asked him: "Where did you meet your wife?"

At once he was alert. Some vestige of interest after all?

With assumed carelessness he said: "At a party."

She laughed.

"I suppose most people meet at parties. It's mundane, isn't it? But I suppose that's what they're for. I met Rob at a party too."

He looked at her, perplexed, thinking of Robby Robertson. Then he remembered.

"Oh. The American."

"Yes."

She spoke, calmly and with neither grief or bitterness, about Rob, who had been her lover during the years she had lived in Spain. They had met at a party in Malaga, given by two homosexuals who wrote delicately bitchy and vastly successful unauthorized biographies of celebrities. Rob was their favorite would-be writer. She found him charming, and after the party he moved in with her.

Rob had a mysterious second income about which he would never answer questions. Periodically men would arrive from the States and for a time he would be very busy, having closeted meetings with them. Afterward he would stop work on his novel and eat in the superior restaurants and buy everyone drinks in the best tavernas.

Finally he had to move to Madrid because of this other occupation and she went with him. They had a tumultuous affair that lasted for the better part of three years. Then she left him.

"What was he like, this man?" Deon asked, repelled and yet curious.

"He was, oh, I don't know, not even very good-looking." She gave him a faint smile. "Not as handsome as you."

"But he obviously had attraction."

"It was this air of excitement about him. Everything we did together was new and brilliant and witty. He started a magazine once and it was going to be a combination of the *Esquire* and the *Atlantic Monthly* of the Old World. It only survived one issue. Then he was going to make films and he talked some old woman into putting up the money, quite a few thousand dollars, and somehow it just melted away and he never even finished the script. But the old woman never complained. He had charm, especially with women. And there was an air of menace about him, especially when he was in a mood. He would lie on the bed for days on end, doing nothing, not even answering when you spoke to him. And suddenly he'd switch out of it and be back chasing some new fantasy. Living with him was like living on the edge of a volcano."

"He sounds a bit paranoid to me," Deon ventured. "Why didn't you leave him sooner?"

"I wanted to go away, but I couldn't. It was like giving up a child, betraying one's own child." She looked toward where Giovanni was playing in the sand.

"What happened in the end?" Deon asked hastily.

"I left him eventually and returned to Malaga. Then I went to Italy."

"And then you got married?"

"Yes. But it took me a long time to get over it. Even today . . ." She shook her head wonderingly. "Women are funny creatures. I think we must be born with an infinite capacity for inflicting pain on ourselves."

"Women aren't alone in that," Deon told her.

"Perhaps not."

"Did you ever see a film called *Brief Encounter?*" he asked her suddenly.

She had been playing with the sand. Now she stopped and looked at him. Her knees were together and the fashionably long skirt was draped gracefully round her legs.

"What was it about?"

"It was about a man and a woman who had a love affair."

"Was it based on a play by Noel Coward? I think I did see it. What about it?"

"I was just thinking about the end. It was wrong. Fake."

"Why?"

"Well, this woman gave up her lover and went back to her husband. There was a scene at the end where I think he was sitting at the fire and he looked up and said something like: 'So you're back.'"

"That's right. There was a double meaning to it. You were led to understand that he had known all along and that now she was back it didn't matter."

"Quite right. Well, it was faked."

"Why?"

"Because it made believe she could quietly slip back into the old ways. You know. Life as usual. Forgetting what had happened, but it's not really like that. Men don't forget. Nor women either. Once you've been in love you can't simply stop. You've changed. The world has changed."

She did not say anything, and after a moment began to trickle sand between her fingers once more.

"Do you ever come up to town?" he asked, a little desperately.

"Not often." She sounded distant and evasive for the first time. He had gone too far, but now there was no turning back.

"If you do come up, would you have lunch with me? Or dinner?"

"I don't know. I don't think so."

"Well, if you change your mind . . . how can I find out if you've changed your mind? Your father hasn't a telephone."

She laughed suddenly. "You do seem to know a lot. His neighbor takes calls for him when necessary."

"What's the number?"

After a moment's hesitation she told him. "But I don't think there would be much point in your calling."

"We'll see," he said stubbornly.

Trish stood up decisively and called to her son. He came to her at once, carrying bucket and spade.

"It has been pleasant meeting you again, Deon," she said briskly.

"May I offer you a lift back?"

"Thank you, but we always walk. We need the exercise."

And she smiled brightly, dismissingly.

He bowed his head, equally formal. "I hope we meet again."

She continued to smile and said nothing.

Eight

An absurd line kept repeating itself in his mind, like one of those tenacious advertising jingles which he sometimes found himself humming and then could not banish.

"The dog it was that died."

Where it had come from and how it had sneaked into his thoughts he did not know. But there it was, like a phonograph record stuck in a groove and endlessly repeating.

"The dog it was that died."

He had felt chastened and disgruntled at first, driving back to the city, taking the mountain road again because he was in no mood for scenery, no matter how attractive. He began to drive faster, taking deliberate chances on the corners, putting his foot down on the straights, as if to place as big a distance between himself and Trish as quickly as possible.

A bend that had started as a lazy curve became sharper and he was traveling too fast for it. The outside wheels touched gravel and he felt the car go. He corrected the skid too roughly and the rear wheels came the other way. He looked through the windshield at a long drop down a heather-covered hillside, coming straight toward him. But he resisted the urge to hit the brakes and put his weight and full strength against the locked steering wheels. It came free at last, but so close to the edge that he hit a white marker stone a glancing blow and the engine screamed as the rear outside wheel spun in air.

He drove on a little farther, to where the gravel shoulder widened, then stopped the car and got out. His hands were trembling and he felt as if someone had struck him unexpectedly, low in the stomach. But he could walk anyway. To prove it to himself he walked round the front of the car to inspect the damage. A mudguard was badly dented and a sidelight shattered.

"Damn!" he said. "Bloody fool."

But at once, quite reasonably, he felt a resurgence of that vitality he had experienced earlier, driving the other way. He was alive and free and acutely aware of everything around him: the chilly smell of the mountain air; the cries of a pair of sparrow hawks dipping and swinging along a cliff face far above; the blue, fading mistiness of distant hills; the grating feel of gravel under his shoes.

He was aware of everything and understood.

"The dog it was that died."

The idea that had come to him as a flicker of light earlier in the afternoon had now taken on a steady radiance of its own. It had been there in the darkness all the time, but had freed itself and come floating upward, glowing brighter as it rose.

He thought with wonder about the fact that down in the oceanic abyss there were fishes that lived in eternal darkness and were blind. Yet, for some inexplicable reason they were able to give off luminescence, to light up the waters around them that they would never see.

He knew now what he had to do. He knew how to repair a tricuspid atresia.

The morning started off well enough, in spite of the dreary weather. As if begrudging the single day of sunshine, the late autumn rains had settled in again, and it had been drizzling since Sunday morning.

But Deon was whistling in time with the gay tune on the radio as he took the lucky road down the mountain. The rain had left the roads slippery and he drove slowly and with care to the children's hospital, remembering, with a small shudder, how close he had come to killing himself on Saturday.

Once there, as he routinely prepared to operate, a part of his mind was still somewhere else, winging its way alone, drifting like a bird, untroubled and free.

Immediately upon his return from Hermanus he had telephoned Moolman to discuss the new idea. They had tried it yesterday and so far things seemed to be going well. Moolman had phoned this morning, very elated, and although Deon tried to be restrained, he too, deep down, was convinced that it was going to work. If they could get a dog to survive for four days he would be happy to accept that the procedure was feasible for humans too.

He was still whistling as he walked jauntily toward the theater, where Robby would already have completed the first stages. He was glad Robby was assisting him and Tom Morton-Brown was the anesthetist. They worked well together.

Robby and he had seen Peter Moorhead's niece, the little Irish girl Kathleen, in the ward yesterday. She was still shy and they had tried to get her talking.

"Who's your hero?" Robby had asked.

"Donny Osborne," she told him seriously.

"What? I thought I was your hero!"

"You're my third hero."

"So? And who's your second hero?"

She hid her face in her pillow and pointed at Deon. "Him."

Robby put his hands to his sides. "That's what always happens. I'm much more handsome than he is, but all the girls fall in love with him."

The pillow had shaken with her laughter.

Deon smiled again at the memory and went through the scrub room door to stand behind the anesthetist's screen.

"How's it going?"

Robby replied without looking up: "Fine. Ready for you in a minute."

Deon lingered a moment longer to look at the opened chest cavity and the grossly enlarged three-chambered heart, mentally revising the steps he had worked out to repair the deformity. Then he returned to the scrub room.

They linked Kathleen's circulation to the heart-lung machine without a hitch. It was as if today everyone had become infected by his driving self-confidence and shared it. He tightened the tapes around the catheters and looked over the screen at the anesthetist.

"Line pressure okay?"

Morton-Brown glanced at the manometers and then at his clipboard. "Everything's fine."

"Full flow," the technician called.

Robby looked at Deon and his eyes crinkled above his mask. "Second hero," he said.

Deon turned to the nurse. "Knife."

He used a stiletto-bladed knife to make a small cut in the wall of the right atrium and then with a pair of scissors he extended this into a long horizontal incision. He slipped two retractors under the left edge of the opening and gave them to Guido Perino, who acted as second assistant. Robby sucked the cavities clear of blood and Deon looked inside Kathleen's heart.

He stared as if mesmerized. He could see right down into the ventricular cavity with valve leaflets hanging from their chordae like flaps of skin dangling from a raw wound. He had never seen anything like this before.

Deon asked for a dissecting forceps and with one in each hand he pulled the leaflets apart, but still the inside of Kathleen's heart would not reveal its mysteries.

Jesus.

He looked up. Robby from his position could not get a clear view of the interior of that hollow heart and continued to assist Deon undisturbed.

"Hell, Robby. I haven't got a clue what's going on here."

The fucking cardiologists.

Deon bent down again over the open chest. Again he pulled the leaflets apart. He had never encountered this type of defect before.

The surgeon stood back to think. It was impossible. He did not know where to start to reconstruct all this.

Robby had noticed his confusion and peered over to get a clear view of the inside of the heart. Deon moved aside.

"See what you make of it!"

The words came out in a harsh screech. Guido was still holding up the retractors. He looked up, startled.

Deon cleared his throat. "This is an absolute mess." He gestured despairingly. "I think both the atrial and ventricular septa are missing. The inside leaflets of the mitral and tricuspid valves appear to have no basal attachments. This is a single-chambered heart!"

"Where are the damn cardiologists now?" he shouted at no one in particular. "Why don't they come and tell us how to fix this heart? How the hell did they miss the diagnosis?"

Tension partially relieved by the outburst, he turned to examine the heart again.

Once, on a visit to Europe, he had met and befriended a sculptor named Arkhiv. Elizabeth and he had been invited to Arkhiv's studio and there, lying in the dusty backyard, Deon had spotted half a dozen large blocks of marble.

He had stood at the big south-facing window and called to Arkhiv who, with delicate movements of his hands, was explaining something about a half-finished nude to Elizabeth.

"And those?" Deon had asked. "Why don't you do something with those beautiful pieces of marble?"

Arkhiv came to the window beside him. A black cat walked arrogantly across the rough-paved yard, making for a row of trash cans. The air was dusty and filled with soft-filtered sunlight. Arkhiv looked thoughtfully at the carelessly jumbled blocks and then smiled at Deon.

"Because, Professor," he had said, "I still cannot see what is inside them."

It had sounded obscure and even a trifle pretentious, but now Deon understood precisely what the sculptor had meant. He was looking at a heart and he could not see what lay within that heart.

The best thing would be to close it and do nothing. Leave it alone, prudence advised. At least you won't do more damage than has been done already. Try patching those bits and pieces and you'll end up with a complete disaster. There's no way of telling where the conducting bundles run. You'll have heart block for sure.

And yet a compelling and rebellious part of his mind would not accept defeat. There had to be a way, if only he could see it.

"Guido."

The Italian, usually so cocksure, had caught the fatal contagion of uncertainty. He looked miserably over at Deon.

"Go out and phone Peter," Deon told him. "Tell him the damn cardiologists made a mistake. Tell him there's no ventricular septum either. I don't think there's anything to be done. I'm simply going to close up again. Ask him whether he agrees."

Guido nodded and moved away from the table. A nurse helped him untie the back of his gown. The pneumatic device on the door closed it behind him with a sucking noise which was startlingly loud in the silent theater.

"Nobody could do anything with this," Deon said angrily to Robby, as if defending himself against unstated reproach, although Robby had not even looked at him. "It's quite impossible. If I'd known it was a single ventricle I would never have considered operating."

Robby nodded agreement, but it did nothing to diminish the hollow horror of defeat. Deon knew that he had no need to vindicate himself before Robby or anyone else in the world.

Except himself.

They stood at the table in silence and terrible inactivity.

Unable to bear the gray despair for one second longer, Deon started pulling the unattached leaflets of the tricuspid valve first, and then of the

315

mitral valve, into various positions. He peered down to the very apex of the heart. He could see the openings of the pulmonary and aortic valves. Each of them should rise from a separate chamber. But how? Where did you start?

The door sighed again. Guido, pale under his olive skin, and sweating.

"Peter says . . ." He gulped and started again. "Peter says you must do whatever you think is best."

Deon laughed within himself, without humor. What was it you were trying to get? Reassurance? A decision? Did you want him to say soothingly: "All right, Deon. Close up."

Then, at the moment he was about to ask Colleen for a suture, it happened. The mist in which he had been moving lifted and vanished, so that the sun shone and he could see exactly where he was going.

Like Arkhiv's block of marble, Kathleen's heart had fashioned its own shape.

"Guido, scrub up again," he said. "Okay, Robby. Let's try it."

Robby's eyes widened fractionally. Then, with seeming casualness, he nodded.

Their first task would be to create a ventricular septum. But he could not do it all through the atrium, so he would have to make another approach. He made a transverse incision through the front wall of the right ventricle, a little below the pulmonary valve. He avoided a branch from the right coronary artery. Kathleen would need everything going for her after this.

Robby and Guido held the cut open with retractors. The heart continued to beat.

The view into the ventricle was more familiar now, for this was the approach he normally used to repair ventricular septal defects. He studied it carefully. Mitral and aortic must be on the left; tricuspid and pulmonary on the right. He would have to place a row of interrupted sutures to map out the boundary. Like fence posts; and he thought fleetingly of his father and of Wamagerskraal.

"Sutures. Four-O."

The scrub sister handed him a needle holder. He pulled away the tricuspid's flaps and began to place the stitches. But he could not see what he was doing. He had hoped he could keep the heart beating while he was doing the repair. Then, should a suture hit a vital nerve, the electrocardiogram would immediately show it. But it was going to prove impossible to achieve. He would have to have a still and relaxed heart.

The heart-lung technician sat alertly at his console.

"Cool," Deon said.

316

The technician flicked a switch.

"Cooling on," he said promptly. "How long do you want it, Prof?"

"Until the heart is fibrillating."

Deon picked up the heart to place a vent into what would become the left ventricle. Already he could feel the muscle cooling. The beat was slowing. He secured the small plastic tube with a stitch and gently lowered the heart back into the pericardial sac. At that moment the coordinated contraction of the muscles stopped, as each fiber took up its own squirming rhythm.

"Fibrillating now," Morton-Brown said.

"Okay. Stop cooling. Aortic clamp, sister."

Now that they all knew what he was trying to do, the comforting sense of routine was reestablished. Sutures were stitched and clamped with almost automatic precision. Once again his and Robby's and Guido's and Colleen's hands moved together in symphony as if they were interchangeable parts of the same flawless machine. What they were doing was new and risky, as if they were acrobats on the high trapeze, trying a maneuver no one had dared try before and with no net below to catch them if they fell. But the techniques were those they had used many times, and this helped them keep their nerve as they swung in long curves and patterns from their dangling ropes, gripping and counter-gripping without effort, and unmindful of the emptiness below.

When the sutures were placed, Deon fashioned a piece of plastic felt to the correct size and shaped it into a U. He passed the stitches through it at the bottom and then along both limbs of the U. Robby lowered the patch into position while Deon held the sutures taut. He tied each securely and cut them short.

"Looks good," Robby said.

"Hope to hell I haven't caused a block," Deon told him grimly.

He switched to the incision in the right atrium, so as to have a clear view of the atrioventricular valves and the top of the U-shaped patch. Working with the meticulous care of a seamstress making stitches in fine lace, he fastened the inside leaflets of the valves to the top of the patch.

To test them he injected water into the two newly formed ventricles. The leaflets ballooned out. They closed perfectly. Perhaps there was a small leak of the tricuspid, but it wasn't important.

He shaped the second piece of dacron felt and built a wall to divide the common atrium, taking care that the veins from the lungs drained on the left.

He straightened up at last and held his head back for a moment, letting his breath go in a weary sigh.

"That's about all. Let's close it."

"Start warming."

"Warming on," the technician said.

The pump that circulated hot water through the heat exchanger's jacket began to whine. Deon released the aortic clamp and heated blood began to flow back into the heart muscle. He closed the long atrial wound.

Now that it was all done he became more and more nervous. His tremor increased so that he could hardly steady the needle holder.

While he had been remodeling the heart he had tried to suppress thought of consequences. But now all the damned-up doubt came flooding back. Would it, could it, possibly work? There were so many unpredictables. Heart block. Leaking of the reconstructed valves. So many others that he hadn't even thought of.

The atria had taken up a regular beat, but the ventricles were still fibrillating. It was as if the heart were uncertain how to go about pumping blood through its new form.

"What's the temperature?" he asked.

"Esophageal, thirty-four," the anesthetist said. "But the rectal's still a bit low. Twenty-eight."

"Can't you warm faster?" Deon asked the technician impatiently.

"The water's forty-two, Prof. That's the best I can do."

"I don't want any cheek from you, do you hear?" Deon shouted.

The technician looked at him sulkily from under his brows.

The blood coursing through the heart was now at normal temperature, but the heart continued to fibrillate. He would have to shock it.

But as he lifted the trembling muscle to place one paddle behind it, it kicked to life under his fingers, as if he had already jolted it with an electric charge. It seemed to hesitate. The atria were pouring their signals to the ventricles as if to encourage them in their flagging effort. Another contraction. Then the two newly created pumping chambers burst into regular and, to everyone in the operating room, beautiful sinus rhythm.

Robby stretched up to his full bony length and closed his eyes.

"I don't believe it," he said.

Then he raised his gloved hands high and showed them to Deon. They were balled into fists with the thumbs held hard in each fist.

Afterward, in the recovery room, there was a phone call from Peter Moorhead. "You take it," Deon said urgently to Robby. "Tell him I've already left. Tell him anything you like."

To speak about it now, to anyone, would subtract from it. He needed to conserve it and to do so he had to hold it within himself, not sharing. It could not be shared.

Deon found Philip Davids working in the small laboratory that led off his office. Philip looked only mildly surprised to see him, although they had made no arrangement to meet. In fact Deon had intended returning to his office, but had found himself instead going to the building next door, where the Department of Genetics was housed.

He had knocked, but there had been no reply. Finally, feeling a little uncomfortable, he had pushed open the door. Behind a farther door marked "laboratory" were a couple of people in white coats. They looked at him. A short, fox-faced man with rimless glasses approached, frowning officiously.

"Yes?"

Then, with a double take so dramatic that it was almost comical, he recognized Deon.

"Professor van der Riet! Good afternoon, Professor."

"Afternoon. Sorry to interrupt. I'm looking for Professor Davids."

"Oh," the other man said. Then, with less enthusiasm: "He's in the office down the passage."

The office door was open, and so was the laboratory door beyond it. Through them Deon could see Philip, sitting back from the microscope over which he had been leaning.

"Hello," Philip said. "Come through."

They shook hands and Philip indicated a chair. "Sit down. I won't be a minute."

"Sure."

Deon sat down and looked around with interest. It was a laboratory much like all the others he had seen and worked in, although possibly tidier than most. That would be Philip. He had always had something of a compulsion about cleanliness, even when they had been children together, washing under the outside tap after grubbing around in the mud.

There was an animal smell. He saw rows of numbered cages against one wall. A scampering movement behind the mesh. Mice. And rabbits in the lower cages.

Philip sat back from the microscope again, made a note on a scratch pad beside it and swiveled round on his padded stool.

"So," he said. He smiled. "What brings you here?"

"Sorry it's been such a long time. You know how it is."

"I know."

"How's the work going? Did you manage to get everything you needed?"

"Yes, indeed. The university has been very generous. I've got everything I need for the time being. It was kind of you to put me in touch with the right people."

Deon grimaced.

"The way things are, my recommendation may have done you more harm than good. I'm not exactly a blue-eyed boy anymore. No; they're not stupid. They could see the university was going to pick up a lot of credit for this."

"Still. Most people wouldn't have bothered."

"Anyway, are you making progress?"

"I think so. Nothing to set the world on fire just yet. It's a question of simply doing one experiment after the other till you've got enough data. Some people would be bored stiff. I like it."

Deon laughed. "I don't think it would suit me. I prefer life to have a bit of dash and drama."

"No doubt," Philip said drily.

"Like this morning." Deon began to describe the operation he had just completed. He had imagined it would be impossible to communicate his feelings about it to anyone, but he found himself speaking easily. He did not dramatize the story, for there was no need to do that. He knew that Philip would understand.

"Yes," Philip said at length. "That was quite something."

They talked on, content with one another's company.

"Have you found any abnormalities?" Deon asked.

"It's too early to say."

"Will the knowledge that you gain now and the techniques you perfect someday be applicable to humans?"

Philip smiled good-naturedly. "Who knows? But whatever we find out will bring us nearer the truth. To know is enough," he said mock-heroically, and smiled again.

"Okay, that's all very well. The basic scientist in his lab, looking only for knowledge. But what you find out here today may help someone else to complete the whole development of a human fetus in artificial conditions. 'The Baby Factory' prophesied by Aldous Huxley many years ago."

Philip frowned. "All I'm trying to find out is whether the injury inflicted on the genetic material by handling it can change the message it carries," he said stiffly. "That's all."

Deon, his mind still wound up from the morning's tension, plunged zestfully into the argument. "Wait a minute. You can't escape the consequences that easily. You can't say: 'I won't do it, so it's none of my business if others do.' That's like a physicist splitting the atom but washing his hands of the atom bomb."

"I accept that."

"Then where do you stand? If someone were to make a test-tube baby, would you hail it as an important scientific advancement or an immoral act?"

"In my opinion it would be both."

"That's precisely my point. Even you, even a sane and responsible person like you . . ."

"Thank you," Philip said with an ironic half bow.

"No, wait," Deon said. "I'm serious. Even someone like you has an ambivalent attitude. Take the work you're doing now. It's all very scientific and remote. At present you are working on mice and rabbits. The next logical step will be to see whether your findings also apply to fertilized human ova."

Philip swiveled the high-backed stool from side to side, watching Deon impassively. "Yes," he said finally.

"Now, do you apply the same rules, the same standards, toward that human life you've created as toward the animal? Can you also take the human embryo you have cultured and kill it or wash it down the sink when you have completed your experiments?"

Philip continued to twist the stool. "To start with, you have to define what you mean by human life. Remember that the embryo you're talking about is at most no more than a blastocyst, less than a week old. It's only a pinprick of matter. Some highly respected scientists today believe life should only begin after a child has been born and has been found to be normal."

"I know. I know. But you are missing the point I'm trying to make. Those few cells, or as you called it 'only a pinprick of matter,' which resulted from the in vitro fertilization of the ovum have the potential to become a normal, healthy human being. In other words, passed the final test of your so-called respected scientists. So, how can you just destroy them? I want to ask you one more question: What do you think of asexual reproduction? About reproducing any individual as many times as you like by transplanting his nuclei?"

"I'm glad you mentioned that." Philip appeared to be filled with new enthusiasm. "You are ignoring a basic fact. We may not have gained very much from putting a man on the moon, but there's great value in the spin-offs from the research that enabled us to get him there. Already the technique of cell fusion, which to you only means the production of a clonal man, offers one of the best avenues for understanding the genetic basis of cancer. Now, all over the world, cancer cells are being fused with normal cells to pinpoint those specific chromosomes responsible for given forms of cancer. If you turn round and say 'Stop such research,' using the argument that cloning represents a greater threat than a disease like cancer, you are likely to be considered irresponsible by virtually any man able to understand the matter."

Suddenly Deon seemed reluctant to continue the argument. "Well, I don't know," he said with an abstract air and got up from the desk on which he had been sitting. "I've got to go now, but we'll take up the argument some other time."

Philip put out a restraining hand. "There was something else I wanted to ask you. A further request. Anyhow, since you obviously don't approve of my work, perhaps I should forget it."

"Now hang on," Deon protested. "I've never suggested I don't approve. It would be presumptuous of me in any case."

Philip shook his head. "No. You've got to go."

"Don't be so damn foolish. What did you want to ask me?"

"You were quite right, Deon. I want to move on to experiment with human ova."

"I told you," Deon said with a mischievous grin. "And you want me to help you get hold of some?"

"Yes. Professor Gleave has been trying his best for me, but he just hasn't been able to persuade anyone to help us. I don't think he has enough influence or knows enough people."

"What's the legal position?" Deon asked suddenly.

Philip spread his hands. "It's rather obscure. We haven't been able to establish it exactly."

"Hmm-yes. That's one problem. And the other is that you'd need volunteers. You would collect them by laparoscopy, I assume?"

"Of course that would be ideal. But there might be too many complications. To start with I'd be happy if I could get the use of freshly removed ovaries or pieces of ovaries. Then I could collect ova from them."

"That might not be too difficult to arrange. I know a couple of gynecologists pretty well. I could speak to them. The only thing is . . ." He pulled his lips to one side, hesitantly.

"Is what?" Philip asked quickly.

"I don't think I'll tell them why I want the ovaries. You know how small-minded some people are." Deon saw Philip's expression harden. "Look, I have nothing against the work you are doing and there are many others who won't, but I still think it is better to keep it quiet."

"Naturally. But if you think the risk is . . ."

Deon silenced Philip with a hand gesture. "Don't get on your high horse now. I'll arrange that you get the ova you need. The only thing is that it must be kept absolutely secret. Even Gleave mustn't know. That's fair enough, isn't it?"

"Fair enough," Philip said.

Deon obtained the ova—under false pretenses.

For reasons he did not wish to analyze, Deon had used the doctor's phone outside the deserted lecture room, so that the call did not have to be placed through the hospital exchange.

He had dialed the number Trish had given him, and when the call was answered had asked, very politely, to speak to her.

"I'll have to call her from next door," the woman said. "Who shall I say wishes to speak to her?"

The inquisitive tone irritated. "Tell her it's a friend." But that might make the woman more curious. "Please tell her it's Deon."

There was a long wait before the receiver was picked up.

"Hello." That deep voice, with its suggestion of resonance, made his throat go suddenly dry.

"Hello, Trish." As casually as he was able. "Deon."

"I know."

Deon decided to be equally direct.

"I have something important to tell you."

"What is it?"

"I would rather tell you in person . . . Will you be coming in to town some time?"

"It just so happens I am coming in tomorrow to see the travel agent."

"Would you have lunch with me?"

"Thank you."

Stumbling slightly over the words he had made the necessary arrangements of time and place.

Now, walking side by side with Trish up Adderley Street, he felt the same incoherent awkwardness. It was twelve thirty and the pavement was crowded. He gave silent thanks for the press of people that made conversation mercifully impossible.

Her first question at their meeting had been: "What is it you want to tell me?"

323

But he had shaken his head and said: "Not here on the street. Later."

He guided her, a hand lightly at her elbow, into the small, discreet restaurant he had chosen. They went down a shallow flight of steps into warmth and a comfortable air of seclusion. The busy street at once seemed miles away. A headwaiter came smiling and bowing to meet them. He recognized Deon and his eyes flickered toward Trish, but he was silent as he escorted them to a table.

For a while they were occupied with menus and choosing from the wine list, so it was not necessary to talk, except in standard, polite phrases. But finally the waiters and the wine steward withdrew and they were alone.

Trish leaned across the table toward him. "Now. Now you can tell me."

"Let's have a drink first."

He could not explain to himself his reasons for delaying, for tantalizing her. It was not cruelty, although perhaps there was a slight degree of it, an endeavor to find revenge for her aloofness. But mostly it was a need to retain her interest for a while longer, even if the means were as crude as withholding information she desperately wanted.

She watched his face for a moment, her eyes searching. Then she gave a small shrug and looked around her. The restaurant was all rich bronze and gold and polished wood. It gave the impression of having endured for centuries.

"I don't remember this place," she said lightly.

Obviously she had decided to humor him, to play the game by his rules. And, paradoxically, he was at once disappointed by her acquiescence.

"Opened last year," he told her with a mocking smile. "All these timeworn oak beams and ancient paneling are just window dressing. Anyway, I can recommend the food."

She laughed. "That's a relief."

"Anyway, we wouldn't have been able to afford this kind of place in those days, would we?"

She did not show, by word or gesture, any reaction to the rather obvious move toward a special relationship, based on shared memories.

"No," she said.

"Have you decided when you're returning to Italy?" He dreaded the answer, but it was the only question he could think of.

"At the beginning of next month. I've come in today to make the necessary reservations."

Three weeks. Less than three weeks.

"So you're not planning to stay on a bit longer?"

WINTER

Nine

A hot berg wind was blowing out of the north.

Deon thought, as he climbed out of his car in front of the hospital, that the wind probably marked the end of the fine weather. For almost a week, now, one golden-warm day had been succeeded by another, and people had begun to speak optimistically of an early spring. But this wind, which seemed to carry with it the hot, dry breath of Africa itself, threatened otherwise. The worst of winter was yet to come.

A berg wind always unnerved him. He knew that he would have a headache by midmorning. When he was a child his father had always told them that this wind came straight out of the mouth of hell. And, coincidence or not, it had often presaged some evil, even if it was nothing worse than a cold or a bout of flu.

He started ward rounds with a feeling that, in that dull heat, his clothes were too tight for him. He vented his irritation on his staff, hunting for faults, finding them and issuing frequent harsh reprimands. The discovery that the patient on whom he had performed a mitral valve replacement yesterday still had not completely recovered consciousness was the final straw.

He rounded angrily on the recovery room registrar, a comparative newcomer from somewhere in Middle Europe.

"What the hell is going on here? Why didn't you let me know?"

The registrar stammered an incomprehensible reply. Quite unreasonably, it provoked Deon to further anger.

"What are you saying? Speak up, man!"

Robby Robertson intervened smoothly.

"I imagine you got a little air into the heart when you went off by-pass," he said. "It went into the brain and now there's a bit of anoxic damage."

327

Deon curled a lip toward Robby. "I can work that out for myself, thank you."

"You can't blame this youngster for it, can you?" Robby asked with spirit.

Several people shifted their feet uncomfortably and looked at the monitors, the charts on the wall, the ceiling; anywhere but at Deon and Robby.

Stung, Deon retorted: "Maybe. But he could have taken the trouble to let me know, not so? What was he going to do? Phone me after the patient was dead?"

Robby shrugged. "What could one do, except wait and hope for the best? No one could do more, could they? Not even you."

The taunt was as unmistakable as it was unexpected. There was a tense, listening silence all around them. Deon's eyes narrowed.

"Look, Robby. While I'm in charge of this unit I want to know everything that happens in it. Everything. Is that clear?"

Robby turned away with another shrug. They completed rounds in strained and unhappy taciturnity.

By the time Deon had left the hospital his anger had faded, to be replaced by shame and regret. He really should try to curb the habit of lashing out at one of his staff in front of all the others and even, at times, in the presence of patients. Blame it on the weather. Blame it on the way things were. Blame it on the way he was made.

Nevertheless it was true that a degree of animosity had crept in to spoil his and Robby's long and easy relationship. Robby had never been particularly respectful, but he had always acknowledged Deon as unquestioned leader and head of the cardiac department. Lately, however, he had become very prone to answer back, or to question decisions and instructions.

This morning he had been decidedly in the wrong. Even if he felt that criticism was irrational (as, with a twinge of conscience, Deon recognized it to be), he should have kept quiet. Now he had presented himself, whether consciously or not, as a defender of the juniors on the team, and this could easily lead to dissension.

Deon climbed the stairs of his office building slowly, feeling suddenly old and weary. Something was happening to his dream. The old loyalty and comradeship had vanished.

Blame it on the heat, he thought plaintively. Blame it on the heat.

One thing he had to do was to get more staff. The unit was desperately short. Both Guido and the Frenchman, Carrére, had resigned suddenly and had not yet been replaced. Only two of the seven registrars' posts were filled.

That's the reason we're all so edgy, he thought. The boys are having to work too hard. Perhaps I should cut down on the volume of work for a few weeks.

He would phone Professor Snyman at once about his promise to recruit registrars for the unit from the general surgery pool. When had they spoken about it? At least two weeks ago, and still nothing had happened. Surely the old man couldn't have forgotten?

It was different in the old days, Deon reflected bitterly. Then he was only too happy to give me everything I wanted: staff, equipment, lab space, money for research. Now I have to battle merely to get a full complement of registrars.

At one time a rotation scheme which allowed all surgical registrars to serve six months in the cardiac unit had assured him of staff. But the system had been changed abruptly, with no convincing reason given.

He went in through the outer office, passing Jenny with no more than a brief nod. He needed solitude and silence; time to think and find direction. He felt suffocated.

The wind, he thought. It's only the wind.

On his desk was a note. Professor Snyman wished to see him. Would he telephone Miss Arensen to arrange a suitable time?

Maybe this was the answer to the staff problem, and, if not, he would have an opportunity to mention the subject. Feeling suddenly cheerful, he rang Snyman's office.

Yes, Miss Arensen said. Professor would be free shortly. Would Professor van der Riet please come to his office at once?

Professor Snyman was silent and unsmiling. He did not rise as Deon came in. He had a typed sheet of paper on the desk in front of him and shielded it with one hand. He began speaking as soon as Deon sat down, his voice high and querulous.

"I am disappointed in you, Deon. Deeply disappointed and saddened. I never thought it of you."

He paused, lowering his head to look down at his bit of paper. This withdrawal of his gaze was carried out slowly and deliberately, as a further sign of his displeasure; of the distance he was placing between them.

Deon stared at the cockscomb of white hair which was all of Professor Snyman that he was now permitted to see. His mind raced through the events of the past few days. How the devil could he have offended the old man?

"In the future," Snyman said heavily, "when you have surgical problems, please don't refer them to my firm. I am no longer prepared to take care of your complications."

Deon was astounded. "Sir . . . ?"

Consultation and cooperation between the surgical departments was the cornerstone for the whole edifice of the division. It had always been standard and unquestioned practice. A change in the procedure was unthinkable.

"I don't understand. What . . . why . . . ?"

"I am sick and tired of you blaming us for the death of your patients," Snyman said viciously.

Deon shook his head like a boxer who had taken a snap blow on the jaw. "Blaming you?" He tried to put on a look of mock perplexity, as if it might all be a joke. "I'm sure I've never done that."

"I have my sources of information," the old man said. There was an edge of triumph, of the cock crowing from the top of the dunghill, about his tone, which began to annoy Deon. When he replied he kept his voice down.

"Professor, to the best of my knowledge I have never blamed you or your firm for the death of any of my patients."

The triumph was very evident now.

"Then what about that van Heerden case? The man who had peritonitis?"

Van Heerden. Van Heerden. Yes. Couple of weeks ago. Man of about forty. Mid-forties. He had replaced both the mitral and aortic valves.

"I remember van Heerden."

"Well?"

The patient had done well until the second postoperative day. Then he had showed blood in his stools. Professor Snyman had been consulted and had done a laporotomy. He had discovered a volvulus of the small bowel, with gangrene, and had resected a portion of the bowel. However, bleeding had continued and, two days later van Heerden was explored once more. This time a duodenal ulcer was found and it was oversewn and a vagotomy performed. The patient seemed to improve, but three days later he ruptured his wound. A third operation was performed to resuture it. Soon afterward there had been evidence of gross infection in the peritoneal cavity and the patient had died.

"What makes you think I ever blamed you?" Deon asked.

"Never mind," the old man told him brusquely. "Just take your patients somewhere else in the future."

There was little point in taking it any further. Snyman's mind was closed. Someone had come to him with this bit of venom and he had been only too ready to listen and believe.

"Very well." Deon tightened his voice. "If that's the way you wish it."

Snyman glowered, but said nothing.

Deon continued in the same clipped tones: "May I ask, Professor, whether you have made arrangements about getting more staff for me from the pool?"

Snyman lowered his head and again nothing was visible but the ridge of hair. "No."

"Oh? I'm five registrars short, you know."

"I tried," the old man said. "I certainly tried." He looked up now, with a faint smirk. "It might interest you to know that I asked no fewer than fifteen of the registrars if they'd be prepared to work in your unit. Every one of them refused. So I'm afraid I can't help you."

"Fine, Professor," Deon said as nonchalantly as he was able. "No problem. I'll have to look for help myself, won't I?"

If the old bastard had been in earnest he could simply have instructed the registrars to join the cardiac firm, as he would have with orthopedics or gynecology or any of the other specialized departments. "Don't worry," he said again. "I can manage."

"You needn't try to be sarcastic," Snyman said. His face had turned a dull red. "In case you don't know it, no one wants to work for you. It's as simple as that. They all said they'd rather resign than move to your firm."

"And you, Chief of Surgery, let a bunch of registrars tell you that? They were bluffing, and you know that perfectly well. Good God, do you think any of them would have risked his career by defying you if you had told them to move their tails over to cardiac surgery, or else? I'm sorry, Professor. It just won't wash."

The old man, his face now white with anger, was agitatedly hunting among his papers.

Nothing I've said can now be unsaid, Deon thought. Now I might as well get it all out.

"I'm sorry to say this to you, but I have lost faith in you both as friend and as my chief. I don't know precisely what has happened between us, but perhaps it's because I'm not one of your professional committee sitters. God knows you've got enough of those round you."

Snyman flung his arms out angrily, sweeping a clutter of papers on to the floor. "How dare you? How dare you say . . . ?"

"Allow me to finish, Professor. Let me remind you about your new

331

research block. Named the Patrick Metcalfe Research Institute, if you remember. Named for my father-in-law, oddly enough. Why? Because he donated the money for it. Very altruistic, and so forth. But he was going to give it away for some other cause until I persuaded him that we could use it here. So you have a nice new building for research, and when I ask for some space in it for my own work, what happens? The part I played in getting the money is forgotten. The committee sitters have got in before me."

He pushed his chair back, looking dispassionately down at the seated man. He's getting old, he thought coolly. Old and envious and malicious.

"There was a time when you were prepared to look after my interests," he told Snyman. "But no longer. I think this place is becoming too small for both of us, Professor."

He turned on his heel.

"Yes," the old man shouted after him. "It is too small for us. But I can assure you that I'm not leaving."

Long ago, Philip had schooled himself against showing emotion. He knew himself to be a tense person and had taken a painful pleasure in curbing a tendency toward demonstrativeness. Even as a child he had despised those of his own race who wore the fact of their color like a wound; who used it as an excuse for excess.

Perhaps it was his chill demeanor as much as her infantile ambitions that had finally separated his wife and himself. He often wondered, just as he had wondered during their brief marriage, what it was that had brought them together. Sexuality apart, they had almost nothing in common. Had it been a residue—something that in today's jargon would be called a hang-up —of resentment after the frustrations of his affair with Elizabeth? A fading sadness, a glow he had tried to rekindle with another woman who was both white and blonde? And failed because he himself was too cold to be warmed by any fire?

It was not until he finally developed a duodenal ulcer that he had come to realize fully the impossible demands his will was making of his body. He must learn to let go sometimes, the understanding physician who had treated him ordered, and Philip had complied; to a point. His aloof public manner was too ingrained, too much a part of himself, to be lightly abandoned. So he had developed the habit, when he felt pressure building up toward explosion point, of seeking solitude, anywhere: in a lavatory or a corridor or a quiet corner of a room where he could keep his face hidden, and through clenched teeth and in a voice only audible to himself mutter every profanity he could think of. It was childish but it worked. Once or twice he had almost been caught at it, had been unable to compose his face in time for an unexpected interruption, or had caught the startled look on the face of a passing student or colleague. These occasions had frightened him, for he feared ridicule, but had also caused him great and secret glee, for he would dearly have loved to break out, to show the world his true wildness. But he held back, through force of habit and because of the iron control he exercised over himself.

This afternoon, inside his own office, his privacy was assured and he could afford to relax his grip. He crouched behind his desk, swearing in a menacing monotone, his voice contorted with rage.

Professor Gleave had been profoundly enthusiastic about the genetic manipulation study right from the start. He was an ambitious man as well as a pleasant one, and it would do his professional career no harm to be associated with such an investigation. Clearly he had been relieved to know that his restricted budget would not have to bear any of the cost, and in sudden generosity he had offered Williams' services as a full-time assistant for Philip.

Philip had been dubious. His relations with the chief technician had remained formal, and he had tried to keep dealings with the main laboratory to absolute essentials. On the other hand, there was a lot of time-wasting routine work that Williams could handle.

Things had worked better than he had expected. True that he and Williams were far from being friends, but at least they were not open enemies. Both had scrupulously avoided chances of a confrontation and had succeeded until now.

Until today.

They had been working in the draft-free enclosure set up in one corner of the laboratory by the simple expedient of curtaining it from floor to ceiling with a plastic sheet. Philip was flushing out newly ovulated eggs from the ovary duct of a dead mouse with a thin pipette.

"Where do we get the spermatozoa?" Williams asked unexpectedly.

"Hm?" Philip said absently. He was struggling to position the fine point of the pipette. "Are you ready with that culture dish?"

"I'm ready," Williams said. He repeated his question. "Where do we get the sperm?"

This time Philip took his eyes off what he was doing to stare at the technician in surprise. "What for? The eggs are already fertilized."

Williams looked baffled. "Fertilized? But how . . . ?"

"But good lord, surely you know? We've been doing it for months."

333

Philip recited somewhat testily, as if to a child: "You put the males in with the females and the next morning you select the female mice which have a vaginal plug, indicating that coitus has . . ."

Williams flapped a hand dismissingly toward the animal cages. "I don't mean those things. I'm talking about the human ova."

Philip's gaze sharpened. "What do you know about human ova?"

The technician managed to look both superior and sly. "I'm not exactly stupid, you know. But how do you fertilize them?"

"I use my own," Philip told him shortly. "Let's have that dish. We've got to get these into the incubator."

Williams did not move.

Philip had slipped the ova he had just collected under a microscope. He did not see the angry flush which had come to the technician's face.

"Dish, please, Mr. Williams."

Williams put the dish down, deliberately out of reach, and Philip looked up then, astonished.

"Do you mean to tell me that your . . . that you use . . ." Williams' voice was trembling and his glasses had dropped far forward on his nose. "You . . . you're . . . It's disgusting."

Philip put down the pipette. He was still baffled by the technician's reaction.

"Come now, Mr. Williams. It surely can't be something new to you? Man, it's standard laboratory practice throughout the world to use volunteer donors." He decided on a jocular, man-to-man approach. "Why, hell, we all masturbated when we were kids, didn't we? It's just a stage toward maturity. So what's wrong with doing it now for the sake of science?"

He reached out to give the technician a friendly pat on the shoulder. Williams jerked away. His mouth was working so that he could hardly get the words out.

"Some of those human eggs may have come from white women," he said.

He took off his glasses and wiped them crossly on the hem of his coat. Without them his face had a curiously naked, defenseless appearance.

Philip surveyed the man with the same scrupulous but remote attention he might have shown toward evidence which supported some regrettable scientific theory.

"Does that make any difference?" he asked finally.

"Of course," Williams snapped. "You're a Coloured."

He had been expecting it, of course. It had been inevitable, from the very beginning of their exchange. But it still hurt.

"Mr. Williams," he said in a soft, dry voice, "I think you had better leave this laboratory now. And, while you're about it, go to the police and ask them to charge me under the Immorality Act."

Williams put his glasses on again with an abrupt movement.

"Don't you worry about that. I'm going all right. I refuse to take part in this filthy business."

He whirled around and tried to stalk away in outraged dignity, an exit spoiled by his having to fumble with the plastic drapes.

Only now, behind the locked door of his office, did Philip feel free to express his feelings in the words he should have used. "You miserable, dirty-minded little bastard," he said in deadly rage. "You miserable little white bastard."

He rose, his mind made up. Gleave would have to act. There could be no backing down. And yet, as he walked to the door, deep inside him was a small anxious question. Would they do it? Would they discipline a white man because he had insulted a Coloured man?

You're Philip Davids, he had to remind himself. You're Professor Philip Davids. And to hell with it.

Elizabeth was at her dressing table, leaning forward into the hard glare of its lights, lipstick in hand, when Deon came padding softly, barefooted, into the room. He stopped at the door to watch her. She was dressed only in flimsy underclothes and her body was trim and supple as she half sat, half stood so as to get closer to the mirror. Her hair, long and blond (how much of its golden gleam was due to the hairdresser's careful attention he did not care to know) hung thickly down her back.

He felt a familiar, possessive warmth at the sight. She was beautiful and she belonged to him. He was fortunate.

From this angle he could see her only in profile, but he knew that she would be watching the glass with a slight frown, causing tiny wrinkles to appear at the corners of her eyes. Superficially, this was almost the only difference between the Elizabeth of now, at thirty-eight, and the Liz he had married nearly nineteen years ago. If there were other differences they lay on the credit side: maturity, poise, knowledge of people, all the social skills. Perhaps she was no longer as ardent in bed as she had been, but nothing could last forever, could it?

She was beautiful and he was proud of her.

This admission caused a sense of guilt so powerful that it was almost tangible; it made him flinch as from physical force.

You have this; why risk it? his angry conscience reproached.

335

His wife turned suddenly and saw him at the open door. She opened her eyes wide after the brightness of the dressing table lights. She smiled at him uncertainly.

"Hello, darling," she said. "Am I late?"

"Hell," he said. His voice was rough. "Hello, darling. Take your time. I'm not quite dressed either. But it's only a cocktail party. Doesn't matter if we're a bit late."

And his traitor's voice went on and on inside his own head.

Ten

One of the junior reporters, the one who dressed very modishly and wore his hair rather too long to the taste of the conservative-minded chief reporter, was chatting with the girl at the editorial reception desk. Neither of them noticed the little man standing at the sign saying: "Reception" in both English and Afrikaans. Only when he coughed did they look at him and at his pinched, stubborn-looking face. Something about him made the girl decide immediately that he was a teacher.

"Excuse me, miss," he said. His voice sounded choked and he coughed again.

He had used Afrikaans, but it was clear from his accent that he was not accustomed to the language, so the girl addressed him in English.

"Can I help you, sir?"

He, however, stuck determinedly to Afrikaans, perhaps in the belief that the use of the language in the office of an Afrikaans newspaper might favor his mission.

"I want to speak to the editor, please."

The reporter, disassociating himself from the proceedings, feigned intense interest in the framed drawing, an original by the newspaper's cartoonist, behind the reception desk.

The girl had been faced with this request often and had developed a standard reply which she now began to deliver in the same briskly cheerful way as she operated her telephone exchange.

"Sorry, sir, the editor is in Johannesburg, at our head office. This is only a branch office. Would you like to speak to the chief reporter?"

The little man looked disappointed and dubious. He took off his glasses and the girl realized now that it was these, the fact that they were rimless, which gave him his pompous air and had reminded her of the history teacher she'd had in high school. Without the glasses he was only another short man with a sharp, inquisitive face.

"I don't know," he said, and gestured at her with the glasses.

The receptionist had never liked that history teacher, so she was inclined to be a bit quick with the little man.

"What was it in connection with?"

"I can't tell you." He seemed keyed up by his own sense of self-esteem. "But it's very important."

The girl was used to cranks too. She turned away with a shrug. "Then you'd better see the chief reporter."

"All right," he agreed unwillingly.

The exchange buzzed again and the girl reached toward it.

"Frans," she said to the reporter. "Will you show this gentleman to Mr. Lategan's office, please?"

She thought, as she manipulated switches and pulled out plugs, that she had rid herself of two potential nuisances. She observed the injured-looking stiffness of the reporter's back as he preceded the little man into the newsroom. She sniffed derisively. He really did fancy himself. She dismissed him from her mind and thought instead of the dance club she and her boyfriend had joined last weekend.

By choice, Deon stuck to routine heart surgery that week. But he was insecure, even doing relatively simple procedures. He noticed it and knew that his staff was aware of it too. He was quick-tempered and clumsy at times. He reminded himself sardonically of what Professor Snyman had once said about a particularly inept surgeon: that the man had four thumbs and a big toe on each hand. Even more disturbing, he found his concentration slipping. During an operation in the middle of the week, as he was about to insert the arterial cannula, the anesthetist had warned him hurriedly that the patient had not yet been heparinized. The omission could have killed, for the blood would have clotted.

In the laboratory, at least, things were different. He and Moolman operated with great success on a dog; closing the opening of the tricuspid valve to simulate atresia, then diverting blood from the right atrium to the lung. It worked. They were ready.

On Thursday afternoon he met Trish at the children's hospital and helped her through the admission formalities. Giovanni followed them to the ward. He trusted Trish and Trish trusted Deon.

338

Moolman was waiting in the ward. Deon had moved him from the laboratory to the hospital. For the next three weeks his only responsibility would be this child. He would do the work-up before surgery, assist during the operation, and then stay with Giovanni every minute of the day during the postoperative period.

Trish kissed her son lightly on the cheek and turned away. Giovanni began to cry. Moolman tried to distract him with a toy, but he merely cried more loudly. Deon saw Trish hesitate, but then, her face resolute, she left the ward. Walking together down the corridor they could still hear the child's cries.

Deon thought that she probably needed distraction, so he drove to a beachfront hotel and bought her a drink in the ladies' bar. They talked for a while about Giovanni and the operation, then began to exchange reminiscences from student days. Trish was very serious, but not poor company. When he invited her to have dinner with him she accepted. Afterward he took her home to the flat she had rented to be near Giovanni. She asked him in for coffee.

The room was bright with moonlight. Trish did not turn on the lights at once. Instead she crossed to the window and stood looking at the glitter of the moon path on the sea. It seemed to Deon to be a signal and he went to her side and tried to take her hand. She freed herself promptly but calmly. He felt foolish and stood with his hands hanging awkwardly at his sides.

A late-flying gull moved soundlessly below them. It made a sharp silhouette against the shining waters, so that it might have been merely a shadow, or the ghost of a gull.

"The seagulls come to my window every evening to be fed," she remarked quietly.

He imagined how the birds would come planing past on the wind, making constant delicate adjustments with their wings, heads greedily turning to watch her. What did she feed them? Bread? He could picture her flinging out chunks of bread as a gull wobblingly reached the stalling point of its flight, and then swept swiftly downward after the morsel.

She would smile gravely from behind the window at the ease and freedom with which the gulls flew.

Almost without meaning to he said: "You're a darling."

She smiled at him exactly as he imagined her smiling at the seagulls. Then, without saying anything she went back to the door and turned on the lights.

"Coffee?" she asked.

"Thank you," he said.

There was a kitchenette, compact as a ship's galley, off the living room. He watched her fill the electric kettle and put out the coffee mugs.

"Are all these things yours?" he asked.

She shook her head.

"It's a furnished flat. The only thing here that belongs to me is that watercolor. I bought that yesterday."

He walked over to examine the painting. It showed a street scene. In the Malay Quarter, he thought. He did not recognize the signature.

In a wire rack below the watercolor were several glossy magazines. The top one was a German journal, intellectual-looking and devoted to the arts. Idly paging through it, he found a full-page color photograph of Trish.

Trish, wearing paint-daubed denims, stood at an easel with a half-completed painting of a plaster horse. The photographer had captured her intent, questioning expression.

There were additional photographs on subsequent pages: Trish in a garden; with Giovanni on a hillside, both of them laughing; Trish in a barnlike studio. Reproductions of paintings: a bowl of yellow flowers, five figures against an oddly cubist background; a desolate beach landscape.

He stumblingly translated the captions, guessing at the words. "Like a comet out of the heavens of art . . ." ". . . Patricia Sedara, painter of genius . . ." ". . . executed with the grace and vision of a true genius . . ."

He started on the text of the article itself, but then Trish came from the kitchen, carrying the steaming mugs. He took his from her, then showed her the magazine.

"I hadn't realized you were famous."

She glanced at the book and shrugged. "Oh, that. A friend of mine sent it to me."

"But seriously. I didn't know you were that good."

She seemed to weigh her answer. "Of course, I'm not as good as they claim. You know how these people exaggerate. But I am painting well, and I think I'm getting better."

He put down the magazine and drank his coffee quickly.

They talked of Giovanni again. He told her what would be done during the next few days: the blood analysis and cross-matching; X-rays to ensure that the lungs were clear; urine tests to exclude kidney disease and diabetes. All of them routine things, he assured her. Moolman was a gentle young man. Giovanni would be fine and happy.

Then he sat back in the skimpily padded lounge chair and smiled at her.

"And here I find you a famous artist. But that day on the beach at Hermanus you told me you couldn't paint. You had discovered you couldn't paint. Something like that."

"That was in Madrid," she said. "When I realized I was living that awful fake life. Yes, I stopped painting then."

"And you started again after you were married?"

"Yes."

"That's often the way, isn't it? It takes some sort of jolt to . . . well, to stimulate creation."

She gave him a distant look.

"I think that's very seldom how it happens. People get unnecessarily romantic about the creative process. An artist works at his painting like anyone else. If he's distracted, as I was in Madrid, he doesn't work well. That's all there is to it."

"And you've been painting ever since?"

"Yes."

Before he could think of anything else to say she rose to take his coffee cup and when she returned from the kitchen began to talk about Giovanni once more.

He could sense that she wanted him to go, but he wished to stay, though he knew that she did not need him. He tried to switch the conversation back to her paintings; she answered him noncommittally but he persisted.

Finally she offered him a drink and he accepted. He heard himself rambling on, recognizing a compulsion to speak but unable to control it. He looked around at the chilly, sparsely furnished little flat high above the sea and knew that it was dear to him. He felt carefree here. Nothing and no one could reach him. He would have liked to stay here all night and to hell with tomorrow's tortured explanations.

He remembered that Elizabeth had also had a flat like this, once. Elizabeth and Deon. Elizabeth and Philip. Had Philip, then, regarded that flat the way he now thought about this one: as the only place where nothing, whether it was a call to duty at the hospital or the need to consider one's race, could intrude?

Was that what it had been? Merely a refuge? Over the years he had wondered: what exactly was there between them?

He still could not answer the question.

He put down his glass and stood up.

"I must go," he said.

* * *

341

The copy editor was starting to feel desperate. Two inside pages were due to go away and he did not have a decent lead for either of them. He shuffled through his pile of copy again. Not a thing. There was that divorce story, but it was poorly written and hard editing would reduce it to nothing. And a lot of guff from Reuter via Sapa about the Middle East, and who the hell cared about that anymore?

"I need a lead for page six," the chief copy reader reminded him unnecessarily.

"Dammit, I know," the copy editor said in a hard, bitter voice.

Some of the other copy readers at the horseshoe-shaped table looked up at them.

"Got to have a lead, you know," the chief copy reader said.

It was an old joke between them, its origin founded on some long-forgotten crisis. The copy editor grinned and relaxed, combing his fingers through his hair again, but less agitatedly this time. Friday afternoons, when the pressure was on, were always bad. It would probably have to be the divorce story, badly written or not. He wished it were Sunday. He and his wife liked to go fishing on the river on Sundays.

The pneumatic tube at his elbow made a belching sound and a canister plopped out. He unfolded the wad of copy inside. The top sheets were stock exchange prices and he put them aside. The second story was datelined Cape Town and came from the branch office there. He read the introductory paragraph.

"Good God!" he said.

The chief copy reader, who had been ruling something on his layout sheet, looked across at him.

"Hell!" the copy editor said, still reading. Then, excitedly: "This is a great story, Daantjie. It's from Lategan in the Cape." He handed over the top page and went on reading. He was feeling very elated now. That was page six taken care of, at any rate.

Deon woke into that feeling of hollow desolation without, at the moment of waking, being able to identify its cause. Sunlight came in through the bedroom window and lay at an angle across his bed. The rising heat of morning was causing him to sweat under the blankets, so he kicked them off and lay back again.

He and Elizabeth had quarreled last night, ostensibly about Lisa, but really about something far deeper, something that was beginning to dominate their lives. He had felt a fever inside his wife. She seemed like a wild animal, caged and intent on escape. But he didn't know why.

Was it something in himself, a change of attitude she had sensed? Could she, in turn, be aware of what had caused it? Did she know, or guess? Feminine intuition? Nonsense. He kicked off the sheets as well.

Had he, in fact, had a change of attitude? What did he really feel? Below the superficial attraction he felt toward Trish, and the illusion of youth restored, was there anything more?

He shaved and showered, turning the water to cold at the end, twisting the tap to full volume, so that the stinging spray hissed down over his upturned face and chest. But even the feel of the cold water against his skin did not restore him, could not wash away the deep, bleak feeling of doubt and despair.

It was Sunday, so he dressed casually in slacks and an open-necked shirt, pulling on an old sweater, for it would be chilly out in spite of the sunshine.

Elizabeth was in the kitchen, busy with breakfast. The smell of frying bacon and eggs and of bread toasting made him suddenly hungry and reminded him that they had hardly eaten anything last night. The fight had started before dinner and had continued during it, so that the food had gone back to the kitchen virtually untouched.

"Morning," he said tentatively.

Elizabeth glanced briefly at him, but did not reply.

So, he thought. That's the way it is.

There was coffee bubbling in a glass percolator on the stove and he poured himself a cup, matching her silence. He drank it black and bitter, then put down the cup and went to the door.

"I'm going down to town to fetch the papers," he told her.

She did not even glance at him this time and still did not say anything.

"Well, screw you then," he said loudly to her unresponsive back and banged the door behind him.

He was still angry when he reached the small store, near the city center, where he customarily bought the Sunday newspapers. Silly bitch! Did she think that being spiteful would gain her anything?

His appetite had vanished and he did not really feel like returning home. If it was silence she wanted, let her have it. She could have blissful silence all day long, for he wouldn't be there.

But where would he go? It wouldn't be pleasant down at the wintry sea. To the hospital? He had told his staff yesterday morning that he would skip Sunday rounds, so they would all have finished by now and left for home.

343

Trish?

It was tempting. Ten, fifteen minutes to her flat. Only a quarter of an hour separated him from the woman . . .

Yes, what? The woman he loved. The woman who was the new Light of his Life?

Or the woman he pitied and grieved for, so that he imagined that pity to be a form of love?

There was the excitement of anticipation, the quickening pulse at the thought that he might see her again, soon. But was it real? This breathlessness, this urging of the loins, this haste to be there, near her, at her side. Was it indeed passion, a need so great that he could and would tear down everything to fall with him as he fell? Or was it the trite old story; the folly, humorous at best, of a middle-aged man suddenly aware of life slipping by?

He sat in the car outside the small shop that sold fruit and vegetables and candies and cigarettes and ice cream and the Sunday papers. He began to page desultorily through the one on top of the pile, the *Afrikaans Sunday*. He glanced at a headline here and there, read a caption to a photograph. He turned a page and there was a faint shock of recognition.

The headline was bold and clamorous, bannered across the top of the page: S.A. COLOURED DOCTOR MAKING TEST-TUBE BABIES.

A subheading, in lesser type, proclaimed: "Woman's egg experiment at Cape laboratory."

Below the headline was a photograph of Philip standing with his head cocked slightly, smiling quizzically at the camera. It was one of the pictures taken on the day he had given his lecture.

"Oh, my God," Deon said out loud. He scanned the long report rapidly. He did not find his own name. Thank God for that, anyway.

He started to read the story more attentively. It had been neatly put together to give the impression of being factual and objective, but the writer's personal wrath and revulsion came through clearly. An unidentified informant had disclosed that human eggs and sperms were being used in the experiments. The source of these eggs was a mystery.

The Coloured doctor in charge of the whole affair was a Canadian citizen, although he had been born at the Cape. What was especially serious was that some of the ova might well have come from white women. The informant had not disclosed where the human sperm to fertilize these eggs had been obtained.

The inference was clear. Any reader could take an educated guess.

Deon read the story through twice, from beginning to end. No, his name was definitely not mentioned. One mercy, at least. Now he had to make sure Philip didn't drag him into this mess.

From the accuracy of the report it was clear that the informant had inside information. But he had said nothing of the purpose of the research. The reporter claimed to have consulted several top scientists, all of them anonymous. None of them could see any scientific reason for the experiment, so the reporter had chosen to put his own construction on this satanic meddling which was being permitted within the borders of the Republic. Artificial life was being created by a so-called scientist seeking to defy God's mastery, playing at God games for the sake of personal glory.

I must stay out of this business, Deon thought. If they so much as get a hint of my involvement . . .

If only the fools had bothered to check on the real purpose. But that would have spoiled the story. Easier to believe the sensational lies of a man off the street. Who the devil had it been? Obviously someone with a smattering of medical knowledge and an old score to settle.

He had to get to Philip. Stop him from giving out further information. Try to help him. Quite evidently his race was the critical factor, the catalytic element that had caused this particular reaction. He would have to be saved from them, from the dog pack, those shrill voiced harriers already eagerly on the scent, clamoring their knowledge that the quarry was near. Philip would not break and run. He would not try to escape. And so, deprived of the excitement of the chase, they would fall on him and slaughter him.

He had to be helped. Not officially, of course. From behind the scenes. That was the best way to handle the whole sorry business.

Deon started up the Jaguar. He would warn Philip and at the same time impress on him that his own help would be of all the more value the less he was personally implicated.

A burly man was sitting in a hotel bedroom on the Foreshore, the remains of an ample breakfast on a tray by his side. He was drinking a second cup of coffee and going through the newspaper page by page, disregarding the stories he did not care for, choosing mostly those which concerned politics, running a thick thumb down the side of the column as he read. Occasionally some item would cause him to give a grunt of gratification or disparagement.

He turned a page and a photograph caught his eye. He read the caption and then the story itself, holding the paper close to his eyes.

345

He threw it down abruptly so that it fell in a jumble of pages, to join the sports section, which already lay spread on the carpeted floor. His always ruddy face had become darker, but it was hard to tell from his expression whether this was from rage or exultation.

"Martie!" he called loudly.

After a pause, his wife replied from the bathroom. "What?"

"That bloody Hottentot I told you about. That one in the elevator."

"What?" she called back uncomprehendingly.

He scowled to show his annoyance at her obtuseness. "The so-called professor. The one who cheeked me."

"Oh?"

He knew that she had still not remembered and was angry with her for being able to forget anything which touched on his dignity.

"He's in the newspaper," he said shortly.

"What for?"

"He raped a white woman."

He grinned with pleasure at the resultant squawk of alarm from the bathroom and poured another cup of coffee before resuming his contemplation of the photograph.

His name was Johannes Jacobus Hendrikus du Toit and he was a Member of the Provincial Council for a highly conservative, predominantly farming constituency in the northwestern Cape. He was in Cape Town for a National Party congress and was due to speak on several items on the agenda when the congress resumed tomorrow.

The Dutch Reformed Church minister was reading the newspaper behind the closed door of his study. He knew that he was safe from interruption, for the closed study door was a signal to everyone in the household that the dominee was not to be disturbed.

He came every Sunday to read the paper in the privacy of his study. He had never consciously reflected on his motives for closing the door, but he did at times think of the weekly ritual as being distasteful. His church's and his own interpretation of morality was strict and narrow, so that he did not doubt that his action could be interpreted as sinful. For a Sunday newspaper was a thing of evil. However, he regarded the reading as a bounden duty. This particular newspaper went in for titillating sensational display of stories of wide popular interest. The dominee believed it was essential for him to know what subjects were occupying the minds of his people. Some of his strongest, most successful sermons had been based on a chance item picked up while he read the newspaper on a Sunday morning.

Elizabeth met Deon in the hall as he came into the house, papers bundled under an arm.

"I have to make a call," he said shortly. "I'm going through to the study."

"Do you want your breakfast there?"

"No, thanks. I won't have breakfast."

She nodded distantly and turned away at once.

He hesitated. Should he mention this business to her? Better leave her out of it.

He had noted down the number at which Philip could be reached. He dialed it now, fumbling between two digits in his haste and, cursing, had to start from the beginning. The ringing tone buzzed like a monotonous-voiced insect trapped inside the receiver. He perched on a corner of the desk and slung his long legs over the arm rests of the leather-upholstered chair. It had been, he remembered, Elizabeth who had chosen it and decided how it was to be placed. As with so many other things he was unable to fault her taste.

No reply. He joggled the receiver rest, waited for the dialing tone and tried again.

Still no reply.

After half a minute he banged down the receiver, rose from his seat on the desk and paced a few times round the room, touching a book here, a painting or a framed photograph there, as if to ensure himself that these things existed, that there was another reality behind the turmoil which was his own mind, that there was a continuity to life, a pattern which could be perceived if only it were possible to stand far enough away.

The telephone rang and he answered it quickly, expecting to hear Philip's voice.

Instead a strange woman, sounding faintly surprised at the prompt response, asked: "Professor van der Riet?"

Flatly: "Yes."

"This is Winifred Anderson of the *Mail*. Sorry to trouble you on a Sunday, Professor. Probably you don't remember, but I once interviewed you and Professor Philip Davids. I don't know if you recall, but it was at the beginning of the year. At a lecture which Professor Davids . . ."

Plump face and hair in a bun. Hard to shake off.

"I remember," he said brusquely.

"Well, the Afrikaans paper this morning had a very interesting story about an experiment Professor Davids is doing and we thought a comment from you would . . ."

"I'm sorry, but I know nothing of Professor Davids' work." Perhaps he was being undiplomatically harsh, but he could not help himself. "I'm a heart surgeon, you know. He's a geneticist. We work in utterly different fields."

"I know, Professor, but we thought that seeing you are such close friends and . . ."

"I'm sorry. I have no comment," Deon said firmly and cut the connection. He held the switch down firmly and when he lifted his finger the dialing tone started again.

The Monday morning newspapers repeated the substance of the report in the *Afrikaans Sunday,* suitably condensed and tricked out to appear up to date. Professor Davids could not be reached for comment. Both the Minister of Health and the President of the Medical Council had said that the matter would be investigated and appropriate action taken.

One newspaper devoted a brief paragraph to a sermon given by a Dutch Reformed minister in a suburban church. He had, predictably enough, labeled the experiment as the work of the devil.

Deon had tried all evening, but had still been unable to raise Philip. So far he was in the clear, but how long would it last? One incautious word . . . Again and again he listed the good and valid reasons why he should not be involved in this controversy.

A small group from the cardiac unit waited for him outside the ward. Fewer than usual. Still no solution to the staff shortage problem either. So many things to think about. So much undone. He exchanged greetings distractedly.

Robby was already in the doctors' room. He was shrugging his narrow shoulders into the white coat which always seemed too big for him and he turned as they trooped in.

"Hello, Deon."

"Morning."

Robby's ironic gaze surveyed him.

"I see friend Philip has been getting himself into a lot of trouble. Trying to find new ways to make babies. What's wrong with the old way? Or is he a bit queer maybe?"

A couple of the registrars laughed uneasily, but there was immediate silence when Deon looked up and they saw his face.

"I thought he was your friend too, Robby?"

Robby laughed too, looking away. "Well, of course. I . . ."

Deon added contempt to his cutting tone. "And even if you have given him up as a friend he remains your colleague."

Robby blinked. Then, obviously deciding to play it off as a joke, he put up his hands in an attitude of surrender. "Don't shoot, sheriff. I'll come quietly."

Deon pulled on his own coat, anger still in his face, and walked to the door.

"I'm only pulling your leg," Robby was saying placatingly. "Don't get so hot and bothered about nothing." He grinned at Deon's back. "Don't tell me you've been making babies too!"

Deon was already out of the room. Now he spun round, and Robby, taken unawares, cannoned into him and staggered back.

Deon watched him, shoulders hunched, as if he was about to leap. His voice was like a knife.

"I have nothing to do with his work. But he's my friend, even if he isn't yours. And I would help him as if he were my brother."

The ward round was carried out in an atmosphere of acute discomfort. Everyone watched Deon's face anxiously and there was a great deal of furtive maneuvering to find places safely out of harm's way at the back of the group.

There was little discussion as the registrars reported the bare details of the progress of each patient. Deon walked from bed to bed, taking it all in automatically, from habit, but haunted all the time by an odd feeling that he was not really there.

"I would help him as if he were my brother."

Had he really said that?

He left halfway through the round, with a quickly thought out and probably unconvincing excuse about being late for an appointment in his rooms.

Surely Philip must be available by now?

He was already on the ground floor, halfway to the door, when Moolman came pounding down the stairs.

"Professor! Professor!"

Deon halted grudgingly.

Moolman's spectacles had slipped down almost to the tip of his nose. He peered over the top of them.

"That dog we did last week is still great!"

"Oh? Well, that's fine."

The registrar was obviously taken aback by Deon's lack of enthusiasm. He folded his arms protectively across his chest.

"I think we can pack up the experiments now," Deon said. "How is Giovanni?"

"F-f-fine." Moolman breathed in hard to control his nervous stutter. After a moment he said: "Of course, there's a high hemoglobin and hematocrit, but apart from that the blood tests are normal. And he's quite happy in the ward."

"Good. You're keeping an eye on him?"

"Yes, sir."

"Okay."

The note of dismissal had been there, but Moolman had apparently decided to ignore it. He kept pace with Deon as he went toward the outside doors.

"Ah . . . Prof?"

Deon turned, frowning. What the hell now?

Moolman was earnestly insistent. "I just wondered if you'd seen this article in *Thorax*, sir?"

"What article?"

At once Moolman pulled a double-folded journal out of his coat pocket. He opened it at a dog's-ear mark and held it out toward Deon.

"I'm afraid it seems the French have beaten you to it, sir." There was real sympathy in his voice.

A single glance at the diagrams was enough. Deon did not have to read the text. Before him was the technique he had thought out and developed in the laboratory for the repair of tricuspid atresia.

He recognized the name of one of the authors. They had met once at a congress in London. The Frenchman had been rather dour, rather tight-lipped. But he had thawed once they had started to talk, and had proved to be pleasant enough.

"Have they done any patients?"

"No, sir." Moolman turned a page. "They say they have some cases waiting, but so far they haven't operated on any of them."

Deon attempted a light smile. "So we still don't really know if it's going to work with humans."

Moolman nodded his head slowly up and down.

"It's tough luck, Prof."

"It's not really important, is it?" Deon said, and hoped that he sounded convincing.

You didn't show it. The rules of manliness prescribed that you dared not show it. You had an inspired idea and you worked out every little detail and you sweated blood over the things that went wrong until they came right again and you practiced it over and over to perfect the technique. Then someone else in a different part of the world who'd had the same idea, only earlier, came out of the unknown and passed you at the winning post. And, although your instincts were to snarl and slash at him like a tethered dog, you had to smile and congratulate him decently on his victory.

Everybody likes a good loser. Although they soon forget his name.

"We'll still be going ahead, sir?" Moolman asked uncertainly.

"Of course."

"Oh, good," the young man said, then blushed at having revealed his feelings.

The boy's disappointment at discovering that he was not to share in the glory of a pioneering venture had obviously vanished. If, indeed, it had ever been there. Possibly not. Possibly Moolman had been concerned throughout only with the experiment itself and with its ultimate goal, not with the personal benefit it might bring.

Deon watched him covertly, asking himself: Was I ever like that? And, if so, where has it gone? That compassion, that indignation, that determination to change the condition of man, that serene faith that medicine could achieve this. That certainty that the only thing I sought was to mend the broken bodies which were brought to me.

I had it once and I have lost it.

Not all of it. Be honest and fair. I still feel pity, and a rage at the too-early coming of the night. But my pity is not unmingled and my rage not always long-sustained. Once the stream ran pure, but now it is muddy and I cannot see the gleaming pebbles on its bed.

He went to his office and for the rest of the morning and all that afternoon Jenny tried without success to find where Philip had gone. He tried to concentrate on the French researcher's article, but time and again his mind wandered. He would find himself staring into space and then would slap the side of his head angrily, in school-masterish rebuke to the unwilling brain behind the skull.

Late in the afternoon his buzzer sounded.

"Yes?"

"A call for you, Prof. But the gentleman won't give his name." Jenny sounded faintly disapproving. "He says it's personal and very urgent."

Philip. Must be Philip. At last.

"Put him through."

Then, without preliminaries: "Deon? What the hell's going on?" The voice was both breathless and guarded, as if its owner was looking over his shoulder after each sentence. Deon recognized it with misgivings.

"Oh. Hello, Barry."

"Hello, hell! You lied to me. That cock-and-bull story about wanting ovaries for hormonal essays! Do you know what kind of spot you've got me into?"

Deon held the receiver away from his head, looking at it distastefully. The sputtering sound of the now muted voice continued. After a while it ceased and he put the instrument back to his ear.

Anxiously: "Hello? Hello?"

"All right, Barry," Deon said. He made his voice into a deliberately casual drawl. "I can hear you. But now listen."

"Look, it's not a question of listening," the other man interrupted shrilly. "If those goddamn ovarectomies are traced back to me, it's the bloody end. Let them find out I had anything to do with it and I might as well close up shop. My practice'll be shot to hell."

"Listen!" Deon said in his most strident voice.

The lament at the other end stopped instantly.

"Okay. Now, in the first place you're not to blame for anything. You performed a number of perfectly legitimate operations, with the only difference that instead of incinerating the excised ovaries you preserved them and passed them on to me for scientific purposes. No. Wait!" he said sternly to halt the renewed torrent of sound. After a moment he resumed. "Secondly, there's no chance of anything being traced back to you. I'm the only person who knows where those ovaries came from and I'm not saying."

The other man's voice changed at once, into equally breathless gratitude.

"Jesus, Deon, that's great of you. I can't tell you what a burden this is off my shoulders. I've been worried sick, ever since the damn papers . . . Anyway, if you're prepared to shoulder the blame then . . ."

"And finally," Deon said in the same sergeant-major's voice, "I don't know why the hell you're in such a panic. It's Davids and his experiment they're gunning for. The point about where the ova came from is purely incidental."

352

There was a moment's stricken silence.

Then: "Dear Lord, where have you been? Don't you know what's going on?"

"What do you mean?"

"But that's what all the fuss is about!"

"What fuss?"

"My God, man. They're planning to bring it all up at the faculty meeting this afternoon. And the point they're going to hammer at is where the ova came from. Haven't you heard the rumors?"

"I don't listen to rumors," Deon said with a vain attempt at dignity.

The other man gave a short, harsh laugh. "Well you'd better start. You might hear things that'll interest you." He paused, then asked sharply: "Did you know there was going to be a faculty meeting today?"

"Yes."

It was not exactly a lie, for he had known. Jenny had put the notice of the meeting, and the agenda, on his desk as always at the beginning of the week, and as usual he had crumpled it up and thrown it into the wastepaper basket.

"Are you attending it?"

"I don't know. I haven't decided."

"I suggest you do. Seeing that it's your own chief who's going to lead the attack."

"Chief?"

"Old Snyman. He's asked for a special debate on the subject as a matter of urgency for the whole of the faculty."

"I see."

That certainly warranted some thought.

"You didn't know that?"

"No."

"Well, the rumors are that it's your scalp he's after. But that couldn't be, could it?" Suddenly pleading: "For God's sake, he hasn't got onto anything, has he?"

"Impossible."

"Are you going?"

"I haven't decided."

"Please, Deon. Don't mention my name."

"I won't."

"I can't ask you to swear to that, but you know what it means to me, don't you? My practice'll be bust, and hell, Deon, it's taken me half a lifetime to get it where it is and there's the kid at university and if a word of

353

this gets out, well, I might as well close up and start as a G.P. in the Free State or something. And you did say to me . . ."

The whining tone began to irritate.

"Look, I've told you I won't say anything. Isn't that enough?"

"And what if they start putting on the pressure?"

"Shut up!"

Deon forced himself to be calm. "Barry, I usually keep my promises. And anyway this thing won't even come back as far as me. Professor Davids is the only person who knows about my involvement and he'll never tell them."

"A Coloured guy?" Skeptically.

"A Coloured guy," Deon said. "And let me tell you something else, my friend. Compared to that Coloured guy you're nothing but a little shit."

He listened briefly, with grim pleasure, to the sounds of indignation at the other end.

"Goodbye, Barry," he said softly.

He put down the receiver. But, he realized at once, it wasn't going to be easy to end it all quite so firmly and unequivocally.

Snyman.

That, indeed, was something to think about. Had the panicky little bastard on the phone been right, and had the old man picked up some rumor somewhere? What was it he had said, that day they'd had a row? "I have my sources of information."

Snyman was hunting him. Was this a weapon? What had he heard? What did he know? What was he guessing at?

The meeting was usually in the early afternoon. Plenty of time. But he had to decide now. Should he attend? Would it be wise? Once his blood was up he wouldn't be able to remain silent. But would that be the most intelligent way to serve Philip's cause? He had been determined to stay behind the scenes. Would anything be gained from seeking an open confrontation?

The dry charade of committee meetings was his particular dislike and he could picture the astonished stares of the regulars, were he to turn up this afternoon. Snyman's knowing look. The baited questions. The glib assumptions.

"Hello, Deon. What brings you here?"

"Hello, Deon. Come to the circus?"

"You look worried, Deon."

"Your friend's for the high jump, Deon."

"Hello, Deon. What are you? Counsel for the defense?"

354

Defense.

The hell with them. He would defend Philip. He would explain the high scientific purpose of the research, explain his part in it, and his reasons for participating. He would confound them, with their narrow legalistic minds. He would refute their arguments; knock down their Establishment-orientated doctrines.

And then? And then?

With his own career in ashes, what would he do then?

For they would not, could not, allow him to go unscathed.

And then a solution occurred.

Gleave would be there.

He seized on it with desperate relief. Gleave will be there. Gleave is head of the department after all. It's his responsibility. He'll explain it to them. He's the geneticist. He knows all the answers.

But I must tell Philip. Warn him. Tell him I am backing him all the way, but warn him against my being involved.

He dialed the number again. The bell began to ring—continued to ring—endlessly echoing the emptiness of his soul.

Eleven

Deon turned off the freeway into the narrow, tree-lined drive, up to where slender Grecian pillars stood among tall trees.

Philip had arrived before him and was waiting; he could see the cream Volkswagen parked beside the entrance to the memorial building. Philip looked about when he heard the crunch of tires on the gravel and, smiling, climbed out of his car.

They had agreed, speaking on the telephone earlier this morning, that it would be inadvisable to be seen together, so they had chosen this place, away from the hospital, but not too far away, for their meeting.

They greeted and walked out onto the terrace. Philip looked up to where a brooding statue sat at the head of the flights of granite steps. He read the chiseled inscription aloud in a tone that was marveling: "To the spirit and life work of Cecil John Rhodes, who loved and served South Africa."

He turned to look northward to the pale hills. Their slopes were covered by a suburban sprawl.

"'There is your hinterland,'" Philip said. "Didn't he say that once?" He glanced up behind him to examine the statue once more. It faced the hills with calm and constant assurance. "Amazing how confident they were. The people of that generation. Never a doubt. Never a thought that there might even be doubts. I think that's where we differ from them. We've learned there are a lot of answers to any one question."

"Yes," Deon said distractedly. He was not looking at the hills, but down toward the hospital. The hospital building itself was out of sight, but odd bits of the medical school were visible from the corner of the forecourt. Its bulk was suitably reduced by height and distance to a casual arrangement of tall blocks haphazardly scattered among other, smaller blocks. Wooden blocks such as a child might use for toys. It pleased him to see it all like that, of no more consequence than a toy, having no real substance. Scaled down by perspective, how could those blocks be large enough to crush a man?

"We must talk," he said.

"Of course," Philip said with prompt courtesy, and joined him at his vantage point.

"What are you going to do?"

Philip looked briefly at him, then away and down at the distant buildings. "What do you suggest?"

"If I were you, I'd sit tight and let things ride. It'll blow over soon enough."

"You think so?"

"I'm sure of it." Deon turned away and kicked with needless force at a loose stone on the terrace, catching it with his toe and sending it spinning far out into emptiness, falling in a long curve to the grassy slope below. "Of course, I'll do everything I can to help you."

Philip nodded slowly, but he did not speak.

"It was a clever move on your part not to drag me into it," Deon said. He looked down to where the stone had fallen. "Old Snyman is gunning for me, you know. Once my name is mentioned I'll be powerless."

I'm talking too much, he thought. Protesting too much. What does he think? That I am going to betray him like the rest of them?

Philip was not looking at him. "Of course, you must not get yourself into trouble for my sake."

His tone was ambiguous.

"It's not that at all," Deon said vehemently. "It's just that I can be of far more help if I appear to be a disinterested outsider."

"Of course."

There was a moment of stiff silence.

"You don't appear to believe me," Deon said.

"That's completely irrelevant. You have every right to stay clear. It's my responsibility, for it was I who got you involved in the first place."

"You don't seem to want to understand."

"Perhaps I understand only too well."

Deon started to say, slowly and menacingly: "Look, don't you bloody well . . ."

He broke off abruptly. We're fighting, he thought. For God's sake, we're on the verge of a fight. Then it occurred to him. We are brothers. And it's even more than that. We are having to *be* brothers for the first time.

357

"Sorry," he said. He kicked at another stone. It struck the edge of the terrace wall and rebounded. "I'm on edge. I've got a hell of a lot of problems. And it's not always easy to know what solution is right. Have you any idea who started this affair? Who gave the story to the newspapers?"

Philip, too, was clearly relieved to end the tension. "It must have been Williams."

"Who's Williams?"

"My ex-technician," Philip said grimly. "He denies it, but it could only have been him."

"Why would he do a thing like that?"

"We never got on particularly well. And finally we had a hell of a row. It started . . ." Philip hesitated, then clearly changed his mind about what he was going to say. "Anyway, it was an unpleasant episode and I realized we couldn't work together, so Professor Gleave had him transferred to another department."

"So you're on your own now?"

"Yes. Actually it's unimportant, because I've been told to stop my work."

"What! By whom?"

"The dean called Gleave and me to his office this morning and told us the council had met and instructed him to see that my research came to an end."

"And what did you do?"

Philip shrugged. "What could I do? It's their lab and facilities. Gleave was as mad as hell and he wanted to hand in his resignation at once, but I managed to dissuade him. There's no point in both of us going and breaking up all the work he's done in the genetics department."

"What do you mean? You're not resigning, surely?"

"I am."

"Jesus, Philip."

"I can hardly stay on, can I?"

"Well, it's a bloody shame."

They stood side by side on the roughly paved terrace and watched traffic moving on the road below.

"Never mind," Philip said with precise emphasis, and smiled. "It's not the end of the world. There is our hinterland." He pointed to the north and slapped Deon lightly on the shoulder.

Standing next to Philip on the heights, on the edge of the stone wall which rose like a rampart above the slopes, Deon had a sudden feeling of assurance, of unassailable strength. They were alone together and would stand together, united on the towering walls of a city capable of withstanding any siege. They would share in adversity and calmly endure it.

"You're right," he said. "The hell with them."

Philip looked at him with a degree of amusement. "I'll see the thing through and then I'll resign."

"See what through? What else is there?"

Philip looked at the hills again. "Perhaps you haven't heard. There's a flap about where I got the ova. Apparently the question was brought up at a faculty meeting yesterday, and although Gleave tried his best, there was a lot of loose talk about unethical behavior and . . ." He broke off to examine Deon's face fleetingly. "You're on the faculty, aren't you?"

Deon worked his shoulders under his jacket.

"Yes. But . . . I was busy with . . . I was a bit tied down, so I sent my apologies. I hardly ever go to those meetings anyway."

"I see."

"So what happened?"

"They agreed to an inquiry into the whole thing, and the dean had to ask me where I'd obtained the ova."

Deon caught his lower lip between his teeth. "You didn't tell him?"

"No."

"And now?"

"There's to be a full-scale inquiry. I have to appear before it."

"But good lord, man! What's wrong with it? You've been doing straightforward research."

"No. Because I wouldn't tell them where I got the ova. It's all a bit confused and I don't think the dean likes it very much. But it seems your professor is pressing the point."

"Is that so?"

It was a certainty now. Snyman knew. He was out to get him.

And the wall on which they stood was no longer secure. Already there were cracks; already you had to step carefully where it edged upon the precipice. It was possibly this sense of precarious balance which caused him to say, a moment later: "Philip. I'm in trouble."

Philip turned an attentive face toward him and immediately Deon knew that he could not, would not, say what he had intended saying, which was: "I'm quitting. I'm sick to death and I'm quitting."

Instead he said, "It's . . . everything. The job . . . my unit. It's falling to pieces. It's sheer hell to see everything you've planned, everything you've worked for, hoped for . . . to see it all . . ." He shook his head, infinitely weary. "And my family too. Elizabeth. I'm damned if I know what to do."

Philip was silent and withdrawn.

And so Deon was obliged to continue, trying to say the unsayable. "Lisa. Well, you've seen for yourself. And Elizabeth. There's a . . . I don't know . . . a kind of vacuum. God knows. And now there's someone else," he said bleakly, without meaning to say it.

"It's Trish, isn't it?" Philip asked gently.

Deon could not rouse himself sufficiently to show dismay or even surprise at common knowledge of what he had had every right to believe was his private concern. It was easier merely to nod. So he nodded.

"I must tell you that Elizabeth has spoken to me," Philip said. "She phoned to ask if she could talk to me about something. And naturally . . ." He made a quick, distorting movement of his mouth. "Well, anyway we met yesterday afternoon."

Deon smiled with delight at having a small mystery explained. It obscured for the moment the larger mystery which he did not yet wish to consider.

"I tried to reach you by phone all yesterday. That's why I couldn't find you."

"Yes," Philip said with compassion.

Unwillingly, Deon asked the necessary question: "Why did she want to see you?"

"She wanted my advice. She had been informed that you were seeing Mrs. Sedara. And she felt I could help her."

Deon nodded in full comprehension; even approval.

Philip watched him anxiously. "Are you all right?"

Deon looked up with a careless smile. "All right? Sure, I'm all right. I'm perfectly fine."

He plunged on: "You said I was informed on. Elizabeth was informed, I mean."

"Yes."

"What do you mean, *informed?*"

"Apparently someone wrote to her."

"Wrote to her about what?" he asked crossly. Anger was a good restorative. Anger was a fine aid to forgetting.

Philip looked at him. "Deon, there are strange people in the world. It seems someone decided to spy on you and even went to the length of hiring a detective agency to watch you and make inquiries. This person sent the agency's report to Elizabeth in the mail. With an anonymous letter."

"Jesus! Who would do a thing like that?"

360

Deon remembered a sharply inquisitive backward glance at a restaurant door and thought, with instant certainty: Gillian Moorhead.

"It was a woman. Wasn't it?"

"It was a typed letter. Signed only 'Your Friend.'"

"Lovely," Deon said. "Absolutely bloody lovely."

Gillian Moorhead, he thought, but without anger. I'll lay you a hundred to one that's who is was. Crazy bitch. Crazy as a witch. She's a witch all right. Poor Peter.

"What did this report say?"

"Do you really want to know all this?"

"What did it say?"

"They checked on Mrs. Sedara's background. Found out you had known one another at university. That kind of thing. She was married before, wasn't she? In Spain?"

"Well they got that wrong," Deon said with vindictive satisfaction. "She wasn't married. She was living with someone."

"I see."

"And what else?"

"Don't you think that's enough?"

"What else?" Deon demanded fiercely.

"Dates. Times. Places where you met. Telephone calls. That kind of thing."

"It just goes to show how the most innocent thing in the world can be twisted and misconstrued," he said angrily. "Trish was consulting me, damn it. I'm operating on her child tomorrow."

Philip said nothing.

"Don't you believe me?" Deon asked in fury which was also anguish. He pointed toward the distant pile of the children's hospital. "The kid's in hospital right now. I could go and show him to you. I told you about him. Well, I'm operating tomorrow for tricuspid atresia."

Still Philip did not reply.

"You believe me, don't you?" Deon pleaded.

"I believe you if you want me to."

Deon turned away. "But you don't. What do I do?" he asked finally. "What do I do now?"

Philip surveyed him calmly, almost disinterestedly.

"I can't tell you."

"I don't know," Deon said slowly. "Dear God. I just don't know."

* * *

It was late in the afternoon and he sat alone in the common room across the corridor from the theater where he had completed his last operation of the day only minutes ago. His assistants would still be at work there, closing the incision, and with part of his mind he was linked to the theater and to the deft, unhurried movements of the people around the table. They would be relaxed and would be making small jokes among themselves, for the operation had gone well. A part of him was there. But another part had been severed completely, as if the corridor had become a chasm, too wide to leap across, and he was fated to spend all the rest of his life in isolation on this side of it.

He sat alone and the newspaper lay on a chair opposite him. Had it been deliberately placed on the arm rest just so? Where he would see the headline the moment he came into the room? Yes. Then, by whom? Someone of his staff harbored this secret malice; wished him ill; could plan and carry out an act of revenge. He did not care to learn who. His eyes had caught Philip's name and that other title in juxtaposition to it. When his mind had made sense out of the headline writer's stylized slang, he had sucked in his breath.

Boldly across the page: Surgery Chief Raps Davids. And: "Big names involved in embryo experiment."

With a growing sense of disbelief, Deon read on: Professor Tertius Snyman, Professor of Surgery, had at a Press conference this morning condemned the experiments on human embryos carried out by the famous Coloured geneticist Professor Philip Davids. Professor Snyman believed the tests to be immoral and unnecessary. University authorities were conducting an urgent inquiry, in conjunction with government health officials, into all aspects of the experiment, particularly in regard to the source of the human ova used by Dr. Davids. Prof. Snyman had indicated that startling disclosures were expected and that eminent medical personalities were possibly involved.

He read on, down to the final paragraph, and again he made that hissing sound between tongue and teeth, as if in pain: Professor Snyman had also announced at the conference that a new Director of the Department of Surgical Research had been appointed. He was Dr. A. G. Robertson, who had previously worked with Professor Deon van der Riet in the Department of Cardiac Surgery.

He and Philip were alone.

He tried the thought on himself, sliding into the concept like a bather reluctantly entering cold water, wetting himself piece by piece, accustoming himself to the chill until it was all around him, until he was afloat in it, hanging weightless and numbed in the cold and bitter sea and it no longer caused pain or even anything stronger than a feeling of mild discomfort.

We are alone, he thought.

He considered telephoning Robby.

Now, in this state of frozen indifference, he could do it quite easily. Robby had not operated this afternoon. Perhaps he would be in his office at the medical school. Not in his new office, that of the Research Director, comfortably next door to the Professor of Surgery himself. Not yet. More likely that he would be in his old office, clearing his drawers, throwing advertisements from pharmaceutical firms into the wastepaper basket, emptying out bent paper clips and a couple of corroded flashlight batteries and a pocket diary for 1969 with the initials E.A.O. stamped on the cover and a map of the London underground inside (wondering, as he sifted through this accumulated clutter, the debris of the years of waiting: "How did that get there? To whom does it belong?" And perhaps, above the muffled and drumskin-tight beating of his heart: "How did I get here? Where am I going?").

He could imagine how the conversation would go. Robby: uncertain, fumbling for the correct phrases, a little ashamed and therefore defiant. Himself: curious above all, in this moment of cold awakening. Not angry; not yet. But curious to know all the deep intricacies of the process of betrayal; to discover motives and long-hidden angers and the tortured reasoning which had (which must have!) preceded the moment of decision.

"Congratulations."

"Thank you."

"It's quite a step up."

"Thank you."

"You'll probably be the next head of surgery. When the old man goes."

Quickly and defensively: "That doesn't necessarily follow."

"Still, you'll be the obvious choice."

"Maybe."

"Why?"

"What?"

"Why did you do it?"

"I don't know what you mean."

"Why are you switching sides? Without even telling me you were going?"

"I wasn't aware I had to tell you of my plans. We both happen to work for the same department and I've been offered another job in the department. That's all there is to it."

"So that's it."

"What do you mean?"

"You resented working under me. You didn't like always being second."

"I don't know what you're talking about."

"I think you do."

"Look, Deon, if you want plain talking then you can have it. I've got something to tell you. Your ground isn't as sure as you may think it is. You're not the only surgeon in the world, you know."

"Thank you."

"What?"

"Thank you, old friend. Thank you, Doctor Robertson."

"You're welcome, Professor."

Robby. Red hair and freckles and spectacles and cheerfully mocking grin. Old Robby, ever smiling, ever ready with a quick joke, a rude retort. And, behind the smile, the cancer of discontent, the concealed envy, ambition's fervent prompting. Old Robby.

No. He would never make that particular telephone call.

Twelve

Again he stood at that table which was, simultaneously, dock and witness box and judgment seat. And where, equally, he was the judge and the chief accused.

The smaller of the pair of overhead lights was poorly focused, so that a shadow obscured the pulmonary artery. He glared at the offending light and a student, one of the ring of closely concentrating observers, reached up to shift it.

"Too far," Deon snapped. "Back to the right."

The spot of light moved.

"Okay."

He grunted perfunctory thanks and leaned over the opened chest once more.

When they had opened the pericardium, Peter Moorhead, working opposite him as first assistant, had given a light whistle of surprise. Deon had nodded somberly. The enormously bulging left ventricle and the miniature right ventricle clinging to it (like two balloons, he thought; one inflated and the other pricked) had been exactly what he had expected to see. That, and the appearance of the rest of the heart, confirmed the diagnosis about which there had never been much doubt. Tricuspid atresia.

Peter pulled the aorta out of the way and Deon pushed the needle from the pressure machine gently into the right pulmonary artery. He looked over his shoulder at the heart-lung technician.

"What's it read?"

"Fourteen. Fluctuating between twelve and sixteen."

"Okay." Peter was his first assistant, but Deon spoke to Moolman, at the end of the table. "That shouldn't be too high?"

Moolman shook his head.

"It is quite a good sized artery too," Deon said. "Okay. Let's go." He turned to the theater sister. "Dissecting forceps and scissors, please."

He had seen Trish earlier this morning, waiting in the corridor outside the Intensive Care Unit and he had wanted to stop, to speak kindly and reassuringly. But his legs had taken him past, as if by their own volition, and he had given no more than a curt nod in reply to her greeting. He knew that she was watching his back as he walked away from her, and there was still time to turn, time to go back to her. He did not turn. He went in through the door marked "Operating Rooms" as if plunging into the sanctuary of a church.

Why? He always found it difficult to speak to the parents of a child on whom he was about to operate. But Trish? Surely to heaven not with Trish?

He freed the superior vena cava from where it entered the right atrium to where the jugular vein joined it, and then freed the right pulmonary artery as far as its bifurcation.

"Bulldog clamp," he told the nurse.

There was a moment's interruption to the rhythmic, patterned movements of his and the two supporting pairs of hands while the girl searched among her instruments. The break was somehow offensive, as if a deliberate impiety had been committed in the midst of a long and elaborate ritual. Both Peter and young Moolman lifted their heads. The nurse found the clamp and gave it to Deon.

He paused to withdraw his mind a little; to consider each step he now had to take in order to shunt blood from the superior vena cava into the right lung. He would achieve this end by dividing the right pulmonary artery, isolating a portion of the superior vena cava with a side clamp and making an incision here, then anastomosing the severed pulmonary artery to this opening. Finally he would tie the opening of the superior vena cava to the right atrium. All the blood in this vessel would then flow into the right lung.

If only it were possible to solve all problems so tidily, by applying mechanical laws.

He thought about the odd contradiction that medicine, that the study and practice of medicine, exposed its acolytes to life at its most severe, that nothing of life's brutality was withheld from them; yet at the same time medicine sheltered them too, kept them innocent and perhaps even pure. They had a particular knowledge and a particular view and because of this were somehow never able to comprehend the full agony. They were not

366

required to examine life from aloft, to watch the slow-wheeling, far-below world with amazement and some alarm and, yes, with a kind of fascinated loathing; watching all the squirming and crawling and wriggling and crazed contortions and little eruptions, now here, now there; and the urgent mindless rushing movements to and fro and the jostling and scrambling and the strange, sad posturing and hopeless maneuvering and terror and faith and courage too, blind courage which was also sad; which was almost as sad as hope. And love, which was the saddest of all.

All the best doctors he had ever known were very simple people. They had in common the absorbed look of a group of well-behaved children. And you knew, simply by looking at them, that they were innocent children, *good* children, like well-scrubbed orphans at a clean, bright institution run by charming and efficient nuns. They did not have the time to become complicated and so were safe from corruption. But they did not have a full vision of life, for to have that, to have the steadiest and most unwavering vision, you had to be corrupt.

He had passed Trish in the passage with a nod and had not turned to go back to her.

Earlier, he had said farewell to Elizabeth with a light, unemotional kiss and had gone down the steps to the garage without looking back.

I don't know, he thought. If there is an answer, I don't have it.

I have to divide the pulmonary artery. To do this I must ligate it near the bifurcation, then place the bulldog clamp where the artery enters the lung.

Will the anastomosis be the right size? Won't the pressure in the pulmonary artery be too high?

I don't know.

He thought that possibly it was the first time ever that he had been faced with an insoluble problem. Its dimensions were those of life itself.

Perhaps I too have always been an essentially simple man. My ambitions and strivings have never been particularly complex. I haven't thought very far or about any particularly troubling subjects. Perhaps I am guilty of that. Guilty of innocence.

Must I change? Or do I go on as before?

There was no solution, and he thought that perhaps this was the penalty you paid for having tasted knowledge: to know that the only certainty of all was uncertainty.

He applied the small Cooley clamp to the side of the vena cava and, using a stiletto-bladed knife, made a careful cut, a quarter of an inch long, into the isolated bit of vein.

"Suture. Five-o."

He began sewing the cut end of the pulmonary artery to the opening in the vein with a running suture.

"Follow me, please, Peter."

He was working well, he noticed with impersonal pleasure. His hands were steady now, and each stitch was placed with absolute precision.

It worried him for a moment that he was able to observe his own work with such objectivity. Should you not be involved? Should you not share in the agony and the anguish, bleed even as your fellow man bled? Weep when he wept?

He remembered something Philip had said yesterday morning as they had stood before the Rhodes memorial.

"You can't turn your back."

They had been talking of Philip's plans; of what he was going to say to the inquiry committee.

"I'll simply hand them my resignation. That should be enough."

"And then?" Deon had asked. "Are you going back to Canada?"

Philip hesitated. "I'm not absolutely sure. In fact I have been considering returning to Beaufort West."

Deon stared at him. "You're joking. What for?"

"To be a doctor."

"You mean general practice?"

"Yes."

"You must be crazy."

"That's a matter of opinion."

"But dear God, Philip, you can't possibly do that. To give up everything and go and practice in a dusty little town . . ." Deon had laughed, shaking his head incredulously. "I'm sorry, Philip. That would simply be bloody stupid."

"As I've said, that's a matter of opinion."

Deon tried a more rational approach. "You'd be wasted there, you know. Without trying to flatter you, you must be one of the best-trained geneticists in the world today. And you tell me you want to go off into the Karoo to treat colds and backaches? Come now!"

"I'm not so sure. I was trained as a doctor to start with. Remember? Mendel made his discoveries in a monastery's pea garden. Maybe I'll do my best work in the shade of a thorn tree."

"I can't believe you're serious."

Philip thrust his hands deep down into his trouser pockets and flexed his shoulder muscles. Deon was momentarily startled to recognize, in this, a duplication of one of his own familiar gestures.

"Absolutely serious," Philip said. "It's not just a whim. I've thought it all through very closely. We have to straighten out our sense of values every now and then, don't we? And what is more important, treating an under-nourished baby in the Karoo, or preventing another mongol being born?"

"But you are trained to be a geneticist."

"True. But I am also trained to be a doctor. And now, for a change, I think I should do something for that child in the Karoo."

"You'll only be allowed to treat Coloureds, do you realize that? Even in the hospital?"

"Yes. Why?"

"You won't be allowed to have white patients."

Philip watched him and was silent for a while. Eventually he sighed and said: "I know. It makes me very bitter sometimes. But at other times I wonder. Does it make such a great difference how and whom you serve? Does that alter the fact that you do serve?" He looked away and added, almost shyly, as though making a confession: "You can't simply sit down and cry out about injustice all the time. You can't help from the sidelines, Deon. To contribute, you have to get involved. You can't turn your back."

The two clamps had been released and all the blood from the superior vena cava now flowed directly to the right lung.

Deon peered over the sterile barrier between him and the anesthetist. "What's the venous pressure?"

"Twenty-two. But it's still falling."

"Hell! It better go lower than that."

"It's still dropping, Deon. Twenty now." The anesthetist counted off slowly: "Nineteen . . . eighteen . . . sixteen . . . fourteen . . ." A pause. "It seems to be settling at fourteen."

"That's better. That's not bad at all."

Deon glanced at the clock. Two hours since they had started. Now they were halfway. He had decided to do the earlier part of the operation without bypass, but now came the tricky part. Now he was going into unexplored territory, and no one could know what pitfalls lay hidden ahead. He looked across at the technicians standing waiting beside the heart-lung machine.

"Okay. Are you ready to go on bypass?"

Both of them looked up suddenly, as if startled by the sudden realization that they, too, were now to be drawn into the vortex: that circle which had as its center the child on the table, around whom revolved fluid forces, deceptively weak-seeming, until the victim was caught in them and started struggling vainly against the reality of their implacable, drowning strength.

Victim? Yes, Deon thought. Judge and executioner and finally victim too. The present has its roots in the past. What I am depends on what I have been. What this child is depends on what I was. So both of us are victims.

I am responsible for his suffering. Not in any neatly abstract way, because of our shared humanity. I am directly, personally responsible. If I had acted in a different way he would not be here; would not be what he is. So he is in my charge and also charged against me.

None of us can escape. We do what we do because we must do it.

And what must I do?

Stand by Philip? Or betray him?

For that is the simple choice, shorn of all the obscurities, the vague generalizations about high ideals and duty and obligation. The choice is there; and it's so simple.

He is going and I am staying. But before he is permitted to go he will be forced through the indignity of appearing before an inquiry or tribunal or whatever they would choose to call it. Like some disobedient child he will be asked for an explanation.

Of course the question of the ova and its source was now quite beside the point—a minor triviality. What was at stake really was authority and its harsh demands.

An individual—and the man was a Coloured, to make it even worse!—was standing up before that authority, contemplating its ponderous, pompous dignity, and saying: "To hell with you."

Must I go there too, and stand beside him and say it too?

How had Philip phrased it? You can't turn your back.

Will he be happy, working as a general practitioner in Beaufort West? Perhaps happiness is not his concern. He is going back to his origins. He will be taking his mother with him, to live and eventually to die among her own relatives. He is going back and her presence will make his return so much more complete—as if he had never left.

I could not do it. I try constantly to cut my ties with that past. I have grown away from my mother, from Boet. I care for them only from a sense of obligation, of family duty. But I could not go back, for that would be a retreat and a confession of failure. For him it is a challenge. No, a problem, to be tackled with the same cool scientific curiosity as any other problem.

He remembered what his daughter had said to him one evening, a long time ago now. She had sat on her bed, naked to the waist and unashamed.

"You have not achieved anything with your life," he had told her. "I have made a success of mine."

And she had asked: "Have you, Daddy? Have you?"

He could still recall his exact response to the question: the first blank astonishment; the succeeding feeling of resentment that he should be asked such a question and by a child; the pause to consider what retribution should be exacted. And then the giddy rush of guilt as he understood the question's serious intent. Have *you? Have* you?

He shook his head slightly to dispel memory and concentrated instead on the next necessary moves which would bring about hypothermic arrest of Giovanni's heart.

Would Trish still be waiting, in that corridor outside?

Probably.

Where do we go from here? Is there in fact any place to go, together? Do I wish to go with her; she with me?

Probably not.

Having acknowledged this, what then? He pictured Elizabeth's familiar face: its planes and shadows, the arch of the eyebrows, the once-loved downward twitch of her lips as she began to smile, the unposed abandon with which she carried her body.

Elizabeth and Etienne and Lisa.

And Deon?

I simply don't know.

"Do you want me to cool any lower, Professor?" the technician at the heart-lung console asked.

"What was the temperature when the heart fibrillated?"

"Twenty five, sir."

"Okay. Leave it at that."

Now he would breach the obstruction formed by the underdeveloped tricuspid valve with an aortic homograft. He and Moolman had collected it at the police morgue: an aortic valve and three inches of aorta from a young girl who had been knocked off her bicycle and killed. Her parents had mastered their grief for long enough to give permission for the vessel to be used. The radiotherapy department had sterilized it by irradiation with a cobalt bomb and now it lay waiting in the kidney dish on the instrument tray. One end would be sewed on to the left pulmonary artery and the valve end to the opening in the right atrium.

"Do you think we should copy the French and run it behind the aorta?" Deon asked Moolman. "Or in front, as we've done in the lab?"

Peter Moorhead answered for Moolman. "Maybe the French method is best, Deon."

"How can you be sure? And anyway, why should we just imitate them?"

Stubbornly, he laid the graft in position over the aorta. He could not quite explain his decision. Was it really the best way? Or did he simply want to do it differently? To be original.

It had worked best this way with the dogs, he reasoned. It was true that dogs had deep chests, but there still seemed to be plenty of room behind the breast bone. Of course it would work. In the dogs it had worked, every time.

Trish would be waiting outside for news of her son.

Elizabeth would be at home, waiting too.

You can't turn your back, Philip had said.

Would he be able to retain that definition now, when he was treating septic wounds and fractures and chronic diseases among the Coloureds in their desolate, windswept township on the fringes of Beaufort West? Would he be able to close the door to his other world so firmly behind him?

And again the thought returned: will I let him stand alone, or shall I stand with him?

There were valid reasons why I should not have been involved, and they still haven't changed. He's going away in any case, so what purpose will it serve to try to make a martyr out of myself at this late stage? In fact, wouldn't it be taking an easy way out? To say to them: all right, here I am as well. If you force him to go, then, because I helped him, you'll have to force me to go too. And then I can quit everything, get rid of all my problems in one go, be free to go anywhere I want to. Leave wife, children, patients, hospitals, colleagues, strife—the whole bloody lot of it. And with a clear conscience. I stood up for what is right and it's not my fault all this has happened.

But what is more difficult: to live with a clear conscience and no problems or with problems and a sense of guilt and doubt about your true motives?

Last night he had made a telephone call.

The man at the other end had been suspicious, especially when told the object of the call. However, after some persuasion, he had agreed to a brief meeting and Deon had set off on the two-hour drive to the home of P. J. Joubert, the Nationalist Member of Parliament, the father of a child named Marietjie, who had once given a white toy rabbit to a black baby.

Joubert was frigidly polite as they sat in the living room among heavy and glossy pieces of stinkwood furniture. There was no sign of his wife, the plump and pleasant woman, or of the daughter.

He answered Deon's inquiries curtly. "Marietjie is very well, thank you. Our doctor saw her last week and he said he's very happy."

And his lips were compressed once more while his long nose lifted as if he had detected some unwholesome smell. There was no point in observing the social conventions.

"You're probably wondering why I've come to you about Professor Davids' experiments," Deon said.

The shrewd eyes moved with a degree of complacency over the big clumsy chairs and display cabinets. Joubert would not look at Deon. After the waiting moment had stretched too far he nodded impersonally.

"It's because I know you have a lot of influence. And if you understand the reason for the experiments you'll see how necessary it is that he should carry on with his work. Besides, it'll do a lot for our image overseas."

"This work is not in the interest of South Africa."

"How can you say that till you know what it is?" Deon asked challengingly.

"It is against the teachings of the church," the other man said, as if Deon had not spoken.

It was impossible to move him. Finally Deon left. Joubert escorted him outside. Only when they stood at Deon's car did the other man show a spark of warmth.

"I'm sorry I can't help you. Especially after what you did for my child."

"You don't owe me anything," Deon burst out. "All I'm asking is that you listen, and think."

"It's a pity you let politics get into it."

Deon turned on him incredulously.

"What the hell are you talking about? No one's said anything about politics."

"The English press, man. They're saying we're persecuting this doctor because he's a Coloured. So we can't back down now."

Deon understood. With his own political career at stake (and was that Cabinet plum being dangled ever closer?), P. J. Joubert, M.P., could not afford to support the cause of a Coloured man.

What strange creatures we are, he thought. Our technology supplies our eternal dream of a world of plenty. And yet half the world starves. We can send rockets into the dark mystery of space, or explore the mysteries of the human body, as I am doing now. And yet we can watch indifferently as

R

others suffer. Our moral sense has not changed. Like the beasts that we were we continue to obey the mindless laws of self-preservation.

Philip had said: "You can't turn your back."

And long ago a middle-aged man, now old, had told a young man, now middle-aged: "The best you can do is try."

I don't know.

But by saying: "I don't know," did you imply that you would never know, or was there a concomitant although unstated vow: "I shall find out"?

It hit him then and he paused momentarily, so that both Moolman and Peter Moorhead looked at him, puzzled.

Of course, he thought. That's it exactly.

"Not knowing, I shall find out."

Behind his mask he gave a slow smile to acknowledge the unexpected irony of the revelation. He considered it, and all its permutations, with the same scrupulous attention he was giving to his examination of the suture with which he had just finished stitching the homograft into place.

I must do it. No matter what the cost. For how can I know it if I have not experienced it? I shall find out. Philip and I will stand together as brothers before our accusers and, together, we shall look into the unknown.

I'll be damned if I'm going to Beaufort West with him. I won't, in fact, have to go anywhere probably, because I very much doubt they will do anything to me. Of course old Snyman will be triumphant and the cardiac unit and I will be in bad favor for a time. But the only real cost will be the courage it will take to join Philip.

So I must do it.

Deon looked across at Moolman.

"What do you think? Will it work? You've done this often enough."

Moolman looked alarmed at being thrust unexpectedly into prominence. He flinched, as if the lights had become too bright for him. He looked at Giovanni's half-repaired heart.

"It should."

"Hold this end out of the way," Deon said. "No, not with your hand, man. Forceps. Hold it to the left."

He made an incision and, unhesitantly, closed the hole between the upper chambers; that hole which had acted as a safety valve and had kept Giovanni alive. Now there was no retreat.

He sewed the end of the graft to the cut he had made in the atrium.

It was done.

He stepped back half a pace, as if to give himself the advantage of a broader field of vision, of a slightly elevated and therefore more remote position.

Trish would be waiting.

"Rewarm," he said. Immediately there was the whirring sound of the pump starting.

"Warming on."

They waited as life returned to Giovanni's heart: first as fine fibrillation, then coaster fibrillation and finally, happily, they saw it burst spontaneously into sinus rhythm.

You're on your own, Giovanni.

You're on your own too, Deon told himself.

Once you have made that admission: I don't know; and then taken on the consequent burden: But I shall find out; then loneliness becomes your essential condition. Far from fearing it, you should welcome it.

The temperature had risen to thirty-six and he told the technicians to turn off the pump. He examined the beating heart with meticulous attention. The right atrium seemed to be coping well with its new burden, pumping blood to the left lung.

"What's the venous pressure?"

"Twelve," the anesthetist told him.

"Arterial?"

"Sixty-five. The urine is coming well." There was a note of elation in the man's normally unemotional voice. "I think you've got a winner here, Deon."

"We'll see," Deon said. He turned back to the heart-lung technician. "Let's do a right atrial pressure." He took up the pressure line's needle.

"Flush."

"Flushing."

"Any bubbles in the line?"

"No, Prof."

"Okay. Here's your zero."

"I've got zero."

Deon pushed the needle through the atrial wall.

"Are you getting a tracing?"

"Yes, Prof."

"What's the mean pressure?"

The tension around the table had spread to the ring of spectators, to the silently waiting floor nurses, to the students peering over one another's

375

shoulders. Perhaps it had spread even beyond the confines of these antiseptic walls, to a corridor where a lone woman waited.

The technician hesitated. Then he squeezed his eyes tightly closed, as if he could not believe what they had perceived.

"Seven, Prof."

"Fantastic!" Moolman shouted, and both the scrub nurse and Peter Moorhead smiled at him. There were murmuring voices all around now.

"Bloody good!"

"Nice work, Deon."

Peter Moorhead: "Great going, Deon."

"That was some operation."

He had to get away.

Swallowing hard, he stepped back from the operating table.

"Peter, will you boys check the bleeding and then close the chest for me?"

He walked absently through the double doors into the scrub room, took off his gloves and gown, and washed his hands.

Should he go out and tell Trish the good news?

No, he would wait a little.

Deon wandered dazedly into the tea room. The tea was cold. Thank God the operation was over and Giovanni was well.

He had repaid a debt. A debt of long ago. The slate was clean.

His memory went back to that night. Trish, without showing emotion, relating the details of the abortion until finally she had burst into tears and admitted that it was awful. Trish staring at the fetus lying on the toilet seat, shouting: "You've killed it."

Now he had given back her son, alive.

"Come quickly, Deon!" someone called in the distance. "Come quickly. You're needed urgently."

He stared blankly at Professor Snyman standing in the doorway of the tea room.

"For Christ's sake, Deon! That kid has collapsed! They want you in the operating room!"

No time to think about where the old man had come from. No time to consider why he had come.

Deon ran.

Only one thought occupied his mind as he grabbed a cap and mask and entered the operating room: How am I going to tell Trish?

"What's happening?" he shouted.

Peter Moorhead tried desperately to explain: "Everything was fine till we closed the sternum. Then the venous pressure shot up and the blood pressure dropped to hell."

He had known it. Had feared it. The graft was being compressed by the front bones of the chest. He should have taken it behind the aorta after all. Now the blood flow was being obstructed.

He had blundered.

She turned as he came up to her. Her body was in that attitude of absolute stillness, but her eyes were steady enough; very steady and apparently calm as they looked deeply and wisely into his.

She read the answer on his face before he gave it, and her own face changed.

But, as if it was a formula which had to be copied exactly, or a rite, the success of which depended on the strictness and fidelity with which each prescribed movement was carried out, she asked the questions anyway.

"Is he all right?"

"He's fine."

"Did everything go off well?"

He was weary, but he could not show it. Not for a time.

"A little bit of trouble when we closed the chest. The graft was being pushed flat. But there was no problem, because the heart-lung machine was still sterile. So we could switch the graft round again. No problem."

No problem at all, he told himself. Except that I very nearly killed your child. But fortunately surgical details meant very little to Trish.

"Will Giovanni be all right?"

"One can't be sure, Trish. But I think so."

"Thank God! When can I see him?"

"In a little while. We'll be moving him to the recovery room and as soon as he's settled we'll let you have a peep at him."

"Yes. Thank you."

They walked a little way down the corridor.

"How are you?" she asked.

Deon hesitated, then asked evasively: "How do you mean?"

"You're not very happy, are you?"

It had never been any good trying to lie to her. Now, nevertheless, he lied again.

"Oh, merely minor problems," he said lightly.

She watched his face.

"Nothing I cannot solve," he said.

"I must go now," he said, after a moment.

"Yes," she said. "Thank you. Thank you for what you have done. Thank you, Doctor."

He looked at her, startled by the sudden formality. And then he realized that it had not sounded strange after all.

Yes, he thought. That's right. I *am* a doctor.

He nodded to her and went in through the swinging doors, back into the operating rooms. He returned to his patient.